T0278948

THE BLACK GIRL SURVIVES IN THIS ONE

THE BLACK GIRL SURVIVES IN THIS ONE

HORROR STORIES

Edited by Desiree S. Evans
and Saraciea J. Fennell

FLATIRON
BOOKS
NEW YORK

This is a work of fiction. All the characters, organizations, and events portrayed in these stories are either products of the authors' imaginations or are used fictitiously.

 Printed in the United States of America. For information, address Flatiron Books, 120 Broadway, New York, NY 10271.

www.flatironbooks.com

Designed by Donna Sinisgalli Noetzel

The Library of Congress Cataloging-in-Publication Data is available upon request.

ISBN 978-1-250-87165-7 (hardcover)
ISBN 978-1-250-87168-8 (ebook)

Our books may be purchased in bulk for promotional, educational, or business use. Please contact your local bookseller or the Macmillan Corporate and Premium Sales Department at 1-800-221-7945, extension 5442, or by email at MacmillanSpecialMarkets@macmillan.com.

First Edition: 2024

10 9 8 7 6 5 4 3 2 1

For all the Black girls who have been aching
not only to see themselves in horror
but also to come out on top as the Final Girl—
this is for you.

CONTENTS

CONTENTS

FOREWORD

TANANARIVE DUE

> "If bad things can happen to white kids, it'll be even worse for you."
>
> —JUSTINA IRELAND, "BLACK PRIDE"

"*Can we live?*"

That frustrated phrase has become a battle cry, but rarely is it as literal as in horror movies and fiction. Whether it was through the complete erasure of Black women and girls in horror or through their quick demise as the "spiritual guide/sacrifice" (as in the horror film *Annabelle*), the message to Black women in much of horror is that we are not meant to exist—and especially not meant to survive.

Many people have heard of horror's "Final Girl" trope, coined by Carol J. Clover in her book *Men, Women, and Chainsaws: Gender in the Modern Horror Film*—but it isn't a term that has often included Black women. In fact, Black women—if we existed at all—have roots as "voodoo queens" in films like *Ouanga*

(1936), starring Fredi Washington as a woman scorned by her white beau who tries to wield her mysterious powers of "Black magic" out of jealousy and ends up dead as the film's vanquished monster. In horror films and literature, we traditionally haven't been able to enjoy the vicarious thrill of seeing Black girls use their courage, strength, and wits to survive. In the past, if Black characters appeared at all in horror, they often existed only to advise or to sacrifice themselves for the good of white characters, or a white Final Girl. There were exceptions in films like Ernest Dickerson's modern classic *Tales from the Crypt: Demon Knight* (where Jada Pinkett Smith not only survived but vanquished a demon!), but tropes and exclusion have made Black women and girls all but invisible in traditional horror.

Black women were mostly absent in horror in the 1940s–1960s (with some exceptions), not gaining further visibility until the Blaxploitation era of the 1970s, with films like *Ganja & Hess*, *Blacula*, and *Sugar Hill* showcasing roles for Black actresses both as heroines and monsters. The '80s saw many of those roles disappearing, aside from standouts like *Angel Heart* and *Vamp*, starring Grace Jones. The '90s gave birth to a new renaissance in both Black cinema and literature—with films like *Eve's Bayou*, Rachel True's role in the ensemble film *The Craft*, and the emergence of horror literature by writers like me and L. A. Banks (the Vampire Huntress series) who were able to create horror stories thanks to the literary boom kicked off by mainstream commercial Black writers like Terry McMillan. The early 2000s brought us Angela Bassett in *Supernova*, Naomie Harris in *28 Days Later*, and Halle Berry in *Gothika*—but too many roles for Black actresses were still as support for white protagonists. As Rachel True said in the documentary *Horror Noire: A History of Black Horror*, so many parts she was offered were simply repeating the line: "Are you okay?"

Despite the tropes and erasure, many Black women and girls have loved horror for generations. The first horror fan in my life was my late mother, Patricia Stephens Due, a civil rights activist with whom I coauthored *Freedom in the Family: A Mother-Daughter Memoir of the Fight for Civil Rights*. From the time she was twenty years old, she wore dark glasses even indoors most of the time after a police officer threw a tear gas canister in her face in 1960, when she was leading a nonviolent protest against segregation as a student at Florida A&M University in Tallahassee.

Maybe it was Mom's lifelong sensitivity to light, her most visible battle scar from the 1960s, that drew her to the darkness of horror. So it's no surprise that she passed on her passion by watching old Creature Feature movies with me, like *The Mole People* and *The Fly*, when I was probably too young. She also gave me my first Stephen King novel, *The Shining*, when I was sixteen and firmly supported me when I started publishing horror novels in 1995.

Seeing monsters on-screen validates our fears because they look like what we are feeling, whether those monsters are sympathetic or terrifying. Or both. And watching characters fight to survive feeds deep-rooted drives that can help keep our nightmares at bay. After all, horror in fiction and movies wasn't nearly as scary to me as coming of age as a Black girl. For my mother, it wasn't nearly as scary as her memories of being tear-gassed and jailed, or fearing for the safety of her unborn grandsons and granddaughters.

Horror's primary preoccupation is simply *survival.* Watching characters find ways to survive under the greatest stress of their lives is a nutrient I can't get enough of. And when I write stories about my own worst nightmares coming true through the veil of horror, I hope I'll give myself just enough strength to vanquish my own monsters.

Today's Black horror renaissance is showing signs of more staying power—and many more opportunities for Black women and girls to thrive. Jordan Peele no doubt helped open the floodgates in cinema, with his film *Us* as almost a primer on survival behavior, led in a tour de force performance by Lupita Nyong'o. A slew of other horror writers and filmmakers are now centering Black women and girls in their storytelling—especially the writers included in this anthology.

The Black Girl Survives in This One is a groundbreaking project that rebukes and revises Black women's invisibility and servitude in horror. *We* get to be the heroines, and *we* get to survive. Cultural value is reflected in the arts, and the Black women in this anthology are asserting that *we* matter. From a werewolf story from a Black perspective we've never seen, to a tale of telepathic powers gone wrong, to the discovery of an ancient, mysterious journal, these diverse stories show rich characters with their own hopes and dreams who sound like us and people we know. These young Black women protagonists are navigating a dangerous world that puts their survival, or their sanity, at risk—and they show us how to overcome.

Which is exactly what we love about horror stories.

Tananarive Due teaches Black horror and Afrofuturism at UCLA. She recently published a short story collection, The Wishing Pool and Other Stories. *Her latest novel is* The Reformatory. *Her website is tananarivedue.com.*

HARVESTERS

L.L. MCKINNEY

"I'm gonna kill him." My grip tightens on my phone until my fingers start to ache.

"Who? Not Eddie." My best friend, Missy, somehow hears me grumbling over the music pounding from speakers strategically placed around the room for optimum hearing loss.

In lieu of answering, I just turn the screen toward her.

She lowers her drink and leans in, her brown face scrunching up while she reads. It might take her a minute; the text is at least two paragraphs long. I didn't make it past the first two words.

So sorry

I don't have to. I know what the rest says without reading it.

The way Missy's expression twists tighter the more she reads means I'm right.

"Asshole!" she hollers, then knocks back the rest of her drink. "Look, forget his corny ass, okay? You look amazing tonight. I told you this dress was the one."

The dress in question is deep red and hugs me in all the right places from my shoulders to my knees. I wear my braids in a bun, so the keyhole back is visible. Initially, I wanted to wear this beige romper. It was cute, but Missy found the dress in the back of my closet and blocked my bedroom door until I tried it on. I'm glad. Paired with matching 1s, we *cute* cute.

Missy says, "And Brandon Miller has been eyeing you since we walked in." She wiggles her eyebrows conspiratorially and pulls her lips to the right.

It takes everything in me to pretend to check my phone while I glance around "casually." Sure enough, Brandon is tilted against the far wall, cup in one hand, the other in his jacket pocket. He's talking to someone, but like Missy said, his attention is on me.

Our eyes lock. His smile widens. My face warms.

That was *not* my intention.

I cannot lie. Brandon is three kinds of fine. Has been since middle school, back when we talked more. Less busy, I guess. And I got feelings for Eddie, I really do, but the way he's been acting since school started got me fucked up.

Brandon winks, and the heat in my cheeks intensifies. I manage a little smile, then turn back to Missy, who looks ready to burst.

"See!" she squeals, and the music is so loud I'm sure no one else heard her, but I feel my stomach go a little squirmy anyway.

My eyes dart around. "Quit yelling! And yeah, I saw."

Her smile widens to fill her round face. Even in the dim party lighting, I can see that twinkle in her eye, the one that means trouble for me. She latches onto my wrist. "Come on."

I plant my feet. "Where?" But I already know.

The look Missy gives me means she knows that I know. "I'm gonna refill my drink. *You're* gonna go talk to Brandon."

"I don't think that's a good id—"

Missy narrows her eyes, then steps in close. I can smell the oil from her press just under the sweetness of whatever perfume she's wearing. "Why not? Eddie's bum ass? Jo, he been ignoring your texts, letting your calls go to voicemail. He don't like or comment on nothing you post anymore, and damn near every time y'all supposed to do couple stuff, he either don't show up or gets there so late there was no point to him coming at all."

Damn, that don't sound good laid out like that. But Missy is right, especially since she's the one I complain to every time Eddie starts with some mess.

I jump when Missy snatches my phone and pulls up the text I just showed her.

"And now he wanna act like he ain't know about tonight?" She wrinkles her nose and reads, mocking Eddie's deep voice. "Ahem, 'So sorry babe, I didn't realize the party was this Saturday,' like the whole school ain't been talking about it all month. Whatever, nigga. 'I have a previous engagement so I can't go, but I'll see you this weekend for the bonfire.' Since when has Eddie *ever* used the phrase 'a previous engagement'?"

She has a point, and I don't have an answer. So, I shrug and fold my arms. There's no reason for me to be irritated at Missy. She's just telling the truth. I'm in my feelings, though. The way she pats at my elbow tells me she knows this, too.

"Six months is a long time to be with someone, but it's only gonna get worse from here. I ain't saying go over there and jump on Brandon's . . . well, I ain't *not* saying it." She sticks her tongue out, and I crack a grin. "But talk to him. Feel him out. Maybe word gets back to Eddie, and he gets his act right. Or maybe he stay on some fuckshit and ghosts. Who cares? Just do it. For me." Missy lays her hand, and my phone, over her heart. Her lower lip pokes out in a very dramatic pout, and I roll my eyes.

What did I say? Trouble for me. "I'm not—I can't talk to another dude when I'm with someone. Even if said someone *is* being a jerk."

"Grade-A certified bitch made liar, but proceed."

I aim a look at her. "I won't cheat. Period."

"This ain't cheating." Missy comes around to my side again, loops her arm through my folded ones, and hauls me forward.

I don't fight her this time.

"This is a conversation," she continues. "Y'all friends. You can talk. Laugh at some of his jokes, politely take his compliments."

"So, flirt."

"Con-ver-sa-tion." She steers us over to the archway that separates the living room from the dining room and kitchen.

This house is huge. It belongs to Reggie, one of the more popular kids. Their parents are loaded, lawyers or writers or something. Which is why they can afford a big-ass house practically in the middle of nowhere.

Okay, it's not exactly the middle of nowhere. Matter of fact, my neighborhood is just a couple of miles away. Walking distance on a nice day. But most of those two miles is grass and some fields and stuff. The fields gradually fade into denser neighborhoods, so the house is close enough to civilization but still far enough that Reggie and their family don't have to be bothered unless they want to.

Missy stops at the archway, squeezes my arm, then hands back my phone. "I'm gonna get a refill, wait for me!" She waves at some people as she slips for the kitchen, essentially abandoning me five feet away from Brandon.

He returns Missy's wave, then turns those dark brown eyes on me. The way his smile lights up makes my stomach warm. This is such a bad idea.

"Hey," he says.

"Hey."

We stare at each other as the house moves around us. Music shakes the walls and floor. People bounce and roll to the beat. Someone somewhere smells green as hell, and I kinda wanna find out who so I can hit it real quick. I don't know why, but my body feels tight. There's an energy racing beneath my skin, like there's no room for the rest of me, but the energy has nowhere to go.

"You good?" Brandon straightens out of his tilt. His drink is gone, both hands in his pockets. He's still smiling, but he looks a little worried.

My face is on *fire* with embarrassment. "Y-yeah, yeah, I just . . ." I gesture at nothing. "Got a lot on my mind. I know that's cliché, but it's funny how true it can be."

"I feel you. I'm glad you aight." The faint frown smooths away, and all that's left is his gorgeous grin. "And it don't sound cliché. I remember you used to be a lil' spacy sometimes."

The incredulous squeak that escapes me is genuine, but he's

still *smiling*, and I can't help but smile back. "I wasn't spacy, you just didn't have nothing interesting to say!"

"Hey!"

"That ain't my fault."

"Wait a minute, now."

"Be less boring."

"Good god, woman, I yield."

And I laugh. We settle into easy conversation. He asks about my granny. I tell him she fine, cantankerous as all hell. When he's done laughing at my word choice—which is perfect, by the way—I ask about his family. His dads are thinking about having another baby. Stuck between two brothers, Brandon is praying for a sister. We swap numbers. To keep in touch. Friend shit.

By the time I notice it's been almost half an hour and Missy ain't came back from the kitchen, I'm torn. Losing myself in talking to Brandon shouldn't have been that easy, and definitely not that deep, but it was. I can't lie. Which is why part of me, a real big part, wants to stay here and keep talking.

We've switched places, me tilting back against the wall, him standing just off to the side. With his arm bracketed a couple of feet away from my head, he leans in over me a little whenever he laughs. Each time, my heart leaps to my throat, my stomach drops to my shoes, and I'm stuck in the middle trying to keep myself together.

Another, smaller part of me is worried about Missy. It knows there's a chance she's staying away on purpose, having set this whole thing with Brandon up, but she hasn't responded since I texted her asking if she was cool just a few minutes ago.

"Hey, um." I sigh and shut my eyes as the worry wins out. "I need to check on Missy. She been gone a minute."

Brandon blinks as if he's not sure what I'm talking about, then realization glints, and his eyes widen. "Right, she . . ." He glances over his shoulder. "I'll go with you."

I brush past him and head for the kitchen. Moving through takes a little time, and more than once I either back into Brandon or he steps forward into me. Either way, his hand ends up on my shoulder, so we don't get separated. I try to ignore a few looks when people notice us together.

The second we break through the crowd, my phone vibrates. It's a message from Missy saying she's fine; she was just giving me some space.

I spot her just then, pressed against some white boy's side while he tosses something at a table of Solo cups. A chorus of cheers, and he drinks.

Missy waves me over. I send an apologetic look to Brandon, who just shrugs, still grinning.

When we arrive at the table, Missy loudly introduces us to Mason. It's unnecessary; we all go to the same school and are at least aware of each other. We don't run in the same circles, but I know he's Reggie's cousin, as well as a neighbor in another mansion not too far away.

"Both of our names start with M, so people are gonna call us M&M," Missy says, clearly starting to feel her drink. She's not *gone*, but I'll probably be driving tonight.

Mason doesn't look much better. He throws up a peace sign and bites his lower lip, trying to look hard or something? I don't know, but I'm having a difficult time not busting out laughing in his face.

Missy mimics the gesture, and I damn near explode. She wrong for that, and for gassing this boy up like this. But that's how she do. By the end of the night, she'll have him wrapped around her finger, and if he don't cause no problems, he might even last a whole season.

I glance up at Brandon to gauge his reaction, but he's frowning and looking off to the side.

I nudge him lightly with an elbow. "What's wrong?"

"You smell something? Like . . . gas?"

I sniff a couple of times, but all I smell is weed and liquor. "Just somebody's blunt."

The lines in Brandon's face deepen for a split second, but then he just shrugs it off.

"You guys wanna go?" Mason gestures to the table full of cups arranged in what vaguely resembles a diamond. Or someone's tanked attempt at a diamond. A Mexican boy I recognize from calc tosses something at the cups, misses, but drinks anyway.

"I'm good," both Brandon and I say at the same time.

"Maaaaaasoooooon"—Missy drags his name out like a melted piece of Laffy Taffy—"was telling me the yard is haunted!"

"The fields," Mason corrects, then holds up a finger and takes a swig from his drink. "And I didn't say haunted, exac-eh-tally . . ." He chops the word up in a tipsy lisp. "I said no one knows who owns them. We don't—you never see anyone out there *doing* anything, but there's always corn! And *someone* harvests it every year."

Brandon and I exchange amused looks while Missy plays with one of the strings on Mason's hoodie.

"I appreciate a man with his own ghost corn," she croons.

I can't help rolling my eyes this time, but a chuckle slips free as well. Ghost corn? Man, I wish I'd recorded that for when she inevitably tries to claim it never happened.

Another chorus of cheers goes up around the table as someone wins. Or loses? Either way, cups are lifted to lips and backs are smacked afterward.

Missy flings her arms into the air like she's signaling a touchdown. Her sudden movement jostles Mason. He quickly wraps an arm around her waist, his other hand holding his cup out and away.

"Looks like you got your hands full, man," Brandon says, one corner of his mouth ticked upward.

I wonder what those full lips might feel like against mine but quickly shove the thought aside.

Mason looks like he's about to protest good-naturedly, but the smile falls from his face. "Reg?" He stands, dumping Missy into his chair.

Before I can turn to see what's wrong, someone shoves past me and nearly sends me sprawling. I feel arms wrap around me, and I'm tugged against a hard body. Brandon's breath warms my cheek as I raise my face to his.

You good? he asks with his eyes. His tight hold is the only reason I remain on my feet.

I nod, my face hot for a number of reasons as I glance around for who ordered this ass whupping.

Reggie—wearing a bright green outfit I would've complimented them on if they hadn't *pushed* me—frantically gestures at Mason. "I can't find the extinguisher! It's not in the kitchen!"

"Your dad had it out back for the pit last night," Mason says. "Why do you need—?"

He doesn't finish the question before the answer makes itself apparent when people in the living room start screaming. At the same time, a flare of orange light fills the room.

"Those idiots!" Reggie shrieks, then races out into the living room as the light grows brighter, accompanied by the sound of whooping and hollering.

"Uh-oh," Mason mutters, then follows, leaving a mess of people, including us, staring after him.

Fifteen minutes, one ruined couch, and an equally ruined party later, I sit on the hood of Missy's car, watching kids pour out of the house. Some knuckleheads got drunk and thought it was a good idea to turn the big, fancy fireplace in Reggie's living room into a flamethrower. Like when you hold a match and blow hairspray or something to make a fireball. At least, that's how it works in movies.

They wound up accidentally setting an expensive couch on fire, and probably some other stuff. By the time Mason fetched the fire extinguisher, it was almost fully burned. Then Reggie, after turning white, then green, then three shades of red, told everyone to get the fuck out.

Can't blame them. I wouldn't wanna have to explain to my parents why their favorite ottoman was charbroiled.

News spread pretty quick, and soon the yard and massive circle drive are full of people climbing into cars, screaming at each other, trying to figure out where to go next to keep the party rolling.

"What's taking so long?" Missy complains from behind me. She's spread across the hood like a starfish.

I look back at her. "You could always go help."

She groans and throws her arm over her eyes. "I'm conserving my energy."

"You're wasted," I correct. "And you lost your keys."

Brandon and Mason had walked us out to the car, only for us to discover we couldn't get into it because Missy's pockets were empty. Except for her phone. Reggie wouldn't let us back in, but Mason argued with his cousin until they said *one* of us could go.

Missy was too drunk to be of any help, and I couldn't leave her alone, so Brandon volunteered, even though it was gonna cost him his ride. I offered to give him one, since Missy and I now owed him.

I spend the next ten minutes scrolling through videos, and only glance up when I hear footsteps approaching. It's Brandon and Mason, and they don't look happy.

Brandon winces before saying, "Mission failure. Didn't find them."

Missy groans.

So does my spirit. I purse my lips and bite back my irritation. "Really? Damn, now what?"

Mason glances up and down the drive. "The car will be fine right here. It's out of the way of anyone trying to pull through. When I come over tomorrow to help Reggie clean up, I'll look for the keys, too."

"My hero," Missy hums.

"That doesn't help us tonight," I mutter. "How are the three of us supposed to get home? It's almost midnight, ain't no Ubers coming out here."

"I could take you," Mason volunteers. "My house is about a twenty-minute walk from here. I'll take you home tonight, call Missy tomorrow when I find her keys. Cool?"

Any other time, I would've declined and called my parents. They would come get us, but that would lead to lectures about making better choices and them watching over my shoulder for the next month.

I rub at my knees and look to Brandon instead of answering.

After a few seconds of contemplation, he shrugs. "Sounds like a plan to me."

There's a faint twisting in my stomach. Something about this doesn't sit well with me, but I can't explain what or why, and I don't have a better suggestion. "I don't know if Missy will make it."

"I'm fine," she blurts. "Just . . . tired. Help me up." Her hand shoots into the air, her fingers wiggling. She didn't address anyone specifically, but Mason comes around to carefully pull her to her feet.

She smiles, sinks against him a little, and murmurs a quiet but heavy thank-you. I swallow a groan. Maybe *I* won't make it.

Paired off, we start walking. The last few cars drive by. People honk their horns and hang out the windows. Mason waves at a big red pickup with two guys in matching letterman jackets standing in the bed and howling at the moon.

Missy cups a hand to the side of her mouth and hollers, "Go Timberwolves!" after them.

Brandon shakes his head, but he's grinning. I swat his arm for laughing at my friend while fighting my own smile.

We reach the end of Reggie's ridiculously long driveway and stop at the road. The night is quiet and dark. The only light available is from the lamps on the large gate that guards the property. Outside the hazy halo, the darkness thickens.

"I don't like this," I admit.

"Since when are you scared of the dark?" Missy asks, standing a little straighter with Mason's help.

I shoot back, "I'm not. But it's pitch-black out here, and there are no sidewalks. We'll have to walk in the street. Drivers won't see us until they're on top of us."

"We'll see them, though," Missy says. "We can move."

"Or." Mason points at an open field on the other side of the street. "We can cut across that pasture." The clouds part briefly, and moonlight shimmers over the hill, barely illuminating it and a few bales of hay. "There's a small cornfield on the other side. I go that way all the time. It'll take five, maybe ten minutes off the walk."

"Hell, yeah," Missy says, and starts pulling Mason that way. She doesn't wait for the rest of us to give our input.

Mason follows obediently. Little finger.

Brandon eyes me as we reluctantly fall into step behind them. "I see she ain't changed much."

"Nope," I murmur. Missy has always been the kind of person to take charge of a situation. She just does shit and expects people to follow.

"Didn't think she would. How about you? You change?" He smirks down at me, and I feel warmth in my face again.

"It's only been two years," I say.

"Two years is a lifetime." Brandon nudges me with his elbow as we walk, his hands in his jacket pockets again. "Good to see you."

"You, too." And it is. It's real good. I'd forgotten how fun and funny Brandon was. Is.

Missy's shrill giggle snatches at my attention briefly. She throws one arm around Mason's neck, and the two of them stumble briefly but catch their feet before going down.

"Those two gonna be okay?" Brandon asks, his baritone dipping in a light laugh.

I refuse to acknowledge what that does to me.

"Mmm, right now? Yeah. In the morning, though?" I hike my shoulders in a shrug, and we both chuckle as the other two pick themselves up and shuffle forward again.

We walk in silence for a bit, with the sound of insects and the crunch of dead and dying grass beneath our feet serenading us. A chill catches in the air like cloth on a loose nail. Goose bumps slide down my arms, and I rub them away.

The weight of fabric and faux leather falls around my shoulders. Brandon's jacket, I realize. His warmth clings to it and embraces me, banishing the cold.

I turn to thank him, then freeze. Several yards off, something moves, a shadow skulking low over the ground. It stops and angles around to face me. Disembodied eyes glitter in the dark. My breath catches. I blink, and it's gone.

"What's wrong?" Brandon asks, glancing that direction, then back to me.

The words are stuck in my throat. I shake my head and shut my eyes while I take a breath. It was probably an animal. A coyote or a fox. We are on the edge of the country, and I've nearly hit more than one while driving out here.

"N-nothing," I breathe. "Thought I saw something."

Brandon hesitates, scrutinizing the area I'd been staring at a moment before. He makes a thoughtful sound, clicks his tongue, then starts forward again. I silently agree and follow.

The cornfield Mason told us about is still a short ways off, at the bottom of a small hill, and I can just make out Missy and Mason maybe thirty feet ahead of us. Their voices carry in the still air. I can't hear what they're saying, but she gives that little laugh again and rests her head on his shoulder.

"You talking to anyone?" Brandon asks.

"What?" I must look so shocked that he lifts one hand as if to fend off his own question.

"Just curious! You don't have to answer if you don't want."

"No, I . . . I didn't hear you."

Brandon chuckles. I doubt he believes me. "I asked if you talking to anyone? Boyfriend? Girlfriend? Partner?"

In name only, is what crosses my mind, but I don't say it. I don't wanna lie because then all this talking we doing becomes more than a conversation. But I also don't want Brandon to stop looking at me like that or stop thinking about me in whatever way made him ask in the first place.

"I . . ." I pause, staring straight ahead, my heart once more in my throat.

"You *don't* have to answer," Brandon says.

"It's not that," I say around my rising panic. "Where'd they go?"

We stand at the top of the hill. The moon is bright enough for us to see clear down to the cornfield, only there's no sign of him. Or Missy.

"In the corn?" Brandon suggests.

"Missy!" I shout, already halfway down the hill. Why didn't she wait? "Missy!" At the bottom, I break into a full run.

I'm nearly about to slam into the wall of corn when something rustles, and my best friend seems to materialize from the stalks and shadows. "Girl, why you yelling?"

Mason appears behind her.

The relief, and my screaming lungs, have me doubling over and panting for breath. I hear Brandon jog up.

"We didn't know where you went," he answers for me.

"Right here," Missy says like there was no reason to be worried, like she ain't just disappear into the night with some boy she barely knows. "Come on, my feet tired." She takes Mason's hand and leads him into the corn.

Brandon hesitates, giving me a look.

I roll my eyes—I'm doing that a lot—still a little out of breath, and gesture him forward. Our steps rustle in the grass. Stalks shiver as we brush past them. The moon dips in and out of the clouds, spilling light across the world in fragments. Eventually, it slips behind one and seems to get stuck. The world goes dark. And I mean *dark*. It's thick and dense, pooling around us with an almost physical force that herds me closer to Brandon. I feel his fingers brush the back of my hand.

The shiver that moves through me has nothing to do with the cold, but I shift to pull his jacket on properly. It swallows me, the sleeves long and a little cumbersome. I work to push them up my arms in the dark.

Randomly, I remember hearing from a cousin or uncle or something that on nights like this, out in the country and away from the lights of the city, it gets so dark that you can't see your hand in front of your face. Wanting something to focus on other than the unease twisting in my gut or the definitely-an-animal I spotted earlier that might be in here with us, I decide to test this. For science. My wrist flexes this way and that as I move my hand farther, then closer, then farther, trying to gauge when I can no longer make out my fingers.

Another burst of moonlight reveals both my hand and Brandon's grin. He arches an eyebrow in an expression that asks, *What are you doing?*

I'm embarrassed at the truth, but I tell him anyway. The next time the moon disappears, I can just make out his form beside me and hear his clothes rustle as his hand moves back and forth. A snicker catches at the back of my throat.

"You two okay?" Mason asks from somewhere ahead of us.

"All good," Brandon replies. "How much further? Feels like we've been walking for longer than fifteen minutes."

"We're almost there," Mason says.

My phone buzzes against my hip. I fish it out from my pocket. My eyes go wide as I stare at the screen.

Missy: Girl, where you at? We lose you?

My head snaps up, and my eyes ping to Missy's back. She and Mason walk hand in hand, her phone nowhere to be seen.

I fire back a message: Right behind you.

We keep walking. I watch Missy carefully, squinting to see in the dark for when she reaches for her phone. She never does.

Everything in me goes cold. A stab of panic in my chest feels like my heart has stopped.

When my phone buzzes again, I grab Brandon's wrist.

He looks at me, puzzled, but then I hold up my phone, and the reply from Missy.

> Stop playing. We sitting on Mason's porch. His house bigger than Reggie's!
> If you and Brandon need a second, I can have him give me the tour.

Brandon's eyes get so big, they nearly take up half his face.

"Something wrong?" Missy and Mason have stopped to look back at us, still holding hands. They stare, and I can't tell in the dark, but I don't think they are blinking. Missy isn't stumbling anymore, and Mason is steady, too.

"Y-yeah, it's . . . fine." I squeeze Brandon's arm, my hand trembling. Or maybe that's him shaking.

"It?" Mason asks.

"My phone!" I offer quickly, hoping I don't sound terrified. Because I am. I can barely get my mouth to work. "You know my mom. I'm trying to explain what happened, and I think I'm grounded."

I wish I *was* talking to my mom. Or my dad. I wish I had called them earlier.

"Keep up," Mason says. "People get lost out here sometimes." There's a sort of hissing that accompanies his words. I didn't notice at first, but everything around us has gone quiet. The insects, the animals, all of it.

Brandon tenses beside me. He's still staring. Silent.

"Don't worry about us." I wave my hand. "Missy knows I can't walk and type at the same time. I'll fall on my face. We'll catch up."

The two of them exchange glances, and I swear my skin is ready to jump off my bones. We have to get away. Now. But something tells me if we run . . .

"We shouldn't leave you out here alone," Missy drawls. The hissing is there, under her voice, too.

"I'm not alone!" I blurt. My words echo in the dark, loud and wavering. I take a breath and force a smile. "Brandon's with me. He'll make sure we get to Mason's if I fall behind." My grip tightens on his arm. My nails dig into his now bare skin.

That snaps him out of it. "Yeah!" he wheezes, then clears his throat. "Yeah. I'll . . . get to Mason's. I mean, get her to Mason's. We'll be there."

Missy and Mason look back and forth between us. Their heads bobble like synchronized swimmers. At the same time, they smile and let go of each other.

My phone buzzes again. Another message from Missy, asking what the plan is. I don't know what to say. I have no idea how to explain what's happening, but before I can even begin to think it over, my phone rings.

The screen says it's Missy.

And yet "Missy" is standing maybe ten feet in front of me.

She asks, "Are you going to get that?"

My fingers shake so bad I almost drop my phone. It takes both hands to hold it to my ear and I stammer, "H-h-hey, Mo-o-m."

"Mom!" Missy's voice explodes from the speaker. "It's me! You sure you not the drunk one?"

I don't answer. I can't, because I'm staring at something wearing my best friend's face and smiling in a way that would've been reassuring if not for the needlelike teeth glinting in the slowly vanishing moonlight. Her face fissures, her features stretching. Her body does the same.

"Mason" bears a similar set of fangs. He raises too-long arms and spreads his fingers.

No.

Claws.

"Run." Brandon nearly yanks my arm out of the socket. "Run!"

All the air leaves my lungs. I turn and bolt into the corn.

Something, one of them, shrieks behind me.

My heart thunders in my ears, mimicking the sound of my feet pounding the ground. Stalks of corn flicker in and out of my vision, raking at me with long leaves and tufts before vanishing into the night. It feels like razors snatching at me, cutting into my cheeks and then my hands when I try to protect my face. I smell and taste blood.

I can't tell if Brandon is with me. I can't hear anything over the sound of my pulse pounding as I barrel forward through the night.

My feet catch on something. I go down hard. A rush of cold falls over me. There's hissing all around me. Or maybe that's the blood rushing in my ears.

Something yanks at Brandon's jacket, pulling me up. I lash out, the bottom of my shoe connecting with a warm, hard body.

I hear it hit the ground with a thump and a low grunt. But I don't care. I'm free and scrambling away, fast as I can. I don't care which way, I just go.

Part of me wants to call out to Brandon, but if I open my mouth, I'm going to scream. And never stop screaming.

I break right. My legs burn. My lungs burn.

A howl splits the air.

Don't look back, my mind shrieks. *Don't look back!*

The ground gives beneath my feet. My legs buckle. I go down again—I can't go down again!

Pain erupts through me when I hit the ground and tumble several feet. When I stop, I immediately curl up and pray whatever happens, happens quick.

"Jo!" Hands grab me and haul me across the grass, trying to lift me.

I kick and flail and keen. "NO!" My fear is alive in me, trying to claw its way out.

"Jo! Ow! Fuck, why you kick me?" It's Missy's voice.

Her real voice. No hissing.

I blink through the hot tears and, in the glow of a porchlight about thirty feet off, can make out Missy's worried face and Mason's beside it. Their actual faces, flushed with booze and worry.

I lie on my back, staring up at them, my chest heaving, my body buzzing. A perfectly manicured lawn stretches out around us, the cropped grass going right up to the edge of the cornfield. Seeing the stalks, I scramble up and away.

"Nononononono!"

"You okay?" Mason asks.

"Does she *look* okay!" Missy asks, still holding her hands out toward me.

"I-I . . ." I try to speak, but the words won't come. Only harsh, quick breaths and the beginnings of sobs.

"Oh, thank god," says another voice, and I turn just in time for Brandon to scoop me up. His arms are like iron. They hold me up when my legs won't. He cups the back of my neck with one hand. His words rumble through me. "You made it."

I wrap my arms around him and squeeze, burying my face in his chest. The smell of him mingles with the scent of blood and dirt.

Blood. And dirt. Blood . . .

The sobs finally break free. I melt into him. I'm only partially aware of Missy hovering around us, asking if I'm all right, asking what happened to me. Brandon doesn't answer.

I can't answer.

By the time they manage to calm me down enough to get me to the porch, a friendly white woman who turns out to be Mason's mom has appeared with glasses of freshly made lemonade for all of us and a blanket and first aid kit for me. She flutters around, clearly concerned.

Mason manages to convince her I fell in the field because it was so dark. It's not far from the truth. I did fall. And came tumbling out into their yard. He and Missy saw the whole thing where they were waiting for me and Brandon on the porch.

They did not see what had been chasing me, but thank god it didn't follow.

My eyes drift toward the field, then dart away every handful of seconds. I want to get up and run again, to keep running, put as much distance between me and it as possible. My fidgeting makes it hard for Missy as she bandages the cuts on my hands and face. She keeps pitching me worried, questioning looks. I haven't told her what happened because I don't know.

And I don't think she'd believe me.

Once I'm put together enough for her liking, she tells Mason to get the car.

"I need to get her home," she murmurs, squeezing my hand, our roles effectively reversed. She doesn't let go as we pile into Mason's Jaguar, which would've been impressive if I gave a single damn. But I just want to go home.

Mason is behind the wheel. In the back seat, Missy sits on my left, Brandon on my right. I'm braced between the two of them. It's a good thing, too. Without their support, I would shake apart.

As we pull out of Mason's huge garage and reach the end of his driveway, my phone buzzes on my lap. Missy put it there. She'd found it in Mason's yard and kept it for me. It takes a gargantuan effort to free my hand from Brandon's and pick it up.

A text. I open it just as Mason pulls onto the street and into the night.

Eddie: Hey babe, how was the party?

Almost immediately, another slides in beneath it.

My stomach drops.

Brandon: I got out

Darkness swallows everything but three terrible words.

Brandon: where are you

WELCOME BACK TO THE COSMOS

KORTNEY NASH

Momma's hologram wavers in the air between me and the window, flickering in and out of existence every few seconds.

"You're staying out of trouble, right, Danika?" I watch her eyebrows crease against the backdrop of the ever-expansive Andromeda galaxy. She's sitting in bed, bonnet still on.

"Of course, Momma." I can tell by her expression that she doesn't believe me one bit.

To be fair, my team and I aren't up to anything *too* bad. There are four of us: me, Paloma, Jared, and Moe. All of us are eighteen, except for Jared, who turned twenty last week. It's Jared's second term on the *Orbiter IV*; he helped train the rest of us in piloting the ship and filling out reports.

We don't hurt anyone or tell lies. We just like making detours from our assigned route to poke around in the ruins of charred rocket shuttles and deserted deep-space residential colonies. We take things that people left behind. Things that can't be stolen because they don't belong to anyone anymore.

"It's not good, being up there in space. When people die up

there, there's nowhere for their souls to go since they never get buried." She pulls her robe tighter around herself as if warding off the chilly hands of death.

For a second, I catch my reflection in the window behind Momma. On our zero-gravity ship, everything floats. My locs hover around my face like Medusa's snakes, looping through a wayward string of pearls among the rest of the knickknacks lingering in the air. My green Yosemite Falls T-shirt bobs above my shoulders like a buoy in turbulent waters.

"I'm not going to die up here anytime soon." My sentence is punctuated by a silver Eiffel Tower keychain floating into the frame and bopping my nose.

Momma sighs with the weight of someone at their wit's end. "I know you're not going to die. You die, and I'll bring you back to life and kill you myself. I'm talking about all those people who already died, they—I don't know, but I do know that something bad is going on. So many people disappear up there, and the ones that don't are different when they come back to Earth. They—"

My eyes glaze over as she keeps talking. We have the same conversation every time she calls, about how people change in space, about how people go missing in space. She spends all her free time reading conspiracies on Reddit forums that tell tales about bodily possession and nightmarish supernatural encounters among the stars. The fact of the matter is people go missing on Earth, too. People change on Earth, too.

Eventually, I interrupt her. "This is my job, Momma, I'm not just here messing around. Why can't you be happy that I'm trying to do something with my life?"

We look at each other in tense silence.

I've been out in deep space for the last six months; it's my first gig after graduating high school. My twelve-month contract includes free room and board; plus, the work is easy. When we're not creeping around space ruins, I'm painting my nails with Paloma or helping Moe buzz their undercut. Occasionally, Jared and I read together on the observation deck. At the end of my service term, in addition to my paycheck, I'll get a grant that I can put toward tuition at any trade school or university. As often as Momma nags me about going to college, she tends to forget about that last part.

There's been a government-sponsored effort within the last few years to clean up distant galaxies and reinvest in interplanetary colonies. Build new factories to bring the labor force back out to the cosmos. Launch a line of affordable, emission-free space shuttles so the whole family can nip over to the Triangulum Galaxy for a weekend of excitement.

The sanitation teams collect trash (abandoned satellites, scrap metals, spaceships dilapidated beyond recognition). The engineering teams renovate infrastructure that was built and abandoned decades ago. And the demolition teams destroy anything that's been deemed unsavable. But before any of that can happen, my team surveys the landscape in the USS *Orbiter IV*. While easy, it's a horribly boring job; it doesn't even include leaving the ship. What's the point of being in space if all you can do is watch it from your window?

We're just supposed to sit at the observation deck and record the coordinates of every structure we encounter, as well as any hazardous waste, like dead bodies. We've never seen any dead bodies, though. A lot of empty space suits with the helmets cracked open or the visors punched out float past. But never any actual bodies.

"Anyways . . ." Momma starts, gently patting her head through her bonnet. "You'll be home for your sister's birthday, right? She misses you."

"Of course," I answer automatically, then say after the silence starts to stretch on again, "Well, I've got to go. Bye, I love you."

I hang up before she can reply.

As if on cue, a new space suit floats past outside. I put my nose to the window to see if I can make out the date on the singular mission patch decorating the left breast panel. It's red and triangular with an acronym I don't recognize. The suit is otherwise unremarkable. It looks similar enough to the ones we wear aboard the *Orbiter* that I can tell it's probably also from a government-funded expedition (the private enterprises get sleek, aerodynamic outfits).

It drifts alongside the ship for a little while, and I begin to grow strangely fond of it. When the suit starts trailing behind us, and it's clear we're leaving it behind, I wave farewell.

It waves back.

My heart leaps into my throat, then it evacuates my body when a firm grip shakes my shoulders.

"We'll be at the US ISS factory in ten; you ready to suit up?" Paloma asks. Considering how smug she looks, she's aware of how badly she startled me.

Paloma swats at an empty cow-shaped saltshaker, and then at a sage green scarf before they can collide with her face. "When we get to the factory, *please* don't bring anything stupid back this time."

She makes a sweeping gesture at my room with one arm, using the other to push away loose strands of hair that have escaped from the long braid trailing down her back. The braid itself is winding through my collection of keys of varying colors and sizes that lead to cars, houses, and offices I've never been to before.

"Souvenirs are the best part of any trip." I shrug, then say with a sly grin, "You're just jealous I always find all of the cool stuff first."

"I don't want half the stuff you find. I don't want my future dorm room to look like . . . this." While my post–USS *Orbiter IV* plans are a bit hazy, Paloma signed up for the sole purpose of that tuition grant at the end. She's already gotten into some school back in the States and deferred her enrollment while she fulfills her contract here.

At the sound of Jared's voice calling us, she floats out of my room, leaving me behind.

I pull my hair back and glance at my window one more time. The suit from earlier is long gone.

By the time I get to the observation deck, Paloma and Moe are already taking turns zipping each other up. Our space suits are a garish lime green with several thick reflective strips circling the arms, legs, and torso. We're *technically* only supposed to suit up in case of emergencies, but boredom is an emergency that strikes daily in deep space.

"Nice of you to join us, Danika," Moe says by way of greeting, their short hair pulled into two high ponytails to keep it out of their face. Jared nods at me but otherwise doesn't budge from where he's inspecting the backside of Moe's suit, his ring-adorned hands well-practiced at straightening creases and checking for punctures in the fabric. Jared won't be leaving the ship with us. Instead, he floats around in his typical khakis and sweatshirt combo, glasses perched high on his nose.

I grab a suit, sliding into it with ease, and drift toward Paloma to get her to zip me up.

We make quick work of attaching our helmets and securing our oxygen tanks. By the time we're filing into the entrance of the airlock chamber, we look indistinguishable from each other. From the outside, our helmets are an opaque black, paired with our identical horrifically bright suits. Still, I can imagine Moe's pierced eyebrow twitching in amusement behind their visor when I accidentally bump into them one too many times while trying to stay upright. And it's easy to imagine Paloma's freckled face scrunched in silent laughter when the suit to the left of me trembles at the shoulders.

"Danika, this isn't bumper cars; get it together." Moe's voice, laden with static, travels to the speaker of my helmet via Bluetooth.

I try to bump into them again, on purpose this time, but they dodge me easily, though the minimal momentum is enough to send me head over heels.

Paloma turns on her mic just to bark a sharp laugh while I use the wall to try to rotate my body around like the hand on a clock.

I'm barely right side up again when we hear the entrance to

the airlock chamber click shut, meaning Jared finally finished locking up behind us, and we can exit the ship.

We're stalled about fifty yards from the US ISS factory; after we deboard, Jared will pilot our ship through the rest of our route and loop back around in two hours to pick us up. We do all have an actual job to be doing, and this time it's up to Jared to make it look like we're all doing it. Last time, it was Moe. Next time, it'll be me.

We propel ourselves toward the factory entrance using any galactic debris we can get our hands on. Paloma lands on the platform first and throws us a victorious middle finger while Moe and I play leapfrog with fancy space trash to catch up to her.

The factory itself has an overbearing presence, like a huge windowless shopping mall in the sky. The metal double doors at the entrance are ajar, bent at odd angles like someone busted them down with their fists.

"When did this place shut down?" I ask once we're all standing in the foyer.

"It was condemned about . . ." There's a pause while Moe thinks. "Forty years ago. It failed a routine facilities exam but operated illegally for about eighteen months after that."

Moe's mind is a wealth of niche information on everything space related. They're the only one on our team who doesn't see our job as a quick gig so much as the beginning of a long career that culminates in titles like lieutenant or commander.

"Something about the machinery killing too many of the assembly-line workers, right? Or is this the one where there was some type of nuclear meltdown and all the employees disappeared?" Paloma asks, completely ensconced in darkness for a moment before I turn my flashlight on, illuminating the entire room in stark clarity.

There's a blur of movement in my peripheral vision, quick like a roach scurrying into the shadows when the lights come on, but when I glance to the side, nothing's there.

"It's the second one; this was the US ISS's satellite spare part assembly factory. It was when companies first started implementing paragravity, but it wasn't stable enough for long-term usage yet," Moe says, following Paloma deeper inside. Paragravity had been the wave a while ago. People were thrilled at the prospect of making synthetic gravity widely available, but after several catastrophes aboard various ships, stations, and intergalactic factories, developers had called it quits.

"This is the one where the families all started filing missing person reports, and when the inspector showed up to the factory, it was just completely empty, right?" I say, vaguely remembering my mom telling me this story with the same tone used to tell someone they have less than a week left to live.

"Creepy," Paloma comments, but her voice stays as upbeat as always.

Dust floats around the lobby like a snow flurry put on pause. There's burgundy carpet, which was probably bright red during the factory's glory days. High ceilings and cream-colored walls. An enormous chandelier fills the center of the room, more fitting for a hotel than a factory.

A large U-shaped desk sits against the wall opposite the entrance, which Paloma is already rifling through. On both sides of the desk are doorways to corridors leading in opposite directions. The other walls are stacked with gray lockers, floor to ceiling.

I start going through each locker methodically. I end up finding a bit of jewelry (a handful of wedding rings, a heart locket with a photo of two women inside), some clothes (a wide variety of sweatshirts and jackets), and a rusty letter opener with a floral-patterned handle. I keep the letter opener and the locket.

By the time I've finished one wall, Moe and Paloma are long gone. Before I can move across the room to start raiding the other set of lockers, a shadow moves on the outer fringes of my vision. I whip my head around as fast as I can, but once again, nothing. I do a slow 360 of the room to be sure. I guess I let my mom get into my head with her space horror stories.

Still, I'd rather not be in the lobby anymore.

I head toward the door on the left. The carpet changes from burgundy to royal blue at the threshold, the walls a lighter blue with piss-yellow stars painted on in seemingly no pattern. Eventually, the hallway opens into a huge office space featuring row after row of gray cubicles. Hundreds of loose-leaf papers float through the air—a mix of unfiled tax returns, PTO requests, and employee records.

I rummage through a couple of desks and find empty prescription bottles, an unfinished needlepoint, and unused rolls of reflective tape resembling what we have winding around our own suits. I watch the tape unspool through the air like parade streamers in slow motion.

I'm about to retreat to the lobby when I notice a sliding door peeking out from behind one of the cabinets across the room. I'm moving toward it before my mind has time to catch up; the best finds are the hardest to get to. Gold-plated dentures wedged in the far corner of an intergalactic vacation home's crawl space. A porcelain tea kettle tangled in the ropes of a flagpole at a cosmic military base.

I try to move the cabinet out of the way, but it's—predictably—nailed to the floor. It takes a lot of patience, but I'm eventually able to maneuver my gloved hands into the seam between the door and the wall and wiggle them around until I have enough room to slide it open. The space between the top of the cabinet and the top of the doorframe is a tight squeeze, especially with my helmet, but I shove myself through with all the grace of a watermelon sliding through a keyhole.

The room on the other side looks like it must've been the assembly-line floor. The ceilings here are even higher than in the lobby. Large cranes are bent at odd angles over an empty conveyor belt as if frozen in the middle of a task while countless gears, nails, and sheets of metal float in the air.

Before I can take a step farther, I feel that telltale nagging deep in my hindbrain that says I'm being watched. As soon as I turn around, my flashlight dies, plunging me into complete darkness. This is all punctuated by what sounds like the door sliding shut behind me with shocking finality. The funny thing is, sound isn't supposed to travel in space.

"Ugh, guys, my flashlight just died," I groan into the mic.

A beat, and then two voices at once.

"Sucks for you." (Paloma)

"That sounds like a personal problem." (Moe)

"Did either of you pack extra batteries?" I ask, already inching back toward the door I came from.

"That's something only Jared would do," Moe answers.

"Don't tell me you're afraid of the dark," Paloma immediately follows.

"I'm not scared, but I can't see anything." This is only a partial lie; it really is hard to see like this.

"Then go wait outside. If you see a shooting star, you can wish for Jared to bring the ship back around early," Paloma responds while Moe snickers.

Both of my teammates being as annoying as ever helps to calm my fraying nerves enough for me to stick my arms out in front of me and begin groping my way through the room. Like hell am I going to twiddle my thumbs in the lobby for the next hour just because I lost my light. We've visited places twenty times creepier than some washed-up factory.

Just when it seems like I'm getting nowhere, I feel my hip knock into something hard and almost scream before I realize it's only the conveyor belt.

I drag myself along its winding path, flinching every time my helmet bumps one of the miscellaneous items in the air, until the belt veers off into a shaft in the wall. It's just large enough for me to shimmy into. If I'm lucky, I'll end up somewhere close to either Moe or Paloma, or at the very least someplace less dark.

I brace both hands on either side of the passageway and slowly inch myself forward through the tunnel. The labored sound of my breathing bounces around in my helmet and gives me a headache. It feels like the farther I go, the tighter the shaft gets; at this rate, I worry I'll dislocate both my shoulders trying to maneuver my arms through the tight squeeze.

I try to distract myself by imagining the factory in its prime—people filling every cubicle, the decadent chandelier in the lobby greeting them each morning, going through their lockers after work, and chatting with the receptionists up front. People standing at the conveyor belt sifting through products, operating the cranes, and watching the bits and bobs slide out of sight into the shaft I'm currently crawling through. There must've been hundreds of people buzzing around. Hundreds of people who just never went home one day. Hundreds of people who were never seen again.

"Oh my god."

I bite back the urge to jump at the suddenness of hearing another voice.

"I just found the paragravity switch in the control room," Moe continues, basically screaming into my earpiece.

"No way," Paloma interjects. "Flip it; let's see if it still works."

"I already flipped it like ten times; nothing happened. It's probably busted." I can hear the disappointment in Moe's voice.

"Well, *I* found something way cooler than some broken paragravity switch." Cue dramatic Paloma-esque pause. "Vintage peanut M&M's still in the wrapper."

"Dude, that stuff will get you crazy sick," Moe groans.

They bicker over my earpiece while I continue my slow crawl through the shaft.

"And you, Danny? Find anything new to add to the clutter in your room?" Paloma asks.

"Nothing as cool as a wrecked paragravity switch and expired candy." I snort. "Besides, I already told you my flashlight died. I can barely see anymore."

Paloma blows a raspberry. "Boooo, where are you?"

As I begin to answer, my arms suddenly meet no resistance when I reach forward to scoot myself along the passageway. "I've been crawling through some type of tunnel; I think I just made it to the end, thank god."

I heave myself free and stretch my arms above my head. The room is completely empty except for the vague silhouette of a large rectangular hole in the middle. It looks like the indoor pool at the Y back home. As my eyes adjust, I can make out what looks like tile lining the floors, walls, and ceiling. The relief I feel from leaving the shaft quickly vanishes once I realize it's both the entrance *and* exit.

I float to the edge of the pool. Whatever liquid is in there is eerily still, like molasses. It takes a moment before I can make out my own reflection staring back.

"Guys, I might've actually found something cooler than a paragravity switch," I start, "or at least weirder.

"There's a pool here; I don't know what they used to use it for," I continue. "It's super creepy. The room doesn't have a door or anything, or even any furniture; it's just this pool."

A beat.

I feel the beginnings of a frown. "Guys?"

Silence.

"Guys? Hello?" I try to sound more annoyed than afraid, but my breathing is already speeding up, and my palms are getting clammy inside of my gloves.

This must be some type of dead zone. It happens, just like losing phone service.

After it becomes clear no one can hear me, I lean away from the edge of the pool, ready to head back to the passage. But as I move backward, my reflection surges forward, and I realize it's not a reflection at all.

A near identical suit swings at my helmet, leaving a thick streak of slimy liquid on the glass. I yelp as they throw their full weight against me, fully drenching my suit in mucus-y gunk. They aren't floating like I am but standing solidly on the ground. As if the paragravity switch worked on them alone.

"You guys." My voice trembles and cracks, shouting into a mic that I know doesn't work. "*Please*, you guys—someone—*something* is here."

I try to run away, but I'm only able to manage a big, clumsy backpedal, my body still very much weightless. I spin myself around and lunge for the passageway, but a foot in my side upsets my center of gravity, and then everything is upside down.

There's a moment where my mind goes from 100 miles per hour to zero so abruptly that I think I'm already dead. That this thing has killed me. But then every one of my senses kick-starts at once, and even though I don't know what the thing whaling on my helmet is, I do know one thing for certain: Momma ain't raise no punk.

I yank the belt on my attacker's suit to send them stumbling into the wall, and for my efforts, they grip both sides of my helmet almost lovingly before slamming it into the ground with all the force of someone trying to crack open a coconut. I manage to brace my arm under myself before they slam me down again, so my visor violently collides with my gloved hand instead of the unforgiving tile floor. I can't help the ragged cry that escapes me, but I roll onto my back more deftly than I thought possible, blocking their next attempt at gripping my helmet.

A strong kick to my sternum sends me pinwheeling across the room until I hit the opposite wall. They're running over instantly, slugging at my helmet three times in quick succession before I can block them. Unrelenting fingers alternate between prying at the seam between my helmet and suit and tugging at the tube of my oxygen tank. They're determined to disrupt my air supply.

I use one hand to try to push them away while the other digs around in my pocket. I feel the tube start to give in and have a nightmarish vision of my oxygen flow stuttering to a halt, leaving me to asphyxiate in a room where no one would ever find me.

A particularly hard blow leaves me with whiplash, dazed, my vision going fuzzy at the edges. I bite my lip until I draw blood, the sharp pain shocking me back into focus.

Finally, I find the smooth handle of the letter opener in my pocket. I'm aiming it at their stomach with a guttural scream before I even have time to think about it. They jerk in shock, knocking our helmets together in the process. The force only snaps my neck back, but it sends their helmet clean off.

I blink hard against the darkness, trying to make out their face. The shadows seem to jump and dance around their head, leaving them completely obscured no matter how hard I squint.

Then, it dawns on me: there's nothing to see. No head inside of their suit, just a blank space where I can see the rest of the tiled room.

Momma said people disappear in space, but I didn't realize she meant like *this*.

For a few long moments, we stare at each other. Or I stare at the space where I imagine a face would be. Tears well up and overflow in my eyes, floating uselessly and obscuring my vision.

Standing this close, I can tell their suit is the same shade of green as mine but covered in dust and slime. The resemblance stops there; they don't have any of the reflective tape snaking around their body, and on their left breast panel sits a red triangular mission patch.

Soundlessly, they bend down to retrieve their helmet, reattach it to their suit, and then walk toward the crawl space I came from, hoisting themselves up and leaving me behind. I fight the urge to vomit, clutching my stomach and closing my eyes for several long moments, my breath shallow and unsteady. I keep my eyes trained on the conveyor belt entrance. I don't let go of the letter opener.

I don't know how long I stay in the same position, waiting for the thing to return to finish what it started. The awful mucus-y residue on my suit has time to dry up and then flake off. It isn't until I hear a static-riddled, cut-off scream on the Bluetooth that I'm shoving myself into the crawl space and scurrying forward. I can't tell whether the panicked cry belonged to Moe or Paloma. I try calling out to both of them several times but receive no response.

I feel phantom hands reaching for my body and pawing at my face the whole time I wind my way through the assembly-line floor until I find the door leading back to the rows of cubicles, neatly shut where I had previously left it open. At some point, my Bluetooth regains connection; I can hear idle chatter now over the suit's sound system. I feel some of the tension leave my body at the sound of Moe and Paloma's bickering. They're both okay.

I'm the last one to arrive in the lobby.

"Thought we'd have to leave without you," Moe gripes.

"Who screamed earlier? Which one of you?"

Two expressionless visors stare back at me.

Finally, Paloma speaks up, a note of concern leaking into her typical irreverent tone. "What are you talking about?"

"On the mic, I—one of you also fought that thing, right? That's why you screamed?" I'm desperate for an explanation.

"Fought what? What do you mean?" Moe sounds genuinely confused.

Suddenly, the anonymity provided by our helmets feels unwelcome. I wish I could scrutinize both of them, stare into their eyes and determine who's lying. My desire to tell them about the thing that attacked me earlier is smothered by my sense of unease.

Slowly, the *Orbiter IV* creeps into view outside of the lobby entrance.

"Let's get out of here," I say, and I don't turn around to check if either of them follows me.

Jared lets us back on the ship with little fanfare. We de-suit quickly and quietly; if Jared notices anything is off with us, he doesn't mention it. I basically flee to my room and shut the door. I even lock it, something I almost never do. After a prolonged internal back and forth, I end up calling Momma.

I can tell she's at work, maybe on an early lunch break, her braids pulled into a neat bun while she sits on the curb.

"Can you tell me more about the people who disappeared? In space?" I ask.

She raises an eyebrow but doesn't protest. "You know the stories people tell, at all those factories and what have you, where one day everyone went into work, but nobody left. And when they go to look for them, it's just empty space suits at the workstations and desks."

"But—well, do you know what happens to the suits? Or, I mean, do the suits *do* anything to people?"

"They steal faces," Momma says as if she were reciting the weather. As if these words all make sense when strung together like this.

"They what?"

"I told you, Danika, it's no good dying in space. The spirit gets lost up there; it jumps around and finds a new body like a hermit crab." She smacks her lips together once, twice. "I kind of have the taste for a seafood boil for dinner; you wouldn't believe how much snow crab is going for these days."

We chat only a bit longer before her break ends. My mind is already trying to rationalize everything from the past two hours. Maybe I hallucinated the entire experience, but that doesn't explain why my left hand is achy and stiff, or why no one acknowledged the scream that I know I heard. *They steal faces*. With my rush to get to my room, I didn't get a good look at Moe or Paloma when we'd de-suited. Even if they do steal faces, do they steal mannerisms, personalities, memories, and inside jokes? Nothing seemed particularly off about either of them, and yet there's something keeping me on edge.

It takes time for me to gather the resolve to venture back out to the observation deck to remove the few things I'd managed to collect from my space suit's pockets. I inch toward the corner where our uniforms are floating in a tangled mess and blindly stick my hands in the pockets of the first one I pick up. I don't feel the letter opener or the locket, but something flatter and rougher.

When I pull it out, I recoil so violently, an observer would probably think I'd been shot. The red triangular mission patch floats directly in front of me. I pat down the suit with shaking hands and find thick collections of dust in every crease. During my manhandling, one of the reflective strips starts peeling off the arm as if it were taped on in a rush.

I can't remember who had been wearing the suit when we got back.

They steal faces. Momma's voice rattles around in my mind over and over and—maybe one of them found the patch and picked it up by chance. It's something I would've done. I repeat this to myself until I believe it before moving on to the pockets of the next suit. I breathe a sigh of relief once I can tell I got it right this time.

I roll the mission patch between my fingers and float down the narrow hallway where our bedrooms lie. I hover in between Paloma's and Moe's rooms, trying to find the strength to knock, to offer them the souvenir they left behind. To see if either of them has an explanation for why their reflective tape is floating away in limp ribbons.

Before I can decide whose room to enter first, Paloma's door slides open, and she and Moe exit together.

"Sheesh, Danny, you basically ran away once we got back. You feeling okay?" Paloma asks while popping M&M's in her mouth, likely the same ones she'd pocketed earlier.

I give a stilted nod and hold up the mission patch, ready to ask my million-dollar question when Moe interrupts me. "Please don't tell me that's one of the things you chose to bring back with you this time. They had whole rooms full of valuable metals and you bring back—what is that? A Girl Scout badge?"

Paloma and Moe laugh loud and long, the sound echoing as they head toward our small kitchenette.

Fighting off a full-body chill, I float backward into my room. I let go of the locket, letting it find a place among the rest of my floating bounty, but I keep the letter opener in one hand. The red mission patch is in the other. I lock my door again before settling into my usual spot by the window.

At first, I don't see anything except for the vast nothingness I've grown accustomed to out here. But when I press my whole face against the glass, I think I can see something bright in the distance. I lean in impossibly closer, straining my eyes until it hurts. It's human shaped and neon green. Reflective bands winding up and down the arms, legs, and torso.

Helmet ripped clean off.

GHOST LIGHT

ERIN E. ADAMS

"Transition Four—um. Four-One." Janine took a breath and then repeated, "Transition Four-One: Run crew, Lights 224 through 230, Sound 70 through 85 . . ." Janine whispered into the mic of her headset. "Standby."

"Lights," Sarah, the board operator, confirmed.

"Sound," Tim, the sound designer, echoed.

Where's run crew? Tight hairs along the nape of Janine's box braids prickled. Her finger hovered over the call button. Below her, the actors onstage moved swiftly through their lines. A quick flash of red on her headset relieved her. "Crew" finally popped into the channel, and Janine allowed herself a deep breath—all the pieces behind the scenes were set, ready to dazzle the full house below. Everyone in school had come to see the fall show's opening night performance.

Janine was the first sophomore anyone could remember being production stage manager—not assistant stage manager or splitting the duties with a senior—Production Stage Manager. This was her opening night, her theater, her show, and her first time calling it alone. Thankfully, the nerves in her voice didn't make her hands shake. Instead, she beamed with pride and stood so straight her shoulders ached.

Some holy angel
Fly to the court of England and unfold
His message ere he come, that a swift blessing
May soon return to this our suffering country
Under a hand accursed!

The actor playing Lennox boomed, his voice bouncing off the back of the house.

The dark animal of the audience rippled at the actor's yell. Some proud parents nodded in agreement. Other bored siblings shifted in their seats, uncomfortable, ready for the play to race toward its conclusion.

Janine's parents were absent at her request. Opening night was too much pressure. Unlike some of her peers, her parents loved that she did theater. Dad said he couldn't wait until she was working on a Broadway show, like *The Lion King*. She didn't have the heart to tell him she much preferred plays to musicals. And to get anywhere near *The Lion King*, she had to successfully call her high school production on her own.

She got her parents tickets for mid-run and—even better—closing night. Mom always asked Janine if she loved making "magic" when she controlled scene changes, lights, and sounds, but Janine didn't see what she did as magic. Janine didn't believe in the "magic of theater" because performance, especially this one, felt all too real.

"I'll send my prayers with him," a lord responded. Then came a long beat of silence. The entire play hung in the air, waiting for the next moment. Janine glanced down at her script. Multicolor-coded cues and blocking notes covered it. She was sure she'd memorized it, but when she traced her finger down the page the missed cue was . . . her. *Janine* was what the actors were waiting for. She fumbled in the dark until she double tapped her headset. All the other headsets lit up in response.

"Lights 224, g-go!" Janine's voice jumped. She swallowed and watched intently as the lights relieved the performers below, washing them in a deep blue. The over-ear headset made the whole right side of Janine's face break into a sweat. She shifted it, allowing some cool air to hit her skin. Actors shuffled in the dim light, moving from memory, guided by glow tape tracing a map that only made sense to the cast and crew. "Sound—Sound 70, g-go."

Sarah chuckled. "You see a ghost or something?"

Janine felt her face heat up. Sarah was a senior. Sarah had been sure she was going to call the fall show, not Janine.

"Not funny," Tim said in a harsh whisper.

Sarah groaned. "There's no such thing as ghosts."

Janine silenced them both. "Clear channel, please."

Everyone knew about this theater's ghost. Kids said they would see a girl in the lights, watching. They said she had been a vicious understudy overcome by ambition. She'd poisoned the lead in the school play to take her part. However, she'd never gotten to go onstage. The girl had met her demise on opening night. Some say it had been a car crash on her way to the show. Others said she'd made it to the theater but fell into the orchestra pit during her put-in rehearsal, breaking her neck.

Tim made sure he got the last word. "Every theater has a ghost."

Janine breathed to steady her voice. "Sound 70.5, go."

The cue picked up. It was something vaguely musical, enough to set the tone. Janine hummed along just loud enough to feel the vibrations in her throat but not let the sound escape. If it did, she would have been on beat but out of key. Janine was a theater kid, but she didn't have those kinds of theater skills. Sitting in rehearsal taught her the rhythm of the text, but she had no desire to speak lines onstage. The thought made her throat tighten.

Instead, Janine knew how many seconds of dark she had before the lights completed their fade. *Five*. She knew how many set pieces had to move before the stage was safe for the performers to enter. *Three*. She knew the crew backstage was waiting on her to say one word. That would come when the sound cue reached a combination of notes that made her hair stand on end. They felt more like a scream than a chord. The music climbed up, up, up, then the speakers in the theater emitted a cry that worked its way all the way to the rafters.

Janine took a deep breath. "Run crew, go." The run crew, true to its name, raced out to shift the set. Once the glow tape was covered, Janine directed, "Lights 226, go." The lights faded up. "Sound 75, go." The sound cue faded out. "Lights 228, go." A crossfade of color pushed in from the sides of the stage, mimicking a sunset. "230 and 80 . . ." The run crew scurried off. Janine held her breath, waiting for the last of them to clear, ready to launch the next cue. "Go." The lights completed, revealing a totally new space and a part of the set the audience hadn't seen before. Judging by a few gasps and murmurs, some people didn't think a high school production was capable of such a feat. Janine smiled as the audience marveled at her well-rehearsed machine.

"Oh man, that was *rough*!" Sarah said. She followed the remark up with an equally boisterous laugh. Janine turned to silence her. "What? It's true."

Janine pulled the mic down from in front of her mouth. Sarah rolled her eyes. Janine sought them out. When she finally had Sarah's gaze, Janine held one finger to her own lips. A simple moment, but still condescending—infantilizing—something a teacher would do to a student. Any other time or place, Janine would have cowered under Sarah's words. But during the show, in the booth, Janine was in charge, and Sarah had to listen to her. The booth was a place for quiet.

"No one can hear us up here," Sarah added in full voice as she watched the lighting cue complete. This time, both Janine and Tim flinched at her volume. "You two take this stuff way too seriously."

Serious was the only way to take being a techie. Forget the football field, the theater was the most dangerous place in the school. Kids wielded power tools, hammered sets, and used ladders to hang lights from the grid. The only reason no one really got hurt was they took their duties seriously.

Below them, the witches started one of the most famous scenes in the play.

Round about the cauldron go;
In the poison'd entrails throw.
Toad, that under cold stone

Days and nights has thirty-one
Sweltered venom sleeping got,
Boil thou first i' th' charmed pot.

Janine remembered from auditions that this was one of the hardest sections. The rhythm was strange. Iambic pentameter gave some actors more than enough trouble. The way the witches were written was not at all how people spoke.

"This part always gives me chills." Sarah let the fight go but refused to whisper.

"It's supposed to," Tim offered, lowering his voice even more, hoping to inspire her to speak softer.

Sarah ignored him. "Why?"

Janine cut in. "They speak the opposite way everyone else in the play speaks."

"That's not it," Tim corrected.

"It is." Janine insisted, "The meter is—"

"It's 'cause it's real," Tim replied. "That's why it's freaky. It's a real spell."

Sarah scoffed. "What does it do?"

"Like most spells." Tim's voice dropped even lower. "It opens a door."

Sarah frowned. "Every time?"

"I mean, it closes when they finish the spell, but—"

Sarah sucked her teeth. "No way they put a real spell in *Macbeth*!"

Tim and Janine froze. Sarah seemed content to sabotage the play by spiritual means if necessary to prove her point.

"What?" Sarah challenged. "I can say the name if we're doing the play."

Tim's energy moved from annoyed to serious. "That's not how it works, and you know it. Turn around three times and spit. Now."

Sarah frowned again. "Ew. No."

Janine split her focus between the show and the cardinal theater sin Sarah had committed. "Sarah, just do it."

Sarah's eyes burrowed into Janine. "Don't tell me you actually believe in that stuff."

Janine didn't. Just like the magic found in theaters, the ghosts that haunted them were all too human: technical difficulties due to a distracted board operator, a misplaced prop, a forgetful actor—missing pieces in the machine.

Pop!

With a bright flash of light, part of the stage plunged into darkness.

"*Double, double toil and—*" The spell became a shriek as the witches panicked on the darkened stage. The smell of smoke invaded the booth. A shower of glass rained down from the lighting grid. Thankfully, most of it landed between the scenery and backstage.

"Blown light," Janine assessed. She tapped the headset. "Can I get eyes on the deck and make sure the actors are okay?" Janine turned to Sarah. "How bad is it?"

Sarah moved quickly, assessing the lighting situation.

"Actors are fine," the deck crew reported. "How about lights?"

Sarah didn't respond; she just continued to work. Janine

rested her finger over the God mic. She'd never used it. Ever. If she turned it on, it would send her voice booming across the theater—to audience and performers alike. The show she and her classmates had worked so hard to make would be revealed for what it was: pretend. The idea of speaking in front of an audience, even in this capacity, made the two words needed to stop the show, *hold please,* hide in the bottom of Janine's chest.

"Sarah?" she asked again, barely able to hide the desperation in her voice.

"We're good." Sarah popped her head back up. "What cue are we in?"

"*Double, double toil and trouble—*" The witches' voices wavered, failing to find the strong unison they had before.

> "*Round about the cauldron go—*"
> "*Fillet of a fenny snake—*"
> "*Scale of dragon—*"

Janine's stomach dropped. "They're lost."

"Totally," Sarah mumbled, barely able to hide the delight in her voice. The show was falling apart. She turned to Janine. "What're you gonna do?"

Tim leaned in, trying to catch a cue. "They'll get the lines; give 'em a second."

Janine checked her binder. The actors were jumping all over the place. The blocking was wrong, the lines were wrong, and they were in the wrong cue. Someone in the audience began to cough.

"*Double, double toil and trouble— Double, double toil and*

trouble—" they repeated again and again like the curse it was, but the spell never completed.

Janine scanned her script for a moment to unite them. There were too many cues, too much blocking. The best one was, "Transition Four-Two, standby." She started to rattle off the sound and light cues and warned the run crew.

"You're gonna jump the scene!" Sarah rushed back to the board with an eagerness that irked Janine even more. Any decision that delighted Sarah was the wrong one.

"*Double, double—*" the witches continued in the loop.

Janine tapped her headset. "Transition Four-Two, go!"

Cue after cue, Janine righted the show. She never took her eyes off the stage for the rest of the performance. Sarah didn't distract her, content that Janine had bungled it enough. Every so often, Janine would be drawn to the spot lacking light just left of center. The blown light. It was the missing piece in the machine of her show.

After Janine called the last cue, after the house lights came up, after the applause died and the audience began to file out of the theater, Janine finally took off her headset. "Sarah, we need to talk." Janine turned over her shoulder only to see Sarah racing out of the booth. Janine followed. As she did, she heard snatches of conversation.

"I can't believe she skipped the best scene—"

"What else was she supposed to do?"

"I'd be so embarrassed if I was—"

The conversations only seemed to build as Janine passed by. Sarah burrowed deeper and deeper into the gathering thrall of worried actors, busy dressers, and judgmental crew.

"Sarah!"

Everyone turned to look at Janine. This wasn't the booth. The play was done, and Sarah didn't have to listen to her anymore. Sarah smirked and plowed out of the theater. Janine froze and faced all the questioning eyes in front of her.

"There were . . . um . . . we had technical difficulties." Her voice shrunk. "Sorry." Her eyes burned, but she refused to cry. Being on the crew was more welcoming than being an actor as long as you proved you could do the work. Janine rolled her shoulders to dissipate the tension in her body. She moved through her post-show to distract herself. The rhythm of resetting the space helped her tune everything out. She barely noticed that nearly everyone had left until someone tapped her on the shoulder.

"Janine?"

She whirled around and came face-to-face with a girl with long natural hair neatly plaited in two French braids under a black bandanna. She wore all black. When Janine tried to focus on the exact make of her clothes, her mind went all fuzzy. This girl was painfully nondescript. Janine searched her mind for her name and came up short.

"Yes?" Janine replied. The girl looked young; she must have been a first year. And she was staying late. Ambitious or lost? There was always a rotating crew doing odd jobs during the run, but Janine prided herself on knowing everyone's names. "I'm . . . I'm so sorry. What's your name?"

"Mary," the girl said.

When that still didn't ring a bell, Janine thought she knew why. "You with costumes?" Costumes always had people in at odd hours and sectioned off from everyone else. "They're usually done quick and out early. I bet you can go if you want."

"I want to help." Mary smiled.

"Umm . . ." Janine thought through her remaining duties. Set the props for tomorrow. Sweep. Strike the buckets of stage blood. Leave the ghost light on. Janine reached for her back pocket to grab her phone to check the time. It was gone. She felt over her person for it. "Have you seen my—?" Janine turned back to Mary only to find the girl buried in her phone. No, not the girl's phone, Janine's phone. Janine touched her back pocket again. She hadn't even felt Mary grab it. "Do you need me to call your parents for you? Come pick you up?" she asked, reaching for her device.

Mary continued to look at it. Its glow lit her face. She didn't seem to scroll or tap; she just stared into the light of the thing. Janine watched her for a second and was reminded of how her parents thought kids were sucked away from the world and into their phones these days. In reality, that couldn't be further from the truth. There was a whole world in there. Mary was drawn to the screen like a moth to a flame.

Janine grabbed a heavy broom from the wings. "Let's have you sweep," she said. "You make dirt as you go. Sweep. Stomp." She demonstrated by smacking the head of the broom on the ground after every sweep with decided strength. A small cloud of dirt lifted off the bristles and landed in a line in front of the broom. "Sweep. Stomp. Sweep. Stomp." Janine worked her way across the stage. She turned over her shoulder to check on Mary. The girl was still in Janine's phone.

Janine stopped. "Mary? You see that?"

"Uh-huh."

Janine frowned. "If I come back here and find a streaky mess, you're gonna have to sweep again. Can't mop a dirty floor." Janine handed off the broom. "Can I get my phone back?"

"But . . ." Mary took the broom, using only the tips of her fingers. "I like it." She clutched Janine's phone in her palm so tight her knuckles went white. Janine remembered a time when she, too, was desperate for attention. She'd never done anything like taking a phone to get it, but it was obvious: Mary was another lonely first year looking for her crowd.

Janine considered insisting on getting her phone back, but the screen was locked, and they were almost done. "Uh. Okay. Fine. Don't answer any texts." She shrugged and headed stage left.

Though she was used to closing down the theater by herself, Janine was thankful for the help. Even with a new set loaded in, she knew the nooks and crannies well and moved quickly. She peeked on stage to check on Mary. She was sweeping. Slowly. She took time to follow the motions Janine showed her to a tee. She cradled the broom like she was still figuring out how to hold it. Janine stopped clearing buckets of stage blood and grabbed a broom. Working in diminishing parallels, in a few minutes, she and Mary met center stage.

"Are your parents waiting for you?" Judging by the silence in the lobby, everyone had left for the night.

Mary stared down at the phone, tracing a fingernail over the glass.

"I can give you a ride home if you need one," Janine offered. She held out her hand, insisting on getting her phone back. "I'll need my phone, though."

Mary clutched it tighter. Janine didn't press Mary any further. She knew she'd end up waiting in the parking lot with this girl. No way she was going to leave her here. But Mary looked so sad. Before they were done, she wanted to do something special for her.

"Wait here," Janine said. "This is my favorite part."

"What?" Mary called after her.

"Don't move." Janine returned with a freestanding light. It looked like it belonged with the theater's red velvet curtains and wooden seats. Brass. Tall. Heavy. With a naked light bulb. Janine set it in the center of the space and then rushed back into the wings. "Don't move!" she repeated. Mary stayed put.

Janine cut the work lights, plunging the theater into darkness.

"Janine!" Mary yelled. She held the phone. It illuminated a short space in front of her. Janine turned on the light at the center of the stage. It shone like a beacon, cutting through the dark. For the first time that evening, Mary's gaze stayed up with the bulb.

"This is the light that always stays on at the end of the night," Janine said as she crossed back to center. "The ghost light." Seeing Mary's face fully, Janine noted the wonder on it. Janine stood up a bit straighter. "It's for safety. We have to leave it on so no one falls off the stage or, even worse, into the pit." She pointed to the orchestra pit at the front of the stage. It'd been repurposed as part of a forest, with trees rising out of the depths and branches descending on a few flats from the grid, for the last act. "But still. It looks pretty cool."

"Why is it called the ghost light?"

Janine couldn't help herself. "Every theater has a ghost,"

she said, repeating Tim's words. Then she added her reasoning. "They're harmless as long as you leave the light on. Keep 'em company." No matter if the light was for safety or to comfort a lonely ghost; if a performance stopped because of a distracted stage manager, or from naming a cursed play, in the end the show must go on.

The parts between Janine's box braids caught a chill, and her whole body trembled. She reached up and pressed her fingers against her scalp, warming the skin there. Janine turned to go, expecting Mary to follow. Instead, she stayed with the light.

"Mary?"

Mary reached for the bulb. She scratched down its side.

"Careful, it's hot."

Before Janine could pull Mary's hand away, the bulb burst, casting both of them into the dark. For the second time that night, glass showered the stage.

"Mary?" The dark echoed Janine's fear-filled voice back to her. She thought of how far away the wings were. Then how far the lip of the stage was. She started to move toward the wings. "Mary? You okay?" A light glowed away from Janine. Her phone. "There you are. How did you get over there?" Mary stood to the side of Janine, which meant she was near the pit. "It's okay. I'm almost to you."

Mary pulled the phone close to her, under her face. The glow made her features stretch and distort. Her face looked like the tragedy mask: her mouth tense and downturned, her eyes dark and hollow.

"I'll get you, and then we can feel our way to the wall." Janine reached Mary only to realize she was farther away than she thought. Janine reached out for her again, leaning ahead until she felt the lip of the stage under her foot. "What?" Janine stopped. Mary was impossibly beyond the edge of the stage. "Mary?"

Mary's expression in the dim phone light shifted from tragedy to comedy as a harsh smile bloomed across her face.

"*Mary*." Janine's voice darkened in a warning. She was scared but did her best to keep it to herself.

"What happens if you don't keep the ghost company?" Mary reached out. She wrapped a cold hand around Janine's forearm and pulled her forward. Janine managed to yank herself back. "You're supposed to keep me company."

"What?" Janine's mind struggled to wrap around what Mary just said.

The girl's frown returned. She dropped Janine's phone into the pit. It clattered through the false forest before shattering on the ground below, plunging Janine back into the dark. Janine's stomach lurched. Her muscles stung, wanting to run, but the dark stopped her. Mary was lonely and seeking company, but Mary was no girl. Janine reached for anything familiar in the vast expanse of the stage. Her hands grasped at nothingness as the reality of her situation fully dawned on her: Mary was a ghost, this theater's ghost, and she didn't intend to be the only one by the end of the night.

Janine felt a cool breeze rush over her fingertips. A draft. But from where? Surely the wings. Janine started to crawl in that direction. She felt grit under her palms and her knees—Mary hadn't swept well. *How did she sweep? How did she grab me?*

Janine's loneliness struck her. She'd driven to the theater by herself. Her parents knew to expect her home late. While she could count on her father to wait up for her, like he always did, he had a bad habit of "resting his eyes" only for a moment. Most of the time, she came home to Dad asleep in front of the TV. She was the one to wake him up and send him off to bed.

Pop!

A sound Janine knew well—a blown light, but the grid was powered down for the night. Still, glass rained down on the stage and over her. Janine covered her neck. Then she heard a deep groan above her.

Pop!

The burst of light that followed was just enough for her to see what was happening. Directly above her on the catwalk, a heavy light plummeted from the grid. Janine lurched back. The twisted metal landed where she had just huddled. Mary laughed. Janine's mind raced.

How does a harmless theater ghost become a full-blown poltergeist? The ghost light and the light in the show broke after Sarah had said the play's name. Janine had skipped the witches' scene, so they hadn't finished the spell and closed the door—in the end, no matter who started this, Janine was going to have to fix it. She could meddle in the details of blame, or she could survive.

Janine got to her knees. She knew what she had to do. Getting her feet under her, Janine turned over her shoulder three times and spit. She waited. She did it again. And again.

Firm hands pushed her shoulders forward. She did her best to catch herself, but she slipped on the shards of glass, crashing back to her knees. A few thin pieces found a home between the fibers of her jeans, cutting her.

"Wrong one." Mary laughed. She didn't feel Mary take her

phone because she'd literally slipped her hand through her pocket. But over the course of the hour, she had built her power. Soon after Mary had gotten her phone, she could clutch it. She'd taken her time handling the broom before she used it. She shattered the bulb before bringing down the lights. Each time, Mary was discovering how she could manipulate objects. Discovering the power to kill Janine.

Janine scrambled to her feet. She had to get out from under the grid.

Flash!

Crash!

Another light fell. The smell of burning filament filled her nose.

Flash!

Crash!

The flashes blinded Janine. She squinted as she made her way to the theater's back wall. The wings were closer but filled with lights—more weapons for Mary. If Janine could make it to the back, she could reach the fire exit.

To get there, she'd have to navigate the set.

The blocking images she'd sketched in her script came to her mind. There was a path around the benches placed on either side of the center and then straight up the platform that held the throne. When her fingers touched the platform's painted wood, she gripped it and hoisted herself up. Crawling around the throne, she felt the topography of the stage. There were two feet of clearance behind the platform, then an opening in the back curtain. After that, the exit would be a few feet away. Janine crouched down and jumped off the back of the platform.

She landed in blood.

A whole bucket of it. The thick syrup coated her foot and made the ground slide out from under her. Janine fell hard on her hands, sending white-sharp pain through her wrists. The medicinal smell of stage blood filled Janine's nose. Hash syrup, bitter cornstarch, and deep red food coloring. She tentatively rolled her wrists. Thankfully, for all the gore, she was fine. Her foot squelched as she moved. She didn't need to look up to know that Mary was working in the rafters above her.

Janine smelled Birnam Wood before it fell.

She threw herself back before the set piece dropped from its storage in the fly space high above the stage. The terrible din of it crashing rattled the air.

"Help!" Janine screamed. "Help!" Useless tears stung her eyes. Even if school was in session, the theater was a void. A soundproof place where people could be loud. Where they could imagine violence and pretend delight without being told to be quiet. Couple that with after-hours and night—no one was coming to help her.

"I need you to stay here with me, Janine!"

There was only one way left. The way Janine had retreated from earlier.

The pit.

Janine made her way to the front of the stage. To the most dangerous part. She moved quickly and carefully. Before she knew it, her toe found the edge again. She sat on the lip of the stage. Her breathing, sharp and heavy, echoed in the pit in front of her. She twisted and lowered herself over the ledge. A few brittle branches met her but quickly crumpled under the weight of her body. They wouldn't support her. Once they snapped, her feet would hang in the nothingness below.

Janine let go.

When she landed, her stage-blood-covered foot stuck to the ground. Her balance failed, and her opposite ankle rolled under her. The pain told her all she needed to know. It was broken. She screamed into her hand, feeling the wetness of her tears and the heat of her face. Her ankle began to swell. She grabbed a long branch and used it like a cane.

The theater was a dangerous place, but under the stage, she didn't have to worry about what could fall on her from the catwalk above. Also, all the supplies were down here:

Gels.

Extra props.

Old set pieces.

She knew the place like no other. This was her opening night, her theater, her show. Janine steadied herself. She wasn't going to run and hide. She was going to fight. Mary had proven how well she could trap Janine, but Mary's weakness was light. She was drawn to Janine's phone and the ghost light. They kept her docile. In the dark, Janine found what she needed: a replacement bulb for the ghost light. Janine grabbed it and headed for the stairs.

She was in her home territory now. Janine didn't know much about center stage, but she knew backstage like the back of her hand. Though she was injured, she used the edges of the space to support herself and keep a steady pace.

Wrong one. Mary's words echoed in her mind.

Janine kept climbing backstage. If Mary wasn't responding to the name of the play, maybe she was responding to the very real spell in it. The witches hadn't finished the spell. They'd opened the door but never closed it. Now Janine had to. She arrived stage left in the wings. Mary waited for her in the dark.

Janine had been working on the show for months. She'd recited all of it under her breath during rehearsal. She knew these lines. She stepped back out onto the stage. Her fright tried to take over, but the pain from her ankle overrode it.

"*Round about the cauldron go*," she started.

Mary howled like a monster cornering its prey. Janine moved toward the broken light.

"*In the*"—she grabbed the cool brass—"*p-poison'd entrails throw.*" Janine reached up and found the broken bulb; she twisted it out of its socket.

Flash!

She braced herself.

Crash!

Another light from the grid fell. It was so close, it rattled the stage under her feet. Janine twisted the new bulb into place.

"*Double, double toil and trouble; / Fire burn, and cauldron bubble.*"

She rattled through the rest of the spell, listing ingredients and instructions from the text. The light spilled over her hands when she got the bulb in the right place.

Up in the rafters, Mary froze. Janine watched her as she floated down to the light like a moth drawn to a flame. Once Mary got close enough, Janine shoved the light into her face. The girl's hollow eyes filled with the light. Her face distorted in agony. The theater groaned with her scream. Janine held the ghost light steady and finished the spell from the Scottish Play.

Make the gruel thick and slab.
Add thereto a tiger's chaudron,
For the ingredients of our cauldron.
Double, double toil and trouble
Fire burn and cauldron bubble!

Silence filled the empty theater. Janine leaned on the light and used it to explore the space. Nothing.

Scratch. Scraaaaatch.

The sound came from the bulb. The light made her eyes hurt, but in its depths, Janine saw a face. Hollow eyes stared back at her, and a mouth twisted between the comedic smile and the tragic frown. Janine blinked, and it was gone, as if by magic.

She shuddered and took in the empty proscenium. Her attention to the elements that made the play had helped her, but that was only a part of it. Owning the magic—*her* magic—in the machine of the show had saved her life. Janine held that knowledge close as she limped out of the space.

Later, she'd decide how to explain what happened and choose what details to share. Now, only one thing was important. Before she closed the doors to the theater, and locked them for good measure, she was absolutely sure to leave the ghost light on.

THE BRIDES OF DEVIL'S BAYOU

DESIREE S. EVANS

Aja dreams of broken girls.

Girls like the one sitting at the edge of her bed tonight. This girl is smiling at Aja, but the girl's teeth are all missing, leaving a mouth full of bleeding gums and gaping holes. Aja wants to speak to the girl, to ask her who she is, but she can't make a sound. She can only watch as the girl crawls closer, as her toothless grin widens.

Everything inside Aja is screaming to move, to run, to get away. With a count to three, she forces herself into motion, scrambling out of bed and tumbling onto the floor. When she looks up, she sees the girl moving toward her. This close, Aja notices how the girl's face is a Halloween mask of bleeding scars and crusted wounds.

Aja opens her mouth, finally able to screech, "*No!*"

The girl reaches out a hand as if to help Aja up from the floor.

"No," Aja whimpers again.

"*One!*" the girl rasps out.

At that moment something grabs Aja from behind, and she screams until she blacks out.

When Aja wakes, she remembers where she is.

She sits up, gasping like she's been underwater. It takes her a minute to relax enough to slow her breathing and to let her eyes adjust to the dark—she's back home. Or what used to be home, a tiny shotgun house on the outskirts of Devil's Bayou, Louisiana. It's the first time Aja has been back since her daddy took her away when she was twelve.

Aja throws off her blanket and looks around her old childhood bedroom. It feels weird not to be back in her freshman dorm room at Sycamore College in North Texas with her snoring roommate, Chelsea, and her Tweety Bird alarm clock. Aja shakes off the sense of wrongness that sits deep in her belly, the way she feels foreign even though she's back in familiar territory. Homesickness long ago settled in her spirit, a constant feeling of missing a part of her past she can't ever get back.

Aja knows time doesn't stand still. She's no longer a child running through the swampy grove, chasing fireflies and mysteries. She's eighteen now, an actual adult preparing to take on the world. Right? *Yeah, right.* Most days, Aja feels clumsy in her body, sloppy and unready for the tasks at hand. Like the task she now finds herself facing, having returned to Devil's Bayou, the land of her mama's kinfolk.

Two days ago, Aja took her last exam of the semester, and then convinced her best friend, Letricia Moseley, to fly to

Louisiana with her for the weekend. She and Letricia had arrived at the house earlier that evening, after driving two hours from the airport through winding rural backroads. The plan is to celebrate Aja's nineteenth birthday in two days here in her old hometown, heeding the advice of Aja's therapist from the campus health center: *Go to the source of your fear and let it go.*

Aja still can't believe it's been seven years since her daddy had told her they were leaving this cursed bayou forever. They'd resettled out in Fort Worth, and he'd forbidden her to ever return. Told her that staying away was for her own good, that the town gossip and rumors wouldn't follow her around anymore. But then the nightmares began a year ago, and the only thing Aja has been able to think about since is coming back to Devil's Bayou.

Aja checks the time on her cell phone: *11:15 p.m.* She'd slept for three hours, which for her is a pretty good run, considering her insomnia. Glancing at her phone's lit screen, she notices another missed call from her daddy. She swallows back her guilt. She hadn't told him about this trip, knowing he'd be upset. In fact, she's been ignoring his calls for the past three days, shooting off quick texts of *I'm fine!* and *Exams are killing me!*

Aja climbs out of bed and winds her way through the dark house before stepping outside onto the porch. She takes in the wild expanse of her family's land. The quarter moon sits huge and heavy in the sky beyond the bayou's bend, and the trees in the yard—full of moonlight and shadows—cocoon the house on all sides. Aja can't believe her ancestors had lived out here alone for generations. That Memaw Abbigail had died out here alone, too, nearly two years ago.

Needless to say, then, Aja is shocked when she turns to see the old woman seated in her favorite porch rocking chair, as if she'd been waiting for her.

"I'm still dreaming, ain't I?" Aja breathes out, the realization making her dizzy.

Memaw Abbigail chuckles, rocking away. She looks much like she did the last time Aja had seen her seven years ago. Thin and regal, with light brown skin and a head full of kinky silver hair. Her face, even in old age, had always been soft with few lines, giving her an ageless appearance.

"It come for you," Memaw Abbigail says to Aja, her voice rough but familiar.

"Memaw, stop with the ghost stories." Aja sighs, exhausted by the old tales and superstitions, the very reasons her daddy had taken her away in the first place. She turns from her grandmother and gazes out at the tangled yard, at the blue glass bottles that dangle from the branches of the oak tree out front. Like the witch knots that hang from the porch ceiling, the bottles are meant to trap evil spirits that make it across the bayou. Memaw Abbigail's old-time beliefs fill so many of Aja's childhood memories of home.

"Now that you a woman, that demon gonna come for you," Memaw Abbigail says again, gazing out at the darkness. "Gonna make you its bride."

"I ain't being no demon bride, Memaw!" Aja huffs, shaking her head.

Even here in Aja's dreams, her memaw is stubborn in her belief in their old family legend. Its origin story is one Aja heard throughout her childhood. Her ancestor, a young enslaved girl named Mosi, made a pact with a demon she'd summoned out in Devil's Bayou. In exchange for freedom and safety, the girl had promised the demon five generations of her bloodline's eldest daughters.

"*Cara. Margaret. Anna. Catherine.*" Aja whispers the names of the four young women in the family who had vanished into the swamp on their nineteenth birthdays. Never to be seen again. According to the story, Aja should be next, as the eldest daughter of the fifth generation descended from Mosi. Growing up, everyone in town would whisper about Aja's inevitable fate, about how she was the last of the cursed girls, the final bride promised to the demon of Devil's Bayou.

This piece of family folklore used to scare Aja more than anything in the world, but her therapist had told her these stories were just a way her family had tried to make sense of the horrible things that had happened to them.

"It's how we try to understand tragedy," Aja repeats aloud, into the quiet of her dream. "This swamp is full of natural dangers. Those girls either got hurt in the swamp, ran away, or killed themselves. No reason to blame a monster."

Wary of the family's influence on her, Aja's daddy even forbade her from attending her memaw's funeral two years ago. Now all Aja has left of her memaw is the crumbling, empty house she'd inherited from her. And these dreams.

Silence for a long time, and then Memaw Abbigail asks, "What do you dream about?"

Aja chuckles softly. A dream asking about a dream—how fitting. Yet it's true that all her dreams these days are like this one—murky, strange.

"What do you see?" her memaw continues.

"You. This house," Aja whispers, recalling her dreams of late. "Snakes swarming me." Her dreams are often filled with slithering things creeping and crawling across her body in the nightmare dark. Two weeks ago she'd begun to see the broken girls, but tonight was the first time one actually spoke to her.

"It's calling to you." Memaw Abbigail's voice echoes in the night. Then: *"Find the bone. Send it home."*

Before Aja can even process her memaw's last cryptic words, she sees a disturbance in the overgrown front yard. Something glistening in the moonlight, rising up from the tall grass. It takes Aja a moment to understand what she sees.

A teenage girl silhouetted against the night sky. She climbs out of the ground, her white dress mud-ravaged and bloody. Her dripping, tangled hair is plastered across her face. The girl has no eyes.

Aja watches in horror as two long snakes slither out of the girl's empty eye sockets, circling around her neck like a noose just before the girl collapses back to the ground. Down in the grass, the girl croaks out one wet, phlegmy word: *"Two."*

"Hell nah," Aja says, backing away slowly. "You're not real. I'm still dreaming." She wills herself to believe this as the girl begins crawling forward through the grass, her eyeless face grinning, ghastly.

Wakeupwakeupwakeup! Aja tells herself.

From inside the house, the family's old grandfather clock chimes five times.

Aja wakes to predawn shadows crossing the empty porch and

the emptier yard. She knows the dream is over, but her memaw's strange words linger.

Find the bone. Send it home.

Sleepwalking is nothing new for Aja, so she's not surprised she'd managed to make her way onto the porch last night. Images from the dream flicker in and out of her thoughts, feeling so real. Aja spends fifteen minutes in the bathroom, gathering herself. She looks at her reflection in the mirror, her honey-brown skin ashen in the fluorescent light. She traces her broad nose and full lips, which remind her so much of her absentee mama and dead memaw. She leans over the sink, turns on the faucet, and splashes water onto her face. She takes off her head-scarf, and her dreadlocks spill out wild and unruly, circling her face like a Black Medusa. She'd dabbed a little rose oil into her locs before wrapping them, and the scent of it fills the air, centering her. *She's awake.*

In her Introduction to Psychology class last semester, Aja had learned dreams were the mind's way of processing the information it takes in. Sorting out random thoughts and imagery from people's memories. Her therapist had said the same thing, adding that Aja's nightmares were her mind dealing with the rupture in her childhood.

Aja frowns at her puffy, bruised eyes and tired face. Despite whatever her daddy and dream memaw think, she's safe and finally *home.*

In the kitchen, Aja dons her memaw's old "Praise the Cook" apron and preps breakfast. As she scrambles eggs and fries up some pork sausage patties, the hiss and splatter of grease in her memaw's sacred kitchen space feels like another homecoming. She's in the middle of taking buttermilk biscuits out of the oven when Letricia springs into the kitchen, bright-eyed and bushy-tailed.

"Morning, love," Letricia sings before giving Aja a wet smack on the cheek.

"Go make the table, I'm just finishing the grits," Aja says, smiling.

Aja and Letricia met during freshman orientation and had hit it off right away. Letricia had grown up in Biloxi, and she and Aja bonded over their love of frozen custard and the graffitied study carrel on the fifth floor of the campus library. Letricia is funny and sarcastic, and completely stunning: tall with Southern-girl curves, dark brown skin, and long Senegalese twists that fall down her back in waves. Today she's wearing a form-fitting black tank top over camo cutoffs and ridiculously high cowboy boots, obviously ready for the country life.

"Did you sleep well?" Letricia asks, her big blue hoop earrings swinging and catching the light as she takes a seat at the kitchen table.

There's something cautious and soft in her friend's voice that makes Aja's gut twist. "Did you hear me sleepwalking?" Aja asks, worried.

"Nah, but the look in your eyes tells me all I need to know,"

Letricia says. "The dreams haven't gone away just because you're on home soil?"

Aja sighs. She'd come home hoping it would put an end to her dreaming, but so far the dreams feel more alive than ever. "I'm glad you could make it," Aja responds instead.

"I was not about to miss my girl's legendary haunted-ass birthday," Letricia says with a soft laugh. Then she quietly adds, "Plus, I knew coming back here would be tough for you. I wanted to be around in case you needed me to sing loud and off-key nineties slow jams to cheer you up."

Aja returns the laugh, then turns her attention to bringing the food to the table. They go quiet as they sit and eat. The buttermilk biscuits, fresh from the oven, crunch sweetly as Aja bites into them. Her memaw's old recipe, just another taste of home.

"Did you clear out our entire bookshelf?" Aja asks, nodding at the stack of paperbacks Letricia had brought with her to the table.

Letricia smiles around a mouthful of jam-filled biscuit. "Your grandmother had quite the collection. But sis, you didn't tell me they have whole-ass books about *you*."

Aja groans, taking a long sip of orange juice before glancing at some of the familiar titles. *Local Folklore of Fournier Parish, Louisiana. The South's Most Haunted Swamps. Tales of Voodoo in the Bayou.* And her favorite: *The Cursed Brides of Devil's Bayou.*

Aja picks that one up and examines the small black type. It's an original copy, dog-eared, worn. It was written back in the 1970s by a Tulane grad student collecting local folklore. Aja had grown up with these campfire ghost stories, but this book recorded her family's actual memories of the four disappearances.

"When your therapist said go home and confront your demons, did you tell her you had *actual* demons?" Letricia asks.

Aja snorts. "We have talked at length about what it means to be Abbigail Guilbeaux's grandbaby, the Devil's Bride."

"Are you still mad at your dad for making y'all leave?"

"Not really," Aja admits. She'd forgiven him a long time ago, understood why he did it. Her daddy had never believed all these old stories, and he'd hated that Aja had spent the early part of her childhood scared of her own shadow, scared to go to sleep, barely able to function. The teenage years she'd spent in Texas had brought some normalcy.

Aja doesn't believe the stories anymore, but there will always be a part of her that still freezes up with fear, a part she has tried hard to bury that can't help but worry something terrible will happen. She came back to put an end to these fears. Aja's therapist wants her to face the stories head-on and to see the family's curse for what it always has been—a fiction.

"I spent most of my childhood thinking the boogeyman was going to get me," Aja explains into the quiet between them. "Now I'm trying to understand why people believed something so crazy. How they still believe in it."

Letricia inclines her head, watching Aja closely. "Are you saying you don't believe *any* of the stories? You're not scared of the curse?"

"I don't believe, and I'm not scared," Aja says resolutely. She swallows a big gulp of juice to clear her suddenly dry throat.

"Well, I'm creeped out," Letricia says, lips twitching. "But I'm a true believer."

Aja meets her best friend's eyes and cracks a knowing smile. Letricia loves a creepy story; she spends hours trolling through online forums dedicated to weird urban legends and creepypastas. Aja herself hates scary stories, since she's grown up in her own version of one.

"Not to mention, your boogeyman is so old-school," Letricia adds with a little awe.

"What do you mean?"

"Think about it. We're in the age of photoshopped internet memes. But this is no meme, no Slender Man, Siren Head, or Man with the Upside-Down Face," Letricia says, ticking each name off with a finger. "Your boogeyman is an old-school baddie. Blood curses. Demon deals for souls."

"Yeah, I guess so," Aja says, scraping the last of her eggs around her plate.

"Your dreams are freaky, too. And they've only gotten worse the closer you are to nineteen," Letricia says, frowning.

"My mind is messed up, that's all. Which is why I'm here. The only way to deal with the past is to confront it head-on." Aja gets up from the table and takes their empty dishes to the sink to let them soak. As she runs the water, she glances out of the window above the sink. The flimsy white curtain ripples, and the swamp in the distance looms like a wild and strange old friend.

Aja jumps at the sudden movement outside the glass. A face stares at her through the open window, a teenage girl with dead-black eyes, bulging veins, and twisted, bloody lips. The girl is whispering, but it sounds more like she's hissing when she says: *"Three!"*

Aja closes her eyes, inhales and exhales several times. She opens her eyes to an empty window. No broken girl. Just trees rustling in the wind.

That afternoon, after Letricia leaves to pick up some groceries in town, Aja settles on the porch to nap. When she opens her eyes to the sound of crunching gravel, she's not all that surprised to find Miss Louisa, the family's closest neighbor, pulling her car up in front of the house. Word travels on the wind in these parts.

Miss Louisa climbs up the porch carrying a big picnic basket and a familiar smile. Her hair is cut short, a cute salt-and-pepper bob that flatters her brown skin and dark eyes. A few small creases around her eyes are the only testament to the years that have passed since Aja last saw her.

"Sugah, look at you! So grown!"

"Good to see you, Mama Lou," Aja tells her as Miss Louisa takes a seat across from her in the porch's wicker chair.

"I fixed up a couple of your favorite dishes," she says, pointing to the basket of food. Then she quiets and adds, "Oh, honey, I'm so sorry about Abby. We all miss her."

"Yeah, me, too," Aja says, swallowing through the thickness in her throat.

Miss Louisa's eyes are sharp on Aja's face as she says, "Your birthday's tomorrow. I'm worried."

"I really don't believe those old stories," Aja says, although her voice goes whisper-soft, recalling the morning's waking dream.

"But you came back; some part of you must believe."

"Miss Louisa," Aja sighs. "*Please.*"

"Don't you go giving me that look, girl," Miss Louisa scolds. "Your mama ain't had the sense she was born with, running off when you were little, leaving you behind. Scared the demon would come for her even though she was the youngest of Abby's girls. I watched your memaw help your daddy raise you. She took good care of you. She swore she'd not let that thing get you like it got her Cathy."

Catherine Guilbeaux, the fourth girl who disappeared. Memaw Abbigail's oldest daughter. Aja doesn't respond for a moment, the hidden wound of her mama's long-ago abandonment sitting next to the more recent loss of her grandmother.

"Your memaw knew that your daddy taking you away wouldn't change things. The curse would follow wherever you ran," Miss Louisa says.

"My daddy never believed," Aja says. "When Mama left us, he blamed this town. And he thought leaving here would free me from going crazy like Mama and everyone else."

"Believe or not, you need to cast it out," Miss Louisa says. "Your memaw knew that much, had found a lady who worked roots to protect you."

"I'm just here to say goodbye," Aja insists.

"Give me your palm, baby," Miss Louisa says.

Aja looks at her, surprised. This was a game Miss Louisa had played with her, pretending to read her palm like a fortune teller when Aja was little. Aja raises her hand and opens it, palm up. Miss Louisa cradles it, making soft tutting noises.

"What do you see?" Aja smiles, indulging her.

"Strange." Miss Louisa frowns, her thumb pausing for a moment, tapping at Aja's life line.

Aja's smile slips. "What is it?"

"It's already been visiting you."

Aja pulls her hand away. "Please—"

"*Find the bone. Send it home,*" Miss Louisa whispers.

Aja is surprised to hear the exact words from her dream. "What did you say?"

Miss Louisa shakes her head as if coming out of a trance. She looks at Aja with worry and squeezes her hand tight. "I think . . . I think maybe your memaw left something for you in this house before she died," she says. "Find it and be ready."

Aja looks closely at her empty palm, dread settling in her chest. She and Miss Louisa embrace for a long moment before the older woman leaves. Aja grabs the basket of food, stretches, and heads back inside the house. She can't let this town get to her. As Aja enters the living room, she startles when she sees movement on the sheet-covered couch. She looks back toward the guestroom but remembers Letricia is still out getting groceries. No one should be inside the house. Aja looks at the couch again, at the sheet somehow moving by itself.

"No fucking way," she whispers, shaking her head in disbelief. This must be another dream.

Even in the dim light, Aja can make out a solid lump moving under the white sheet. The sheet slowly bulges outward and then inward, as if something breathes beneath it. When the sheet rises up from the couch on its own again, Aja gapes. Slowly, the sheet gains definition: the impression of a nose, a forehead, eye sockets, and a moving mouth. Breasts and arms curve into place, creating the silhouette of a tall, thin woman.

"*Four.*"

The word is so soft that Aja can barely hear it.

"No," Aja says. *Not again not again not again.*

The sheet collapses onto the floor as if there were never anything beneath it at all. Aja shivers in a sudden cold sweat. She's by herself in the living room. Wide awake.

That night, Aja dreams she's lying flat in bed, unable to fall asleep.

She can't move her body; the commands she sends to her limbs go unheeded. Sounds boom in her ears: floorboards creaking as if someone is walking in the other room; the grandfather clock ticking; water dripping from old pipes; the slithering and hissing of a thousand snakes moving along the floor, closer, closer, and ever closer. Her mind spins in fear.

This is just a dream, she tells herself. *I'm in a dream.*

The thought settles her until the voice comes, the hissing turned into whispered words. Words hard to make out at first, but slowly taking shape until they fill her mind: *Do you hear me?*

If Aja could move her mouth, she would scream as the voice, brittle and terrifying, asks: *Will you let me in?*

Goawaygoawaygoaway, Aja thinks.

The voice hums as if satisfied. *Mine.*

You're not real, Aja insists.

Look up, it says. *I'm real.*

Aja looks up, and that's when she sees it—the mass of rolling shadows moving across the ceiling. It slithers down the wall to the floor, arranging itself into a monstrous figure with two glowing yellow eyes. Its arms and legs are like strips of storm cloud woven together.

Her demon.

Obey, it says with a voice that sears into her.

You're not real, she tells it.

The demon's body ripples with sparking white light as if an electric current pulses through it, and then it opens its mouth to release a sound like a steam engine screeching against the tracks. The noise fills the room, fills Aja's head until her brain is close to exploding.

Stop! she tells it.

The demon closes its mouth with a crunch and lowers itself over her. The hot, heaping weight of it smothers her, crushes her down deep into the mattress. It feels like every bone in her body is on the verge of breaking. But she can't move, can't fight it off.

The demon crawls over her, smelling of rot and wet earth, the stench of the deep swamp. Its foul breath tickles her cheek as it leans in and says again, *Mine.*

Aja feels close to vomiting as its long fingers grip her face, its claws raking against her throat. Its jaw distends and widens as if it is readying itself to eat her alive.

In the midst of her terror, Aja notices movement from the front of the room, realizing there are more horrors to come. Four young women stand in the darkness watching them. They are teenage girls like herself, their bodies broken and mangled. As one, they turn their battered heads to gaze directly at Aja.

Her nightmare girls.

They each raise an arm to point at her, and images flash through Aja's mind. She sees the young women whole and alive, wearing school uniforms, talking with their families, holding the hands of friends and lovers. She sees one of the girls playing jacks on the porch of Aja's family home. One of them working at the counter of a local grocer. One of them running through the tall reeds of the bayou, laughing. In that moment, Aja understands who these girls are—her ancestors—and she's shocked she hadn't connected the dots earlier. The images stop as suddenly as they came, thrusting Aja back to the current dream. The girls all turn away from Aja and point down at the floor. They scream as one, a wailing that spills across the room.

The demon jerks his body above Aja as if surprised, leaping up and bellowing in anger before turning to rake his claws across Aja's thigh. Blood splatters. The world disappears.

Aja wakes in the same position on the bed as she'd been in her dream. The sensations of her body return slowly, a thousand dancing pinpricks across her skin. When she's finally able to sit up, a throbbing pain rolls down her thigh. It's only then that she looks down. Her pajama shorts are stained in blood, the fabric torn to reveal four slashes across her thigh.

Fortunately, the cuts aren't deep, so there's no need to rush to an emergency room. Letricia has enough camp counselor first aid training that she goes full-on Florence Nightingale the minute Aja stumbles into her room in tears. The two of them huddle in the bathroom, Aja seated on the closed lid of the toilet while Letricia kneels in front of her. Letricia cleans away Aja's blood with gentle strokes of a warm washcloth, adds antibiotic cream, and then bandages the wounds. Aja has managed to stop crying; she tries not to think about anything at all and concentrates on watching Letricia's steady brown hands.

"All done," Letricia says, sliding a bandage over the last scrape. She stands up and snaps her first aid kit shut.

"Thank you," Aja says. She hates how her voice sounds so scared.

"How are you feeling?" Letricia asks gently, her eyes lingering on Aja's patched-up thigh, on the red stains seeping through the bandages. "Does it hurt?"

"Just a little," Aja admits, pinching her lower lip between her teeth, trying to stamp down the fear, the tears. Her hands shake when she leans on the sink to stand. She looks at the pile of bloody towels on the floor, her heart in her throat. She needs to understand what is happening.

As Aja and Letricia clean up the bathroom and change the bloody bedsheets, they review a list of theories.

Theory one: Aja scratched herself in her sleep. It could make sense, but her nails are cut short, and there's no blood on them.

Theory two: Aja sleepwalked and cut herself on something sharp. But Aja and Letricia circle the house three times and find nothing that could have made the marks, and there's no evidence Aja left the house in her sleep again.

Theory three: Aja is, in fact, being haunted by a demon.

Aja no longer knows what's real. The skepticism she'd worked so hard to cultivate over the past several years, the skepticism her therapist had backed with sound scientific explanations and promises of eventual healing, is fading fast. *The demon is a manifestation of your trauma.*

Aja came back home in hopes her bad dreams would go away, thinking it was her guilt that was fueling them in the first place. Her guilt for leaving Devil's Bayou. Her guilt for missing her memaw's funeral. Her guilt for not understanding how to help her damaged family.

But if the demon was *real*, if everything she'd been told as a child is real . . . she doesn't know what to think.

"What the hell is happening?" Letricia whispers as they settle down at the kitchen table over cups of coffee and an open internet tab.

"I don't know," Aja says, the fear in her voice from earlier replaced with something harder and more self-assured. "We need to figure it out."

Aja spends the rest of the night on her laptop deep in research mode, searching the internet for any and all articles on demons and demon deals. Letricia puts her chatroom skills to good use in online forums and communities dedicated to creepy things. They find articles on possessions, on curses, on hauntings. They examine photos, case histories, firsthand accounts of Catholic exorcisms. They read until their eyes glaze over, jotting notes down. When Aja finally looks up from her own laptop, the warm light streaming in from the kitchen window tells her it's morning. Finally.

She's nineteen.

"The demon called on the girls several times before taking them," Letricia reads aloud, slamming the screen door as she makes her way onto the porch. "And then the girls all vanished the night of their nineteenth birthday."

"From *The Cursed Brides of Devil's Bayou*?" Aja asks from where she's seated in her memaw's rocking chair, watching the sky blush pink over the bayou.

Letricia holds up the book. "Yeah. It says each girl told friends and family about months of hallucinations, nightmare visits."

"So I'm not crazy. Just haunted," Aja confirms, still feeling absolutely batshit crazy.

They spent the morning hours learning more about demons, digging for clues in old family albums and searching the house for bones, any bones.

"Why does it happen on your nineteenth birthday?" Letricia wonders aloud. "Is there some numerological significance?"

"Legend says it's 'cause Mosi was nineteen at the time of the deal," Aja says. "So that's all the time the girls get."

Letricia frowns. "Imagine being on the run at our age, scared and alone in the swamp, all those slave catchers coming for you."

"Doing what you have to do to survive," Aja says.

"Like making a demon deal," Letricia says.

Aja glances at her phone, sees her daddy's text message wishing her a happy birthday. She hasn't responded yet. Aja doesn't know what she would say to him if she called him right now. "I just . . . I don't even know if I believe any of this," Aja says aloud. "How can I?"

"Believe it," Letricia says, fervent. "That demon tried to carve you up for dinner last night!"

"Happy birthday to me." Aja gives a broken laugh, curling her legs under her chin. Even that slight movement causes her thigh to sting. Another reminder that this is all too real. After a few beats, she asks, "What does the bastard even want?"

"It's not like these other possession stories we read about," Letricia says, pointing to their stack of demonology printouts from the internet. "I think this thing wants to claim your soul."

Aja considers the four young women standing in her room last night, showing her their lives. "The girls' spirits could be trapped, tied to the demon in some way," she says. She recalls how each girl had come to her in dreams this week, telling her their number, the generation they'd been taken. Warning her that she was next. Number five, the final bride.

"To free them, you need to break this curse. You need to take back the power," Letricia says firmly. "I think your memaw was telling you how."

"*Find the bone. Send it home*," Aja recites.

"Miss Louisa said it came to her as she read your palm, right?" Letricia asks. "It can't be a coincidence you dreamed it, too."

"But we've searched the house all morning, no 'bone' to be found," Aja says. She looks up at the sun's position in the noonday sky. The night is coming much too fast. She can admit she's really scared now. If this is real, if that thing comes for her tonight . . .

"Let's get to work on the backup plan, then. We have rituals to perform," Letricia says, picking up the printout called "Banishing Evil: A Starter Kit."

"I can't believe this is happening," Aja says. "My birthday . . ."

Letricia reaches out and squeezes her shoulder. "The party's just begun. We have a demon to banish and a cake to cut. It's not over until it's over."

Aja stands and gives Letricia a tight hug, a gesture she hopes says: *Thank you for being here. Thank you for battling demons with me.*

By late evening, they've tried four different rituals from just as many religions. Holy water and Latin; charms and incantations; sage and incense; chants and prayers for protection. The house remains quiet throughout each attempt. No demons, no waking dreams, no ghost girls.

"How do we know when it's been banished?" Aja wonders aloud. They're in the living room, lighting candles and drawing sigils on the hardwood floor.

Letricia frowns. "I think you'll feel it. Like that book says, he's connected to you by oath and blood."

"I guess," Aja says dubiously. "So what's next?"

Letricia holds up a piece of loose-leaf paper with her own writing on it. "This rite isn't from the internet; it's from my mama's people in Mississippi. Old Delta hoodoo stuff, you know. We start off by throwing salt in the four corners of the house, and then we bury a bottle of it under the house."

The skin on Aja's neck tingles. For the first time all day, something in her mind clicks into place. She thinks back to last night, how the girls all pointed down to the ground right before the demon slashed out in anger.

Aja runs to her bedroom, Letricia on her heels, and they stand over the very spot. When Aja taps her foot against the wood, the floorboard groans.

"What's under the house?" Aja asks.

"Um . . . your crawl space?" Letricia hazards.

"Yes, exactly." The house sits about six feet off the ground, a bayou flooding safety precaution. "Memaw Abbigail used to tell me how folk used to hide old sacks of luck under their houses back in the day. For protection, to ward off evil. I would see her down there sometimes, digging around."

Aja smiles at the memory of her mud-covered memaw climbing up from under the house, whistling. She turns to Letricia. "I think I know where the bone is."

The house sits raised on large brick beams, and there is enough space that Aja can crawl under it without much difficulty. Aja had insisted Letricia wait in front of the house, just in case something happened, and she needed to go for help. Her best friend is currently armed with an old rosary, internet prayers, and Florida water—ready for battle.

"We got this," Aja whispers to herself as she directs her cell phone flashlight toward the area of the crawl space where her memaw would bury her luck bags. Aja doesn't know what she expected to find under the house, but the biggest obstacles are the tangled growth of weeds that slows her movements; the spiders, whose thick cobwebs catch on Aja's clothing; and the muddy ground, still waterlogged from an early-morning rain.

As she crawls forward, Aja's eyes widen. Her memaw had placed big rocks in a circle around a spot in the center of the house. Aja takes out a small shovel and begins to dig in the marked location, and it's only a couple of minutes before she hits her prize: a medium-size tin can, which she opens to find a small red flannel sack just like the luck bags her memaw used to carry around. *This some good gris-gris*, she'd say.

The instant Aja's hand closes tightly around the rough material, a hissing noise surrounds her. She recognizes the demon's presence, can feel him creeping from the house's woodwork, the swirling cloud of his body reshaping itself in the shadows of the crawl space. Aja's pulse skips.

For a moment, her mind goes blank. She can't think or move, and she feels herself falling into the mess inside her head. Every childhood fear she's ever felt claws its way inside of her. Every nightmare, every snaking terror.

"Aja, hurry!" Letricia yells from in front of the house.

Aja snaps out of the fear and sucks in a deep breath. *We got this*. She tucks the bag into her shirt pocket and rushes back toward the surface. When she crawls up from under the house, the night erupts.

The demon rages like a tornado, the gray cloud of its mammoth body whipping through the trees, thrashing branches to the ground.

Aja grabs Letricia's waiting hand, and they race together through the storm, finding cover beneath the trees lining the edge of the front yard. They turn to watch the demon coalesce into a swirling storm cloud right above the house.

Aja turns to look at Letricia, their bodies racked and breathless. She sees raw terror etched in Letricia's expression, a sure mirror of her own. Panic courses through her body, but Aja squeezes Letricia's hand and says, "I need to go and do the spell now."

Letricia looks unsure but nods and says, "Be careful."

Shaking, Aja turns and runs toward her memaw's house, her house now.

Everything slows down then, the moment stretching out like taffy. Aja sees debris and broken branches hurtle across the yard, sees Letricia kneel in the mud to pray. Aja's heart races; her throat burns with each wheezing breath. She feels faint. She doesn't think she's strong enough to face this. Pressing her eyes shut tightly, she wills herself to wake up.

But she knows this isn't a dream. Aja knows this is real. She is here, face-to-face with her demon. Her tears blur the moon into a bright smudge beyond the sprawling canopy of trees. Aja doesn't feel strong enough; she's not her memaw. She doesn't know anything about this old magic, about the way of dirt and bones. All she knows is this constant fear that she's lived with all her life. *I am not strong enough*, she thinks. Then she hears her memaw's voice in her head arguing with her, like always, saying, *You are more than strong enough.*

Aja reaches into her pocket for the red sack—the protection bag she found beneath the house—and empties it into her palm. A pile of herbs, feathers, and stones. And in the middle of it all, a sharp white finger bone. Aja wraps her hand around it, and she knows instantly that it's Memaw Abbigail's. The vision plays out in her head. She sees Memaw Abbigail slicing into her own hand, carving off her finger, sacrificing it for the banishment ritual. She knows her memaw did it to save her, not wanting to leave Aja defenseless. In that moment, Aja misses her memaw so much that it hurts.

Above her, the demon stops swirling, the gray mass solidifying into a shape with arms and legs. It approaches Aja with a wicked laugh, reaching out as if to embrace her. *Come to me*, it says.

"I'm not yours!" she screams as the demon wraps itself around her body, dragging her onto the ground. The demon hisses as Aja begins reciting every prayer and incantation she's learned over the past day. Memaw Abbigail's voice comes to her on the wind again: *"You must banish him now!"*

Aja breathes in and summons all her strength. "I banish you from this place forever!" she bellows. "By the blood of my ancestors, I banish you!"

You are mine, the demon growls.

Aja can feel its anger, raw and all-consuming.

"I spent my entire life being afraid," she tells it. "Waiting for you to get me. But guess what? You can't have me."

Mine, the demon hisses, crushing her arms between its hands.

"I don't belong to anyone but me!" Aja shouts. "I banish you back to wherever you came from!"

The pain of its hold intensifies, and she thrashes as it picks her up off the ground. But through it all, Aja holds onto the bone, and says as loud as she can, "You are no longer bound to my family. The deal is broken! We are protected!"

Aja's mind flashes to the girls who had come before her and to Mosi, the desperate ancestor who had struck this bargain to begin with. She hears them in her head, their collective voices pouring from her as she screams, "*We are free; you are banished. There will be no more demon brides in Devil's Bayou!*"

The demon screeches, releasing her at last, and Aja thuds to the ground. As the demon reaches out for her again, Aja lunges forward and stabs the bone into its chest.

The demon explodes into hundreds of pieces of twilight glow that dissipate like smoke as they hit the ground.

The world goes quiet. Aja feels the sharp rupture of their connection. She collapses onto the wet soil. Her body aches, and she is exhausted down to her toes.

"Aja!"

She turns her head in relief at the familiar sound of Letricia's voice. Letricia rushes to her, and Aja reaches out and pulls her close as Letricia throws herself on top of her.

"Hi," Aja murmurs into her best friend's shoulder.

"Hi," Letricia says, tears in her voice. "You're so badass."

Aja laughs, feeling it deep inside. She did it. She's free. "We're all free," Aja whispers to the bayou, to the missing girls, to her memaw.

"Happy birthday, bestie," Letricia says, squeezing her tight. "Can we finally cut the cake now?"

Aja's eyes are closed against the aches in her body, but she still manages a small smile. "Yeah, we can," she says. Then her eyes slide open to see the bowled heavens spinning above her, the purple sky tipping toward morning.

TMI

ZAKIYA DALILA HARRIS

1.

"What's with the flip phone, baby?"

I lower my phone and look up from my blanket to see who's disrupting my quiet time. He's exactly what I expect: tall, muscular, early twenties. We've never met, but I know he hangs around this park almost every day, catcalling new mothers, geriatric nannies, barely legal teen girls, and everything in between.

Usually, I ignore any stranger who calls me "baby." But not today. Today, I remove my sunglasses and pat the area of grass beside me. "Depends. You got time for a story?"

A flash of surprise crosses his face. Then, a satisfied grin. "You can tell me anything you want, baby," he says with a wink. "I'm yours."

He sits so close I can smell the coffee on his breath. I want to turn and run far, far away, but I don't. I *can't*. This guy might be the best chance I get. So instead I lean forward, put on my brightest smile, and ask, "Have you ever heard of Etta Vee?"

II.

It's a stupid question, really, because every warm-blooded American has heard of Etta Vee. There was a time when she was everywhere: on the couch of every morning show, behind the microphone of every podcast, splashed across every magazine cover. You probably saw her promoting a new novel or a new collection of short stories, or—toward the end of her career—a memoir she would refer to as her passion project.

To entertainment critics, Etta had raw, natural talent. No one wrote a word about her without reminding readers that her highest degree was from Beacon Prep, a small private high school in northern Connecticut.

If you'd asked anyone in the Beacon Prep community, though, her success could be attributed to Beacon itself. The facts—at least, the reported ones—didn't lie: she'd walked through Beacon's distinguished doors a scholarship kid and left a superstar.

And a few years later, toward the end of my junior year, Etta came back to Beacon.

"I read somewhere that she *never* does events like this. Every appearance she does is usually prerecorded. Something about fear of crowds."

"I'd be afraid of *this* crowd if I were her. Have you *seen* this auditorium since we got here? Total fire hazard. It's wild."

The two girls sitting in front of me swiveled their heads around. I followed suit, anxious to avoid potentially awkward eye contact. But once I turned, I couldn't stop looking. The auditorium was wild, indeed. You would have thought we were at a Hollywood movie premiere instead of an optional first-period assembly. Every single seat was taken. Students who hadn't shown up early enough either stood behind the back row of seats or crouched in the aisles. And everybody—students and faculty alike—was joyfully snapping selfies, thrilled to tell the world they were about to see our generation's latest sensation in the flesh.

I turned back around, my limbs buzzing with an unfamiliar sense of community. I couldn't remember when—or if—I'd ever felt like I truly belonged at Beacon Prep. I'd joined this club and that club my freshman year, striking up as many conversations as I could. But no matter how hard I'd tried, I'd never learned how to speak the same language as any of my classmates.

Eventually, I started trying less and observing more, and here's what I noticed: my unmissable status as a scholarship kid who took a thirty-minute bus ride here from the other side of town. My absence on the annual ski trip—a trip that likely cost more money than Mom made in six months at her nursing job. And perhaps the most telling of all, my itty-bitty, pay-as-you-go flip phone.

But somehow, I'd managed to make Beacon work. I'd sifted through the toughness to find the cozy parts, like Kim, the bus driver who always greeted me like a friend when my day started and ended; or Ms. Hernandez, a teacher who sometimes let me eat lunch in her office while she watched telenovelas. And now, I had Etta Vee. Etta Vee, who'd survived these very same classrooms as a Black scholarship kid from the other side of town. Etta Vee, who'd gone on to become a household name practically overnight. Seeing her up on that stage would help me remember why I was here in the first place: a chance at a better future.

Flash!

The girls in front of me giggled as they peered at the selfie I was certain I'd unintentionally photobombed. I groaned and flipped open my phone. Times like these often called for a game of snake. But before I could attempt a new high score, the lights dimmed, saving me from my loneliness.

"What the hell *was* that?"

"I don't know. But my *god*, it was awful."

"Right? That was worse than that drinking and driving thing they made us sit through last month."

I recognized the last voice: Mallory. We'd been lab partners in freshman biology for an entire unit. We'd even dissected a baby squid together. If I'd really wanted to, I could have turned and joined the conversation that was happening behind me. *Leave Etta alone*, I might have said. *She wasn't that bad.*

But I couldn't. Because they had been right.

When Etta had first stepped out onstage, she was met with so much applause that it had taken Vice Principal Frederickson five minutes to get everyone to settle down. But the Etta we'd all gotten to know from the internet disappeared the moment she opened her mouth. She seemed uncomfortable up there onstage—almost like she was frightened. She could barely finish a sentence without forgetting where she was going with it. The entire time, she seemed more focused on the long French braid that stretched over her shoulder than any of the questions she'd been asked.

Now, as I followed the crowd out of the auditorium and into the lobby, I couldn't help but wonder: What *happened*?

"Hot take," I heard Mallory say. "She did this because she felt like she had to. The Beacon Alumni Association *can* be pretty stalker-y about bringing famous alumni back. I heard that's how we got our homecoming emcee last year."

The guy sucked his teeth. "I bet she did it for the money. I heard famous people can make up to twenty-five thousand just shaking ten students' hands."

"Well, in that case . . . she doesn't need me to buy her book, then. You waiting in this line? Or do you wanna head to the cafeteria?"

"Fuck this. I'm hungry."

I stole a quick glance at Mallory and her friends as they exited the lobby along with countless other students who'd decided to forgo meeting Etta. I felt a pang of guilt, $25,000 be damned. Maybe Etta was having an off day. Maybe she had cramps. Whatever the reason, she of all people should be allowed to phone it in at *least* once.

When I found the meet-and-greet table, there was no line.

"Hi! Thanks for waiting," Etta said dryly. She was smiling, but it barely reached her brown eyes. She regarded my empty hands. "Not one for reading, huh?"

My face grew hot. "I, uh . . . I've read every single book of yours," I said. "But I get them from the library."

Etta's eyes softened as she stopped fiddling with her braid. "I love libraries. I used to work part-time at the main branch back when I was at Beacon."

"They're really nice there," I agreed. "They always wait to kick me out until the very last minute."

"They used to do that for me, too." Etta chuckled, then sighed. "God, I miss that place. I can't really spend too much time in libraries these days. You know . . ." She gestured at herself, then the small army of adults behind her that I could only assume were her entourage. "Because of all of this."

I nodded. I did know. Kind of.

"So. You're a junior, right?"

"Good guess. Although people always take me for a freshman," I admitted. "The whole five feet tall thing, I guess."

Etta laughed. "I get that. Do you know what you're gonna do after you graduate next year?"

"I'm thinking of taking time off after graduation. Maybe get a job and try to save up for community college."

When I dared share this plan with somebody at Beacon Prep, it usually garnered a pair of raised eyebrows or a simple *Huh*. But Etta just nodded approvingly. "That makes so much sense," she said as she reached for a book from the stack beside her. "What's your name?"

"Sam."

"Sam. This is from me," she said, picking up a pen. "On the house."

"Oh, wow . . . thank you!" I beamed as she signed the title page in big swooping letters. "Um, would it be possible to take a photo with you? We'd have to use your phone, though, because . . . well . . ."

I pulled my flip phone out of my pocket and showed it to her, bracing myself for judgment. But to my surprise, Etta let out a loud, high-pitched squeal. "Oh. My. God! Check this out."

She dug into her bag and held up a rectangular piece of plastic. A shiny red rectangular piece of plastic that looked an awful lot like my own flip phone.

We both gasped.

"Are they the same? Can I see?" Etta asked, wide-eyed. I handed it over. "The exact same kind," she murmured, turning the two phones over in her hands. "Amazing."

I shook my head. "I've never seen another one out in the wild before!"

"We definitely *have* to get a photo now. Hey, Phil—will you take a photo for us?"

At the sound of his name, a tall, mustached man peeled away from the posse behind her and came over.

"This is my uncle-slash-manager, Phil," Etta said as I joined her on the other side of the table. Once we'd taken a few photos, she sprang out of her chair and gave me a hug. "Best of luck to you, Sam! And congratulations—you're almost free."

I thanked her and turned to leave. But Etta called for me to wait before I could float too far away. She slipped something cool and familiar into my palm. My phone. "You might want this."

III.

I spent the rest of the day convinced I'd tripped and fallen into an Airbnb on cloud nine. Nothing could get me down—not even the discovery that my phone had died shortly after first period. Since I couldn't play snake during lunch, I started rereading Etta's novel, perfectly content with eating solo for once. I reviewed three chapters for the art history final I had the next morning during study hall, and two more on my bus ride home.

My entire world wouldn't change until later that evening.

"He's staying over *again*?" I regarded the three place settings on the table with disdain. "This is the third night this week."

Mom emptied a box of rotini into the pot of boiling water on the stove and shot me a look that said, *I bet he can hear you*. I shot her one back that said, *I don't care*. It wasn't that I didn't like Nigel. I just didn't like having to *perform* for Nigel. He was always asking me questions about prom and friends and football games—questions that made me suspect he'd had an annoyingly idyllic high school experience. But what bothered me even more was that Mom wasn't always home for dinner. I preferred to spend the few nights she didn't have to work late at the hospital with *her*. Not with Nigel and the cast of *Pawn Stars*.

"Come on now, Sam," Mom said, stirring the pasta. "You know he's a good guy."

"*Who's* a good guy?"

Nigel breezed into the kitchen and wrapped an arm around Mom's waist. I planted my butt on the stool Mom occasionally used when she was too tired to stand and cook.

"You're such a ham," Mom joked, but she kissed him back, far too passionately and too long for my liking. I shuddered and unplugged my phone from the wall, desperate for a distraction. But the second it powered on, something was wrong.

The background. When had I changed it to a sunset?

Before I could make it make sense, the room went white,

and everything went silent. Then, I heard whispers—a chorus of dozens, hundreds, thousands, coming from around me—or maybe within me?—building and building and building until suddenly, finally, my ears popped.

Then, just like that, I was back in the kitchen.

I looked around. Everything *seemed* normal. The food was still cooking on the stove. Mom and Nigel were still cooking, too.

There was just one difference: the television. Why was it so *loud* all of a sudden?

God, this woman feels so GOOD! I can't wait to undo these buttons and—

I cleared my throat pointedly. "Hey, Nigel . . . I don't know *what* kind of family-friendly show you were watching in there, but can you turn it down, please?"

Nigel finally let go of Mom's waist and frowned. "Turn what down?"

I just wish Sam had somewhere else to be just for a few hours so Marjorie and I can—

"Seriously? How do you not hear that?"

Mom reached for the spoon she'd been using to stir the marinara sauce, but she was staring at me like I'd just asked her to shave my eyebrows off. "I'm not sure what you're talking about, honey," she said slowly. "But the TV isn't on."

Is this one of those cries for attention Dr. Schaffer warned me about? I thought Sam was too smart to—

It was a woman's voice this time. My *mom's* voice. That part I was sure of. But her lips hadn't moved at all. She was still staring at me, concerned.

Dr. Schaffer said I should always make her feel heard so maybe I should—

"Love," Mom said, turning to Nigel, "did you leave the television on?"

Nigel shook his head as a voice—his voice, it had to be—rang loudly in my ears:

Such a vibe killer. Sam could really stand to loosen up. I bet she's never even gotten any—

"Air! I really need to get some air." I was beginning to feel dizzy, like I might throw up. But my discomfort with the current situation was strong enough to pull me to my feet. I grabbed my keys from the kitchen counter and started down the hallway.

Mom hurried after me. "But dinner's almost ready!"

"Start without me!" I slammed the door behind me and jogged off into the warm, and hopefully quiet, night.

It was the phone. It *had* to be. I'd opened it, undergone some weird psychedelic experience . . . and now I could hear Mom and Nigel's thoughts. It was that simple.

But *was* it?

I paced through the dimly lit sidewalks of our apartment complex, racking my brain for a more logical explanation. Maybe I'd fallen off that kitchen stool, hit my head, and slipped into a coma. Or maybe the coma had happened much earlier. Had my bus crashed? Had someone bonked me with a basketball during gym? I played my day back in my mind in excruciating detail, pausing on each class to search for a moment when I might have endured some kind of head trauma.

Then, I remembered: *Etta*. We bonded over loving the library . . . and having the same phone. She'd taken my phone. And then she'd given it back to me.

Or, at least, I'd *presumed* she had.

Suddenly, my legs felt too woozy to do anything but fail me. I collapsed onto one of the park benches that lined the quietest part of the apartment complex I could find, turning the phone over and over in my hands. *No way*, I thought. *There's absolutely no way this could have anything to do with—*

Bad idea to be sitting out here all alone where no one can hear you scream—

I whipped my head toward the source of the male voice I'd just heard. A man wearing a baseball cap was making a beeline toward me in the dark, seeming to purposely avoid the path illuminated by the streetlights. I stood up and balled my free hand into a fist, my heart pounding in my chest.

Just never know these days; there are lots of weirdos and rapists hiding in plain—

"Leave me the fuck alone, or I'll scream, asshole! I have mace!" It was a lie, but shouting it made it feel true for some reason.

I heard something yelp. A dog. A small one, it sounded like.

What the hell is her problem?

"Uh. Sorry? Didn't mean to frighten you. I'm just walking my dog."

He stepped into the glow of the streetlights and waved. It was Mr. McManus, an old man who lived with his cocker spaniel a few buildings down. He sometimes helped dig Mom out of her parking spot when it snowed.

"Sam, right?" Mr. McManus considered taking another step forward, then decided against it. "Are you . . . okay?"

I placed my sweaty palm on my forehead. I was not okay. "I'm fine, Mr. McManus. Th-thanks. You have a good night."

"You, too." He waved before pulling his dog in the direction of his apartment.

I sighed, the adrenaline rush giving way to relief as I waited. Fifteen seconds passed. Then, when I was sure I was alone:

Damn Black kids always causing trouble—

The tears came first. Then, the rage: hot, sharp, and surprisingly violent. This *damn* flip phone. Was this how I was going to spend the rest of my life—hearing the thoughts of every single person I came into contact with? If so, I was doubtful I'd survive even the next few hours.

A sudden pair of high beams from an oncoming SUV distracted me from my pity party. I took a couple of steps forward, a plan I hadn't even realized I'd been hatching now fully formed in my brain. Without stopping to worry about the consequences, I chucked the phone as hard as I could into the path of the car.

The loud crunch of plastic beneath tire brought me more satisfaction than I'd felt in a long, long time. I turned and started toward home, feeling famished.

God, yesssss, Marjorie, that feels so good—

My eyes snapped open so quickly, you'd have thought I'd

heard a gunshot in the next room. But it was just Nigel. And my mom. Doing . . . I didn't want to know what.

"No," I whispered, covering my ears with my hands. "No, no, no . . ."

His voice just grew louder and more insistent as he expressed his approval in excruciating detail. I groaned. Falling asleep was out of the question now. I reached over and fumbled for the switch on my bedside lamp, blinking until my eyes adjusted to the brightness. But when they finally *did* adjust, I wished they hadn't.

Because there, sitting patiently next to my lamp, was a shiny red flip phone. A flip phone that definitely didn't look like it had been run over by an SUV.

I scrambled out of bed and backed away from the desk, staring at the phone like it was a persistent cockroach. I'd watched it get crushed. But somehow, this piece of plastic had found its way back to me.

I surveyed my room for another option, zeroing in on a dictionary I'd never once cracked open, then immediately ruling it out. Smashing the phone with something heavy hadn't worked before. I needed something else that would be harder to come back from.

Something like . . . water damage.

I lunged for the untouched glass of water on my desk. I dropped the phone in. And I waited.

I'm not sure what I expected. Not an apocalyptic-style combustion, but *something*. A tiny spark. A staticky fizzle.

But there was nothing. Nothing but my mom's voice now, telling me things about Nigel that were making my stomach turn.

IV.

I skipped breakfast the next morning.

If I didn't have an art history test that would count for 75 percent of my grade, I would have skipped school altogether. The fear of failing forced me out of bed and into the quickest clothes I could find. I paced around my room, waiting for Mom and Nigel to leave for work. There was no way I could face them after last night. And that was just the beginning. Beacon Prep was going to be a nightmare. The sheer number of thoughts I'd hear just walking down the hallway would probably bring me to my knees. And if I thought Mr. McManus was bad, who knew what kind of thoughts my privileged and mostly white classmates would have?

My only consolation came from knowing I had art history first. I could go in, take the test, then pretend I was too sick to stay the rest of the day.

Finally, I heard the front door slam shut. I stepped out of my room slowly and confirmed Nigel had taken his bag and his set of keys with him. Then I grabbed my backpack, shoved a granola bar in the side pocket, and bolted out the door.

The bus was just pulling up when I arrived. At least *one* thing was going right for me this morning.

"Morning, Kim," I said, huffing my way up the steps.

"Just in time! You get some extra shut-eye this morning?" Kim asked jovially. A wave of relief washed over me. Maybe this bus ride wouldn't be *too* bad.

I regarded the handful of classmates who'd been picked up before me as I made my way down the aisle. A few were asleep, their thoughts mostly quiet, nonsensical sounds that were easy enough to tune out. A theater girl was singing a show tune in her head. She was pretty off-key, but another warm wave of relief settled in as I grabbed a seat near the back. I could work with this for the next thirty minutes.

I pulled my art history book out of my bag and flipped to the section I'd had the hardest time getting down: Greek architecture. I willed my droopy eyes to keep reading, using my pinky to underline every key detail. But I was just so . . . *sleepy* . . . and now that we were on I-95, the bus ride was so smooth . . .

I pressed my head against the cool glass window. A little nap wouldn't hurt. Plus, I could use this mind-reading thing during the exam. Only if I needed it, of course. It wouldn't be cheating . . . not technically. And hadn't I suffered enough?

I had nearly drifted off when a low voice wafted over to me from the front of the bus.

I wonder what would happen if I drove into oncoming traffic or maybe even off a bridge—

My eyes popped open. Was that . . . *Kim?*

I shook my head. Kim was kind and bubbly. She was easily the nicest bus driver I'd ever had. There was no way she could possibly . . . it had to be the car beside us, or maybe—

I bet no one would survive. I bet we'd make national news. I bet then they'd wish they'd paid me more—

They're just thoughts, I reminded myself. *She's entitled to think what she wants.*

But still . . . who the hell fantasizes about crashing a bus to make a statement?

I set the book aside and put my head in my hands, deciding what to do. I could scream and carry on until she agreed to let me out in the middle of nowhere. Or I could sit up front and try to chat with her. I could remind her that we were real, actual humans—mostly lower-income ones, it was worth noting. We had families who would miss us. A crash like that would be devastating.

I was rising to my feet, still not sure which option to choose, when I felt something vibrate. I removed the flip phone from my pocket and read the notification window: *You have 1 unread message.*

I felt like my stomach had left my body, jumped out the open bus window, and splattered onto the highway. After twelve hours of silence, I'd figured the phone only had one setting: "on." I'd never sent any texts or made any calls with it because I was too scared. Opening it had already unleashed a Pandora's box of trouble. What if it cursed me with another terrifying ability?

I stared at it for a few seconds, debating. *Fuck it,* I finally thought. *What's worse than being able to read minds?*

I opened it and read the text sent from an unknown number.

> First night down, many more to go! I'll be at Breyer's till 9. Let's celebrate! Xo E

Celebrate? I had no clue what that meant. But I *did* know who "E" was. I sat back down and forced myself to take a breath. Breyer's Diner was a short walk from school. I could return Etta's phone, then race back to school. I'd have to miss the first twenty minutes of my test. But at least I'd be free.

I paused outside the entrance to Breyer's, in need of a pep talk. There were at least a dozen cars in the parking lot. That meant there were at least twelve minds inside—more than I'd ever had to hear at once.

After one long inhale and an even longer exhale, I finally opened the door and hurried into the threshold, feeling a twinge of comfort as a Hall & Oates song filled my ears.

"Can I help you?"

A hostess with curly white hair narrowed her eyes at me. I smiled at her immediately rather than wait to hear if her thoughts about Black people came in the same hue as Mr. McManus's. "I'm supposed to be meeting someone here," I said cheerfully, hoping niceness would thaw her out some. "But I don't see her."

The hostess grunted but didn't move.

You should be in school instead of hanging around here causing who knows what—

"I go to Beacon," I added quickly. "But I'm not feeling well. My older cousin said she'd meet me here and bring me home. Can I grab a stool while I wait?"

She gave me a once-over, then followed my pointed finger to the empty row of seats at the counter. At last, she grabbed a set of menus and motioned for me to follow. "Lenny'll get your order," she said, nodding toward the cook on the other side of the counter.

I thanked her, pleased when her thoughts shifted from me to a waitress who'd forgotten to refill the sugar bowls again. But they were quickly replaced by different thinkers' thoughts:

How in the hell am I supposed to raise this kid by myself?

I didn't even want her story about working late tonight—working late is bullshit!

I bet it's Tommy; she's always talking about Tommy's just gonna keep spitting in their food if they're never gonna leave a tip—

It was nearly impossible to pin down whose voice was whose, except for the last one. The last one—which also happened to be the loudest of them all—likely came from the aproned man who was flipping pancakes a few inches away. No breakfast for me, then.

I closed my eyes and inhaled. *Just focus on Hall & Oates,* I told myself, bobbing my head to the music. *Focus on yourself. Focus on anything but everyone else in this diner.*

"Yes, Sam! It took me months to figure out the meditation trick."

I jumped. The voice *sounded* like Etta's. And yet, when I opened my eyes, I didn't see her. The young woman standing in front of me was wearing thick-framed glasses, baggy black sweatpants, and a faded maroon sweatshirt. A Beacon Prep baseball cap covered her long hair. But the most shocking difference was her piercings: one ring each in her lip and eyebrow, and two in her nose, which she was now wrinkling at me in confusion.

"What's the . . . oh! My new look." Etta pointed at her face triumphantly. "These actually aren't new. I've had them for years. I just know for a fact this shit freaks a lot of middle America out. So I took them out for interviews and all that." She settled into the seat next to me. "How's it all going with the phone, Sam?"

I had to stop myself from screaming, *How's it all going? Seriously?* "Well," I said quietly, motioning to the bags beneath my eyes, "I didn't sleep last night."

"The first night is always the hardest," Etta commiserated. "But don't worry; it gets better."

"I don't see how that's possible."

She nodded again. "I get it. You had a rough night. But once you learn how to adapt, everything will—"

"*Adapt?*" The bitterness in my tone surprised even me. "I don't know why you did this to me, or how," I said, placing the phone on the counter between us. "But whatever it is you did, you better undo it. *Now.*"

Etta blinked at me, astonished. "Wait . . . you're kidding me, right?"

"I heard my mom's boyfriend say things I will never be able to unhear!" I said. "I don't think I can ever go home again. Or ever leave my home. I can't keep this thing, Etta."

Etta sighed. "Let me explain. When I was at Beacon, my biggest dream was to become a writer. But my mom was on her own, which meant I was either always working or taking care of my little brothers. So when this phone came into my life my senior year . . . it was like a golden ticket, Sam. It gave me so many ideas. No, more than that—so much *access*. I learned how to get my voice out in the world. How to actually *be* something I'd only dreamed of. And I couldn't have done that without this phone. Not coming from where I came from."

Etta placed a hand on my arm, her eyes glittering with tears. She blinked them away before continuing. "Now. I won't lie and say it wasn't hard at first. There were a lot of harsh truths I had to swallow. But once I found a way . . ." She shook her head. "This changed my life for the better. It changed my *family's* life. And it could change yours, too. I just need to help you learn how to use it the way my mentor helped me."

I pulled my arm away. "But why *me?*"

"I've been wanting to pass this along to someone else who needed it, and when I met you yesterday, I heard all of the things that were going through your mind. I thought—I *knew*—that this would be helpful for you. So, listen."

Etta pulled a notepad out of her bag. "Phil manages some properties in northern Connecticut. It's quieter up there—we can find you a one-bedroom so you'll have at least a little more peace. Phil can also help get you a job. A personal assistant position usually pairs well with this gift, and it can pay pretty well, too. And I can help you get better at tuning out the voices that don't matter while concentrating on the ones that do. Think about it," Etta practically sang. "You'll be able to mold yourself into the perfect college applicant. You can find friends who genuinely appreciate you for who *you* are. You can even ace that art history test you have today. It's all going to be worth it, Sam. I promise."

Etta was looking at me so intensely that I had to look away. I focused on the cook's latest breakfast order instead, mulling it all over. The thought of my own apartment—an apartment where I'd be far from Mom and Nigel—was tempting. But even more alluring was the idea of acing my SATs. I had done all right on them the first time around, but they could definitely be better. So, too, could my GPA. Like Etta said, I *could* mold myself into the ideal candidate for any college if I really wanted to.

It all just sounded so easy. *Too* easy.

"If it's so great," I said finally, "why are you giving it all up?"

Etta didn't respond. When I looked up again, she was glaring at me, her gaze a wall of steel.

Only then did it hit me: I hadn't heard a single thought of

Etta's since she'd sat down. Like she'd been purposely trying to hide something from me.

But what?

"I just *told* you," Etta said coolly. "I wanted to help you out. I have more than I need now."

But her words sounded too forced to be true. I crossed my arms and leaned forward. "You know what I think?" I asked. "I think you decided to foist this thing onto me because you can't handle it anymore."

Etta pressed her lips together in a hard line. "No."

"You had a hard time up on that stage yesterday," I said. "You were all over the place. Which is fair—I've read about tons of big celebrities getting stage fright. But your reason was different. Because all you could hear were the thoughts of every single person at Beacon. Right?"

"I was *tired*," Etta snapped. "It had nothing to do with—"

"And you're writing a memoir, aren't you?" I pointed out. "Must be hard to do that when you have a million other people's voices in your head."

Etta was shaking her head so fervently that I knew I'd struck a nerve. Good. I jumped to my feet and plucked the phone off of the counter. "I've been treated like a charity case long enough to know when it's happening, Etta. Don't act like you're doing this out of the goodness of your heart. You pawned this off on me because you want to live your life without having to hear what everybody else thinks about it. Well, news flash: so do I. So either help me destroy it, or take it back and give it to someone else."

Etta flinched when I pointed it at her. "Sam, I swear to god, if you hand me that thing, I'm gonna scream."

Her tone was measured, and her voice had barely risen above a whisper. But I knew she wasn't bluffing. We glared at each other for what felt like a lifetime. Finally, I slipped the phone back in my pocket. "Fine. I hope you enjoy the rest of your life knowing you ruined mine."

With that, I started toward the door, ignoring the nosy hostess's stare. I was only a few steps away from the door when Etta called out, "Wait!"

I spun around on my heel and watched, relieved, as Etta started toward me. "We can't destroy that thing. And I can't take it back. But I can help you find someone else to give it to."

The man stares at me for a good fifteen seconds. Then he erupts into laughter so hearty, I almost wonder if Etta was wrong about him.

Almost.

"Yo, that story is *wild*!" The man laughs, slapping his thigh. His eyes flicker up and down my body like it's a tall, cold glass of iced tea. "You got any more stories for me, cutie?" he asks, moving in closer, reaffirming my plan.

I shrug and hand him my flip phone. "Give me your number. I bet I can think of a few more."

BLACK PRIDE

JUSTINA IRELAND

It was getting closer.

Maisie ducked into the tree line, away from the road. There was a creek not too far down the hill. She could lose the creature there. Run through the water so it would lose her scent. Wasn't that how it worked?

Tiny pebbles filled her sandals, jabbing her soles and causing her to stumble from the pain until her feet found purchase in the dead leaves and ferns of the forest floor. But she still didn't stop. Her fear was too great.

The day had been scorching and when they'd left the cabin to head to the lake, Maisie hadn't opted for much more than a halter top and hot pants. Now, as she tore blindly through the woods, brambles and low-hanging branches reaching out with sharp fingers, she wished she'd worn her overalls instead.

But it was a fleeting thought as the sounds of something crashing into the forest behind her stole her wits, fear erasing everything but the need to get far, far away. She looked over her shoulder, expecting to see the creature through the dappled shade of the forest, but there was nothing. Not yet.

There was still hope.

Maisie's lungs burned, and her side ached, and still she ran, crying as silently as she could. If she was quiet, maybe she could somehow escape the monster when Roger, Peter, and Shelly hadn't. But the memory of claws ripping into her friends' soft flesh was too fresh, and she hiccupped on terrified tears. How could this happen in the middle of the day? Monsters belonged to the night.

She had to get away. Someone had to know the lake wasn't safe. Someone had to warn people.

She could be that someone.

Maisie's toes smacked into a partially exposed rock, and she went down with a yelp, rolling over and over. She was close to the creek, and the landscape suddenly dipped, sending her headlong down the incline. She rolled until she was sliding down an embankment, battered and bruised, scraped and sore. She climbed to her feet awkwardly, hopping a little when she tried to put weight on her right ankle. It was twisted, maybe sprained. She wouldn't make it much farther.

But there was the creek, and she hobbled into it, the cold water numbing the pain of her ankle enough that she could limp along until she found a tall stick, grabbing it and leaning on it heavily as she dragged herself downstream.

There was a crashing sound nearby, and Maisie fell into the water. The creek was shallow here but deepened a few yards ahead of her, and she tried to scramble for that deeper part. Maybe she could hide under the water. Maybe she could hold her breath until it was gone. Maybe, maybe, maybe.

The creature snatched her up so quickly that it was only when the sharp teeth were sinking into her shoulder that she realized it was happening.

"No! Nonononono," she screamed, hands finding nothing but fur, so much fur as she tried to fight back. It was pointless, and words quickly became meaningless as the pain took over. Where had the creature come from? It had been behind her, and then beside her. What kind of monster was this, to move so quickly in so many directions?

But then the world was washed in white, her pain gone, and an overwhelming warmth was the last thing Maisie felt before her heart gave out.

"You aren't really going to wear that, are you?"

Sheryl looked up from her duffel bag to where her mom stood in the doorway, gesturing at her with a lit cigarette.

She grinned. "What? You the fashion police now?"

"No, but that halter top is showing a lot of skin."

Sheryl shrugged. "Be happy I paired it with bell-bottoms and not a pair of hot pants."

"I don't like you running around the neighborhood like that. You're a college girl, not one of these loose women who run the streets."

Sheryl took a deep breath and sighed. "Ma, it's 1973. I can wear a halter top and study law. Women can do all kinds of things, and once the ERA finally passes, the world is going to change." Sheryl walked over to her mother and pulled her into a hug. She lowered her voice. "It's a halter top, Ma. I'm eighteen, and it's fine."

Sheryl released her mother and went back to her duffel bag, throwing in a bikini and a pair of flip-flops. "Besides, you should see Tonya in her tube top. Now that is a sight to see."

Her mother wasn't any happier about the outfit, but when the horn honked out in front of their house, Sheryl grabbed her duffel. "That's them. I'll give you a call when we get to the cabin."

"You be safe. There's been talk of wild animals out there at Lake Preston terrorizing folks. A bunch of white kids went missing, and if bad things can happen to white kids, it'll be even worse for you."

Sheryl laughed, swinging her duffel over her shoulder as her mother stepped out of the doorway to let her pass. "I know, Ma, which is why I'll make sure to stay inside of the cabin once it gets dark. I'll be fine. I'll see you Sunday night."

Sheryl ran down the stairs, only stopping long enough to make sure her Afro hadn't gone flat, before she ran out of the front door, her mother's "Be safe!" echoing after her.

Tonya leaned out of the passenger side window of her boyfriend Daniel's Cadillac. "Look at you! You going to the lake or *Soul Train*?"

Sheryl grinned and did a bit of a strut before swinging her hips exaggeratedly like she was working the Soul Train Line. She and Tonya had spent all of their senior year practicing their *Soul Train* stroll, even though neither of them was likely to make it onto the show. Still, it was enough that someone up the street let loose a wolf whistle, and Sheryl felt herself heat with embarrassment.

"Okay!" Tonya said, laughing as she climbed out and pushed

the seat forward so Sheryl could get into the back. "Looks like you got a fan club, Miss Thompkins."

"Ugh, everyone on my street is old," she muttered while Tonya laughed even louder. Sheryl scrambled into the back and grinned as she saw Shep already reclining in the seat. "Shep! I thought you couldn't make it."

"I moved some things around," he said in his sleepy voice. He was a big dude, dark-skinned and soft and sweet. Tonya had invited him because he was friends with Daniel and because she knew Sheryl had a bit of a crush on him, even though everyone said he played for the other team. Still, even if he wasn't interested in her, it would be better than being a third wheel.

Shep held a joint out to Sheryl. "Want some?"

Sheryl shook her head. "No. Maybe later. My mom is definitely watching right now," she said as Tonya got resettled in the front seat and slammed the car door. "Let's get the hell out of Baltimore."

The drive to the lake was a short one, thanks to Daniel's lead foot and James Brown jamming on the 8-track. They drove for a little more than an hour, the city streets giving way to farmland and then woods. Sheryl was just starting to nod off, the warm day and the smooth sounds of the music making her eyes heavy, when Daniel suddenly pulled off the road, fishtailing a little as he pulled into a small gas station with an attached general store.

"Um, why are we stopping?" Sheryl asked, and Daniel laughed.

"There's not much up at the cabin, so I'm going to grab some beer and sodas. Don't worry, this place is safe," he said, climbing out and flipping the seat forward so Shep could get out as well.

"You been here before?" Sheryl asked, squinting at the store. The outside was cobbled together with thick planks of wood, the boards weathered and warped.

Tonya nodded and climbed out as well, holding the seat forward so Sheryl could follow. "Yep. Daniel and I have stopped here every time we came up to the cabin this summer. These are good people. Which you would know if you'd come with us," she said. There was nothing but attitude in her words as all summer she'd been pressuring Sheryl to skip her shifts at the local grocery and spend some time at the lake. But college was expensive, and Sheryl needed to save all the money she could get before she headed off to Howard.

Sheryl ignored Tonya and followed everyone into the grocery store. She got a whiff of something musky and feline and began to sneeze as she walked behind Tonya. "Ugh, they must have a cat," Sheryl said. Tonya gave her a strange look. "What? Didn't you smell the cat piss outside?" she asked, lowering her voice so the elderly woman behind the counter wouldn't hear.

"Girl, you are always smelling things no one else does," Tonya said, going straight for the rack of candy and grabbing a bag of jelly beans. "Also, don't talk to me. I've decided I'm mad at you."

"What? Why?" Sheryl asked, going to a nearby cooler and grabbing a glass bottle of Coke before snagging a bag of Fritos from a nearby shelf.

"My mom talked to yours and she told me that you're still planning on going to Howard next month."

Sheryl took a deep breath and let it out. "How is that a surprise?"

"I dunno. I thought you'd change your mind or something," Tonya said, grabbing a couple of chocolate bars and a couple of packs of hot dogs.

"Well, I'm not. You know I've wanted to be a lawyer ever since my dad . . . you know," Sheryl said, the lump in her throat sudden and thick. Two years before, her father had been arrested, mistaken for someone else, and accused of a horrible crime. The public defender had been awful, far beyond inept, and Sheryl's dad had eventually been convicted and sentenced to twenty years in prison. Not that it mattered. He died six months into his stay, the unfortunate victim of a prison riot. A guard had beat him to death, and no one seemed to care, so Sheryl had decided she would change the world, that she would make people care. Howard was the first step on that path, and when she graduated, she would go to law school and make sure no one ever went through what her father had.

"Yeah, but all those lawyers didn't help, did they? Black folks don't need more lawyers, they need someone to realize the system doesn't work for us because it wasn't made for us. Three-fifths, right?" Tonya said. Her voice had a hard edge, same as it always did when they talked about stuff like this. "How can you get justice when the country was founded thinking we weren't even a whole person?"

"Tee, don't be like this," Sheryl said when Tonya walked

away, her pretty face twisted into a pout. "Becoming a lawyer really is the best way to help. We can change the system from within. Howard is only a train ride away, and I'll be home on the weekends. Nothing is going to change."

"Everything is going to change," Tonya said, looking near to tears. "It already has."

"Hey, you foxy mamas ready to go?" Shep asked, stumbling over, his gaze still sleepy. Tonya moved away, off toward the cashier, but Sheryl just sighed.

They walked up to the register where Daniel gestured for Sheryl to put her things on the counter so the old woman could tally it up.

"Are you sure?" Sheryl asked, and Daniel gave her a dimpled smile.

"Of course. This is my party. The least I can do is pay for snacks."

Sheryl tried to catch Tonya's eye, but her gaze slid away. It was ridiculous. What was Sheryl supposed to do, not plan for her future? For what, more weekend barbecues?

"It's good to see you again," the old woman behind the counter said, her voice creaky. "But be careful up there. They just found a girl torn apart near one of the ravines. Bears, they said. Lots of bad things can happen when there's no one around."

Worry skittered along Sheryl's skin. What was the old woman hinting at?

"Don't worry, we'll be careful, Miss Olive. Wild animals are way less scary than some of those campers on the north side of the lake."

The older woman shook her head. "That was a shame what happened to the Clark boy. Just a shame."

"They ever find them?" Daniel asked.

The old woman shrugged. "Not that I know of. Sheriff said it was probably rednecks that came down from Pennsylvania and beat the poor boy up. He's lucky to still be alive."

Daniel peeled off a few bills and handed them to the old woman. "You tell Mr. James that I said hi."

She gave Daniel an affectionate, toothless grin. "I will. Do you want your brother's special order?"

Daniel shook his head with a laugh. "Nah, he can pick it up. It won't fit in my car. But I'll let him know."

"Okay then. You kids be safe," she said.

Once they were outside, Daniel used his keychain to open Sheryl's soda and handed it to her.

"So, you know that old woman?" Sheryl asked, drinking her Coke before climbing into the back seat.

"Oh yeah," Daniel said, twisting around in his seat to face her. "Mrs. Grayson. Her and her husband have owned the store for forever. My family has been coming to the lake since my dad was a kid. They all know us. Like Tonya said: good people."

"Yeah, she seems nice. Which makes me think maybe we should take her advice and just head back to the city," Sheryl said, shifting nervously where she sat. "First some kid gets beat up, and now some girl got eaten. Are you guys sure the lake is safe?"

Daniel laughed, and Tonya sighed. "We finally get you to hang out with us, and now you wanna flake?" She twisted around to scowl at Sheryl.

"No, it's just, I don't want any trouble," Sheryl said, feeling a little silly. Outside the car, the sun was shining, hot and bright, and there was no one else around. It felt odd to be scared on such a nice day.

"I can promise you that the woods are safer than Baltimore," Daniel said.

Sheryl glanced over at Shep, and he just shrugged, as if to say, *He has a point.*

Sheryl swallowed the rest of her objections and nodded. "Okay, if you guys think it's cool, I'm cool."

Tonya turned back around. "Don't worry so much, Sheryl. It's going to be great. Just wait until you see the lake. You're going to love it."

The conversation ended, Daniel started the car and peeled out onto the main road, the back end fishtailing once again. But Sheryl wasn't so much worried about his driving as she was the warning from Miss Olive, still echoing despite everyone's reassurances.

Just what had happened to that girl in the ravine?

As they pulled away from the familiar picnic areas onto a dirt road, Sheryl leaned forward, resting her arms on the back of the front seat.

"Okay, so where exactly is it we're going?" Sheryl asked, raising her voice over the music. "Because I really do not want to end up torn to pieces in a ravine."

Shep and Daniel laughed even as Tonya rolled her eyes and looked out the window.

"My family has a cabin on the Eastern Shore," Daniel said, accelerating around a curve a little faster than Sheryl liked. Loose stones pinged the undercarriage, and the tires slid a little, but Daniel was unbothered. "It's mostly Black families who have cabins there."

"Just wait until you see it," Tonya said. "You'll wish you'd joined us sooner."

They bumped down the road for what seemed like hours, but was probably closer to twenty minutes, before the trees parted, and there was the cabin, which was really an impressive house that made Sheryl's row house look quaint. A brand-new Ford Ranchero sat out front.

"Oh, this is amazing," Sheryl said as she climbed out of the car. "Whose Ranchero?"

"My brother Alfred's," Daniel said with a grin. "You should go say hi to him."

"Daniel . . ." Tonya said, her voice a warning.

"He's back?" Sheryl said, feeling suddenly self-conscious and more than a little intrigued. She remembered when Alfred had gotten drafted and sent off to Vietnam. She'd been a freshman, and it had seemed so scary and dangerous for him to go to war, especially when his family was affluent enough to get him a waiver. But Alfred had said he was going to do what he had to do. He'd become a bit of a neighborhood legend, his mom sharing pictures he sent back from the war, color photos of him in dirty green dungarees, staring at the camera with an expression that said no one back home would ever understand what he'd lived through. Afterward, he'd come home for a while before taking a sojourn to Africa, traveling across the continent like so many people talked about doing. He was a doer while so many others were just talkers, and Sheryl thought that was admirable.

"Look at her; she's already drooling," Tonya teased, and Sheryl laughed.

"Please. Now are we going to chat about the guest list or go swimming? That water is calling my name."

They unpacked the car quickly. The boys dragged the ice chest up onto the porch while the girls took their bags into the house, lugging them up the staircase directly in front of the door. Tonya pointed toward a guest room near the back. "That one's yours," she said, and Sheryl grabbed her arm before she could turn away.

"Hey, what's up with you?"

Tonya sighed. "There's something I've been meaning to talk to you about."

"It's not another one of your 'lawyering won't save anyone' speeches, is it? Look, Tee, I get it. I'm going to miss you, too. But I have to do something with my life. I have to change the world."

"What if there's another way?" Tonya began.

But then one of the doorways at the end of the hallway opened, and Alfred walked out. There was no mistaking him for anyone else: deep brown velvety skin, broad shoulders in a red shirt, and trim hips made impossibly slim by the bell-bottoms he wore. His Afro was perfect, full and round, and Sheryl's mouth went dry when she spied his sideburns, thick and perfectly groomed, just like Richard Roundtree's. She was a sucker for sideburns, but so few guys her age could grow more than an anemic line.

Alfred, a few years older and a war vet besides, had no such problem.

Sheryl could sense the exact moment he saw them. His gaze was electric, and a delightful flutter started up in her belly as their eyes met. And then Tonya was saying something and skittering away, leaving Sheryl all by herself with the neighborhood legend.

"Oh, ah, hey," she said, trying for coolness. "I don't know if you remember me—"

"Sheryl." He made her name one syllable, so that it sounded like "Shirl." Sheryl's heart did a double beat, but she wasn't quite sure why. He hadn't done anything extraordinary. There was just something about Alfred that was incredibly alluring. He walked toward her with a strange grace, and her gaze locked on him, unable to stop staring. She felt like she'd landed in a Marvin Gaye song. "You grew up," he said, the tone teasing but also complimentary.

"Yeah," she said, feeling like she was dreaming. It was a simple observation, and there was nothing inappropriate about the way he said it, but it made her feel . . . happy and strangely excited, like he was finally seeing her for the first time. She half wondered if she was imagining the way he leaned toward her just so, like he was also interested in her. "I, uh, think I'm in this room."

Alfred reached over and opened the door for her, and Sheryl took the opportunity to breathe deeply, inhaling the scent of him. He smelled of aftershave and something else, musky and seductive, but then he was leaning backward and giving her a slow smile, interested but respectful. "Good to see you again," he said, and then moved past her to the staircase.

Sheryl took a deep, steadying breath, let it out, and went to put on her bikini.

It was a perfect day, even though Tonya was still acting a little weird, watching Sheryl whenever she thought she wasn't looking. But Sheryl wasn't about to have another argument about Howard and leaving for college, so she threw herself into having the best time ever. They swam until the air began to cool and goose bumps ran across their skin whenever they came out of the water. Daniel and Shep built a fire near some rocks while Tonya grabbed the hot dogs from the ice chest, and they perched on the rocks and cooked them over the open flame. Sheryl had only had a couple of beers, but she felt warm and content, happy to be in a beautiful place with people she loved. The sun had gone down, and it was darker lakeside than anywhere Sheryl had ever been. It was nothing like her neighborhood, but she thought maybe that was a good thing.

That was when the screaming started.

The first peal made them all sit up straight, and the second had Sheryl reaching for her shoes, slipping them on and getting ready to run. The old woman's warning about wild animals was still fresh in her mind, and she was not about to tangle with Mother Nature. That bitch had claws.

"It's okay; it's just foxes," Daniel said with a laugh. He began to sing "Let's Get It On" by Marvin Gaye and snuggled into

Tonya's neck, and she squealed and pushed him away. Shep gave Sheryl an apologetic smile as she sat back down. She felt silly.

But then a white girl burst out of the trees, sobbing and running straight for them.

"Please," she screamed, running toward the fire. "Help me!" She wore short shorts and a tank top, and there was a strange, dark liquid soaking the material. It wasn't until she got closer that Sheryl realized the girl was covered in blood.

"Holy shit!" Shep said, standing and moving toward the girl. But before he could reach her, something burst out of the tree line, tackling the girl so that she disappeared, far beyond where the fire cast its light.

Sheryl's fingers turned to ice. The girl screamed once more before the sound was choked off. The wet, sucking sounds of something feeding echoed back to them, and Sheryl's brain shouted for her to run, to flee, the drive to escape erasing all else. But she was frozen in place. No one else had moved either.

Then the cracking of bones echoed through the night, and Sheryl's instincts finally kicked in. She took off running toward the house, Shep, Tonya, and Daniel somewhere behind her.

Sheryl couldn't think. It was ironic; all her life, her mind had been her best asset, gotten her out of tough jams, but in that moment, her brain was all white noise, a high keening that sounded like a wounded animal.

That was when she realized the noise was *her*.

Sheryl missed the first step up to the porch, slamming her shin into the second. She ignored the pain, dragging herself up onto the wooden planks and through the door. As soon as she crossed the threshold, Shep was behind her along with Tonya, and they were pushing the front door closed, Sheryl crying and sobbing and sputtering incoherently.

"Where's Daniel?" she asked, but neither Shep nor Tonya acknowledged her. "Tonya, where's Daniel?"

"Look, you just have to calm down—"

"The chairs," Sheryl said, ignoring Tonya. Sheryl hiccupped on her fear, swiping her hand across her face and pulling a trail of snot with it. She could only imagine her mascara was equally tragic. "We gotta block the door."

Shep shook his head. "We need to get out of here. That thing could just come through the windows."

There was a scraping sound outside, and they all froze.

"What was that?" Sheryl asked breathlessly, unable to quell the hysterical edge in her voice. "Just . . . what was it?"

No one answered her. Probably because they didn't know either.

"Upstairs," Shep said. "We'll be safe up there."

Shep ran up the stairs, and Sheryl followed him, too shell-shocked to do much else. Tonya hadn't moved, and when Sheryl looked back over her shoulder, Tonya looked annoyed as she shouted up the stairs after them. "You both need to just settle! It's not how you think."

Sheryl couldn't understand why her friend wasn't losing it like she was.

Maybe Tonya was just in shock. Sheryl was having trouble thinking, not because of the beers, but because all she could see was that screaming girl, the blood covering her looking black in the firelight, and the way she was there and then just *wasn't* as the beast tackled her from the darkness.

When Sheryl tried to imagine what the creature had looked like her mind went blank, unable to understand what it had been. *Bear*, she thought, but her brain immediately rejected the answer. She'd seen a brown bear at the zoo before. The animal near the lake had been slimmer. More agile. *Wolf*, she thought. Were there wolves in Maryland? She didn't think so. But it was easier to think it was a wolf than anything else.

They crashed into the nearest bedroom and Tonya entered a few moments later, taking her time when she should've been running. Shep locked the door, tilting a desk chair into place under the knob.

"You both have to just calm down and listen," Tonya said. There was something splattered across Tonya's bikini top. *Blood*, a little voice in Sheryl's brain helpfully supplied.

Sheryl shook her head, her brain still molasses slow. "How can we be calm when something just *ate* a white girl?" No, this wasn't real. Life didn't work like this. People didn't get eaten. It just . . . it didn't work like that.

And yet . . . Sheryl could feel the truth.

"We should get out of here," Shep said, and Sheryl dragged her attention to him. His usually sleepy look was gone, and his eyes were wide, the whites luminous in the near dark of the cabin. They hadn't turned on any lights, and there was only the glow of the moonlight coming in through the window.

"Where did Daniel leave the keys?" Sheryl asked, eager to latch on to something rational, something that wasn't massive creatures tearing white girls apart. Part of her was worried that this would somehow be their fault. Who was going to believe a bunch of Black kids when there was a dead white girl torn to pieces? But that was a problem for future Sheryl, when she was happy and back in the city, away from monsters that stalked the night.

Before anyone could answer, the window exploded inward, something large landing in the middle of the room.

Sheryl screamed. Shep was closest to the creature, and the thing grabbed him viciously, sinking its teeth into his shoulder and biting down. Shep yelped and tried to get away, but it was futile. Shep was big, but the creature was bigger, powerful in a way that defied explanation.

Sheryl was closest to the door, and she kicked the chair away and pulled the door open, not sparing a thought for Shep. Part of her knew she should try to help him, but the part of her brain that wanted to live knew there was nothing she could do.

Sheryl ran down the stairs and out the front door, Tonya calling after her, telling her to wait. Tears blurred her vision, and she fell down more stairs. She'd just made it to the porch when she slid to a stop. Someone was walking toward her through the trees, and Sheryl started to flee until she realized it was Alfred.

"Oh my god," she said, her words a half sob. "We have to get out of here. There's a monster, a creature . . . it ate a white girl . . ." Sheryl's voice trailed off as she took in Alfred's appearance: his missing shirt; his dirty, torn pants. Footsteps echoed behind her on the porch. Sheryl turned to see Daniel looking completely disheveled, his shirt as ragged as Alfred's pants.

Alfred was clearly annoyed. "You were supposed to talk to her."

Daniel shrugged. "I thought Tonya did, but she said you interrupted them. Anyway, too late now."

"What . . . what is going on?" Sheryl felt like she was about to vomit. "I thought you were *dead*," she said to Daniel.

He shook his head. "Tonya really didn't tell you?"

Sheryl shook her head, looking from Daniel to Alfred. "I don't understand. What is this? Some kind of sick joke?"

Alfred shook his head. "No. It's an opportunity, a chance to change things in a way people have only dreamed. The Black Panthers are finished, but we can carry on their work in another way.

"When I was in Vietnam, the locals talked about a monster, a creature they called 'lewk-a-roo.' I didn't know it at the time, but they were trying to warn us about the loup-garou."

"Werewolves," Daniel interrupted with a grin.

Alfred didn't share his brother's amusement. "We thought they were just backward. Superstitious. Then something started eating my platoon. Turns out when the French colonized Vietnam, oppression wasn't the only thing they brought.

"After the Army sent me back stateside, I started to do research. After all, if there were French werewolves, maybe there were other monsters as well. I went to Zaire and met a French professor there, a colonizer who had been disgraced for presenting the idea that French colonization had been successful *because* of the loup-garou. He told me about a village that the French Army had steadily avoided, and suggested the answer I was looking for might be found there."

Alfred took a deep breath, and his body began to change. His fingers lengthened, and his torso elongated. His already broad shoulders became impossibly wide, and a tawny fur erupted all over his body.

Sheryl gasped and tried to turn and run, but Tonya was there behind her, and she grabbed her and held her in place, much too strong for her delicate frame. "Watch," she said, the words a near growl, her hands holding Sheryl so that she was forced to see, even as she struggled futilely to free herself.

Alfred was still changing. His nose widened, and his Afro went shaggy, and when the transformation was complete, a massive half lion, half man stood before her.

"Werelions," Daniel said, awestruck. "The first time Alfred showed me, I flipped out. It was so badass I could barely handle it."

"It's terrifying," Sheryl said, feeling equal parts fear and awe. She stopped trying to fight Tonya and just stood stock-still, staring at the sight before her.

"But don't you see?" Daniel asked, coming off of the porch to stand next to Sheryl and Tonya. "This was how that tiny village defended itself against colonizers. And it's how we'll defend ourselves and everyone we love from the Man. My parents are rich, and money just isn't enough. Neither is education. We need something *more*."

Sheryl shook her head, but now she understood the pull she felt toward Alfred, stronger than the silly crush she'd had all those years ago. There was something magnetic about him, like seeing a predator in the wild.

Alfred shifted back, too easily, and Sheryl felt completely unmoored from reality, like she was watching it all happen to someone else.

"I . . . you killed that girl. Both of them."

"The Klan has rallies on the north side of the lake," Alfred said, his voice gravelly even as he was mostly back to his normal appearance. "When the Clark boy was attacked a few weeks ago, I went out to the spot and got their scent. She was there. So were the others who we killed. Otherwise, I get the folks at the grocery to order a couple of full cows for us every month. It handles the cravings."

"Alfred's 'special deliveries.' They just think we're having amazing parties," Daniel said with a laugh.

"I don't—" Sheryl shook her head, still trying to make it all make sense, but there was nothing in her experience that even came close. "I don't understand what you want from me," she said, even though she knew. She *knew*.

But she wanted to hear them say it out loud.

"Join us," Tonya said as footsteps echoed behind them on the porch. Sheryl turned to see Shep grinning from ear to ear. His injury had already healed, the bite sealing itself shut. Sheryl finally understood Tonya's insistence that they needed to talk, her pleas for Sheryl to come hang out at the lake all summer.

"Why did you make me think I was in danger?" Sheryl whispered.

"The chase is part of the fun," Tonya said with a shrug. "We all went through it. I wanted to tell you at first, but we just didn't get a chance. Besides, I'm still a little bit mad at you for blowing me off all summer. So, sorry about all that."

Sheryl looked at her friends, all of them monsters, and wondered what they would do if she walked away. Would they devour her? Forget about her?

Did it matter?

Sheryl thought about her father, doing everything right, working hard, trying to be a good man, and how all of it fell apart the moment the cops needed someone to blame for a crime. Sheryl thought about the lawyer who assured him the system would work, it always did, and then watching as it failed her father time and time again until it killed him, all while her mother cried and every other boy in the neighborhood got swept up into the same broken system.

She wanted to change the world. There was more than one way to do that. Tonya had known that, and now Sheryl did as well. It could be that Tonya's way, justice by tooth and claw rather than lawyers and a system that didn't even consider Black people fully human when it was built, was the better answer.

Or maybe, just *maybe*, Sheryl could forge a path somewhere between the two extremes.

"I'm still going to Howard," she finally said, walking toward Alfred, toward the inescapable pull of his gaze flashing amber in the moonlight. He smiled and cupped her cheek affectionately.

"Baby girl, I wouldn't have it any other way."

THE SCREAMERS

DAKA HERMON

"Amaani, do you need help?" Dad yells from downstairs.

"No, I got it!" My legs tremble as I carry the heavy box up the steps leading to my bedroom. I lean against the wall and struggle to catch my breath. "Why did I choose the attic again?" I mumble to myself.

"Mom, Gabe hit me!" cries my little sister, Jada, from somewhere in the house.

"Boy, if you don't keep your hands to yourself . . ." Mom threatens.

"She started it!" my brother responds.

CRASH! Something hits the floor.

"That fell by itself," the ten-year-old twin terrors say in unison.

I hear the thud of small feet running through the house.

"Gabe! Jada! Get back here," Dad calls out, using his most stern voice.

"Yeah. The attic was definitely the right call." I push off the wall and stumble up the last few steps. Just as I cross the bedroom threshold, the bottom of the cardboard box I'm carrying gives out. Comics, running medals, board games, and framed family photos scatter across the scratched-up hardwood floor.

I drop the empty box. Welp, this is why I *hate* moving. It requires packing and then unpacking, and clearly it's not one of my skills. I stare at the mess for a long moment, my eyes drawn to the photo of me with my older brother, Corey. We're on the beach, near the Los Angeles Marathon finish line. Corey's arm is around my shoulders, and he's laughing—mouth open, eyes sparkling as he celebrates my finishing the race. He believed I could do it, even when I had my doubts.

Kneeling, I pick up the picture and set it on the bookshelf near my bed. "Welcome to Tennessee, big bro, but don't get comfortable; you know we'll be moving again soon. I give it two months. Tops."

You can't outrun grief, but our parents keep trying. Tennessee is just the latest pitstop on our never-ending journey.

"I love you, but I really wish you hadn't created that stupid list of all the states you'd like to visit one day," I say to Corey's picture. "It's like Mom and Dad are determined to hit every one."

With a sigh, I swipe my long braids off my sweaty face and glance around my bedroom. Fading sunlight streams across the room, showcasing particles of dust dancing in the air. Cobwebs dangle from the sloped ceiling beams like sad streamers. My nose scrunches at the old, musty smell that permeates the air. "This might be the worst house yet; no wonder we were able to rent it so fast."

I shove aside dingy lace curtains and tug open the window. It protests but eventually gives way, letting in cool, fresh air. "Wow." The view is amazing. In the distance, the sun sets behind the Great Smoky Mountains. The sky is a mix of purple and pink, while the woods behind our house are bursting with yellow, orange, and red foliage that shouts *fall*. Time passes. Seasons change. The world continues even though Corey isn't here. It's not fair.

As if he's alive and standing right beside me, I hear my brother laugh and say, "*Fair is just a place where people judge pigs.*" He was always saying stupid stuff like that, though he was convinced he was dropping wisdom. My mouth twitches as if it wants to smile at the memory, then I remember I'm miserable and hate life.

Just as I'm about to turn away from the window, something catches my attention. In the backyard, there's an axe placed on top of a large moss-covered tree stump. The dipping sun reflects off the sharp blade. Behind it, in the woods, two small orbs of light appear. They brighten as they weave between the trees, gliding toward our house. They look like . . . eyes! "What the—!"

"AHWAAOOOO!"

I jump, bumping into the bookshelf. Corey's picture wobbles on the edge. I dive for it, but it slips through my fingers and hits the floor with a loud thud.

"AHWAAOOOO!"

My heart in my throat, I spin back to the window and search for the source of that noise.

It's like a wolf's howl but more high-pitched and pained. It reminds me of the sound Mom made at Corey's funeral. My gaze settles on the glowing orbs. They're closer, just on the edge of the woods, staring blankly at me.

Swallowing hard, I take a step back, my hand absently

reaching for the wall near the window. I grimace when I touch something damp and sticky. I glance at my fingertips. They're covered with a reddish-brown substance.

"Ewww!" I frantically rub my hand over my jeans as I inspect the peeling floral wallpaper. There's something hidden behind it. Goose bumps appear on my arms as I hesitantly pull more of the wallpaper away.

I gasp as I reveal a black-and-white photo of a family. Two adults and three kids. They're stiffly posed on the front porch of a house. Two little girls wear white lace dresses and have large bows restraining their long ringlets. The woman, the mother, I guess, is covered head to toe in black. She's so thin and frail looking, she could be a skeleton.

A young, somber-looking boy in overalls stands next to his father, who is wearing a black suit and holding an axe. A creepy smile tilts the corner of his mouth. His eyes are . . . cold, dead. Beside him is a big black animal, more wolf than dog.

"Woof! Woof! Woof!"

An embarrassing squeak pops out of my mouth as I spin around, almost losing my balance. My Jack Russell terrier, Buster, races into the room, barking excitedly. I grab my chest, where my heart is threatening to explode. "Buster! You scared me."

He gives me a slobbery grin and, I swear, rolls his eyes as if I'm being dramatic. Buster was more Corey's dog than mine, but since his death, Buster and I have bonded. We're a team.

"Amaani, time for dinner!" Dad yells.

Buster barks again, as if demanding that I follow him, then races back out the door. "Okay, okay. I'm coming." I pick up the picture and notice a small crack in the glass.

"Dang it!" Tears sting my eyes. I blink them away and exhale a deep, calming breath. Then another. I carefully set the picture frame back on the bookshelf, my fingers trailing over Corey's smiling face. "Wish you were here," I whisper.

A chilly gust of wind bursts through the window, causing the curtains to flutter like ghosts. The room is heavy with a dark and icky vibe. I shake off the foreboding feeling slithering around me as I hurry out the room and down the stairs to the first level.

"Mom. Dad. Guess what I found. It's—"

I pull up short outside the kitchen. Dad has his arms wrapped tightly around Mom as they sway side to side. If this scene hadn't played out a dozen times before, I'd think they were slow dancing. Nope. It's the movement of misery. The hug of heartbreak.

Dad must sense my presence because his head pops up and he releases Mom. She sniffs and wipes her eyes, avoiding my gaze. She rarely looks at me anymore. I often wonder if it's because a part of her blames me for Corey's death. She's not the same; *we're* not the same.

"Hey, you," Dad says with a small smile. His brown skin has more wrinkles than it did a year ago. Sadness ages you. "Food's on the table. We'll be right in."

"Okay." With one last glance at Mom, who still refuses to meet my eyes, I limp into the small dining room right off the kitchen. Gabe and Jada sit next to each other on one side of the table. I stare at their chipmunk cheeks and the cornbread crumbs around their mouths. Busted.

"Ooooh. You're gonna get it." They've snuck food before everyone was seated, which is, like, a dinner crime in this family.

"What?" they mumble, trying to look innocent.

I roll my eyes. "You better chew fast and wipe your mouths before they get in here."

They gulp hard and frantically scrub their hands across their lips. Shaking my head at their antics, I move to sit down, then stop abruptly. There is an extra chair at the table next to mine. Mom has included a place setting for Corey.

My brother once told me, *When someone or something you love becomes a memory, the memory becomes a precious gift*. I'm not sure where he learned that, maybe from a greeting card. Moments like this, when the memories only bring pain and a sense of helplessness, I'm not sure I agree.

With a little whine, Buster sits next to Corey's empty chair.

I slide into my seat as Mom and Dad enter the dining room and sit on opposite ends of the table.

"Gabe, it's your turn to pray," says Dad.

Gabe folds his hands and mumbles something quickly before ending loudly with "Amen." He and Jada scoop food onto their plates and argue over who has the bigger piece of chicken.

"Food looks great, honey," Dad says to Mom. "Perfect meal for our first night in our new home."

Mom smiles faintly as she reaches for the bowl of macaroni. She adds some to her plate, then moves to add some to Corey's empty plate before catching herself. Her hands tremble as she sets down the bowl.

"Daddy, can we have s'mores for dessert?" asks Jada.

"We can make a fire in the fireplace." Gabe talks around the food in his mouth.

"Sure! That's a great idea," Dad says, then turns to me. "Did you finish unpacking? You like the attic bedroom?"

"I guess, but this house is weird. I found a picture of a family behind my wallpaper. What do we know about this place?" There's an eerie vibe here that makes my skin crawl.

Mom and Dad exchange a look.

"What?" When they remain silent, my eyes narrow. "*What?*"

"This house has . . . history," Mom says, reluctantly.

"What kind of history?" I ask slowly, my eyebrows rising.

Dad casts a hesitant look at the twins who have stopped arguing and are now focused on our conversation. "Look, it's complete nonsense, but there were some rumblings that the house is haunted."

Gabe and Jada gasp. Their wide eyes sweep the room as if they're searching for ghosts.

"You moved us into a haunted house!" I shout. "What the hell?"

"Language, Amaani!" Dad scolds.

I roll my eyes. "Really? That's what you're worried about? What happened here?"

"This is not a conversation for the dinner table," Mom says, glaring at me.

I tug my phone out of my back pocket and do a quick internet search of this address. "If you won't tell me, I'll just look it up myself."

My stomach churns as article after article appears with the strange family photo I found. I gasp. "A man murdered his family on this property with an axe, then he killed himself." I scroll down farther. "Wait . . . one of the daughters survived the attack. She tried to save—"

"Amaani, put that phone away right now!" Mom says.

I ignore her and keep reading. "There's like an urban legend that the murdered family haunts this house and the woods, that the ghosts kill people who live here. People say you can hear them screaming and—"

"Mom . . ." Jade whimpers.

"Are we gonna get killed?" Gabe asks, shakily.

"Amaani, you're scaring the twins," says Dad.

"They should be scared. Did you hear what I said? People *died*—"

"People die all the time. Dead is dead. You of all people know that!" Mom cries, swinging her arms wildly. Her hand hits Corey's glass. I watch in horror as it wobbles, then crashes to the floor, the glass shattering.

There is a moment of shocked silence, then Mom scrambles out of her chair and begins to gather the broken glass. "Oh no! I broke it."

I swallow the fiery lump in my throat as Dad hurries around the table to her.

"Honey, it's okay," he says. "Be careful. You'll hurt yourself."

"It's his favorite. I have to fix it." She cries out and holds up her hand. Her palm is cut. Blood slides down her hand and arm. My eyes follow the slow descent as drop after drop hits the hardwood floor, disappearing between the dark panels. I hear a muffled creaking sound, and I swear the house shifts beneath my feet. I glance at the twins. Did they feel it, too? Wide-eyed, they stare back at me, holding tightly to the table edges.

"Mom . . . Dad . . ." My voice is hushed. "There's something very wrong here. I—"

"Not now, Amaani!" Dad presses napkins against Mom's

bloody palm and helps her stand. "Can't you see your mom is bleeding?"

Bleeding. Blood. I'm suddenly transported back to the accident. I'm in the car, staring at Corey. His neck is at a strange angle, and shards of glass protrude from his face and neck. There's so much blood; it's gushing from his wounds. His lifeless eyes are fixed on me.

I jump to my feet, tipping over my chair. It hits the floor with a *BAM*! I'm jolted back to the present. My eyes swing around the room. The concerned stares prickle my skin. I pant out loud breaths. "I . . . I need some air." I walk, unsteadily, out of the room.

"Amaani!" Dad calls out, but I ignore him.

Can't breathe. I race out of the house and collapse against the porch railing, gulping in air. Something presses against my leg. I start and glance down. Buster. He followed me. He lets out a little whine as he watches me anxiously.

"I'm okay," I lie. That vision of Corey . . . I inhale and exhale several shaky breaths, but it does nothing to loosen the tightness in my chest. Buster nudges me again.

"Wanna take a walk?" I can't go back inside that house right now.

Buster barks, and I take that as yes.

I grab his leash off the hook on the porch and attach it to his collar. I swipe at the tears I didn't realize were streaming down my face.

On my sixteenth birthday, 377 days ago, Corey let me drive his classic Camaro. I was nervous because he loved that car, but he kept saying, "You got this."

As usual, he was super patient with me, and eventually I loosened up enough to enjoy the drive. On our way back home, a truck ran a red light and slammed into the passenger side of the car where Corey sat. He died instantly. Nineteen and gone forever. I got off easy. My external injuries weren't too bad. Yeah, my leg was shattered, so no more competitive racing, but it was the internal injuries . . . my heart is a pain puzzle that will never heal because a piece is lost. I can't bring my brother back, no matter how much I want to. Mom is right. Dead *is* dead.

Buster tugs on the leash, demanding I walk faster. I speed up, warily glancing at our car parked in the driveway. I haven't driven a car since the accident. Not sure I'll ever be able to drive again.

Buster leads me down the sidewalk. I'm so lost in my troubled thoughts, I'm surprised when I realize we've reached the dead end on our street. A murky fog has drifted in. It swirls around my feet as the streetlights crackle on, cutting through the darkness.

"Let's head back, buddy," I say to Buster. "It's getting late."

I tug on his leash, pulling him away from the bush he's sniffing. The moon peeks out of the clouds, creating an eerie glow across the sky. As we make our way back home, my eyes dart around the neighborhood. My shoulders tighten with unease as I remember the scariness of the articles I read.

I walk a little faster. As we continue up the sidewalk, I spot movement on the front porch of a house three doors down from mine. My steps falter as I draw closer and hear loud creaking sounds. Someone is sitting in a rocking chair.

"A little late to be out walking," a woman says, her voice shrill and ominous. She's partially hidden by the porch's darkness.

There's a small overhead light, but it doesn't illuminate much; it only casts a sinister shadow across the ground.

"Uh . . . Just on my way home," I respond hesitantly, even as I chide myself. Why am I talking to a stranger?

The woman rocks forward in her chair, and I catch a glimpse of her wrinkled white face. She's wearing shaded glasses despite the darkness.

"See you and your family moved into that house." Her head tilts to the side as if she's studying me. "That's too bad."

I swallow hard, not sure how to respond.

"Folks like to pretend you can escape the past, but you can't. Death lingers, watches, and waits. Waits until it can consume something new."

"Dead is dead?" My shaky response comes out more like a question than a statement.

She cackles. "Not always. Evil can evolve."

My stomach churns. I sneak a peek down the street at my house. Black smoke billows out from the chimney. Dad must have started a fire for the s'mores.

"There's wickedness in these woods. Horrors in that house." Her last words are just a whisper, but they echo through my trembling body. "Don't you know the stories?"

She stops rocking and leans forward in the chair, so the dim porch light illuminates the right side of her head, or what remains. It's concave, like the bones have been crushed, and there's only twisted cartilage where her ear should be. That side of her head is devoid of hair, so I can clearly make out the deep, puckered scars. They're like thick, twisted vines woven in a gory pattern down her neck and shoulder.

I slap my hand over my mouth to hold back the vomit rocketing up my throat.

"Turn, kill, haunt. Turn, kill, haunt. That's what they do." She taps her thin bare wrist as if she's wearing a watch. The dangling skin sways with her movements. "Chop, chop! Time's a-ticking. Tick, tick, tick."

"Wh . . . what?"

"Better git, now. They'll be coming soon." Her menacing words cause my heart to skip a beat. "You still got a chance, but not much of one."

What's coming? A chance at what? I'm afraid to ask. My hands tremble as I tug on Buster's leash. "Let's go, boy."

"Tick, tick, tick," the old woman chants. "Tick, tick, tick."

My heart pounds against my chest in rhythm with her words. Buster growls, baring his teeth as he stares at something behind me. I spin around. A bright, blurry figure appears at the edge of the woods.

Buster surges forward, jerking me so violently I fall to my knees and skid across the ground before I lose my grip on the leash. "Buster!"

He darts across the street toward the glowing figure, disappearing into the dark woods.

"Not much time left at all," the old woman says.

I scramble to my feet and chase Buster. Pain pulsates up my injured leg, but I speed up.

"Buster!" I burst into the woods and trip over tangled vines. I fall against a tree trunk. The rough bark bites into my skin.

I push deeper into the thick darkness. The howling wind whips past me, rustling the leaves above. "Buster!" Panting, I stumble into a clearing and gasp when I spot a small structure covered with twisted dead vines and overgrown bushes. The wood is rotten, with large holes along the side of the house. Sharp pieces of cracked glass are all that's left of the windows, and a red door hangs off the front doorway. Moonlight reflects off the tin roof.

A scream rips through the air. It's terrifying—the combination of a painful wail and a screech. My hands fly up to cover my ringing ears. It feels as if they may explode.

As the horrifying sound fades, the temperature drops even further, revealing the panting breath rushing out of my mouth. Suddenly, Buster races from around the side of the house, followed by a bright white light. Buster leaps into my arms. I stumble back, holding him tight. He's trembling so hard I think I hear his bones rattling.

The bright, blurry figure that chased Buster stops near the porch. It's about knee-high. The light flickers, then its features materialize. It's an animal. A dog. Its dark fur is dirty and matted. Its mouth opens in a snarl, revealing sharp black teeth. Its eyes glow bright white.

I gasp. Those eyes. I saw them earlier in the woods.

The beast throws back its head. "AWHOOOOO!"

That's the sound I heard! It was this *thing*!

Before I can even process what's happening, a ghostly figure emerges on the steps of the house. More materialize, stepping out of the woods. Their glowing forms flicker, going from bright lights to translucent bodies. As they come into focus, my jaw drops. It's the family from the photo in my bedroom, only one is missing. A girl. The daughter who survived. The articles . . . the stories about the murdered family haunting the woods . . . they're real!

With a chilling growl, the dog prowls closer. I'm frozen in place.

"Run, Amaani! Run!" It's Corey's voice in my head that propels me into motion.

I clutch Buster tighter, spin around, and run as fast as I can toward home. Every movement is agonizing as my injured leg cries out in protest. A loud scream blasts through the air, creating sound waves that threaten to knock me off my feet. My ears throb, and I stumble before righting myself and speeding up.

"Mom! Dad!" Trees claw at me, scratching my bare arms. Torn skin stings as sweat trickles down, mixing with the blood from the cuts. I burst out of the woods into our backyard and skid to a stop. My grip loosens on Buster. He drops to the ground, trembling at my side. My parents, Gabe, and Jada stand in the middle of the backyard.

"Mom? Dad?" Their heads turn slowly toward me. Their eyes are white.

"Gabe? Jada?" They look in my direction. My stomach plummets. Their eyes have turned, too. Glowing white tears streak down Gabe's face, leaving tracks on his brown skin. Jada's hair . . . I watch as more of her tight black curls turn until they are completely white.

Out of the corner of my eye, I spot a blur speeding toward me. I'm hit in the side and knocked to the ground with such force I'm momentarily stunned. The beastly dog's sharp teeth pierce my already injured leg. The pain is so excruciating, my mouth opens to cry out, but no sound emerges. It's as if my body recognizes no sound could convey this kind of agony. The dog bites deeper and drags me across the backyard as I kick and beat at it with what strength I have. Buster tries to help, attacking the dog, but he's no match for this creature.

The ghostly figures dash past me to stand near the tree stump. I realize that's where the dog is dragging me. It releases me, and I watch my blood drip from its muzzle. Trembling, Buster burrows into my side.

The glowing figures scream, their bodies vibrating with the force of the violent sound that echoes around us. Crying, I curl into a ball. Something wet trickles out of my ears, sliding down my cheek and into my mouth. Blood.

The tallest figure glides toward the axe. The tool—no, weapon—rises off the tree stump and glows. I hear a loud groan, and my tear-filled eyes jerk toward my family. Horrified, I watch as my parents' jaws drop, stretching down to the middle of their chests as they join in the screaming. The whiteness creeps across their brown skin until their entire faces glow.

Tick, tick, tick. Turn. Kill. Haunt. Tick. Tick. Tick.

The old woman's chant rattles in my head. *Turn. Kill. Haunt.* Was she warning me of what was to come? Turn. You turn into the glowing figure? Kill. You're killed? Haunt. You become one of those things? Destined to haunt the woods like this evil family? Destined to kill and hurt others?

The beastly dog prowls closer to my mom. It laps at the bloody cut on her palm before turning back to me, flashing its teeth in a sinister, bloody smile.

Rage boils within me until it overflows. No! I can't—I *won't*—lose anyone else. These things will not take my family!

They won't take me. There has to be something I can do. My gaze frantically darts around searching for something to help. My eyes land on the axe. It was in the photo. It's what the man used to kill his family. It's what they plan to use to kill *my family*. Somehow, I know it needs to be destroyed.

Gritting my teeth to fight through the pain in my leg, I plant my hands on the ground and suck in a loud breath. My arms . . . they're glowing. Instead of fear, the sight sends a rush of adrenaline through me. With a growl of determination, I stand.

"Hey!" I shout to the glowing figures. "You picked the wrong family to mess with."

I leap forward and grab the floating axe handle.

"*Burn it!*" I hear Corey's voice in my head. I don't question it. I just react.

Fire! The fireplace!

The dog pounces at me. I swing the axe, connecting with the beast's side. *THUNK!* I rip the axe free of its body. Black blood pours out of the wound, and I'm overwhelmed by the scent of rotten eggs. The beast falls to the ground with a loud thud, his glowing eyes flickering.

The silence is terrifying. The air crackles with electricity and rage. The glowing figures converge on me.

My grip tightens on the axe's handle, and I race toward the back door of the house, dragging my injured leg behind me. The pain hammering through my body makes me nauseous. Can't slow down. Must. Run. Faster. Buster's right on my heels as I stumble into the living room and slide across the hardwood floor.

Out the corner of my eye, I see white lights zooming toward me. I fling the axe into the fireplace. My legs buckle. I watch in slow motion as it sails through the air. For a moment, it appears as if my aim is off the mark, then the axe's trajectory shifts as if someone is guiding it. It lands in the hearth and glows brightly in the orange flames.

The white figures scream. Buster growls, standing next to me protectively. I glance at him, and my heart skips a beat. His fur and eyes are white. He's turning, too.

The fire crackles loudly, and the entire house shakes on its foundation. The glowing figures dart away from me and toward the fireplace. The axe. It's on fire, burning! Flames flare up and shoot out of the hearth with a whoosh.

The tallest glowing figure reaches for the axe, but flames leap out, and it shifts away. The other figures vibrate, their light flickering wildly as they, too, try to retrieve the axe. More flames lick out of the hearth, setting the floor ablaze and crawling up the walls toward the ceiling. Dark smoke begins to fill the room. The flames continue to spread—the rug is now on fire. Now the couch and moving boxes. Buster grabs my shirt with his teeth. Growling, he tugs at me, desperately trying to pull me out of the room.

With a painful groan, I climb to my feet and stumble down the hallway, leaving a trail of blood. My family . . . I have to get them away from here. I grab the keys off the entryway table and burst out the front door onto the porch—and freeze. Barking, Buster runs to the car and glances back at me. My hand clenches the keys as I stare at the death trap on wheels. Panic swirls inside me, and black dots float across my vision.

A loud scream rips through the air. I flinch. The windows on the house shatter, raining glass around me. I feel intense heat at my back as the fire consumes the house. Buster bounces around near the car, barking urgently.

I stumble down the steps toward the car. My hands shake as I fling open the door. Buster jumps inside, scrambling into the back seat. I fall awkwardly behind the wheel. The moment my butt hits the seat, I gag. I lean out the door and vomit. Hot tears stream down my face. I can't do this. Can't—

I feel a light touch on my glowing white hand. My eyes fly over to the passenger seat. Corey's ghostly image appears. Not broken. Not bloody. Healthy. Whole.

"Corey?" My voice cracks.

"You have to save them."

I reach for him, my trembling fingers gliding through the ghostly vision.

"I'm here, even though I'm not here. Always," he says, fading away. *"Now DRIVE!"*

I blink away tears and shove the key in the ignition, turning on the engine. I slam my foot on the gas, and the car jolts forward through the hedges. Gripping the steering wheel tight, I speed around the house and into the backyard where my family still stands near the tree stump in their scary daze.

I jab a button on the door. My window lowers. "Get in!"

They don't move or respond, still stuck in their zombielike states.

With a muttered curse, I shove the car's gearshift into park and fling open my door. I limp toward them and one by one, I push my family into the car. Mom is in the front seat with Buster. Gabe, Jada, and Dad are in the back seat. I slam the doors closed, round the car, and jump back inside.

White figures glide out of the house, which is now completely consumed with flames. Two white glowing figures rush up to stand in front of the car. As their forms flicker in and out, I see the mother and little boy. Hate blazes in their eyes. I stomp on the gas and rocket forward. Instead of driving right through them, I hit solid forms. *THUD!* They fly up, hitting the hood, then the roof. *THUD!* I grimace, my stomach roiling.

"What's happening?" Mom whispers shakily.

My eyes dart in her direction. She blinks hard. Her eyes slowly transition from white to their usual brown.

"I'm saving you. I'm saving us all."

I race down the street, but the sight of the old woman standing at the end of her driveway has me slamming on the brakes. The car rocks to a stop. Everyone in the car is thrown forward. I hear my family's startled cries.

The old woman stands under a streetlight, allowing me to get my first clear view of her. She's wearing a long white lace dress, ripped and stained with blood. A dirty bow hangs from one side of her head, tangled in her wild hair.

"Burn! Burn!" She points at our house.

My stomach plummets as a sick realization hits me. She's the daughter that survived the murder. How . . . ?

She cackles. "Burn! Burn!"

"Amaani?" Dad whispers from the back seat.

I glance in the rearview mirror and take in his confused expression, then glance at Gabe, Jada, and Mom. The whiteness has faded from their faces. They look normal.

"We're safe now." I put the car back in gear and speed out of the neighborhood. My hands tighten on the steering wheel.

The whiteness of my hands and arms is fading. Patches of brown peek through.

I stare forward, tears burning my eyes. The headlights cut through the dark, foggy road that lies ahead. We can't go back, only forward. The uncertainty, fear, sadness . . . are almost suffocating. There's no way to outrun death or grief, but maybe . . .

"We're gonna be okay," I whisper to Corey.

My heart flutters, and I think I hear him say, "*You got this.*"

QUEENIUMS FOR GREENIUM!

BRITTNEY MORRIS

"How do you know this isn't a cult?" I ask.

While I await a reply from my sister, I turn to my phone and pump some evidence into my video's comment section.

> *I said clearly in my video that these kinds of procedures should be left to medical professionals only. Stop spreading misinformation or you'll be blocked.*

Send.

I reread the comment I'm replying to, wondering how anyone can be so reckless:

> *Everyone needs to know how to perform this simple lifesaving procedure in case of a choking incident. Can't be too careful!*

Um, yes, you can, Barry. Just because you saw a rogue TV doctor jam a ballpoint pen tube into his own windpipe doesn't mean everyone needs to know how to perform a tracheotomy on themselves "just in case." Leave that shit to the professionals.

Diana looks over, rolls her eyes, and lets out an older-sister-esque *pffffft*.

"Will you stop fact-checking for *one* weekend and let your hair down? And it's not a cult; it's a *lifestyle*," she says, adjusting her grip on the wheel.

"That's exactly what someone in a cult would say."

I reach up and touch my teeny-weeny Afro. "And my hair *is* down."

Not only is my hair on point, but so is my dress. Dark green against my skin is absolute perfection, and the boning around my middle is generous enough that I can breathe in this gown.

"See? *Always* fact-checking. Just stop for forty-eight hours, please, and give this a chance? It's a weekend retreat with my smoothie club. Relax."

"And actually," I continue like I haven't heard her, "*you* didn't answer *my* question. How do you know this 'smoothie club' isn't a cult?" I look out the passenger window at the trees flying by. How the hell did I get roped into this trip to Exactly the Middle of Nowhere™? That's where people get killed.

"It's not a cult because I can leave at any time. And because Greenium has changed my health and my wallet. Look at this rental! Would I be able to afford a Range Rover with red leather seats if the hustle was a flop?"

I sigh, staring down at the seats, noticing the scent of the leather. She's right . . . *something* must be funding this lifestyle of hers. I remember when we were kids, side by side in the back of Dad's minivan that was practically falling apart, each of us picking at a rip in the seat until it was a hole big enough to slide one of our arms inside. We could *never* have afforded something like . . . *this.*

I shake it off quickly, though. It's part of the culture to flaunt a lavish lifestyle, isn't it? All over social media I see people stuck in pyramid schemes, or . . . pyramid-shaped business models. Reminder to self: calling it a "pyramid scheme" will get you sued for libel. Diana is *supposed* to be doing this, I remind myself. This is all part of the marketing.

"It's an MLM," I argue.

A multilevel marketing company with a suspiciously pyramid-shaped-but-definitely-*not*-a-pyramid-scheme business model.

"It's been good to me," she says. "Just give it a taste."

"Wait, you want *me* to drink this stuff!" I practically screech.

"Why not?"

Why not? She knows exactly why not. We've known each other for how long? Right. Since I was born. Nineteen years. And Diana doesn't miss a detail about anything. She knows about my severe allergy to soy and moderate allergies to just about everything else.

I shuffle my feet, which bump into the duffel where I've packed clothes, toiletries, my EpiPen, *and* the immunotherapy allergy shot I missed an appointment for earlier this week. Ah well, as long as I take that one by Tuesday, I'm right on schedule.

"Um, the soy allergy? The grass pollen? The tree pollen?"

"There's no pollen in this!" She laughs, holding out a bottle to me. I can't help it—I recoil just a bit at the sheer thought of having it near me.

"Go on, it won't hurt you through the plastic. Jeez, all that fact-checking has you scared of everything."

"Skeptical, not scared," I say, hesitantly taking the ice-cold bottle in my hands. It's tinted an eerie tan-green with the word "Greenium" written in bold along the side. Underneath that, I read: *Complete nutritional beverage. Vegan, cruelty-free, non-GMO, gluten-free, sugar-free . . .*

I know better than to trust labels that advertise everything that's *not* in the product.

"Okay, so what's in it?"

I spot the words I'm looking for. *Contains soy.* "Yeah, soy is a no-go. I'll swell up like a dead whale on a beach."

Diana looks physically hurt at that joke.

"Sorry."

And I really am. I don't want to hurt her vegan feelings. But honestly? This whole operation sounds like a scam. *Complete nutritional beverage?* I smack my lips.

"There's not even an ingredient list!"

"You don't *need* an ingredient list. Just read the testimonials! Zero adverse side effects."

"Unless you have allergies."

"This smoothie will *cure* allergies. Just think—how long do you have left in your treatments?"

"Three years," I say. To most people, that may seem like a lot. But I'm already having less severe pollen reactions. The soy allergy, though? If I have soy, it's EpiPen central immediately. Immunotherapy shots don't work on that.

And neither will this smoothie. I continue stacking the facts for her.

"No smoothie is going to mitigate a histamine reaction, sis. Sorry."

"It doesn't 'mitigate histamine,'" she says with air quotes, as if I'm talking pseudoscience. "It promotes the circulation of lymph in the body, which moves histamine, so it doesn't pool and cause a reaction."

That's not how the fuck that works, but I keep my response short and sweet. "Let's talk about something else."

She bristles but wraps it up with one of her *let me collect myself before I catch a charge* sighs. "We're almost there."

We are? I look out the window. Still looks like Exactly the Middle of Nowhere™ to me. But then we round a curve and I see it.

The mansion.

I count four stories high, featuring a grand outdoor staircase with curved baluster railings along both sides. Three black cars are parked at the base, and just as we pull up, two women in dresses emerge from one of them. They turn and see us, and I can't help it. I gawk. They look like they've stepped out of *Vogue*. Tulle and organza to the floor. One is in a lime-yellow ball gown that pops against her bronzed skin, and the other wears a summer peach mermaid number with bejeweled off-the-shoulder sleeves. Jewelry glittering, teeth shining, edges snatched, jawlines contoured, collarbones popping . . .

They look like perfect princesses.

I look down at my forest-green bodycon gown with its sweetheart neckline that I was in love with only minutes ago, and I want to evaporate. Maybe I should've worn more jewelry. Or maybe some extra eye makeup? I could've at least left my glasses at home . . . or worn some shapewear.

I look at Diana, who seems to already know what I'm thinking.

"Hey. You're with your sis."

And just as I'm about to give her a grateful smile, she rests her hand on my knee and gives me a sad look in return. "All I'm saying is, maybe Greenium can do more for you than you think. I lost twenty pounds on it, you know."

I shoot her a look, and now that I realize . . . okay, yeah, some of the puffiness is gone from her cheeks. And whatever "double chin" she used to say she had is gone. Her eyes look bigger. Brighter. Even her straight, slicked-back hair looks shinier. Or maybe that's the dangling gold earrings and her glittering gold gown doing that. She *does* look thinner.

But that don't mean my size-eighteen ass is interested in doing the same.

"Thanks," I manage, and I turn to open the door, wondering if this whole event is going to be a mire of health nuts telling me what the hell to eat and do and think and be, as if it's my life's goal to lose weight. It *has* to be, right? Look at me.

With my fingers only inches from the door, it swings open, and faces pour in.

"QUEENIUMS FOR GREENIUM!!!" comes a cacophony of screeching from both inside the SUV and out.

I'm sure my face betrays exactly what I'm thinking: *What the absolute hell?*

"*Diana's heeeeeere!*" sings the chorus, almost in unison. Several other girls scramble over when they hear the announcement that my sister has arrived.

Diana commences with the hand signals and the sorority-esque greetings so warm you'd think *they* were sisters.

"Synthia," says Diana, suddenly shutting the driver-side door and scrambling around the front of the SUV to meet these two. "Meet Christina and Gwen!"

"Welcome to the *houuuuuse*," they sing. Christina, the one in the lime yellow, flips her dark curls over one shoulder and looks me up and down. Her smile has too many teeth.

"Have you eaten yet?" she coos at me, like I'm some kind of baby. I guess I'm the youngest one here, but . . .

"Um, no, I'm good, thanks."

There's nothing here I can eat. Between my soy allergy and the pollen allergies wreaking havoc on my ability to eat *any* kind of raw fruits and vegetables, I'll just stick with the jerky and granola bars I brought with me.

Gwen glances down at my bag, and before I can get it, she snatches it from the SUV.

"I'll get your things! You're the guest of honor, after all!"

I . . . *am*?

Christina and Diana shoot her looks so full of daggers, I wonder if she's broken some kind of . . . house code.

"What?" asks Gwen. "I'm just . . . being nice!"

"I've got it, thanks," I say, taking the bag back with the warmest smile I can manage. Does she really think I'm about to leave this immunotherapy shot—carefully kept on ice in my bag—in *any* of their hands?

Is it just me, or is the blank look she's giving me right now . . . pointed? The hairs on the back of my neck stand at attention, and I take a step back.

"No need to baby her, Gwen."

Christina in the lime yellow leans forward to clean whatever that was up.

"Come on," Diana says, pulling me past Gwen and Christina, "let's at least see what the spread is like! I hear the catering is to die for!"

I wish she wouldn't say that out here in the middle of nowhere, but I follow them inside anyway.

As soon as the doors are open, I'm swimming in a flood of made-up faces, swinging weaves and fluttering lashes, grabby hands and perfume.

I grip my bag and don what I hope is a genuine-looking smile.

"Hey, queeeeen." Three women scramble over holding teeny-tiny plates of teeny-tiny food.

"Hey, girls, heyyyy!" My sister beams right back, squeezing my shoulders a bit too hard. "This is Synthiaaaaa."

"Hi, Synthiaaaaa," they sing together. My face hurts from smiling.

"Have a plate! I'll take your bag."

"Uh, no, thanks. I've got it."

What is with people going after my bag?

"Okay, let's give her a little space," says Diana. Then she turns to me. "All right, Synth. Forgot to mention, while we're here, we've all committed to protecting each other from excess EMF."

"Um . . . Email forwarding?"

Her brows go flat, and there's a silence that lasts a little too long. Then, *laughter.* Hissing, cackling laughter bubbling forth from everyone but me. I scratch the back of my neck and give a nervous chuckle.

"Electromagnetic frequencies," she explains. Suddenly, a girl in a purple gown steps forward, cradling what looks like a huge copper urn.

The *hell* is that for?

"All phones go in the harmonizer!" explains the girl so cheerfully it's almost songlike, smiling up at me like all of this is totally normal. "I'm Bianca, by the way."

"Hi." I turn to Diana. "You want me to leave my phone in . . . this thing?" I purse my lips and point at the urn.

"Just for the weekend." Diana smiles. "This is a time to unwind, y'know? Besides, at least now when we leave and you get all our messages about Greenium, you can batch delete them all at once."

I guess the blog can wait till Monday. A break from replying to comments *would* be great for my mental health anyway. And if I ever need my phone back for an emergency, I can always just ask someone where the urn is. I can just leave the premises if they're all so determined to avoid . . . electromagnetic frequencies. I roll my eyes.

Bianca towers over me, smiling way too big while I hold the off button until the screen goes dark . . .

And I drop it in.

Upstairs, the house feels *way* smaller. In the hallways, at least. It's a labyrinth of winding corridors and bedroom doors, and just when I think I'm going to turn the corner and find the end of the hallway, Diana ducks under an archway, and we're in an even longer hallway with *more* rooms. How many rooms does this place have?

I let out a long sigh, and Diana hears me this time. "Almost there, promise! You've got the Rose Quartz Room."

One last turn, and I'm standing in front of a giant pink door that's almost as tall as the ceiling.

"Is this whole door . . . ?" I trace the cold frame beneath my fingers.

"Made of rose quartz?" She finishes my sentence. "Yes, it is."

Holy shit—the tiny crystals can be hundreds of dollars. This one door must be worth thousands . . . no . . . millions? How the hell—?

"When you sell Greenium, you can afford to stay in places like this," she says with a wink.

The inside of the room is just as lavish. Everything is pink, and I mean *everything*. The bedsheets, the pillows, the bedframe, the carpet, the lamps, the weird cat statue in the corner that I swear is looking at me—

"I'll let you unwind," says Diana. "I'll be in the Onyx Room if you need me."

Oh, and how the hell am I supposed to find that in this maze of a house?

"Wait, how am I supposed to find you if I can't call you?" I ask, just before Diana lets the door shut behind her.

Click.

I take one last look at my surroundings before lifting my duffel onto the bed to unpack, starting with my toiletry bag where I find my toothbrush, my boar bristle hairbrush for smoothing out those edges of mine, and my allergy shot. Not looking forward to giving myself that.

May as well get it over with.

I pull out the bottle, still cold from the ice pack, and—

Click.

I look over my shoulder at the door.

Did . . . did that thing just lock?

My heart begins to race. I jog over and try the handle. It doesn't move.

"*Hey!*" I holler, slamming my hand against the door. "Hey, I think I'm stuck in here!"

Nothing.

I sigh. Fantastic. No one can hear me.

And I don't have my phone? This feels like some kind of movie.

Think, Synthia, *think*.

I look up at the ceiling and spot a vent that should take me literally anywhere but this room where they *know* I am.

That'll work.

The high bed makes for a pretty decent step stool, and the vent unscrews from the ceiling easily with the corner of a credit card from my wallet.

That's all I take with me. My wallet, and . . . well, that's it.

Normally, it would be my wallet *and* phone, but . . . I spot the tiny pink mini fridge on the vanity counter and tuck the precious bottle of immunotherapy serum inside. I'll just have to come back for it when I find help.

So it turns out the ventilation system in this house is just as complicated as the hallways and dusty as hell. Why are they always so clean in movies? And my *dress*! I just know it's going to be splotched gray with dust and lint when I get out of here.

Ugh.

I allow myself the world's shallowest cough against all this dusty air.

My knees are killing me, since my fat ass was *not* meant to do this—no, scratch that—*nobody* was meant to do this. I thought for sure I would've found some kind of exit vent into an occupied room by now, but nope. I passed a room that was all green minutes ago (probably called the Emerald Room) and one that looked like it was all diamond—nah, can't be. Whoever owns this place, they rich, but they can't be Queen of Sheba rich. Has to be cubic zirconia. Or Swarovski. Or plastic.

Then, I hear it. A voice!

"Her phone is in the harmonizer," it says, grave and insistent. Is that Bianca?

"You're sure?" comes another voice, this one I don't recognize.

"I watched her do it myself."

"Location services disabled?"

"Of course."

I freeze. A lump forms in my throat that just won't go down. Are they talking about *me*?

I venture a move. Slowly, carefully, I inch myself forward and around the corner to the voices.

"Then we're good," coos the unfamiliar voice, high and squeaky. "All we need now is for her to drink it. She'll come around."

The *hell*?

Drink *what*? They can't be talking about that Greenium shit. I told them I'm allergic!

"Where is she now?" asks the nameless woman as I look down into the dimly lit room. I can't see much, but a ton—and I mean a *ton*—of red.

Must be the Ruby Room.

Bianca stands there in her purple floor-length gown talking to the other woman who is just out of sight from where I am in this cramped little vent.

"She's in Rose Quartz. I told Diana we should put her in Blue Apatite to help quell her . . . ha . . . *appetite*."

Something dark and heavy settles into my chest and blooms into heat. Rage. Then I remember my sister, and that rage melts into fear. I have to warn Diana and get us the hell out of here. If they're trying to *force* this shit on me . . . she has *no* idea what she's involved with.

"I fucking knew it," I whisper to myself. "This *is* a cult."

"But," continues Bianca, "Diana insisted we go with Rose Quartz. She said pink is Synthia's favorite color."

"Go get her then," says not-Bianca. "It's time to invite her in."

Every hair on my body prickles, and my brain does what it always does when I'm anxious as hell—rapid-fires a bunch of jumbled thoughts. Where do I go? Back to my room? Do I stay put? I can't be here in this vent forever—my neck will never recover. There's barely room to lie down!

But . . . maybe that's it. Maybe if I can stay in here for the night, someone will track my phone here and find me? Unless that ridiculous urn thing really does block enough EMFs to mask my location.

But no. I have to warn Diana! Plus, I left the vent door swinging open in the Rose Quartz Room. They'll find me. I've gotta go back *fast*.

I gingerly turn myself around over the vent, careful to keep my feet away from the grates.

Clang!

I freeze, look down at my shoes where the aglet from one of the laces swings.

I feel the sweat beading on my forehead as I venture a glance down into the Ruby Room where I see . . .

Bianca.

Looking directly up at me.

She can't see me . . . can she?

"There you are," she hisses, her face curving into a dark smile.

Oh *hell.*

"She's in the vents!" her voice screeches as I scramble back.

Fuck, fuck, fuck, fuck.

They can't really strap me down and force me to drink this stuff, can they? If it has soy in it, they'd better be prepared to let me use my EpiPen because otherwise I'll literally swell all up in my throat and die!

Think, Synthia, how do I get out of this one?!

Tears fill my eyes. I knew coming out here was a horrible idea. How the hell did I let Diana talk me into this? A *smoothie club*, she said.

Okay, focus.

Get Diana.

Get my phone.

Get out.

Now how the hell do I find the Rose Quartz Room again! I hear voices. A deep, guttural growl actually.

"You can't hide forever, Synthia!" comes Bianca's now gritty, gravelly voice from somewhere in this aluminum maze. And she's moving closer.

"Just one sip, that's all we ask!"

"Holy shit," I whisper to myself. They really are going to try to force-feed me!

I freeze. I can't go back to the Ruby Room. They're clearly already in the Rose Quartz Room, somewhere nearby. I can hear them rummaging through my things.

"It's sad, really," comes the voice I don't recognize. "A toothbrush? Fluoride toothpaste? Ugh, just wait till she hears about activated charcoal and oil pulling. Her life could be so much cleaner!"

I resist the urge to gag. Oil pulling? Really?

"Shh!" demands the other woman, "Keep looking."

"Sabrina!" calls Bianca—she's already in the Rose Quartz Room. "Is this it?" I hear the mini fridge door shut.

I cock an eyebrow and venture farther down the aluminum tunnel until I trace their voices to a room glowing pink through an open grate in the floor.

"That looks like medication, all right." She paused as if the word "medication" were a swear word. "Read the label."

"Allergy Immunotherapy shot 82," she gasps. "Oh my god, that's so depressing! She's had to take eighty-two of these?"

Rage bubbles up again. Yeah, and what of it? They act like I take this shit recreationally. Unlike their smoothie mix, it's actually *doing* something.

The girl named Sabrina makes a *tsk tsk* and says, "Some elderberry treatments should clear that right up."

"Ugh, there's so much she just doesn't know!" exclaims Bianca, and I can hear the pity in her voice.

"That's why she's here, girl," Sabrina says. "But first, we have to find her. Come on. Help me up onto the bed."

Onto the *what*! They're coming up here, too?

I turn to scramble back down the tunnel and then hear—oh shit—more voices echoing from the Ruby Room.

"Katie?"

"Monica! Where is she?"

"In the vents."

"Ugh, gross."

"I know."

Well, what the hell else did they expect me to do? Just take their franken-smoothie and die? That's it, I decide. I'm out of here. I'll either escape this mansion or die trying.

But do I take on Sabrina and Bianca, with the feral eyes and vampiric smiles? Or do I take on Katie and Monica, the oil-pulling queens who have my meds?

Ugh, I don't know anything about these people! The Ruby Room looked like a blood sacrifice den and may be where they keep all their elixir, like a central holding tank. That's probably where they were trying to take me in the first place, so I head in the opposite direction.

But Sabrina is—

Thump. Thump. Thump.

Holy shit—she's in the vent, too!

There's my answer. I scramble down the clangy metal hallway and around the corner, over the vent to the Ruby Room and farther down the shaft than I've yet been. There's barely any light down here—I can't even see my hands in front of me.

Then suddenly, the floor beneath me begins to . . . *creeeeeeak. No, no, no!*

Everything buckles and twists into a mess of metal around me, and my head hits something cold and hard as I fall. The room is dark and dimly lit, with steam escaping from a pipe across the wall. I groan from where I lay on the floor, broken mangled aluminum all around me. I try to move my legs, to stand, and it's a slow process, but I get there.

I hike my dress up again, and I wish I could rip off the bottom half. Guaranteed I'mma have to run outta here, and it's hard enough to run without being stuck in a dress. Then I notice a particularly sharp piece of aluminum jutting up out of the wreckage, and I step forward. After a little dance involving the most careful spin I've ever done, the fabric falls around my ankles, with only a bleeding scratch or two across my shins to speak of. I smile at my handiwork and decide if I'm getting out of here, I need a defense. I look around for *anything* I can use.

Where the hell even am I? I look around—it looks dark enough to be a boiler room, but it's long. Like, *hallway* long.

Is this a secret passage?

No, wait, I've read about mansions this big. This is a staff hallway!

"Oh, Synthiaaaaa," sings a voice from somewhere nearby, sending a chill up my spine and a shudder through my chest. I spot those hissing pipes, one of them punctured from my fall, and settle my fingers against that one to make sure the steam isn't hot.

Nope.

I rip the pipe from the wall with more ease than I expected and bounce its weight in my hands like some Resident Evil shit.

It feels good in my hands, and I know at least if I encounter one of these smoothie-zombies, they'll think twice before strapping me down and making me drink a glass of death. "Welcome to Raccoon City, bitches."

I take the doorknob and ease the door open, peeking my face out just barely. I see shadows growing on the wall from around the corner, and I hear that shrill voice again.

"Why are you hiding? I *know* success can be scary, but please trust us. We want you to see how easy your life can be!"

Bianca.

Easy, she said. What the hell do they think drinking this shit is going to do for me?

"You don't have to take these allergy shots anymore!" she continues. "You could be free! You could . . . you could lose weight and be happy!"

Ooh, these women are pieces of work. What makes them think I *want* to lose weight? What if my chubby ass is already happy? Who said if I'm fat, I gotta be sad about it? And as for my allergies, once I finish treatment, maybe I won't *have* to deal with the pollen allergies that make it so I can't enjoy fresh fruits and vegetables. Do they think I *want* to live like this?

I feel more tears well up in my eyes. *Not now, Synth.*

Get Diana.

Get your phone.

Get out.

"Just a sip won't hurt," calls Sabrina, *way* too close. I freeze, crouch down, huddle up next to the door, look up, flip the lock, shut my eyes, and hope they don't suspect I'm in the staff hallway.

Please, please, please.

WHAM!

The door explodes against my back.

I scream.

"You *are* in there!" screeches someone's voice.

I scramble away from the door, still clutching the pipe, hurrying for the darkest corner of this room that I can find. I tuck myself behind a stack of boxes marked CATERING and clutch the pipe in my hands, ready to whack some knees if anyone comes around that corner.

But I hear . . . nothing.

Total silence.

Where'd they go?

No way they're letting me off that easy.

I get up, creeping toward the door, my feet silent against the floor, and I watch the door handle, expecting it to turn any minute. A sweat droplet rolls down my temple.

And then I hear it. A breath.

Soft, barely there.

In my right ear.

"Gotcha."

"Ahhhhh!" I whip around so fast I almost stumble, but not fast enough to see who's slammed a bag over my head and yanked me backward.

"Hold her!" hollers a voice I don't recognize.

"I'm trying!" grunts another.

I feel at least four arms around me as I'm lifted into the air, my limbs flailing, slamming into walls and floor and ceiling with a familiar *clang clang clang clang!*

I hear a groan that feels far away, and it takes me a minute to realize that the groan was mine. I taste blood and something else . . . grass? I flutter my eyes open to see a golden haze and several tall, bell-shaped figures above me. As my eyes focus, and my ears decide to work, I hear them.

"She's waking up!" cries one.

"I *told* you the crystals would work—"

"Shh," comes a voice I . . . recognize. It sounds so familiar. My eyes search for the source, but all I see are a dozen strangers' faces peering down at me like some kind of science experiment.

A *pseudoscience* experiment.

I'm in a huge room, familiar, filled with golden light. The ceiling must be forty feet high. It looks like . . . wait . . . the mansion. I'm in the front hall! I'm still in this nightmare.

And then all the memories come flooding back. The pipe, the staff hallway, the vents, the Greenium.

The *Greenium*. They're gonna make me drink that crazy shit!

I wiggle my hands and arms and realize . . . they don't even have me tied up! I bolt out of the chair and dart past all of them.

"Let me the fuck out of here, you sickos!" I scream, just knowing I'll find the door locked. But then, once I grab the knob and turn, the door . . .

Eases open?

It's open! Just like that! And then I remember.

"Where is my sister?" I demand, turning to find them all standing there, ball gowns of every color and shape, faces grinning, eyes sparkling wildly like they think they've already won. "Where is she?" I gasp.

My *she* came out as *thee*.

I reach up, feel my lips. Am . . . am I imagining things or . . . is that a tingling I feel?

I drag my tongue against my upper teeth and feel . . . nothing.

Oh shit.

"Where's my EpiPen?" I demand. When nobody moves, I dive for the first girl I see, a girl even shorter than me in a forest-green sheath dress with her red hair in an updo, and I shake her.

"Where is it? If I don't get that EpiPen, I'm going to die!"

The girl says nothing, just stares up at me with huge, scared blue eyes, her hands around my wrists.

Nobody says anything. Nobody moves to help her.

"Where the fuck is it!" I holler down at her, my grip tightening, her eyes shutting against me.

The only sound in the room is my heaving breathing. I look around at them all staring at me like I'm an animal in a cage. What the hell are they all waiting for?

"You think this smoothie is gonna turn me into a Disney princess?" I ask them. The girl's hands come up around mine, not desperately, but gently, like an afterthought. "You think this shit is going to make me like you all? What makes you think I want to *be* like you?"

I try to chill and take a deep breath.

Calm down, Synthie; panicking won't help.

But before I can launch into this concoction being a bunch of bullshit . . .

"Let the Greenium work its magic, will you?" comes a familiar voice—and the last voice I expect to hear say that.

My whole body goes cold. My grip around the redheaded girl's throat relaxes completely. She scrambles away, coughing.

"Diana?" I ask, turning toward the sound of the voice.

And sure enough, there's my sister holding up the black-and-orange EpiPen that could save my life.

I cough, stepping forward. I can feel the itch creeping into my fingers and hands. "Quit playing and give me my EpiPen."

She's unmoving. Her mouth curves into a smile.

"Diana!" I holler.

The silence that ensues is painful, but it tells me all I need to know. I fall to my knees, coughing even more, and she steps forward, kneels, and holds out the stick to me.

"This is what's killing you," she says. "And those allergy shots? Do you know what immunizations have in them, Synthia? Mercury. No wonder you feel like you're dying."

"It's not an—*cough, cough*—immunization!" Is she fucking crazy? "It's immunotherapy!"

"Conventional medicine has many names—"

"It's the thing I'm allergic to!" I erupt in more coughs and start scratching at my throat. "They give it to me in small doses until I get used to it. But soy . . . I can't . . . *cough, cough*! I can't breathe, Diana, please!"

I lunge for the EpiPen, but my sister yanks it away. My only sister. The one who claims to love me. She reaches into her pocket and pulls out a tiny packet, shakes it a couple of times. I reach up to scratch my neck. Oh god, the itch.

The *itch.*

I breathe in, hearing a faint wheeze as I do.

Diana kneels down before me, holding out the packet.

"This," she explains, "is the Greenium Go-Go Shot. Take this once every morning, and your allergies will fade. I promise."

What the hell do I say? I thought I knew Diana. I thought even with her crystals and her cards and her smoothies and her "go-go shots," she knew the dangers of misinformation. I remember when she first told me she'd found this new *smoothie brand,* but *don't worry, I just drink it for the taste.*

Now she's watching me die and holding out more to me as if it's going to save me. I'm drowning, and she's offering me a glass of water.

"I'm not going to let you die, Synth," she insists, her eyes pleading with me. "I love you. I just . . . want what's best for you. Allergy-free. Immunotherapy-free. I want you to be the size and shape you've always wanted to be. I want you to have energy and feel alive. I want you to be able to eat the things Mom and Dad could never afford!"

My eyes go wide at that.

How *dare* she bring Mom and Dad into this?

Whatever cult she's gotten herself into, worked her way up the chain in, even, Mom and Dad loved me at *all* the sizes I've been. They never once made me feel lesser-than for being the bigger-than sister. Sure, they wanted me to be healthy. And *so do I.* Hence the immunotherapy.

Why can't Diana understand that?

"Now," she continues, with a breath that says she's glad we've gotten semantics out of the way, "I have this smoothie packet here, and your allergy stuff in my clutch. Take the Greenium, give it a chance to work, and I'll let you have the EpiPen. Deal?"

If I don't get that EpiPen, I won't have a *chance* to take more Greenium.

"Deal," I croak, feeling the air pass through my ever-shrinking trachea. My eyes are forced open wide as I gasp for air, resisting the urge to cough, reaching out my hand for the smoothie packet.

She grins a triumphant, yet hesitant grin. *Is this real?* I know she's thinking.

I reach out my hand. She offers the packet, and I lunge for the clutch.

She shrieks, gripping it and ripping it back from me. I dive for her, hands around her throat at first, but then I realize—what use is choking her if I'm already mostly choked out myself?

I. Need. That. Clutch.

My hands clamp over the glittering gold bag.

"Girls, help me!" calls my sister.

They *all* move. They dogpile on top of us, and suddenly I'm buried under a mountain of hair—real and not real—tulle, organza, and jewelry.

I feel someone grip my teeny-weeny Afro and yank my head back, but I decide I don't care. Take all my hair. Air is more important.

Someone else's arms tuck under mine and tear me away from my sister. I feel tension on the clutch as someone grabs the chain, and I hang on to the bag harder until I can get into it.

I unfold the clutch and reach inside, finding the EpiPen

that'll keep me alive long enough to get to a hospital, and the immunotherapy shot that'll knock out the symptoms of my pollen allergies so I can have a balanced diet and keep myself alive long enough to die of old age.

I grab them both and tuck them close to my chest, and I tear away from the mass of girls and bolt.

Out into the rain, down the steps, and across the courtyard, I run, cracking open the EpiPen and jamming it into the outside of my right thigh. The sting is quick and warm, radiating through my quad, but I welcome it because I know what it means.

I continue running, but I feel myself slowing.

Running is hard enough. Try running while suffocating *and* injecting yourself in the thigh.

"Synthia!" shrieks my sister, not far behind me. I feel her hands around my waist as she yanks me backward, "I won't let you keep poisoning your body. I want you to be hap—"

I let out a growl from deep within me, screaming into the sky with the last of my breath.

"I *am* happy!"

Before I can register what's happened, I'm gripping the immunotherapy shot, the needle short, burying it halfway into Diana's neck.

The reality of what's happened sinks in. Her eyes are huge. She's frozen above me, rain dripping down her hair and into my eyes.

"Diana?" I whisper.

Her eyes roll back, and she falls to the ground.

"Diana?" I whimper.

Have I . . . is my sister . . .

No . . . it's gotta be shock! Right? Shock, that's it.

I feel a sob coming forth, but it turns into a fit of coughs. It's been ten seconds, so I pull out the EpiPen needle from my leg and massage my thigh gently.

Behind where my sister lies on the ground, needle still in her neck, I see the flurry of ball gowns pour from the mansion's front door.

"What the fuck!" shrieks Bianca, leading them all. "You killed her!"

Have I? I . . . I don't know! I . . . what happens if you inject someone who's not allergic to pollen with twenty-seven different types of pollen? In the neck? In the bloodstream? They . . . they always inject into my arm fat at the doctor.

Never the bloodstream.

Diana?

I press my fingers to her neck and feel a barely there pulse. It's enough. I know what I have to do.

Feelings or not, I have hours to get myself to a hospital, if that.

I swipe up Diana's purse with her keys inside, and I spring for the SUV.

"Synth," comes a croak from behind me. I stop and look back, the sting in my leg having turned into a dull ache. I heave huge breaths, each one more open than the last. Diana pushes herself to one elbow, her free hand up and around the needle. "What . . . what did you do to me?"

"Diana, no!" I holler, holding out my hand, "Don't take the needle—"

Yank.

Blood spurts from her neck in tiny, rhythmic heartbeats, and her hands come up to stop it, her eyes wide.

The tears come forth full force now as I scramble to her, falling to my knees, taking her in my arms, applying pressure to her neck right where the wound is. The bleeding stops immediately under my fingers, but I know if I let go . . .

I've got so little time to get her help, but I look up at the horde of girls looking on, their hair wet with rain, their makeup running with a mix of water and tears.

"Don't just stand there!" I holler. I point to the redheaded girl I almost choked out a minute ago. "You call 911!" I point to Bianca. "You come here and apply pressure to her neck!" I point to Sabrina. "You get everyone else inside!"

But *nobody* moves.

A few exchange confused glances like I'm speaking a different language. But none of them move to get my sister the help she needs.

I look down at Diana through my tears. I fix my eyes on Bianca, her drenched hair plastered to her cheeks as she stares on in shock. "Press your hands to her neck while I drive," I say, lowering my voice for just her. It's not a demand. It's a question. Bianca, the junior leader. Practically the vice president of this whole operation. She stares on unmoving, her right hand flinching for just a second like saving my sister is something to have to think about. Then, as if snapped from a trance, she looks around quickly to make sure nobody else saw her hesitancy before hiding her arms away behind her.

Some *sisterhood.*

I know what I have to do.

I clutch Diana's bag, push myself to my feet, and heave her, unconscious, up into my arms.

I make for the SUV, slowly, surely.

Nobody stops me.

I open the back door with my pinkie, drag her around, and lift her inside, pushing the whole weight of my body underneath her to get her into the vehicle. I tuck the base of her gold ball gown in so it's free of the door and shut it.

I climb into the driver's seat just as Bianca sprints forward. I shut the door and lock it just as her hands find the handle.

"Where are you taking her?" she screams, suddenly realizing I'm taking their queen from them.

"To a Reiki center," I hiss, turning the key and listening to the engine whir to life.

Bianca's face brightens. "Really?" she asks excitedly.

I put the car in drive and roll my eyes.

With the sourest glare I can muster, I look down at her through the car door and spit, "No, we're going to a fucking hospital."

And I floor it.

INHERITANCE

CAMARA AARON

"Please, please, please try to be normal."

Delany gave a thin smile. "I'm doing my best."

Tamara frowned and reapplied her lip gloss. She'd worn all hers off making out with Tyler Hall. Delany and Tamara sat in a lopsided circle on the floor of Tyler's bedroom, squished between students from their local high school. Her classmates, Delany reminded herself. At least, they would be when she and Tamara started the ninth grade on Monday. "Delany, try harder."

They'd both been anxious about ninth grade all summer. She and Tamara were at the bottom of the food chain again. Tamara bringing her along tonight should've boosted her up the social ladder. Except, she couldn't speak to anyone at this party. If she opened her mouth, Delany imagined her entire summer would tumble out, memories she brought home from her island.

On the other side of Tamara, Tyler was spinning the glass bottle at the center of their circle. He'd explained the game when they arrived, slinging one arm over Tamara's shoulder and leaving Delany to walk after them. "It's like seven minutes in heaven," he'd said. "The bottle decides who goes up. Everyone gets to decide when they come down." *Up* was his attic, its entrance in the ceiling of Tyler's bedroom. When Tamara and Tyler went up, one of his buddies stood on his desk chair, pressing the door closed. It didn't seem that fun to Delany.

Tyler's spin slowed and landed on Miles across the circle. He was a junior like Tyler, swinging a pocketknife between his fingers. Delany felt Tamara's elbow in her side. "You know, you could talk to Miles."

It was the second time Tamara had suggested this. The first time, after Tamara had come down from the attic, it had been Tyler's idea. He had mentioned that Miles had also spent his summer in Dominica. Didn't she think he and Delany, his friend and hers, could get along?

Delany had noticed Miles when she arrived. He was a head taller than anyone else there, picking at a peeling sunburn on his shoulders. He looked almost familiar to her, and that was enough reason to avoid him. Every reminder of Dominica made her skin crawl. She'd find herself running her hands over her arms, then her legs, making sure she was keeping it together.

Tamara tugged at her arm. "You have to talk to somebody. This is a high school party; they've got to like us."

Tyler rubbed his hands together before spinning again. The bottle made a hollow sound as it turned against the hardwood floor. It stopped between Tyler and Tamara. Then Tamara extended her foot and nudged the bottle over until it pointed at Delany. "I'm doing you a favor," she whispered. "C'mon, don't be a baby."

Delany's face burned. Tyler's friends whooped as Miles stood, going to stand below the attic entrance. Beside her, Tamara continued. “It’s just a few minutes. We’ll leave as soon as you come down.” She looped her pinkie with Delany’s and shook it in a promise. When she let go, Delany flexed her fingers. Since she had returned from Dominica, she didn’t like the feeling of anything against her skin.

Delany faked a smile as she stood and brushed off crumbs stuck to the back of her thighs. She shouldn’t have let Tamara dress her in a halter top and these too-short shorts. It made her feel exposed as the rest of the party watched her follow Miles up the stairs.

When they reached the top, the door folded up behind them. The attic was half-lit by moonglow. The rest of it fell in darkness. It was dusty, sweltering, and quiet. There was no sound up here besides the noises that old houses make in the night.

Delany watched dust mites float and flip in the moonlight. She counted her inhalations to track the time. After seventeen breaths, she could feel sweat trickling down her back. By thirty-two, Miles had stepped beside her. At sixty-three, she felt a brush of warm air by her ear before he leaned in, lips puckered. She yelped.

“I . . . don’t want to do that,” she said, looking anywhere but Miles.

Miles raised his hands in mock surrender. “Yeah, fine, whatever.” There was a sharp note of frustration in his voice. “Are you religious or something?”

Delany didn’t know what to say. She tugged at her shorts, wishing she were downstairs with Tamara. When she didn’t answer, Miles scoffed and turned away. In the strained silence, she could hear every creak and moan of Tyler's house and the clicking as Miles played with his pocketknife.

"I'm being a jerk," Miles muttered. She looked up at him, surprised by the remorse on his face. "I'm sorry. I just had the shittiest summer."

"Me, too," It just slipped out. Delany felt relieved to have said it, even though she immediately wanted to snatch it back. She'd meant to keep her summer to herself. Now Miles was giving her a small nod in recognition.

He closed the knife, slipping it into his pocket. "Yeah, Tyler told me you were in Dominica, too. I was up in the mountains. Were you around there?" Delany hummed to keep from answering. She willed the conversation to die. Instead, Miles sat on the attic floor and stretched his legs out. "I was with my dad. But he was at investor meetings all summer for this place he's fixing up, and my mom and my brother stayed here. So I was alone. And that sucked. And then, the place burned down, and my dad lost his hair, and all the investors folded, and we could lose our house. So . . . my summer was cursed." Miles tipped his head back and let out a long sigh. Delany watched the attic door, praying it would open.

Miles lolled his head over to look at her. "Well . . . ?"

Delany bit her tongue. Tamara's warning rang in her ears; these high schoolers had to like them. She couldn't steer the conversation away from where he'd set it without being rude. She could at least play along and guide them away from her secrets. If she didn't, she imagined what Miles would say about her when they came down, what his friends would tell their friends. Rumors hardened into reputation; wasn't Auntie Margot proof of that? It would only be a few minutes of trying to socialize, and then she could go home. She just needed to pass the time.

"I don't have many friends down there, either," she offered. "My aunt Margot isn't popular." With his shoulders hunched, Miles seemed small. Delany felt bad, still standing over him. She sat down as well.

Miles laughed. "Neither is my dad. But we're Americans. I figure they hate us on principle. What's your aunt's deal?"

Delany considered how to describe her aunt. Delany's mother talked about Margot like she was her opposite, but they were the same. All the Evans women were: lean like they didn't eat, with dark skin and large breasts. Delany had the gangly body, the mahogany skin. The boobs hadn't arrived.

The first summer Delany had spent in Dominica, she was ten. On the ride back from the airport, her aunt Margot had let her sit in the bed of her yellow pickup. She later made the mistake of telling her mother, who made Margot promise to never do it again. So now Delany was only allowed to ride in the truck's cab. But that day, Delany was driven under a rainforest canopy, sliding back and forth in the bed with each switchback. The unbroken view had been beautiful: winding through the red clay cliffs of Dominica's east side, then the flat swamp of the north, and finally down the coast, the Caribbean Sea breaking just beside the highway.

Auntie Margot lived in the south in a bright blue house. When Delany visited, the two of them still shared a bed. Delany was getting a bit big for it. On nights when Auntie Margot was home, Delany held herself corpse-still to keep from rolling over onto her. Other nights, Auntie Margot never came to bed and

Delany starfish-ed. She couldn't bring herself to move to the couch.

Margot was the coolest woman Delany knew, and the most talked about. Delany remembered an afternoon a few days into her vacation. She was in the backyard, a thin stretch of dirt that backed into a wall dividing Auntie Margot's property from her neighbor's. It was late afternoon, and Delany was doing her summer reading. She heard a hiss. She went to the dividing wall and pressed onto her toes. The neighbor's son, Jero, did the same from the other side, resting his elbows on the wall.

"You know your auntie a soukouyan," he said. Jero must've grown because Delany could make out his whole face over the wall. There was a bruise on his chin. "Imagine, boy. My fader wake last night and see a firefly in his room. He say de door close; de window close. Everyfing close before he go and sleep. He doh even know how it got inside. But you know, soukouyans can slip through the tiniest of cracks. That's how your auntie do it." Delany smothered her grin. She felt guilty for listening to Jero's stories, but she liked the way he told them, his eyes darting around, his voice hushed and quick.

"But he say she didn't suck his blood. He chase her out, and he see the firefly land right over there." He pointed at Auntie Margot's kitchen window. "Then he say the thing get big until it turn into woman. Mistah say he see her pull her skin on, wi boy? You know, she spoil him. 'Cause now he have a big spot on the back of his head like this." He made a circle with his thumb and first finger the size of his father's bald spot. "That's why he doh have much work. But ya, be safe, eh?" Jero crossed himself and slipped down behind the wall.

"Everyone thinks my aunt's a witch," Delany told Miles now. It felt harmless to tell him a little bit of the truth. But with the words came her memories of the beach, the drumbeat of fear in her chest, the feeling of scrambling across the stones, the bite in her calf burning. Delany shivered.

"Are you scared?" Miles slid beside her, wrapping an arm around her shoulders. He rubbed his hand up and down her bare arm. She fought the urge to cringe. He was being nice, she told herself. "You don't actually believe all that, do you?"

Delany shook her head. "Of course not, they're folktales."

"I heard stories like that. Women who shed their skin and fly across the sky like a fireball. Then they come into your house to suck your blood. My dad has local guys working on his property. They would talk about women in town they suspected. They were like the only people I hung out with." Miles left his arm loose around her as he spoke. Delany leaned out of his grip. She didn't want to hurt his feelings—they were still trapped together. So she stayed sitting, though the trail of his hand on her shoulder felt like spiders on her skin.

"You didn't make any friends?" she asked.

"I had three: Jess, Marty, and Piper. They'd explore with me, go on walks." Those names didn't sound Dominican. Delany imagined Miles running around with other white kids in the bush. "What about you and your aunt? What'd you guys do out there?"

Delany thought of the two places she spent her summer, curled up at Auntie Margot's or laid out by the water. "Read and talk and swim. My aunt's down in Soufrière."

"I know there." Miles was wrinkling his nose. "The beach

there is terrible. It's all rocks." He was right; the shore was stony. But the orange pebbles were so worn they shifted like sand underfoot.

"That's my favorite beach on the whole island. The water's perfect," Delany said. "Warm like bathwater, and it bubbles. How can you not like bubbles?"

She and Auntie Margot went to Soufrière Beach every weekend. In the middle of the summer, they found it cordoned off. "Property of the Sea Breeze Hotel. Keep out," Delany had read. The Sea Breeze was an old lime plantation they were renovating in the mountains. The chain hung between two posts freshly sunk into the ground. Auntie Margot lifted the chain and waved Delany under.

Delany took off her T-shirt and shorts on the shore. Auntie Margot said her bathing suit looked cute, even though it was a tankini and every other girl at Tamara's end-of-year pool party had graduated to bikinis. A breeze brushed over them, and Auntie Margot's dress fluttered around her legs. The sun was setting into the water, washing her aunt in warm light. It almost looked like a lick of flame.

"Why do people think you're a witch?" It came out before Delany could think it through.

Auntie Margot sucked her teeth at her. "I tell you doh talk to that boy. His fader is an angry man that like to full his head with nonsense." Auntie Margot was as public about her dislike for Jero's father as he was for her. Delany thought Auntie Margot had the better reason. Everyone in Soufrière knew how Jero's father beat on him. Auntie Margot refused to hire him because of it, telling anyone who listened why. But few of the neighbors listened to Margot.

"It's more than just Jero," Delany continued. The last time they were in town, Delany had watched a young mother snatch her child back before she toddled in front of Auntie Margot. The woman watched her aunt with such suspicion Delany wondered if they were looking at the same person. "Why don't you tell them they're wrong about you?"

"I doh worry about other people. They like weak women. Women who shut their mouth. That's not me. Doh let it be you." Auntie Margot gave her a look that went right through Delany. She nodded to the water. "Go bathe."

Delany walked into the sea. She turned back to her aunt. Auntie Margot was always alone. Delany wondered if she invited Delany down to Dominica to keep her company. Wouldn't it be worth being a little smaller so her neighbors liked her? So they didn't call her a soukouyan before her back had turned? Delany watched the water lap over her feet, bubbling around her toes. Then she heard a shriek.

Auntie Margot grabbed her, dragging her from the water. That was when Delany saw the dogs. Three of them were charging down the beach. Their brown-and-black bodies kicked up pebbles, their sharp teeth gleaming. Someone had sicced dogs on them, she realized.

Delany scrambled onto the shore, stumbling over the stones. Auntie Margot locked her arm around Delany and hauled her forward. Behind them, she could hear the dogs' snarling breaths and the rattle of their chain collars. They were getting louder, closer. She couldn't breathe. Auntie Margot squeezed her, running harder. Delany saw the beach entrance. The sign whipped in the wind. KEEP OUT, it had read. They hadn't listened.

They were only yards away when Delany felt teeth sink into her calf. She lost Auntie Margot's hand, going down screaming. Delany remembered struggling on the rocky shore. She felt the teeth in her leg burning through her body. . . .

Back in the attic, Delany jolted from her memory. She had felt something brush her calf right where the dog had bitten her. For a moment, she felt its teeth buried in her skin again. She looked down. Miles was touching her, poking at the scar tissue on her calf.

"Excuse me," she said. She jerked her leg away, out of his reach.

Miles cocked his head. "What happened there?"

Delany pressed a hand to the raised scars. She traced the two half-moons of the dog's jaw. Maybe a direct answer would stem his curiosity. "I got attacked by a dog. Kind of ruined my summer." Her legs were going numb from sitting. How long had they been up here? It felt like more than a few minutes.

"How did you get away?" he asked. "It seems like a big dog."

There was something sharp behind his curiosity. Miles was studying her. Delany worried he'd touch her again. She stood and paced, grateful for some space between her and Miles's questions. She stared into the darkened corner of the attic, searching for a good lie. But in the end, she settled on the truth.

"My aunt fought them off."

Delany kicked out at the dog, screaming for it to let her go. When it did, she curled up, bracing for another bite. Instead, she heard a whimper. When she glanced back, the dogs were cowering. One released a low whine from deep in its chest. When Delany looked in front of her, she whimpered, too.

Her Auntie Margot lay there, splayed on her stomach. Her mouth was open, and her stare was vacant. Even when she was asleep, Margot never looked so lifeless. Delany touched her aunt's arm, and it gave way under her fingers, crumpling like a plastic bag. Like the skin was hollow.

The dogs cried again. Delany heard them dancing in place. They were afraid, she realized. But of what? Then she caught a flash above her.

A creature hovered over Margot's skin. Its long body was all pink muscle, which stretched and pulsed as it breathed. Fleshy wings protruded from its back, beating slowly. It burned with a fire that whipped forward as it bared its teeth at the dogs, swiping at them with sinewy arms. The soukouyan had fangs that hooked down to its chin. It also had her aunt's eyes in its skinless face.

The dogs whined and scurried away.

Delany wouldn't have believed it if she hadn't felt the heat of the soukouyan's flame on her face. She buried her head in her arms. She could hear the soukouyan land beside her, the squelching as it slipped back into Auntie Margot's skin. She flinched when it touched her. Auntie Margot looked hurt for a moment. Then she pulled Delany to her feet and walked her home.

Auntie Margot directed Delany to the shower as soon as they got inside. When the water went cold, her aunt wrapped her in a towel. She took Delany's calf on her lap and cleaned the bite. Delany let herself cry harder than she needed to. She had never felt fear like this, a fist around her heart. She wanted to both lean into Margot's touch and run for her life.

Instead, she kept crying as Auntie Margot wrapped her leg, rubbed lotion onto her skin, put her in a nightgown, and sat her at the dining table. She'd made mac and cheese, the boxed kind Delany's mother didn't let her have at home. Auntie Margot squeezed ketchup on top in a spiral, just how Delany liked it. But the sharp red reminded her of Jero's stories.

"Are you going to drink my blood?" Delany hiccupped as she said it.

Auntie Margot laughed. "You shouldn't let that boy full up your head." She tugged Delany's chin. "I protect myself and my own. And I will protect you until you can protect yourself."

As her aunt's words sunk in, Delany gasped. "Am I a soukouyan, too?"

Auntie Margot wrapped her finger around the end of one of Delany's cornrows. This time, Delany didn't flinch. "You doh take foolishness. Call that a soukouyan if you want."

Delany let out a final tear. Then she finished her mac and cheese.

They didn't return to their beach. Every time they passed it, Auntie Margot would grumble under her breath, "That behkay." Delany had never seen the Sea Breeze's owner in person until a few weeks later, at the grocery store in town. He was pale, sweaty in a Sea Breeze–branded polo. Auntie Margot stalked over to him. Delany couldn't hear what she said, but he went even redder under his sunburn. A woman close by crossed herself when Auntie Margot laid a hand on his shoulder.

"She corner the man right there in Whitchurch, wi?" Jero said a few days later. Delany was sunning herself in the backyard, her bad leg propped up to keep her weight off it. "She spoil him, for true!"

The rest of her summer limped by. There was little to do without the sea to visit. She relied on Jero for her entertainment, but Delany couldn't take the same pleasure in his stories anymore. Every time she got out of the shower, Delany would study her skin, wondering if a seam would emerge so she could step out of it. That was the worst part. Not being banned from the grocery store because they were afraid of Auntie Margot's obeah. Not losing her favorite beach to a developer. But dreading a change that didn't come.

"Your aunt sounds insane," Miles said. There was something like awe in his voice. In the attic, Delany felt a flare of protectiveness in her chest. She stopped pacing to look down her nose at Miles where he sat.

"She's brave," Delany snapped. It wasn't the worst she'd heard someone say about Margot, but it irked her from this grabby boy.

Miles scrambled up. "I meant it like a compliment, I promise." He reached out to put his hand on her shoulder.

This time, she was too annoyed to indulge him. She stepped back and left his hand outstretched. She felt like Margot, watching

Miles flush and fold his arms. "My aunt lets people know what she thinks of them. Mr. Sea Breeze or whatever-his-name, she let him have it. She's not afraid of anybody. And I think our time should be up, don't you?"

Delany went to the attic door. She was done playing this game. She pushed at it, trying to force the door open. It wouldn't budge. She pressed her ear to the floor, listening for the sounds of people below. There was nothing.

She almost jumped out of her skin when Miles gripped her arm. He was squatting next to her. "Until now, I didn't know who she was," Miles whispered, his breath hot on her face. "Your aunt really freaked my dad out."

Delany blinked at him, her brain making sense of what he said. Miles's dad owned the Sea Breeze. It was the land he was fixing up in the mountains, how Miles knew her beach. Delany moved back, but Miles held on, his gaze burning into her.

"He told me this crazy lady yelled at him in Whitchurch. He had no idea what she was talking about. He kept asking me, what dogs?" Miles's eyes gleamed as he spoke. "I was way too embarrassed to tell him what I did. He was always complaining about the trespassing. I thought I'd be helpful."

Delany remembered the three friends he'd counted on his fingers: Jess, Marty, and Piper. She tried to reconcile the warmth in his voice with her memory of the three dogs barreling down the beach. She wanted out of the attic. The farther he pushed her away from the door, the harder it'd be to escape.

On Miles's next step, Delany held her ground. He was so close their noses almost bumped. She stared back at him, determined to seem unafraid. "I didn't realize how bad I'd messed up until the hotel burned down. What is it the laborers told us? We'd been spoiled. Your aunt, she cursed us."

Delany was only half listening, planning her next move. She stepped left, then ran right, hoping to dart around him. Instead, Miles lunged. They landed hard. Miles pinned her on her stomach, his hand on the back of her neck, pressing her into the attic floor. The pressure of him squeezed the air out of her. She bucked like a caught fish. She felt just as powerless.

"Please, please, don't do this." As she begged, she could taste her tears. He was bigger than her. Where could she go, even if she broke his grip? And it was that pit of defenselessness that bloomed into anger in her chest. She was not going to let this white boy hurt her just because he thought he could. She let herself go limp. And when Miles loosened his grip on her, adjusted his weight, she twisted her neck and dug her teeth into the soft skin of his inner wrist.

He screamed, and Delany dragged herself away. She didn't expect to like the taste of his blood, but she did. He was sweet. She forced herself to stand. She turned, ready to fight, but Miles was trembling.

She had pulled herself free, but Miles was still holding her. Her skin was loose and limp in his grip. Delany herself was pulsing pink muscle and red flame, her body hovering inches off the floor.

Miles gaped. He fell to his knees, holding her skin in front of him like a shield. "Don't hurt me." Delany sneered at the irony. What had her begging or discomfort meant to him? "Just break the curse—please, break the curse," he pleaded.

"What curse?" Her voice came out croaky and deep. Miles

shrunk back farther, blubbering. "Miles, what curse?" Delany thought back to Auntie Margot at the Whitchurch. Her aunt's hand on the man's shoulder, her smug expression when she'd returned to Delany. Delany flexed her own fingers. What kind of power did she now have?

"You have to help me!" Miles said. He had pulled out his pocketknife. He was pressing it to her skin in his hands. "You need this, right? So help me! And I'll give it back, I promise." His gaze was hard, as was his breathing. Even as she loomed over him, Miles was still threatening her. He was really pissing her off.

Delany surged forward, her flames licking out at him. Miles fell with a shriek. He landed on his butt, dropping the knife and her skin. Before he could recover them, Delany swept forward again. Miles scrambled back, cowering. The moonlight lit his petrified expression. She could tear him apart, she realized, licking her tongue over her teeth. It'd be fun. The thought made Delany stop.

Miles was older and bigger. But now, in this attic, she was stronger. Hurting him wouldn't be for protection; it'd be for pleasure. It was the kind of cruelty Auntie Margot would've despised. She wanted Delany to stand up for herself. The sniveling boy in the corner was proof Delany had. She was no longer defenseless, no longer subject to his power and whims. She didn't have to abuse him the way he had her. She clenched her fists to bank the anger inside her.

"I'll help you," Delany said. She reasoned her aunt had spoiled his father with a touch. Maybe hers could take it back. But she had conditions. "You can't tell anyone about this. And you leave me alone. Don't even say hi to me in the hall."

Miles nodded. She gestured to him to stand. His legs were shaky as he rose. "Th-thank you," he stammered.

"And your dad opens the beach. I want my beach back."

"I promise," Miles said. She landed on the floor soundlessly. When Delany reached for him, he flinched back. He paled, watching the flesh of her hand slide and bunch as she crooked her finger, calling him closer. Miles steeled himself and stepped forward. She laid her hand on his shoulder.

Nothing happened.

"Is that it?" he asked.

Delany didn't know, but her hand went cold. A pulse of energy burst from her palm down into Miles's shoulder. He staggered a step back, then another. Then he plummeted out of her sight. The attic door had opened up underneath him, its open mouth swallowing him whole. Delany heard the heavy thump as he hit the floor. The music cut off, and below her, there was a flurry of gasps and footsteps.

They'd be too distracted to come poking around in the attic, Delany figured, so she took her time stepping back into her skin. It felt like sliding between clean sheets. When she came down the stairs, everyone was crowded around Miles. His expression was dazed as Tyler helped him sit up.

"What happened up there?" Tyler asked.

Miles found Delany over his friend's shoulder. She stared back at him, daring him to break his promise. Miles looked away. "Nothing, man," he muttered. "Leave it alone."

Tyler propped him up against the side of his bed, and the rest of their friends drifted away, breaking up the circle they'd been in. The game was over.

Delany felt Tamara loop their arms together. She glanced between Delany and Miles, questions evident on her face. Delany returned her gaze. She wondered what Tamara would think if she knew what had happened in the attic. What Delany was. That she had screwed up her chance for these high schoolers to like her. But Auntie Margot told her not to take any foolishness. Delany would listen.

After a moment, Tamara snuggled closer with a yawn.

"Are you ready to go home?" she asked.

"Absolutely," Delany said.

The night before school started, Delany slept peacefully. There were scarier things than high school. *She* was one of those things.

BLACK GIRL NATURE GROUP

MAIKA MOULITE AND MARITZA MOULITE

"All are welcome, but please be aware that Black Girl Nature Group prioritizes Black femme-identifying individuals and their experiences. If the prior statement makes you uncomfortable in any way, then this is not the group for you," Lucky reads the text message open on her phone's screen aloud to her mother.

"You heard that, Ma?" Lucky continues, leaning forward from the back seat. "*Prioritizes*. I'll be fine!"

"So you've said," Mrs. Clifton says. "You know I've gotta ask a couple of questions since you want to run headfirst into the middle of a forest. At night. When people are already coming for us just for breathing outside air during the daytime. Not to mention, this is where my sister—"

"Mooom," Lucky says and immediately clamps her mouth shut. If she's going to make sure that her mom isn't texting her Just checking in! every second of this trip, she'll need to drop the whining baby act. She has to be a whining young *adult*.

Lucky recites the response she's memorized in the event her parents wanted to give her any last-minute grief. She clears her throat loudly and speaks as if she were a government official reading a royal decree. “Ma, we talked about this already. I’m going to enjoy this once-in-a-lifetime natural wonder, and you’ll be back to get me tomorrow morning. Although my presence as a Black girl in nature is an act of defiant joy, I really just want to see some stars.” Lucky adds, “Plus, I don’t plan on getting into any kind of trouble whatsoever.”

Mr. Clifton, who has remained largely silent throughout this exchange, finally speaks up. “Don’t take that tone with your mama, young lady. You already know that it’s a big deal for us to even let you go. Your aunt Solange went missing here.”

“Thank you, honey,” Mrs. Clifton says, leaning over to give her husband a kiss on the cheek. “That was a long time ago. No one with a lick of sense plans on getting into trouble. But if it should come looking, you had better send it on its merry way. You hear, Lucky?”

Lucky rolls her eyes and looks out the window. She won’t let her parents ruin this moment with their ghost stories. Mrs. Clifton, in particular, was always going on about ancestor this or spiritual alignment that. Lucky was already on edge because she was here to experience what her mom had called one of the most supernatural moments of a decade. While blood moons happen every year and a half, it’s only every ten years that one appears at the same time as the Crusaders meteor shower. Lucky might have sat the entire evening out if it hadn’t been for her new friend, Patricia.

Patricia’s friendship with Lucky wasn’t exactly expected—she was captain of the cheerleading squad, and her dad was the conservative mayor of their town. But Lucky had been pleasantly surprised by how Patricia had made it her business to not only befriend Lucky but also take her under her wing after she tried out for the squad.

"I'm really committed to learning as much as I can about different kinds of people, ya know?" Patricia had said when Lucky first met her. It was a little much if you asked Lucky, but it was surely better than her being closed off to others who weren't like her. Patricia had even gone so far as to join the Facebook page for Black Girl Nature Group, and when it was hacked, she'd been the one to let Lucky know that they had created a regular group text thread instead. It was more secure that way.

The trees stretch toward the heavens on either side of the moving SUV as the Cliftons continue along their way. Lucky tries to make out the individual lines of towering oaks and maples, but her eyes can't keep up. And are those . . . statues every few feet, hidden behind clusters of plants? The more Lucky continues to stare, the more it seems each jutting branch turns toward her, countless gnarled fingers pointed in accusation. Lucky frowns but shakes it off. She must've imagined them.

"You've gotta understand, Lucky," Mr. Clifton says, glancing at his daughter in the rearview mirror. "When your mom and I were your age, Black folks weren't going into the woods around here on purpose."

"Your daddy is right," Mrs. Clifton says. "Growing up, we didn't live too far from these woods. My grandmama wouldn't let me and your auntie Solange—God rest their souls—outside without speaking a prayer over us. '*This is my granddaughter*

Solange. This is my granddaughter Leticia. Send them back to me whole and unharmed.'"

"And why'd she do that?" Lucky asks in a bored tone.

"Whenever we asked her, she'd say that's what her grandmama did over her so that's what she'd do for us, too. My grandmama was never the same after Solange went missing. She blamed herself for not speaking protection over her that day."

This isn't the first time Mr. and Mrs. Clifton have warned Lucky about the woods on the edge of town at Bear Creek Park. Yet she'd somehow been able to convince her parents that letting her watch the blood moon meteor shower would be her way of helping to break generational curses. Besides, it had been almost ten years since the last person had gone missing in the woods.

Buzz.

Lucky pulls her phone out of her pocket.

> **Patricia:** Hey hey. I hate to do this so last minute, but I can't get out of going to the christening for the alderman's son after all.
>
> **Lucky:** Seriously?!
>
> **Patricia:** My dad's like "I'm the mayor! What will it look like, my only daughter not attending?" Ugh. Have fun at the hike without me though. And please don't hate meeeee <3
>
> **Lucky:** You would have slowed me down anyway.

Lucky erases the last message before sending it. That's the type of joke Jazz would've liked, and Patricia is . . . not Jazz. Lucky's heart twists at the thought of her former best friend. It's honestly a little bit surprising, the way Patricia had stepped up to look out for Lucky since she and Jazz stopped speaking. And it wasn't exactly an easy feat, considering the three of them were partners in chemistry lab.

Their teacher had grouped them together, and no matter how hard Lucky tried, he would not move her to another group. So Patricia had become their buffer, facilitating their months-long game of academic telephone. Lucky was grateful because even though it had been almost nine months since she last spoke with Jazz, their severed friendship was still an open wound. And it was all Lucky's fault.

"All right, looks like we're here," Mr. Clifton says as the car rolls to a stop in front of a large, colorful sign emblazoned with the words BLACK GIRL NATURE GROUP tied to two nearby trees.

Lucky glances around for familiar faces but only sees a few white people milling about the gravel parking lot. It'd been months since she last attended a Black Girl Nature Group event. When Lucky first learned of the local chapter, she and Jazz were still the best of friends. They attended a few of their daytime meetups together, learned foraging tips, even practiced outdoor yoga. Anything to show that nature was for everybody. Back then, there were always all kinds of people who would come to support, but there were usually more Black girls in attendance.

"Uh, this nature group is looking very . . . not Black," Mrs. Clifton says. "When did you say your friend was getting here? What's her name? Portia?"

"Her name's Patricia, Ma," Lucky says, stalling. "And . . . uh . . . she's—"

Honk! Honk!

Lucky glances up to see a tall girl with long ombre braids step out of a dark sedan. The pain she's feeling in the middle of her chest right now has to be a heart attack.

Mr. Clifton pushes the button to roll down his window, and Lucky watches with teeth-grinding anxiety as the squeaky glass slides down. Her dad's voice sounds like it's coming from the bottom of the ocean. "Jazz Walker! Where you been, girl? How's Mr. Walker been?" He waves over Lucky's ex-friend. Gleefully. Cluelessly.

Jazz walks over to Mr. Clifton's car with a smile on her face, but Lucky can tell that it's her *I'm only being polite because my momma raised me right* face.

"Hey, Mr. and Mrs. C. Dad's hanging in there. And I've been busy with basketball and school. Trying to get back into the groove of things." Jazz and Lucky's eyes don't meet. They are two magnets with the same poles exposed, repelling each other.

"That's completely understandable, darling," Mrs. Clifton says, leaning over to look at Jazz. "You hang in there."

An awkward silence descends on the group as Mr. and Mrs. Clifton glance at Lucky, waiting for their daughter to speak up.

Jazz's phone vibrates, and she looks down at the screen. "Oh man, my friend Patricia isn't—"

"Going to be here on time!" Lucky interrupts, finding her voice, if only to prevent her parents from changing their minds about letting her stay for this trip. And why is Patricia texting Jazz on a weekend anyway? Patricia is supposed to be *her* friend.

"Lucky," Mrs. Clifton chastises, "it's rude to interrupt."

"It's all good, Mrs. C," Jazz says, finally looking at Lucky. "Patricia is always running late. It's her thing."

"Well, it wouldn't be a nature group for Black girls without a few people running on CPT," Mr. Clifton says with a chuckle.

Jazz laughs politely and doesn't correct Mr. Clifton's assumption that Patricia is Black.

"Okay, ladies. We're gonna head out so I can spare you Mr. Clifton's comedy hour." Mrs. Clifton smirks at her husband.

"Don't hate the playa!" Mr. Clifton says.

Lucky can't help the groan that rumbles from her chest as she steps out of the car. "Thank you for dropping me off, parents," she says. "I'll see you tomorrow morning, bright and early."

"Okay, honey. Text us if you need anything," Mrs. Clifton says.

Mr. Clifton reaches to shift the car into drive, but Mrs. Clifton places a hand over his. She leans over her husband to get a good look at her daughter before saying, "This is my daughter, Lucky. This is my daughter's friend Jazz. Send them back to me whole and unharmed."

A shiver runs down Lucky's body, starting at the crown of her head, zipping down her spine, and settling at the soles of her feet. Jazz rubs her own arms as if she feels the electricity rushing through her, too.

"*Ma,*" Lucky says in that whiny young adult voice.

"If it was good enough for my grandmama, then it's good enough for me!" Mrs. Clifton blows her daughter a kiss as Mr. Clifton shakes his head, trying to hide his smile.

"See you tomorrow, sweetheart," he says before bringing his window back up.

Jazz and Lucky watch the Cliftons' car drive away until it disappears.

Lucky clears her throat. "Um. . . . Thanks for covering for—"

Jazz doesn't even blink in her direction before walking off.

Fallen leaves paint the forest floor, the technicolor blanket crunching beneath Lucky's feet as she follows Jazz. It's a surprisingly long trail to check in with the Black Girl Nature Group, especially compared to past events where they typically met up in the parking area. Maybe they changed their protocols.

Though Lucky makes a point to keep some distance between them, she is still painfully aware of Jazz's presence. After almost a year of not speaking, all Lucky wants to do now is talk. But clearly the time for that has long passed in Jazz's eyes. And she's right to feel that way. As soon as Lucky had learned how sick Jazz's mom was, she should've squashed everything, once and for all. But Lucky had let her own feelings take precedence. She didn't know how to navigate something so final as death . . . and here she is centering herself yet again.

Lucky focuses on the trail before her just as someone quickly walks by, shoulder checking her as they pass. Lucky strangely feels the urge to follow, but when she turns around, they're already gone.

"Excuse me," a voice says. Lucky faces forward again to find another person standing only a foot away from her. She takes a step back.

"Uh . . . sure," Lucky says.

The middle-aged woman presents the toothless, tightlipped smile given by white women to minorities to feign sincerity.

Lucky continues her walk along the trail, slowing just a bit to make sure that the woman has moved on. When she's certain the stranger is on her way, she continues. Up ahead, Jazz stands before a wooden sign. Lucky stands beside her and reads along.

> *THOUGH BEAR CREEK PARK IS HOME TO VARIOUS FLORA AND FAUNA, IT IS PERHAPS ITS HISTORY THAT MAKES IT ONE OF THE MOST INTRIGUING PLACES TO VISIT IN THE COUNTRY. ITS MARSHY WATERS HAVE BEEN USED AS A MEETING PLACE FOR HISTORIC GROUPS OF ALL KINDS, FROM ENSLAVED INDIVIDUALS FLEEING TO FREEDOM IN THE NORTH TO THE PEOPLE WHO LOOKED TO PREVENT THEIR ESCAPE. NOW, BEAR CREEK PARK IS A PLACE OF CELEBRATION FOR FAMILY REUNIONS, PICNICS, AND EVEN WEDDINGS. GIVEN ITS VARIED USES, LOCAL LEGEND HOLDS THAT THE PARK IS RIFE WITH SUPERNATURAL ENERGY.*

"Are you following me?" Jazz asks.

"Wh-what?" Lucky asks, startled that Jazz is addressing her directly. "No, I'm just walking behind you because you're ahead of me."

"Hmm," Jazz says. The sound holds a treasure chest of unspoken words.

"Honestly, if Patricia hadn't flaked on me, you probably wouldn't even know I was here," Lucky says.

"Flaked on you?" Jazz asks. "She was supposed to be here with me. But then she had . . ."

"A christening," they say in unison, understanding dawning on them.

"Dang," says Jazz. "I really can't believe she played me like that."

"She got me, too. But, I mean, she gave a believable excuse. She's already gone to like four christenings this year alone."

"Patricia and that big ol' politician family of hers," Jazz says.

They laugh. It's an easy one. The *ha, ha, has* land on each other lightly, as if they belong together.

Jazz fidgets with the bracelet around her wrist. A friendship bracelet they'd made together.

"I hope she wasn't trying to get us both out here like in that old *Parent Trap* movie," Jazz says. The laughter in her voice dissipates like a snuffed-out flame.

"Jazz—" Lucky starts, and she knows immediately that her tone has given her away.

"Try not to follow so closely," Jazz says curtly.

Lucky is frozen in place, watching her heart walk away. She turns back to the sign, the words distorted now by the tears she tries to hold back.

NO SMOKING.

NO LITTERING.

NO FEEDING THE WILD ANIMALS.

NO HUNTING.

NO MAKING AMENDS WITH YOUR EX-FRIEND, THE ONE YOU WISH HAD BEEN MORE THAN.

NO CLEANING UP THE MESS YOU MADE.

NO MORE TIME; IT'S TOO LATE.

Lucky sighs heavily, just as a girl about her age with platinum-blond hair stops right in front of her. Lucky nearly bumps into her, but she says nothing as Lucky maneuvers around her. When Lucky looks back over her shoulder, the girl is already gone.

Lucky rubs the goose bumps along her arms, but no matter how many times she swipes her hands up and down, they will not go away. She was silly to shoo her parents off like that without confirming where the rest of the group was first. Just because she'd been out with them a few times before doesn't mean she knows everything there is to know about being outdoors, especially at night. And now here she is, all alone since Patricia wanted to play matchmaker and ditched her with Jazz, who wants absolutely nothing to do with her.

Something rustles near Lucky's right foot, nudging her with enough force to almost change her direction. A scream rises in her throat but Lucky swallows it back down. She really wants to keep it together but with every few steps she takes, another person appears in front of her. Each one stares at her with a widening grin, and even though their teeth gleam with what should be welcome, Lucky feels a trickle of warning slither down her spine. She's used to this specific brand of white person hiker. The ones who are surprised to see someone like her *here*, also enjoying the great outdoors. They cover up their shock with nods. They stand closer than they should, hoping to showcase their tolerance through an *accidental* elbow graze.

Notice how I didn't recoil? I welcome you.

Lucky always smiles in response, in a way that she hopes reads as friendly, not suspicious.

Sometimes it helps. Mostly it doesn't.

The sun hangs low in the sky when Lucky finally makes it to a large clearing in the forest. How much time has she spent walking? She pulls out her phone to check and groans when she sees she has no service. A long table stretches before her, and people stand in disorganized clusters waiting to check in. Lucky scans the crowd, and the unease that's been plaguing her since she started walking the trail alone solidifies like an anchor in her stomach.

Every single person standing before her has blond hair and blue eyes that don't crinkle when they smile.

And Jazz is nowhere to be seen.

"Oh my goodness, Lucky, is that *you*?"

A white woman with curly wheat-colored hair waves Lucky over. All conversation stops as nearly twenty pairs of eyes turn to look at her. Lucky has the strange sensation that she's interrupted a private gathering.

"Sorry—am I . . . at the right place?"

"Of course you are!"

Lucky walks up to the table. Hesitantly. "How do you know my name?"

"You look just like your Bitmoji. I mean, the 'fro is identical. Can I touch it?" The stranger reaches forward as Lucky lurches back.

She chuckles. "Just kidding! I know better than that. Anyway, I'm Rachel! This is Lauren, Brittany, Rebecca, and we'll be here all night if I introduce everyone, but please, say hello."

Lucky frowns slightly. "Rachel . . . ?"

The woman cocks her head. The movement reminds Lucky of Jazz's dog, Ruff Ryder, a slight tilt that occurs when he hears something that only he can perceive.

"Rachel Clifton," the woman says with a slow grin.

Lucky's heart breaks into a gallop.

"But I've met the leaders of this group . . . and they're not y'all." Lucky looks around at the supposed members of the Black Girl Nature Group again, eyes wide as she takes in each pale face one by one. Her mom's words replay in her mind. "*No one with a lick of sense plans on getting into trouble. But if it should come looking, you had better send it on its merry way.*"

"I know we don't seem like the most obvious choice to lead a group like this, but equity and inclusion are such passions of ours." Rachel's Cheshire Cat grin stretches unnaturally and Lucky can't help but think that she reminds her a lot of Patricia.

The crowd at the right end of the table shifts, and Lucky notices a collection of framed photographs with each picture depicting two Black girls. As Lucky scans each face, it's like a timeline through the ages. Bamboo earrings from the '90s. Glorious 'fros from the '70s. Pin curls from the '50s.

"Who are these girls?" Lucky whispers.

"They're the ones who have been . . . lost to the forest over the years," Rachel says.

Lucky's mind fills with even more questions but something tells her that this is not the time to ask them. She takes a step back, ready to return to the parking lot. But her eye catches something in the fading sunlight: a handwoven friendship bracelet covered by brush. Lucky glances back at Rachel, and the woman follows her gaze down to the bracelet.

"Where is Jazz?" Lucky asks slowly.

An eardrum-rattling scream pierces the air.

Jazz.

Everyone moves at once. Rachel shouts at a nearby man to grab Lucky. He races forward, but Lucky is faster. She grabs the bracelet and takes off into the rapidly descending night.

Run. Run. Run. Run. Run.

Lucky can't tell if it's her mind pushing her forward or if there are voices thick in the trees urging her on. Dried branches grab at Lucky's clothes and scratch at her face. What is going on? Where is Jazz? Did Patricia back out of this last minute because she knew something strange would be going on? But no . . . she's Lucky's friend.

A shadow skitters across the ground, startling her, but she keeps running through the forest, fighting spiders' webs and uneven ground until she has to stop to catch her breath.

"Jazz? Jazz, where are you?" Lucky's voice is a harsh rasp. She hopes that Jazz hears her, or at the very least feels her desperation.

Lucky stills for a moment, straining to hear something that might point her in the right direction. She catches the last few snippets of a nearby conversation.

"Rachel, how many times do I have to tell you *not* to say our acolytes' names before they've had a chance to introduce themselves?"

Lucky carefully peers around the tree and finds Rachel's back to her as she faces the woman she introduced as Lauren.

"I know, I know," Rachel says. "But I never get tired of that look of confusion on their faces." Her voice takes on a mocking quality. "'Huh? You know my name? But *how?*'"

"Well, if your little moment of fun makes us miss the ceremonial window, I hope you think it's worth it when our powers are dormant for the next decade," Lauren says. "And you'll have to answer to the mayor, too."

"Yeah, yeah," Rachel says. "That won't happen on my watch. Let's go find her. We need them both here for this to work."

Lucky watches as the women walk away from her. The mayor? If Patricia's dad has something to do with whatever is going on here, does her supposed friend, too?

Night has fallen in earnest now. Countless stars accent the darkness, the finest diamonds ground into living light. Lucky pulls out her phone, but there's still no signal, and now her battery flashes 30 percent.

It doesn't take a rocket scientist to understand there is no Black Girl Nature Group. At least not in the way Lucky knew it. How had these people found her and deceived her so thoroughly? The longer Lucky considers, the more she realizes that there's only one logical explanation. Patricia. She was the one who added Lucky to the new text thread after the Facebook group had been compromised, and Lucky had never actually seen the strange messages for herself because the page had already been taken down by the time she went to look. Not to mention, Patricia was the one who had insisted Lucky join her for this once-in-a-lifetime celestial event in the first place, only to flake at the very last minute. And she'd done the same to Jazz.

I need to find Jazz so we can get the hell out of here.

Lucky weaves deeper into the forest. Heavy branches drape overhead as the trees and shrubs grow more wildly, blocking out the sky. Meteor showers and blood moons feel so far away now.

"Jazz, where are you?" Lucky whispers again into the night.

A frog croaks as if in response, and Lucky spins to see where it's coming from. And that's when she sees her. Sturdy wooden poles of discarded branches are arranged in a cube with Jazz curled up into a ball in the center of the enclosure on the forest floor.

Lucky steps closer, her heart rattling in her chest. "J-Jazz?"

Jazz doesn't move. Lucky reaches toward the makeshift bars to touch Jazz and yelps as her hand bends back. It's as if a force field is stretched over the branches like an impenetrable layer of plastic wrap.

"Can you hear me?" Lucky asks, panic creeping into her voice. "I'm right here! I'm not going to leave you."

Lucky searches for something she can use to reach Jazz. She finds a fairly large rock and raises it above her head, swinging it down against the cage. Once. Twice. Three times. The dull thud reverberates through her arms, but the enclosure doesn't give way. Lucky tries again and again until her hands are cut, until sweat streams down her face in rivulets, blending with her tears. Lucky slides to the ground with the rock still in hand, defeated. She tosses the useless stone aside and leans her forehead against the barrier, shoulders shaking as she tries with all her might to stifle her sobs.

"Jazz, I've missed you so much." Lucky pulls her knees up so she can rest her head against them. The words fly out of her like a confession that's been waiting an eternity to spread its wings. "All this time passed without us speaking, and all I want to do is say I'm sorry. Sorry for literally running away from you when you said you weren't feeling me the way that I was feeling you. Sorry I didn't shake all of that off when I heard about your mom being sick. And the way I spoke to you like we were strangers at her funeral and not like you are my best friend in the entire world? I will never forgive myself for it. If I could go back in time, I would handle it all so differently."

Thump. Thump. Thump.

Lucky looks up quickly at the sound, her eyes flying to the cage.

Jazz. They stare at each other, mirror images of grief for all the time lost and hope for what the future could hold. Jazz's hands are tied together, and her feet are bound at the ankles, but she otherwise looks fine.

Lucky places a hand against the invisible barrier separating them. "We need to get you out of here. Do you hear me?"

Jazz nods, but when she speaks, her voice is muffled.

"The sad, too?" Lucky asks, trying to read her lips.

Jazz shakes her head, stretching her mouth even more, overemphasizing.

"The stat chew?"

Jazz nods furiously, but Lucky still doesn't understand. "The stat chew. Statue? Are you saying statue?"

Jazz looks over Lucky's shoulder pointedly. Lucky turns around and gasps.

A few feet away stand four statues. Twigs, branches, and other debris have been arranged in a circle, and the figures are placed inside, facing one another in an X. The arrangement of stone and nature is strange enough, but it is the twin-size pits that lie in the center that make the hairs on Lucky's arms stand at attention.

"Are those . . . burial sites?" Lucky asks, glancing back at Jazz.

Jazz shrugs, looking just as scared as Lucky feels. Lucky inches closer to the statues. A bronze cube is placed in the palm of the nearest sculpture, shining beneath the sparkling starlight. Lucky reaches for the cube slowly, holding her breath. She glances back at Jazz, who nods encouragingly. When Lucky's hand is an inch away, she closes her eyes and yanks the object from the statue's upturned hand.

"You did it!" Jazz says, her voice normal again, stretching her hands through the bars. "You got rid of whatever that barrier was."

Lucky races back to Jazz, holding the cube in both hands.

"Lucky, we need to go," Jazz says. "When they were tying me up, they were talking about the blood moon and meteor shower. I already knew that they converge only once a decade, but apparently it allows them to perform a ritual that helps them maintain power. And I don't think they're only talking about the political kind."

"If my mom were here, she'd say that a ritual like that only works if you make a sacrifice," Lucky says. "I don't know if you saw those pictures at that fake-ass check-in table, but a part of me feels like those Black girls didn't just go missing out of nowhere."

"I saw them," Jazz says. "If I had to guess, those statues over there have something to do with it, too. We either need to knock them down or get the hell out of here. And if the way people act whenever the likeness of a racist dead white man is pulled down is any indication, I do *not* want to stick around."

"Jazz . . ." Lucky says, realization dawning. "My aunt went missing here like twenty years ago. If what you're saying is true . . ."

"Then we can't waste any more time," Jazz answers. She shakes her head, disbelief etched into her features. "I seriously can't believe Patricia set us up like this. She's the only reason I came here in the first place! I promise, if we make it out of here, I'm going to whoop her ass."

"*When* we make it out of here." Lucky grabs a large rock. "Use this to help cut the rope at your feet."

Jazz rubs the ropes at her ankles against the rock furiously as Lucky uses another stone for the ropes at Jazz's wrists. They work quickly and silently until the knots snap.

"Ugh, finally!" Jazz says, rubbing at her wrists.

Jazz steps up to the wooden bars and turns to the side, forcing the left half of her body through the bars. She's almost halfway but can't quite make it through.

"It's your . . . um . . . boobs," Lucky says, blushing.

"You've got to be kidding me," Jazz says, straining against the opening. "Stick your hands through the bars and push them from the other side."

"Um . . . I . . ." Lucky starts.

"Don't get all shy again!" Jazz says, using her left hand to pull Lucky closer to help her. Lucky pushes hard until Jazz breaks through, falling on top of her.

"Who's trying to make a pass at who now?" Lucky says, the wind knocked out of her.

"Shut up!" Jazz says, laughing.

Lucky wraps her arms around Jazz, and Jazz hugs her back.

"I missed you," Jazz says.

"So did I," Lucky replies, her voice wobbling. "Now get off me before you get me all confused again."

Lucky and Jazz's laughter must act as a beacon because once they've shushed each other into silence, they hear footsteps stomping across the forest floor.

Lucky and Jazz tear through the brush, any attempt at staying quiet forgotten. The moon glows dark red, a watchful guide. Or an omen.

"We're running out of time!" Lucky hears one of their pursuers shout. "The meteor shower is about to start. If we don't get them now, we're going to miss the ritual window!"

"Come on!" Jazz urges. "Keep going!"

"I—I can't," Lucky pants. "Go on! I'll be able to distract them."

"Are you out of your mind? We're not leaving without each other."

"It's—" Lucky pants, trying to catch her breath, mustering the courage to say the words that ruined their friendship, even though it means so much more than it did even then. "It's okay! I love you, Jazz!"

Lucky lets her knees buckle. It only takes a moment for Jazz to realize what she's done.

"Lucky, no!"

It's too late. Lucky is surrounded.

"Do you think it'll work with only one of them?" Rachel asks.

"I don't know, but we're about to find out," Lauren responds harshly. "We're already missing one of the tokens so what's one more headache thrown into the mix?"

The two women continue to bicker and Lucky tunes them out. She is inside of the cage that they had worked so hard to free Jazz from. History has a way of repeating itself. But if you pay attention, you can notice what you didn't before. You can break the cycle.

Lucky searches for something she can use as a weapon. Her eyes land on the bronze cube she had removed from the statue just moments earlier. *This* must be the token they were speaking of. If tonight is Lucky's last, she isn't going down without a fight.

Lucky stretches out her legs slowly so as not to draw attention, grazing the cube with the edge of her foot. Inch by painstaking inch, she drags it within reach and tucks it inside the back of her jeans. It sits cold and heavy against her lower back.

There is no force field holding Lucky in place, but she is still trapped. The Black Girl Nature Group impersonators stand at each corner, grunting as they lift the cage for Rachel to enter.

She grabs Lucky roughly by the arm and drags her to where the others wait by an altar.

Lucky looks around nervously. The group is focused on the sky, the members' faces turned up to the bloodred moon. One by one, the stars begin to move. Only . . . it isn't the stars. It's the meteor shower. The flaming rocks whiz by relentlessly, and Lucky swears she can hear them sizzle.

"It's time," the group says as one. But as they all turn toward her, another sound erupts in the night. The members spin back around, and Lucky sees the trees pull away from one another like a halo of kinky hair being parted.

"Koupe tet! Boule kay!" Jazz screams so loudly it must come from the depths of her soul.

Lucky remembers when Jazz taught her the phrase. One of those random facts she carries around in her mind. Jazz had learned about it while doing her own research after the much-too-short unit they did on the Haitian Revolution in school. *Cut heads. Burn houses.* It was the battle cry uttered by Black revolutionaries. By the ones who'd fought back for themselves and for all those who couldn't before them.

And when Jazz surges forward, she is not alone. Mrs. Clifton's voice echoes through Lucky's mind: *This is my daughter, Lucky. This is my daughter's friend Jazz. Send them back to me whole and unharmed.* Lucky hadn't known who her mother was speaking to then, but now she understands. Jazz is surrounded by a small army of women, some Lucky recognizes—Grandma Tabitha, Mrs. Walker—and others she knows only from the thrum of recognition that vibrates within her spirit. Starlight passes through them, though they appear as solid as Jazz and Lucky.

Lucky watches Jazz race toward the enclosure with a flaming ball of fire in her hands. The braids on the right side of Jazz's head have loosened, the tight coils stretching, reaching toward the sky in their glory. Though the flames should burn her, Jazz does not cry out in pain. Because she has her family with her. Mrs. Walker keeps pace right beside her daughter.

Some of the ancestors who accompany Jazz rush into the circle and envelop Lucky in their protection, Grandma Tabitha standing closest. As they surround her, the statues begin to shake. A slight tremble that grows into a mighty quake.

"What's going on?" Rachel shouts.

There is a great roar as the statue closest to Lucky splits right in two, particles exploding. Someone steps forward from the rubble . . .

It's a girl. A few years older than Lucky. She has her mother's face.

"Auntie Solange?" Lucky whispers.

Grandma Tabitha walks toward her daughter, embracing her with all the pent-up affection she must've held within her spirit in this world and the next.

"Lucky, get back!" Jazz shouts from where she stands outside the circle, raising the blazing ball of twigs, braiding hair, and rubble above her head. Grandma Tabitha and Auntie Solange heed Jazz's warning and race to Lucky, their movements unnaturally swift.

Jazz drops the fire on the circle surrounding the statues, and it catches quickly. Two of the statues quake and tremble, each one ripped clean in two. One by one, spirits pour out. The women and girls who had been memorialized in photographs at the check-in table now stand before them. Free.

In seconds, the flames will enclose the circle. Lucky doesn't have much time. She pulls the token from the back of her jeans. Rachel sees the object flash in Lucky's hands and lunges, but Lucky's ancestors are quicker. They grab the woman by the hair, the arms, the ankles.

"Koupe tet! Boule kay!" Lucky shouts, hurling the bronze cube with all her might at the final statue. Where Lucky expects the sound of shattered stone, she hears a *thump*. As if the power that the statue represents, the power this group of people hoards among themselves, is a real and breathing creature.

A howl erupts from Rachel and her companions. Lucky watches as they writhe, collectively dropping to their knees in apparent agony. She could take joy in their pain, but she won't linger there. Instead, she chooses freedom. Grandma Tabitha and Auntie Solange stand in the path of the roaring flames on either side of Lucky, holding back the blaze for Lucky to escape. Lucky races through and her family follows, just as the last bit of flame rages up, completing the fiery ring.

Outside of the circle, Jazz is there, waiting for her.

This is real. They are getting out of here. Alive. They reach for each other's hands, and the moment their fingers connect, the wall of fire extends up into the night sky, the meteors pulled into the vortex.

Lucky and Jazz stumble away, their ancestors surrounding them like a shield. In a flash, the circle extinguishes itself, and nothing but white ash remains.

Lucky doesn't know how they made it to the foot of the large tree she and Jazz lie beneath. They are curled together, refusing to let go of each other even as they sleep. It's early dawn when they are awakened from their slumber by a gentle presence. The girls wipe the sleep from their eyes, and there they are, the women who came to their rescue just hours earlier. They still stand with them.

"Mom?" Jazz whispers, tears streaming down her face. She stares unblinkingly at her mother, grief and longing and happiness radiating from her.

Lucky reaches out to hold her hand.

Auntie Solange steps forward next, Grandma Tabitha beside her. They cling together, mother and child, fingers locked in a grip that can surely never be broken again. Lucky can't stop staring, and Jazz says what she is thinking.

"She looks just like your mom, Lucky. Like you."

"Auntie Solange?" Lucky asks.

The girl only smiles, but Lucky and Jazz both understand. What happened to Auntie Solange was not an accident. For generations, Black girls and women had been sacrificed at the altar of power for people who considered them less worthy than the soil beneath their feet.

The same fate had been waiting for Lucky and Jazz, but they had overcome.

Lucky thinks back to the times on the trail when she'd felt the unmistakable tug to turn around. She hadn't recognized her ancestors in those moments, but now she knows to watch for their signs. The prickle of her skin. The voice within her spirit. The tugging in her gut.

Lucky and Jazz stare at these women for as long as they can, taking in their beauty to cherish always. When the first rays of sunlight appear, the women surrounding them fade into a mist one by one. Though they're gone from sight, Lucky and Jazz know they are with them all the same.

"Morning, girls!" Mr. Clifton says as Lucky and Jazz climb into the car. He flips through his music for the song he's looking for, distracted.

"Mom and Dad!"

"Mr. and Mrs. Clifton!"

Mr. Clifton's smile widens at this unexpectedly joyful response. He turns to wink at his wife, but the look on her face has him spinning around in his seat to get a better look at the girls. Both are coated head to toe in a lifetime's worth of dirt. Lucky is covered in scratches while one side of Jazz's hair points to high heaven.

"How . . . how was the overnight hike, girls? Where is everyone?" Mrs. Clifton says carefully.

Jazz clicks her seat belt into place. Takes a sharp breath. "We made it through, Mrs. Clifton."

Lucky nods, unshed tears shining.

"Do you want to talk ab—?"

"No," Lucky and Jazz say together.

"Not yet," Lucky adds hastily. Near-death experience or no, her parents do *not* play that.

Mrs. Clifton gives a small shrug. Mr. Clifton turns the radio up and Kendrick Lamar's "Alright" blasts from the speakers.

Lucky and Jazz sit silently in the back seat, each lost in her own thoughts until Lucky's face brightens as she remembers something. She sticks her grime-filled hand into her pocket and pulls out the friendship bracelet. Lucky tosses it to Jazz, who snaps it back into its place on her wrist.

CEMETERY DANCE PARTY

SARACIEA J. FENNELL

"Something about having a good time in a place where bodies are buried seems unhinged," Simone says as we slip on our headphones.

"Of course, you'd think that, Si." I shake my head. "Check out all these horny-ass teenagers here tonight. Do they seem bothered to you?"

Si tilts her head and takes in the scenery. "Aight, so maybe you're onto something." She giggles and points at a couple making out behind someone's resting place.

I laugh. "That's what I thought."

Every year, it's tradition for the president of the graduating class to throw a massive party. Every year, the party gets shut down because of loud music and drunk teenagers and blah blah blah. But this year, since I'm class president, I organized a way for us to get around those two things by: A) hosting a silent dance party (genius, if I do say so myself), and B) hosting it at a cemetery!

I never thought my classmates would go for a turn-up like

this, but it ain't take much to convince them that the Woodlawn Cemetery is *the* best location for hosting a semi-secluded gathering like our senior class party even though it's a famous burial ground. Once I mentioned the level of privacy, plus the freedom we'd have by throwing a silent dance party here, it was a unanimous HELL YES from the graduating class.

Everyone knows I'm into weird, creepy shit. I first fell in love with horror when I watched *Night of the Living Dead* by the Bronx Cuban Horror King—yes, *the* George A. Romero. I'm the chair of the Romero Horror Club at school; he's the reason I created the club to begin with. We host movie screenings and book clubs for Halloween in April. Don't even get me started on how obsessed I am with the genre overall; from *Buffy the Vampire Slayer* to *World War Z* to *Dawn of the Dead* and Resident Evil, I am heavy into the undead.

In fact, I'm high-key so happy I oversaw the planning committee because the party is strong on the macabre vibes! There's a fog machine, fake skeletons spread out across the grass, spiderwebs, glow sticks and necklaces, fake blood splatter—I went all out.

"Yerrr, DJ, throw on that joint we talked about," I shout.

"What do you have planned, Alle?" Si narrows her eyes at me.

"Being the undead geek that I am, this party wouldn't be complete without a 'Thriller' segment. Come on, girl." I grab Si's wrist, and we kick off the dance.

All 120 of us are doing the "Thriller" dance and having the time of our lives—we nod our heads to one side, turn to the other side, and put our arms out.

We dance the full five minutes and fifty-seven seconds of the song. I'm over the moon and sweaty but opt not to take off my cropped leather jacket. I purposefully put on black eyeliner and makeup to look undead like Michael in the video. My brown skin glistens with sweat, and my hair is starting to frizz up as I tap Si on the shoulder and motion for us to grab a drink.

Jamaal rolls over to us with his cooler. I grab a water, and 'Maal hands me a quarter water that's filled with sugar and alcohol.

"This cemetery has some of the greatest people buried here," I say, downing the water. "Like we could be dancing next to Celia Cruz's grave. I feel like she would love to see people having a good time, dancing to her music."

Si takes a sip of her drink and then slaps me on my shoulder. "Sooo . . . you know I *need* you to help me with Tyrellll." She purrs his name, making air claws at me, changing the subject.

I roll my eyes and sit down on a wobbly wooden bench to slide on my compression sleeve, my knee screaming in agony. I can't believe I'm still recovering from my sprain from three months ago. "Girl, you still on Tyrell's tired ass?"

Suddenly, all the commotion around us stops, and three annoying girls stare at us and giggle. Simone's dark umber cheeks are set ablaze.

"*Shit*," I mumble. "My fault, I ain't mean to be that loud . . ."

Simone rubs the back of her neck, the sides of her mouth pulled down.

"Simone, I—"

She sucks her teeth.

Simone's been in love with Tyrell since freshman year, and he has not paid her any attention. I keep telling her to let that crush die, but she won't listen. Annoyed with myself, I poke my head in the direction of the three little gossips. "I swear for life, if you three asshats say ANYTHING about Simone"—I pause and slam my fist into my palm—"you'll regret it."

"Oh, please," Yesika says, waving me off. She pushes herself off the broken headstone she was leaning on. "Ain't nobody scared of you, Allesandra, and don't nobody wants to waste their time or breath talking about Simone and Tyrell." She snickers at Simone.

Yesika and Tyrell had a situationship sophomore year, and ever since things between them ended, Yesika and her friends take any chance they get to mess with Simone. I watch Yesika and her two cronies as they pass me by and smack my lips at them.

"Yo, Alle, looking good, mama! We gonna see you back on the field real soon." Jacquie hustles over, trying to keep the peace.

"We gonna see what happens, sis," I say, grinning, turning away from Yesika and the rest of them. "You know I miss my track girlies."

"Nah, we need you! You the fastest runner we got," Jacquie says in a more serious tone. "Right, Simone?" Jacquie taps Simone's stomach with the back of her hand. "Tell ya girl." She juts out her chin in my direction.

My shoulders tense up as I rub my knee.

"Now you already know my bestie is the fastest," Si says, flipping her hand in my direction.

My cheeks flush from the compliment, and I cover the grin on my face—Si ain't that mad at me, after all.

"Yo, what's good, Alle," Richie says, releasing a puff of smoke from his full lips as he approaches us.

Simone giggles. "Now's your time to tell Richie how you really feel," she whispers in my ear, squeezing my arm. She clears her throat. "Hey, Richie. Take care of my girl. I'm going to find Jamaal. I need a refill." She dangles her empty Styrofoam cup in front of us.

I follow Si's steps and, of course, she's going to get another drink because Tyrell is posted up over there. I throw my head back because I already know Tyrell is about to do some fuckboy shit to her.

"Pace yourself, Si," I yell at her as she jets off through the crowd of dancing bodies. "I'm not tryna deal with your drunk butt," I whisper to myself and turn to Richie.

"Aye, what's good, homie," I say, removing the wireless headphones and falling into step with him. "I haven't seen yo' ass in weeks. Where you been? I miss my workout bud." I bump into him playfully.

"You know I've been chillin'." He shrugs. "Tryna get my act together. I mean, after our conversation about life after high school"—he pauses and licks his lips—"it got me thinking more seriously about my future."

We stop walking and post up on a piece of broken cement. Si's still in my view; I can see she and Tyrell are chatting it up now. He's flashing his golden-boy smile; she's laughing and twirling her fingers through her long purple braids. This dude really has Si eating out of the palm of his hand. If he wants to be with her, then I'm with it, but he's been playing with her feelings like this for months.

"That's great," I say, digging the toe of my sneaker into the grass, trying to focus on Richie.

I'd always hoped Richie and I could be more than friends, but he's always had too much going on. A father in jail, a mother who doesn't give two shits about him or his baby brother. He almost had to drop out sophomore year because he had to work at the supermarket to take care of his brother when his mother disappeared for a couple of months. I covered for him as much as possible so they wouldn't call child protective services on him, but he started showing up just for attendance and then ditching after. It was a mess. I was exhausted and honestly stayed away from him for a bit. But everything has changed over the last year. We've been working out together, and he's been so helpful with my knee recovery. I've missed him more than I thought.

"Check you out, though, you looking good, Alle," he says, reaching for my hand.

I feel my heart drop, suddenly nervous to receive his touch. I lift my fingers toward his, and there's a literal spark that shocks us both.

I jerk my hand back. "What was that?" I murmur. "You Static Shock now or some other secret superhero I should know about?"

"It's all this pent-up energy between us." He tucks a flyaway curl behind my ear.

Damn, he smells good—like cedarwood and rain. I lock eyes with him as he leans in closer. It's finally about to happen. I feel his warm lips start to graze mine, but before we can seal the deal, Simone screams.

"Fuck you, Yesika!" I hear her shout.

I place a finger over Richie's lips. "Hold that thought, please," I say, and turn toward the commotion.

Simone is surrounded by Yesika and two other girls. Suddenly, she and Yesika are swinging at each other while Tyrell and a few of his boys laugh from the corner of a mausoleum.

"Freaking Tyrell. Of course," I say to Richie as we run over to break up the fight.

But by the time we've gotten through the crowd that's gathered, Simone and Yesika have crashed through the mausoleum's door, straight into someone's unstable resting place. Whatever they broke releases a foul stench, and a blackish mist floats into the air.

"Ohmygosh, what's that smell?" someone says from the crowd.

It's like rotten eggs, like death. *Oh crap. What have they unleashed?* I shake my head—that's just me thinking the worst.

"Yo, what the hell do y'all think you're doing?" I yell and shove people out of the way. "How am I going to explain this? Everybody out, out, out! Now!"

Simone and Yesika make their way out of the mausoleum. Si's got a blooming black eye, and Yesika has a missing patch of hair, which appears to be stuck to Si's ring. I pounce on Simone to check if she's okay, but I get distracted by what I swear is something scurrying out of the broken casket. A shiver passes through me as gooseflesh bubbles up and down my arms.

"Alle! Hello? Move! Let's go!" Simone's voice booms in my ear, reclaiming my attention.

"Yo, what the hell, Si? What was all of that about?" I ask.

"Nothing," she says, shooting eye darts at Tyrell. "Let's just go get another drink or something."

I glance over my shoulder, and Tyrell throws his hands up in surrender, as if he's got no clue what that fight was about. "That was not just nothin', Si!" I cross my arms and plant my feet.

Richie gives me a small nod, letting me know it's okay for me to tend to my girl and catch up with him later.

"Fine! We were flirting, and then thirsty-ass Yesika came over claiming that she was his girl and how I needed to get out his face and all that," Si says, gnawing on the inside of her cheek. "You know I don't mess around, so I told her to get out of my face or else . . ." Si bites her nails. "You already know what happened after, do I need to say more?" Her eyes bleed into me, highly annoyed.

We walk away from the crowd, and Simone scoops up her headphones. She puts them around her neck and turns the volume up, heavy metal blasting through the speakers. For a moment, I'm so happy we went with a silent party so everyone gets to listen to their own thing—metal is not for me. I can see how it instantly relaxes Si, though.

Her shoulders drop, and Jamaal walks over to us. "Si, you know Yesika ain't shit. Don't let her get you down. Have a nutty instead." He hands her the semi-frozen alcoholic drink. She grabs it and plucks the top off, guzzling it.

"Simone!" I snatch the bottle from her lips, and liquid spills out onto the grass. "Chill. You don't need to be drinking right now. Let's talk."

"There's nothing to talk about. I hope Yesika gets eaten alive, that stuck-up bi—" Si doesn't have a chance to finish her sentence because screaming and shouting erupts all around us.

"What the hell is going on now!" I whip around to see bodies skittering all over the grass. Someone knocked over the fog machine, and the smoke thickens. The dirt starts to tremble and soften beneath our feet.

Richie runs over to us panting. "We gotta get out of the cemetery."

There's blood on his shirt, and before I can ask if it's his, Si crashes into my back. I trip over my feet and knock into Richie's chest. My headphones fall down to my neck, and I push off Richie's rock-hard abs, setting myself upright again.

"Si, what the hell!" I turn to face her.

"Alle, we've got to get the hell out of here." Her words slur as she points to the ground—

One of Yesika's homegirls is screaming, digging her fingers into the grass, trying to kick something off of her.

My jaw drops. There's a man halfway out of the earth pulling on the girl's leg. His clothes are ratty, but his teeth are sharp as they sink into her calf.

"Help me, help me, please," she cries.

Si and Richie hesitate. I crouch down, ready to pull the girl up, but another body juts from the ground to the left. I scream and fall back. The ground trembles again, and I smell the rot as more bodies begin to awaken. Suddenly, the girl's screams are gone, and I watch in horror as her limbs are ripped apart. Her guts and insides spray the air, raining down over us.

Si and Richie pull me back just before one of those things

wraps its stinky flesh around my ankle. I slap my hand over my mouth in shock. This can't be real, can it?

"Move! Now! It's the freakin' UNDEAD! It's happening—the doomsday apocalypse!" My words ring in my ears.

That's all it takes for me to get into gear. The three of us run, joining the rest of the senior class herd. There's undead all around us, sprouting up from the dirt like Whac-a-Moles. Richie leaps into the air as one nips at his feet. He hits the ground hard, slamming his shoulder into a fallen wooden post. He grunts in pain, pulling out chunks of bloody splinters, but doesn't stop moving.

We run across the cemetery until the loudest screams become distant. My knee aches—it's the fastest I've run since the injury. I welcome the pain because it means I'm one step closer to freedom. One step closer to escaping this nightmare. I see Si in my peripheral, her gait sloppy. She's sweating and panting like a dog. I bet she wishes she ain't drink as much now, but I'll be damned, she never slows, keeping pace with me even as other students get snatched up by the undead.

Jacquie calls to us from a woodsy area. "Over here, over here. We're over here!" she yells until we stop running. "Come this way before more of those things find us!" She's covered in blood like me, Si, and Richie.

Jacquie quietly leads us to an area that has mini statues, some of them broken, and cracked slabs of cement. People are resting on the flat slabs or sheltering under the upright ones.

The air is thick with tension, but we can finally breathe, even if just for a moment. I glance around and realize we're with the people we most dislike—Tyrell and Yesika—and a few others we don't really speak to or could care less about—Jules, Denise, and Franklin. The lucky nine who will likely be picked off one by one if we don't make it out of here. Richie clears his throat, and I move closer to hear what he's saying.

"Listen. I know we all in shock right now. But we gotta stick together. It's the only way we can get out of this," he says.

Richie's always so thoughtful. He's got everyone believing him, hanging on his every word. So charismatic. I stare at his lips, aching at the ghost of his touch on mine just moments ago.

There're several head nods, no words exchanged as everybody tries to catch their breath. I clear my throat. "Not to be the Debbie Downer of the group, but you kidding yourself if you really think the nine of us will make it out of here alive tonight," I say, my voice a little too singsongy. First rule of the doomsday apocalypse: not everyone is going to make it out of this.

"What the hell is even going on?" Jacquie asks, wide-eyed. "I went off to pee, and when I came back, everyone was running. Some idiot knocked over the fog machine, and I couldn't see anything. I hit my head and nearly got trampled."

"Yeah." Franklin jumps up. "If I hadn't found Jacquie and started running, who knows what would've happened to us."

Jules's eyebrows reach for the sky. "These two asshats"—she points at Yesika and Simone—"unleashed something evil when they disturbed that gravesite in the mausoleum."

Yesika smacks her lips, ready to pounce on Jules. "What? Why the hell would you blame me? It's not my fault Simone's an idiot. Dumbass keeps fiending to embarrass herself, pining for Ty–"

"Chill," Tyrell says, grabbing Yesika and yanking her back toward him.

"Ugh, I got some embarrassment for yo' ass right here," Simone growls, dangling Yesika's patch of hair still stuck to her ring.

"All right, all right. Enough with the bullshit," I say. "Jules, what exactly *are* you referring to? Because . . . I ain't gonna lie, I *did* see some misty stuff floating in the air when . . ." I frown and point at Yesika and Si. "Y'all two were tumbling. And I swear I saw something skittering around in that tomb."

Jules nods at me while everyone else stares. I suddenly feel like an idiot for sharing those thoughts aloud. But Jules takes the bait.

"So, I tried to tell y'all that having a party in this particular area of the cemetery wasn't ideal. But y'all ain't wanna listen to me." Jules purses her lips, then throws her hands in the air, pacing back and forth.

"Aight, check this out. There's an urban legend that this part of the cemetery is cursed. Long ago, an enslaved witch put a spell on a white slave owner for him to live forever, only she cursed him for all the pain and trauma he caused her and her family. He died years later, and when his body was moved to be buried here in the early 1900s, he awoke hungry for flesh and blood. It's believed that for the past century he's killed visitors of the cemetery and has created an undead army to feed and force the living into suffering just like him. Like some *Buffy the Vampire Slayer* shit," Jules whispers, hopping onto a slab of cement as if trying not to wake any more dead.

"You think those were vampires?" Franklin busts out laughing. "You're demented, Jules. What's next? You gonna tell us that we need to rub ourselves down with garlic?"

Yesika and Tyrell erupt in laughter, but Richie raises an eyebrow. He's heard me talk about shit like this happening in the world. I swallow hard. "It may not be *vampires*, Franklin. But there's some shady shit going on; you can't deny that." I gesture around. "Look at us, bloodied up, running for our lives . . ."

"What the hell do you two think is so funny?" Si snaps at Yesika and Tyrell. "Stop actin' like y'all ain't just run screaming in terror. Practically everyone is covered in blood." Si turns. "I dunno 'bout no vamps," she says softly, rubbing her temples. "But I know my girl, Alle, is a fan of the macabre." She looks over at me. "What do you think those things were back there?"

All eyes fall on me. "Urm, okay, so." I run my sweaty palms over my thighs. "Bet. I know this sounds crazy, but judging by the smell, the ratty clothes, and the desire to eat us, I'm gonna say zombies." I stare at everyone. "The only way we can protect ourselves is to fight—hole to the head. *Or* . . ." I glance at Jules. "We can use lavender, right, Jules?"

"Lavender—what's that supposed to do?" she asks, searching her pockets.

"It can protect us from the undead. Do you have enough to share?" I ask, holding my breath.

A branch snaps nearby. We all go tense. "Did it reek like rotten eggs earlier?" Franklin asks.

"Yeah, why?" I murmur on high alert.

"Because I think I smell something."

"Ohmywhatthehell," Yesika says, pointing to the woodsy area. "The smell is coming from over there."

I quickly take a headcount. "Where's Denise?" I try to keep the panic out of my voice.

"Oh gosh, she went to find a tree to pee," Jacquie says, alarmed.

Doomsday apocalypse rule number two: never go off alone, especially not to pee in the dark!

"I say we just leave her ass and keep moving," Tyrell says.

His scary ass *would* leave a person behind. I shake my head and turn on my phone's flashlight. I shine it in the direction that Jacquie and Yesika pointed.

"Everyone get ready to move," I say. "I'm going to check to see if Denise is over there. Be ready for anything."

"Absolutely not," Richie says, holding his shoulder.

I didn't realize how badly he was hurt. There's a steady stream of blood dripping from his wound. "It has to be me," I say. "I'm the fastest one here."

"I'll come with you," Jacquie says.

I nod. Richie looks at me like it's the last time we'll see each other. I close the gap between us and squeeze his hand. Before my knees buckle, I bounce up on my tiptoes and kiss him, hard and fast.

When I pull away, he grins. "Hurry back to me."

I let go of his hand and jog away from the group. Jacquie catches up and turns on her phone flashlight as well. We slow down and scour the area. "Denise, Denise, where you at?" I whisper loudly. Jacquie starts to maneuver around a weeping beech tree, and I'm about to lose sight of her when we hear a girl scream. "That has to be Denise!" Jacquie shouts and takes off running.

"Jacquie, WAIT!" I yell as the ground around us starts to tremble. But it's too late. Jacquie comes crashing back through the weeping beech, screaming as Denise's severed head tumbles forward.

"They ravaged her, Alle! Run!" She beams past me quicker than Usain Bolt. I've never seen Jacquie run like that.

The undead moves fast, fast, fast. I do a 180 and take off, already on Jacquie's heels. We yell at the top of our lungs for the others to run. Tyrell is the first to take flight. Richie's pulling Si to her feet just as Jacquie and I reach the resting place. "Run, run, don't stop!"

But it's too late again. As Franklin runs out to the left, the soil softens, and he falls into a giant hole as the undead claw at him. Biting into his body like dogs.

Si, Richie, Jacquie, and I run as fast as we can, but I can't run forever—my knee screams in pain as I trip over a rock and go flying. Richie leaves Simone's side to tend to me. I tell him to keep running, not to worry about me, but he won't budge. Yesika comes crashing into Richie, her left arm badly chewed up.

"Help me, fucking help me, not her!" She punches at Richie with her good arm.

He stares back at her, unsure of what to do. There's no undead in close range, so I tell him to help her. He rips off her belt and ties it around her arm, trying to stop the bleeding. I make it to my feet as Si comes jogging over.

"ALLE! Oh, thank goodness. This way—Jacquie and I found a mausoleum we can hide in."

Yesika's passed out from the pain, so Richie carries her. My legs are fine, but I've dislocated my shoulder, and I'm pretty sure my arm is broken. We make it to the tomb, and Jacquie seals it shut behind us.

"What the fuck," she whispers. "This is NOT how I wanted to spend tonight."

"How are we going to make it out of here?" Richie asks as he lays Yesika down.

It's just the five of us now. We lost Denise and Franklin in an instant, and who knows what happened to Tyrell and Jules. I shake those thoughts from my head. Doomsday apocalypse rule number three: focus on the here and now, what you can do to survive.

"Look, does anyone have a map of this place?" I ask. "We need to know where the hell we are so we can get out of here."

"I don't have a map, but I know that we've got to be close to the entrance. I remember stopping here for photos with some of the track girls." Jacquie shows us a picture on her phone.

"Okay, bet. So we've just got to head in what direction? Keep going forward?" Si asks.

"Yes, exactly. I say we catch our breath, and then get ready to run for the entrance. Just go right, and then run straight. We'll make it to the entrance and out of this bloody cemetery," Jacquie says.

"What about Yesika?" I whisper. "I mean look at her. There's no way Richie can carry her *and* run."

"I say we leave her here, get help, and someone else can save her," Si says, folding her arms.

Richie shrugs. "It's not a bad idea, Alle." He tears off a piece of his shirt and makes a sling for my broken arm.

Si knocks my shoulder back into place; I screech out in pain. "We should vote on it," I say, and look over at Jacquie.

I can tell she's uncomfortable, but we've got no other choice unless she wants to carry Yesika out of here.

"Damn it. Okay, I vote we keep her here."

"Then it's settled. We leav—"

Yesika's body starts to convulse. Her head slams into the ground three times. Richie is closest, so he runs over, trying to brace her head. Si holds Yesika's hands down while Jacquie and I look on in horror. Yesika stops moving. Jacquie runs to her side and checks her pulse.

"Guys, she doesn't have a pulse," Jacquie cries.

I rush over. "Did she lose that much blood?" I hover my hand in front of Yesika's mouth, hoping to feel a breath. But there's nothing. They all back away from her body while I slide my ear above her heart. No beats. I start crying.

"This is unbelievable. We all can't die here tonight," I say as Richie helps me to my feet. I bury my face into his chest and just let it all out.

Jacquie screams. Si does, too. "Alle, look out!" they shout.

I don't know what they mean until I feel Yesika's hand creeping up my leg. "She's alive!" I yelp in excitement, reaching to help her to her feet.

But Richie shoves us both out of the way. Something's wrong with Yesika's eyes; they are glassy, and she's grunting at us. She looks lost as she rises to her knees.

"Holy shit. She's turning," I say.

Si doesn't waste any time. She picks up the funerary art around the coffin and starts throwing it at Yesika to get her attention away from me and Jacquie. She flings vases, decorated rocks—Yesika eats the blows like nothing, stretching her arms toward Si in full-on zombie mode. Si darts behind Yesika and yanks her by the hair. Yesika growls and tries to scratch Si in the face.

"Oh no, you don't," Si says and kicks the back of Yesika's knees, forcing her to the floor.

Richie slams Yesika into the wall; he's got her pinned and yells for us to make a run for it. Jacquie slides the entrance open, and we beeline out. I shout for Richie, and he stumbles out, Yesika at his heels. Si hits Yesika right in the face with a broken tree branch, knocking her back long enough for Jacquie and Richie to escape.

"Just die, you freaking zombie whore," Si screams as she bashes Yesika's head into the cement.

For a moment, Yesika's undead body stops spasming. I can see in the distance more undead headed our way. I shout from deep in my belly: "Run!"

We take off like our lives depend on it—because they do.

It feels like we've been running forever, but I finally see the pathway and a sign that says, THIS WAY TO EXIT.

I ain't think we were going to make it out, but we did. I cradle my broken arm in the makeshift sling that Richie made for me. We're both bloodied and bruised, but we cling to each other. His hand grazes mine, and our fingers intertwine. Richie kisses my forehead, and I lean my head against his chest, his thudding heartbeat a beacon.

"I guess you've made me a believer of the zombie apocalypse after all," Si says, leaning into me.

I smile. "The night wasn't all that bad."

THE SKITTERING THING

MONICA BRASHEARS

Me and Charlotte walk into Windsor. I just keep my eyes on the accessory racks right at the front; Charlotte keeps going on about the pastor at her church who went missing a few months ago.

"Mom said the pastor probably got lost on a spiritual walk and died in the woods."

No birthday sashes on the first rack. I lead us around to the second rack and run my fingers through a spiderweb-looking necklace of fake pearls. "Didn't your mom also say he cheated on his wife?"

"What's that got to do with anything?"

"I'm just saying; that's probably where he's been. With his girlfriend."

Charlotte rolls her eyes, but she still smiles when she points behind me.

There—the sashes.

Above them is a row of birthday tiaras. I just click my nails against them because if I took one down, I'd want it. And that would be too bad, as Mom would say. She usually doesn't even let me get a sash, says it's not right to feel so important, even if just for a day. Mom said she changed her mind about the sash this year "just because," but I know she feels sorry for me after what happened in class last week.

I take a sash down from the hook—the one that's gold like champagne—and rub its grit, pretty glitter dotting my fingers.

I start to head to the register to pay, but Charlotte tugs my arm, and I already know what she wants. Prom ain't even until two more years.

I drag my feet with her to the back, where the gowns hang high so you can see all the thick fabrics. Some soft and velvet, some shining with silk.

Charlotte heads straight to the aquamarine dress like I knew she would; she always says that for prom, she wants to be sea toned.

"Which one do you like?" she asks.

I point to a random dress, but she knows I don't want to go to prom when it's time. But what she doesn't know is that it's not because I don't like dressing up—the sash, duh—but because I know I won't have a date. No one wants to dance with the girl who had a panic attack in geometry.

Charlotte tugs my hand, and we move over to let a girl go by. Charlotte leans in, whispers in my ear: "That girl. She's new at school." Charlotte runs her hand over a teal dress with long sleeves. "Anyway—they already got a different pastor to take his place. I bet church next Sunday will be something else."

"I bet this one cheats on his wife, too," I say.

Behind us, someone asks, "Y'all go to Hickory Baptist?"

It's the new girl: hair tied back in a smooth bun, and the only makeup she's got on is light mascara, which she doesn't even need because her eyes look like Venus flytraps.

"I do," Charlotte says. "Sunny don't because she's afraid of the apocalypse."

I nudge Charlotte, which just makes her giggle and lets them both know I'm embarrassed, which embarrasses me more. I can't be that mad at her because I never told her the real reason why any mention of God or the end of the world sends me into a cold sweat. The real reason is the same reason my mom never made me go to church, the same reason she scrunches her nose up at any man of God: my grandmother.

Anyway, Charlotte doesn't even believe in anything the sermons say. Her parents force her to go to church, and she only likes to go now because of all the gossip about the missing preacher.

"I'm Ray," the new girl says, "and my daddy's the pastor. He doesn't cheat on my mom."

Of all the people in Knoxville who could've heard me talking shit. "I'm sorry," I say.

Ray shrugs off my apology. She hasn't smiled this whole time. "It's cool." She looks down at my sash, then says, "Happy birthday."

After paying, me and Charlotte go back through the mall and step into cold daylight. My birthday is tomorrow—which means tonight, Mom will braid my hair. Which I always don't have the patience for, and it makes my neck stiff. But it ends up beautiful and sleek, and everyone at school says so, even the lunch ladies.

Before we can make it to the bus stop, Ray jogs up to us. Even when she's out of breath, her face is a sort of lit-candle calm.

She doesn't seem anything like a preacher's daughter, and she doesn't have any of that new-kid nervousness. I bet she's never had a panic attack all because someone started talking about how they miscalculated with 2012, how the world will actually end this December.

"You forgot something," Ray says. From the pocket of her jacket, she takes out a birthday tiara.

"You bought this for me?"

Charlotte and Ray both share the same half smile, side-eyeing each other, and then they laugh. Which I don't get because I know for a fact that Charlotte only ever stole once in her life (an Almond Joy, king-size). Her mom caught her and made her take it back in with apologies. But whatever. If Ray can feel good about stealing without a care for damnation, then I can, too.

"Are y'all doing anything tomorrow?" Ray asks.

Charlotte begins, "Actually—"

"No," I say.

"You should both come sleep over," Ray says.

"We kind of have plans," Charlotte says.

What she means is what we do every year for my birthday—I stay over at her house, and we order pizza; we have sheet cake and 7UP punch mixed with sherbet; we watch a movie.

"We could smoke," Ray says. Without giving us a chance to respond, she heads toward the mall to do who knows what else.

I give Charlotte the same look she gives me, an open-mouthed grin, because we've both been wanting to try but have been too scared of getting in trouble to seek it out.

"Okay," we both call out to Ray's turned back. "Yeah, tomorrow, okay!"

On the way to the bus stop, Charlotte slaps her hands together. "I bet her dad will know something about the old pastor."

Charlotte and I catch the bus, then go our separate ways.

Walking up the sidewalk, past all the houses with garden gnomes and sprinklers and BEWARE OF DOG signs, the trees catch my attention. They shake soft in the breeze, and I remember Grandmother saying that in the end, the first trumpet would bring down hail and fire mingled with blood, how it would kill a third of all trees.

The rhinestones in my crown sparkle, match the sash glitter. Tomorrow, I won't look like somebody who cries because they're afraid of the sky suddenly blinking to black. I'll look more like Ray. Put together, chill. I text my mom: Can we do something different with my hair? Like a bun?

After school the next day, me and Charlotte race to the parking lot at the sound of final bell. All day, we've traded guesses about how this slumber party will go—does Ray put her weed in a cigarillo, or in a pretty glass-blown bong, or in a hollowed apple? Does her dad know anything about the missing guy? Does Ray have a TV in her room?

Ray's already waiting in her car with the engine running. I hop in the front—birthday perks. As soon as Charlotte sits in the back, Ray speeds away.

"What part of town do you live in?" Charlotte asks.

"It's near Sweetwater," she says.

Me and Charlotte catch each other's eyes in the rearview mirror and share an unspoken *What the hell?* Neither of us have ever been because there's no reason to go, and it's like an hour away. I only know it exists because of all their tornadoes this past summer, how something within the town's limits seemed to tug down clouds.

"Yeah, it's a little far." Ray twists through the radio stations—commercials, sermon, static. "There's not much around. But we have the Craighead Caverns. Y'all heard of them?"

"Yeah," me and Charlotte both say, even though we haven't.

Ray almost blows through the red light trying to find good music, looks up in time, slams on the brakes.

"Why'd you say you don't go to church?" Ray asks.

The light goes green.

"I just don't like it," I say.

Charlotte starts to say *Ha! Don't lie,* but catches herself right after *don't,* which makes my answer seem even weirder than if she had just called me out, like I'm too fragile to even talk about it.

"It creeps me out," I say. "Like—why's there got to be a whole book on the end of the world?"

We leave Knoxville's city limits.

What I don't say is that my grandmother used to be so sure she'd live to see end times and would talk about the mark of the beast, brimstone, and all the signs. She died before it could happen. I believed it all and feared it all because I was a kid. Now, somehow, I don't believe it, but still fear it.

"Do you know about the underground lake in the caverns? It's the deepest in the state." Ray hides a smile, glances at me out the corner of her eye. "The Lost Sea. It's so deep, people call it a bathtub for demons."

Maybe that's why Sweetwater has so many disasters—it's a little too close to hell. My grandmother read to me from Revelations while I hid under linen on nights too hot to sleep. Her father read to her, and his father did the same. This fear's been passed down from some ugly root too long ago to remember. The sky winters, darkening quick.

Charlotte must sense my thoughts because she speaks up in a too-sweet voice: "Do your parents know you smoke?"

Ray shrugs.

We pass into the Sweetwater town limits.

To our right, a field holds the rubble of a destroyed trailer. Grandmother would shake her head with pity and go on about the four winds of heaven, and where oh where could those angels be?

"I can't wait until we can finally move to Knoxville," Ray says.

She turns left on a dirt road that gets skinnier the farther back we go. At the end, it breaks out into the gravel parking lot of a three-story house. The wood is dark, even darker with night starting to seep in. The first floor's light is on behind the curtains. On the third floor, a thin woman looks out the window and puffs a cigarette. She looks too serious, like those paintings of queens and peasants in history textbooks.

"That's Mom," Ray says. "She makes YouTube videos. Like, tarot readings and verses of the day and stuff."

Which is wild to me because Grandmother wouldn't even let me watch *The Fairly OddParents*, said it was tied to the occult and served as satanic propaganda. Not that I believe in any of it, but Grandmother would say Ray's parents hold hands with the devil.

We all get out. Ray races up to the big porch and fumbles with her key.

Charlotte wraps her arm in mine and whispers, "I just got déjà vu."

I don't ask her what she means because I don't want to know. My stomach churns, anxious as always.

We catch up with Ray once she opens the door. Inside, the house is warm light, polished floors. To the left: an open living room with TV playing a recording of *Thursday Night Football*. To the right: the kitchen with pots steaming on the stove. A chocolate Lab comes over, paws clicking, and balances its paws on Ray's knees, licks her hands.

"Down, Prince," a man's voice calls from the living room.

He swivels the recliner away from the TV, and that's when we see him—Ray's dad, the new preacher man. A Bible's open on his lap, a highlighter with the cap missing in his grip.

"Oh!" He stands and leaves his study material on the seat of the chair. My birthday sash singles me out. "Happy birthday."

Charlotte and Ray step aside, leaving me in the center to blush. He reaches to shake my hand, and I can't help but think of the churches that anoint with oil, only his anointing is neon-yellow ink.

Upstairs, wood creaks. Ray's dad looks up, then nods us along. "Dinner's not ready but will be soon."

Ray doesn't say a word to her dad, just leads us to her room. I've never met a church girl so mannerless. And now I'm wondering if she's really all that free or just a little rude. Me and Charlotte put our overnight bags by the closet.

The walls are bare of decoration aside from one corkboard with a tacked-on Bible verse about happy hearts and cheerful faces. Next to the bed, there's a dresser topped with strange rocks, stacked with no intention. In the corner, boxes are stacked unpacked.

Ray tosses her jacket on the boxes. "I'm not unpacking because we'll be moving to Knoxville soon."

"I can't stand having an undecorated room," Charlotte says.

Ray ignores Charlotte's dig and plugs in her phone charger.

I walk over to the windows, each with no curtains. Her room is on the ground level. Outside it's mostly dark, aside from a little patch of light from the back porch. I can see the edge of an old trampoline. Other than that, it's like there's black velvet over the whole world.

"It'd be so easy for you to sneak out," Charlotte whispers.

"Yeah, if there was any place to go."

What Charlotte really meant was it'd be so easy for something to sneak in. Charlotte joins me by the window and gives my side a light pinch. I feel a little less creeped out because I know she's thinking what I'm thinking—we thought there'd be a picket fence, neighbors close with muffled sounds of dinner parties, streetlights making the edges of it all glow.

Ray asks, from behind us, closer than I thought, "Would y'all rather be lost in the woods or stuck in the ocean?"

"Woods," Charlotte and I say at the same time. I turn to face Ray, to stop looking at all the unknown.

"Not me. I'd pick the ocean."

Now's when I realize Ray might be just as strange as any other preacher's daughter, and I'd rather be home with Charlotte, prank calling the head of the debate team and asking her if water is wet.

Ray plops down on her bed. "Because a shark or whale could have you in their belly before you'd have time to notice. But everything out there . . ." She waves her hand to the window. "Bears and wildcats, snakes. They'll stalk, play with you first."

The room falls quiet. I try to think of a joke, but I can only think of the scariest beast in Revelations.

"And the caves in the woods," Ray says. "You don't even want to know what lives down there."

"Ooh, is it a monster?" I ask.

I expect Charlotte to laugh, but she seems distracted, and without her comfort, my palms dew up.

"They found a Pleistocene jaguar in those caves," Ray says, "and the underground lake . . ."

In Revelations, Grandmother said, the first beast to appear at the end of the world would be the beast from the sea. It would arrive shaped like a leopard, she'd say, only mixed with other parts of wild things—bear feet, lion mouth. It would arrive to bring terror to people of the church.

"What? Full of even more fossils?" I ask.

"Well, let's just say it's not a mystery to me what happened to the missing preacher," Ray says.

Charlotte turns toward Ray while crossing her legs like she's at some business meeting. "What do you mean?"

Ray plays too cool, shrugs and gazes out the window.

"You just ain't going to say anything else?" I ask.

Ray chuckles to herself, and I've met plenty of girls like her. They claim to know the latest on all the gossip, but then if you press for answers, they get quiet like what they know is exclusive, and nobody else can be let in on it. They never really know, and now I'm sure Ray is a liar. She hasn't even said anything about smoking. Probably lied about that, too.

"Girls! Dinner!" Ray's dad calls.

Ray goes ahead of us, leading the parade of my dying birthday party.

I reach for my phone—no service. I whisper to Charlotte, "She's weird. Can you call your mom and ask her to get us?"

Charlotte whispers, quick, "I've been in this house before," then scurries into the kitchen, hungry for more information.

I try lifting my phone high—no bars—then near the window—no bars. Ray calls out my name, and I follow her voice with a curdling dread.

At the table, the food is passed around: hamburger steak with gravy and mushroom slivers, over-roasted brussels sprouts, Texas toast. I soften when Ray's dad begins eating without praying. Ray's mom must be upstairs; her plate waits at her seat.

Ray's dad pours from a pitcher of water. "Best water I've ever had." He swallows some from his glass and sighs out his satisfaction. "Well water. Fresh and clean. Must be why they call this town Sweetwater."

Ray puts down her fork and looks at me and Charlotte. "It's in the basement. Actually—"

Ray's dad clears his throat and forces a tight smile. "Ray, honey. No storytelling tonight, please."

"Is it from the Lost Sea?" I ask.

"Oh, the underground lake?" Ray's dad asks. "I'm not sure."

"This is a nice house," Charlotte says. "But you're moving to Knoxville?"

Ray's dad begins, "Oh, well—"

Ray's mom descends the staircase in an oatmeal-colored dress. Her steps are slow and measured. She takes her seat at the table, face bare of makeup aside from a quick smear of taupe lipstick. Her voice is soft like a secret. "Oh, well, what?"

The preacher talks with a mouthful. "Ray's friend was asking about our move to Knoxville."

Ray's mom pushes out a quiet *huh* of acknowledgment, more concerned with serving herself food.

"Lord willing," says Ray's dad, "but the situation is a little complicated. We were meant to get the previous pastor's home, but—"

Over the scraping of plates, I lean in to hear Ray's mom's interruption. "What's the wife to do?"

"His wife won't leave because she thinks he'll show up," Ray says. "Doesn't seem to understand that he's been missing too long to just show up."

"Ray." The preacher gives her a gentle look of condemnation. "We're staying in his second home while all that's sorted," he says.

Beneath the table, Charlotte kicks my ankle.

"What do you think happened to him?" Charlotte asks Ray's dad.

I kick Charlotte's ankle.

Prince walks under the table, nudging us all with his wet nose in hopes of dropped food.

Finally, Ray's mom speaks in her ASMR way. "What do you say after dinner we play Skitter? Doesn't that sound like a lovely time?"

Back in Ray's room, me and Charlotte sit on the bed while Ray helps her parents clear the table.

"I'm telling you, I've been in this house before," Charlotte whispers. "The preacher had some kind of fundraising event at this house with a Slip 'N Slide and food and shit." Charlotte catches her voice getting louder, softens her words. "What if he's here?"

"What? Like dead in the walls or something?" I try to laugh, to keep my eyes away from the swimming black on the other side of the window. Again, my thoughts veer to the first beast, how Grandmother said it'd aim to gobble up the faithful. My stomach hurts from too much food.

Across the hall, light footsteps make their way to us.

Ray's mom glides to the door; in this small space, she smells like cigarettes and cinnamon and tea. She smiles and directs her voice to her husband in the living room while keeping her eyes glued to us. "Honey, mind the light bulbs."

While Ray's dad obeys, Charlotte and I learn the objective of Skitter from Ray and her mom: to tap into the survival instincts of cavemen or something, to avoid getting caught. Basically—Ray's mom is the Skittering Thing, and her goal is to find us. It's like hide-and-seek. But in pitch-black. Ray's dad removes all light bulbs to 1) avoid cheating and 2) up the level of fear (because apparently, the more fear, the better we get at tapping into instinct). The only way for us to win is to avoid the Skittering Thing long enough for her to tire. If the Skittering Thing enters a room you are in, you have the option to (if you can do so safely) go out the window. But doing so opens the game to both indoors and outdoors (Ray's mom and dad have a home security app on their phones that will alert them of such). The Hour Man (Ray's dad) then shouts "Hunting Hour!" to let all players know that outside is open.

Once Ray's dad twists all the light bulbs out, he goes upstairs with Ray's mom to remove the rest.

"We should stick together," Charlotte whispers.

I nod, even though they can't see me with all our eyes still adjusting to this thick dark.

"That's bad strategy," Ray whispers. "If she finds us huddled together in one spot, it'll be harder to get away."

From upstairs, Ray's dad calls in a gruff voice, one I hadn't heard him use, "Sunset." That means he's taken away the last of the light, and I imagine Ray's mom on the third floor, waking up in a cobweb of cigarette smoke, hungry.

"I'll be in the basement," Ray whispers, and maybe my primal senses are kicking in because I can tell she said this from just past her bedroom door—she's already on her way.

With Ray's exit, the quiet seems as dense as the darkness.

"I'm staying in here," I say.

"What? That's the first place she'll look," Charlotte says.

Upstairs, there's movement. Not like footsteps. More like acrylics on a keyboard, too fast to be a natural gait, and I know they want to scare us.

Before I can argue, Charlotte's crawling out into the hall, so I follow on hands and knees. There was never a moment we decided against walking. Maybe it's just the smaller we make ourselves, the safer we feel. Picking a room too close to Ray's is exactly what the Skittering Thing would expect. We maybe have one more minute before Ray's mom begins looking downstairs. Ahead, I think, is the staircase because I feel the roughness of rug beneath me, and we must be in the foyer. I stop crawling and stretch my hands in search of Charlotte, but I'm met with vacant air.

"Charlotte?" I whisper.

No response.

I roll my eyes and go a little farther because I guess she has her own strategy now.

I remember seeing a closet attached to the staircase. The carpet is nice, silences my approach. I'm once again on cool floor. I'm close. When my fingers find the wall, two things happen at once, and I'm sure I'll be caught: 1) Prince clicks his nails nearby, huffs, and, as comforting as hiding with him would be, he'll give away my location. 2) Ray's mom starts heading down the first staircase. I find the knob to the little closet just in time and open it slow, thankful the hinges don't squeal. I scurry in and shut the door.

I crawl over shoes and try backing against the wall, but instead I feel flesh. Flesh. Soft and warm. My first thought is demon, even though I'm not religious enough for one to be interested in me. A hand presses against my mouth before I can scream, and I know the smell of that palm—Bath & Body Works, black licorice. It's Charlotte.

"How—?" I try to whisper, but her hand presses harder.

Above, Ray's mom announces her descent like a clock; a full second passes between each *tick, tick* of her heels. She pauses after making it to ground level. Me and Charlotte both tense, ready to be found, ready to rush out the door, past the Skittering Thing. But there's no need. She skitters, fast, down the hall, in the direction of Ray's room.

Charlotte lowers her hand.

"I lost you," Charlotte whispers.

"It's the rug," I say. "I must've crawled past you." I hold in my laughter, picturing us both crawling past each other with so much panic in our chests, feeling silly for being afraid of the dark.

The Skittering Thing races by again, up the stairs.

Charlotte keeps quiet, but I hear her fabric shift and know she has a plan. I try to make this game to me what it is to her—stupid, something to win—but when Charlotte reaches across me and twists the doorknob open, my stomach drops.

We crawl out into the hall. Along the way, Prince trots beside us. I imagine he is our protector. He presses his wet nose against my leg and licks, probably savoring the memory of dinner.

Before we reach the basement door, Charlotte hands me the end of something—thin rope, plastic tip, shoelace—and keeps a firm grip on the other end. This is how we keep track of each other as we find our way through the dark.

The door leading down to the basement shuts behind us with a heavy click, and I bite my cheek because I just know the Skittering Thing heard. At least Prince didn't try following us down; he made sure to stop just at the basement.

We stand up to grip the railing and take the stairs one at a time.

Across the room, we hear Ray sigh. "I thought I told y'all," she mutters.

Once off the stairs, I almost slip on the slick concrete. The drinking well must make this basement swell with water. Somehow, me and Charlotte make our way to Ray without knocking into anything.

"Is there a way to the outside from here?" I ask, unsure if I'm facing Ray or whatever furniture they store down here. "We could go out before they'd notice, and she'd search the whole house."

"The home security app," Ray says, "remember?"

At the sound of her voice, I realize I wasn't facing her at all.

"And besides," Ray says, "Prince will bark; he'd see us."

"From upstairs?" I ask.

"Dad tied him up outside. He always goes outside when we play this game."

"Um," Charlotte says.

If that wasn't Prince, then what . . .

"You sure Prince is outside?" Charlotte asks.

"Positive," says Ray.

Grandmother was right. The first beast has emerged from the sea, like she always said, only it's the Lost Sea. The beast must be the reason for the slick floor, as it sloshed its impossible weight out of the well.

"How do we get outside from here?" asks Charlotte.

Ray keeps quiet.

Charlotte slaps her hands against her thighs, making me lose grip of the shoelace. "I'm not playing, Ray. How the fuck do we get outside?"

Ray shushes us. There's silence. Then, above us, the Skittering Thing's high heels rush around.

Ray must grab Charlotte's hand because Charlotte grabs

mine, and we shuffle, one by one, to a window that's just out of our reach. Ray lifts a nearby chair and settles it quietly on the ground. Charlotte steps up first and goes through the sliver of window. I follow, push my way through. The outside air is clean and light compared to the dampness of their underground. A little moonlight, starlight.

I reach out my hand to Ray, but she doesn't take it.

"There's something in your house," Charlotte says.

"You should tell my parents," Ray says. My eyes can just make out her feigned surprise and then a grin that doesn't reach her eyes. "No one will believe you." She tugs down the window, clicks the lock.

From the other side of the house, outdoors, Prince barks.

"What the fuck?" I say.

"Sunny, we got to get out of here right now," Charlotte says.

"How?"

"Now I know you heard him follow us on the way to the basement, and he licked me," Charlotte says. "On our way to the basement, Prince licked me."

I don't waste time trying to show Charlotte I have the same fear because if Ray's dad really has an app, then he knows which window we came from, and I don't know if there's anyone in this family I'd trust.

I take her hand, and we run—from the side of the house to the back, with the thought of us hiding beneath the trampoline, but my gut says absolutely not. I take us just a bit farther, right past the edge of the woods.

I can make out Charlotte's outline better in the natural night, under the stars.

At least I know it's not the end—at least, not the end Grandmother warned about. If it were, the moon would shine red, the stars would fall to the frozen dirt.

But still. There had been an animal with us in the foyer.

From inside the house, the Hour Man calls, "Hunting Hour!"

"What do you think Ray meant just now?" Charlotte asks.

I can't control my breathing; with each breath, my lungs balloon too quick without deflating all the way. It's happening, the panic.

Charlotte locks her arm into mine. I can tell she's trying to keep her voice smooth. "They might hear." I can tell when she says *they*, she doesn't know who or what she means. "Remember what the counselor said."

If I feel the panic settling in, use grounding techniques. There is grass beneath us. The sky is not falling yet. We both smell like sweat and fear. My phone still doesn't have service. The sky isn't falling; the sky is still mounted up where it belongs.

My breathing slows. By now, we're both sure Prince is outside from the crisp quality of his whines, the twinkling of his chain as he paces. "Call your mom," I say.

Charlotte takes her phone from her pocket. No signal. Low battery. "We should've just stayed at my place," Charlotte says. She leans her head onto my shoulder, and her face is wet. We both tremble. "This is a fucked-up joke."

"We should—"

A woman's scream—Ray's mom—from inside the house.

Charlotte lifts her head from my arm, and we search for each other's eyes in the dark, and I wonder if cavemen did this just before getting eaten by sabertooths, if they scrambled for a final glance at a friend.

"Should we go up and check?" I ask.

"What do you think?" she says.

And we both stay still, so we both agree.

Time stretches the way it does in nightmares, every minute pushing against gravity. No other screams or sounds of panic, only the memory of that scream playing in my thoughts like an echo.

Then—

On the third floor, a light flickers, and for an instant, we can see Ray's dad on a stepladder twisting in a bulb. But the room switches back to black.

"Maybe the game's over," I say.

"They could be tricking us," says Charlotte.

"They never mentioned that in the rules."

"But it's the objective." Charlotte unhooks her arm and chuckles to herself, places her hands on my shoulders. "I get it now. They're toying with us, like predators would."

Almost as if to confirm Charlotte's words, a window on the second floor slides open. No one exits. A minute passes, then a window on the third floor slides open.

Charlotte sucks in air, and I know she's ready to yell, *Ha ha, very funny!* I press my hand against her mouth just in time for a window on the first floor to open, for us to make out the shape of Ray limping at a run. She trips once and crawls the rest of the way to her hiding spot, beneath the trampoline. She doesn't see us, even though we're only a couple of feet behind her. She cradles her ankle, rocking back and forth, her sob soundless.

Charlotte wrestles out of my grip, and just before she moves past the tree line, Ray's dad calls from the side of the house.

"Ray, honey."

"Dad!"

"Ray, where are you?"

"Dad! It got Mom!"

"What got Mom? What are you talking about, sweetie?"

"There's something living in the well. I'm so sorry." Ray tries standing but stumbles into sobs. "I let it out. It said it was hungry."

"What on earth are you talking about?" he asks.

Charlotte relaxes and starts to move again, but I hold her back. Because my inheritance from Grandmother isn't just anxiety; it's remembering her stories of evil things loving to trick.

"There's something in the well," Ray says. "It said it was hungry."

"Come here, honey."

Ray struggles to get from under the trampoline, and me and Charlotte see her clearly under the moon's spotlight.

It's the last time.

Once she inches into darkness, her father speaks.

There is a clicking sound beneath his voice: "I'm right here."

Charlotte and I stay quiet as the woods fill with the sound of her screams.

We spend the night on a floor of twigs, hidden by a netting of dead shrubs. I wake from sleep once but keep my eyes closed. The sound of light sniffing. I don't move, tell myself it's a raccoon, a possum, a spotted fawn. But then, the creature huffs disapproval—that guttural clicking just beneath.

Its breath is hot and smells of sickness; its voice sounds like the creaking of old wood. *No faith in these bones. No good, no good.*

When dawn comes and we're still breathing, we know we've won. The Skittering Thing, wherever it rests, has been fed to sleep.

THE BLACK STRINGS

VINCENT TIRADO

I've always been able to see black strings, the physical embodiment of an oncoming death. They just appear, hanging over people's heads when death is close. And when it gets closer, the strings start to unravel at the center, becoming thinner and thinner until—*snap!* The light has gone out from a person's eyes, their heart stops beating, their brain has accumulated too much cell death—the person is *dead* dead. And as far as I know, there's no real way to stop it.

I sat in the back seat, eyes widening as the strings in front began to unravel at the first jolt of the car—

I shook my head and tried to clear my mind. It was just a memory. Get a grip, Mal.

"It was nice of them to book everyone a hotel room." Essie rolled her suitcase into the suite. Just moments ago, as we were entering the hotel, there was an empty space above her head—above all of our heads. A sign of good health and continued living. But the moment we crossed over the entrance, a black string slotted into place for all of us. I quickly looked around the lobby, hoping to find the source of our demise. Instead, I found something worse.

More black strings. At the hotel's help desk, there was a long line of the other people checking in, and each of them had a black string over their heads. Too stunned to say anything, I let Essie check us in and followed her into our suite.

The string over Essie's head was taunting me, filling me with a deep well of anguish that made me want to scream. To keep calm, I focused on the room around us. It was really sleek, with two queen beds, a desk, and a TV that said, WELCOME THE FATES, THREE.

Nora walked in behind Essie with her own black string hanging over her. She eyed me for a moment, a little smirk on her face.

"You just couldn't wait to grab the first bed, could you, Mal?"

I shrugged bashfully. I never really knew how to address Nora. When I was younger, I had a crush on her. But since she was Essie's best friend, it always felt *wrong*. You never date your sister's best friend. Being four years apart didn't help, either—I was seventeen, and she was twenty-one. I once heard her talk about how she could never even look at a person she couldn't go out with for drinks, and I did my best to kill my feelings right then and there.

I don't think I was ever truly successful.

"Stop teasing Mal." Essie cackled, one hand swimming along the bed cushion.

Dad always used to say that if a person has a really good poker face, you can always watch their hands to know exactly what they are thinking. Essie pressed a hand into the bed, sinking into it, and I knew then that she had to be tired.

"She knows I'm joking." Nora winked at me.

I made a beeline for the door. "I'm going to the vending machine," I announced, shutting the door behind me.

"Hurry back soon! We have to meet the assistant in the lobby." Essie said something else muffled by the door, and Nora laughed in a way that still made my stomach flip.

As I walked through the halls, I bumped into several other band members, all here for the same reason Essie, Nora, and I were: to participate in the Acheron Heights Records contest. The winner would be signed by the elusive hyperpop musician and CEO of Acheron Heights, Mr. Hadesly himself. First we sent a CD, then we were invited to play live for him to see if we had stage presence. It was the opportunity of a lifetime.

I didn't know why Essie ever wanted me in her band. Maybe it was because I was family, or maybe it was because I had nowhere else to go, and she didn't trust the extended family to take me in after the accident. Auntie Rose thought I was too standoffish because I didn't like being hugged so hard my bones cracked. Cousin Phil, who was a whole decade older than me, thought I was a narcissist because I didn't like making eye contact. I was always considered the black sheep of the family. Luckily, even though Essie didn't know about the strings, she never minded my personal boundaries.

Maybe that's also why I said yes to being part of the Fates, Three.

When Essie asked if I would prefer to stay with her and be in the band, warning me we would spend a lot of our time practicing for gigs and traveling, I didn't hesitate. The Fates, Three only worked as a name if there were actually three of us, anyway.

The truth was, I didn't even think I really cared that much about music. I understood it from a marketing and mathematical point of view. A steady beat feels danceable. A good harmony feels singable. Put it all together, and people will pay attention. Sure, it was nice to feel life buzzing all around you, an easy escape from the constant reminder that death was always around the corner—but that was all it was for me. An escape. For Essie and Nora, it was a dream to make it as a band, to earn a living by making music. Some days, I felt awful that I couldn't match their enthusiasm. It was easy to notice when we performed onstage. They played with a true love for the craft, and I played with desperation. And off the stage? Essie was just as committed to working on the next song as she was to performing the last one. There were so many times I would find her working on song lyrics in the dead of night. Music was the one thing she really enjoyed.

And I hated to drag her down, so my goal was to help Essie get signed by Acheron Records, then politely leave the band. I'd seen band members get replaced all the time in other groups, so I knew it was possible. It would just be easier if the band was already signed with a record label.

I was pleasantly surprised that we made it past the first round. Hope had a dizzying effect—but all that excitement turned to ash, and it became harder to breathe at the sight of all those strings. Every moment afterward became a question. *Is this the last time I'll see Essie smile? Is this the last time I'll get to play bass? Is this the last time I'll take a full breath?* Even the most mundane activities suddenly became very important. Everything became the Last Time.

Except I didn't want it to be.

I stopped in front of the vending machine. My reflection had the string. I wanted to pluck it and tell it to go to hell but didn't want to cause a scene.

While my reflection maintained a blank expression, my hands shook.

Why do so many people have a black string?

The help desk employee didn't have one. Neither did the room service staff I'd seen on my way to the room.

I could easily rule out a gas leak being a factor, but that was it. Was it . . . part of the contest? Trying to stop death never works—I'd never been able to tell what the cause of death would be until it happened. I'd seen the Final Destination films—you can't cheat death, even if you have a trump card. What if I told Essie about the strings and begged her to get out of there?

Focus, Mal. If you told her about the strings, she'd ask why didn't you save your—

"Hey, are you still deciding?"

The voice was so sudden, I jumped.

A girl with blond hair and cat-eye glasses gave a nervous smile. "Sorry, didn't mean to scare you. Just needed to get a quick snack."

No string over her head. I exhaled slowly.

"You can go ahead." I stepped out of her way. She wasn't dressed like hotel staff but also didn't look like she was one of the rival band members. Most of them wore pilled flannel shirts and studded belts.

"Thanks. I take it you're also here for the contest?" She bent down to grab six different chips.

"I am. You?" I doubted it. The polo shirt and cardigan she wore did not scream punk rock.

"Ha! Can't sing or play an instrument. No, I'm here to make sure you're all settled in."

"You're Mr. Hadesly's assistant?" *That was fast.* I didn't think she'd already be here.

"Yup! I'm Carla. Sorry, I'd shake your hand, but, you know." She held up all the bags of chips.

I nodded. "Mallory. But my friends just call me Mal."

Or they would if I had friends.

"Mal." Carla gave a soft smile, bringing heat to my cheeks. "I think I know your band. The Fates, Three?"

If my chest was tight before, it was now filled with butterflies. "You know us?"

"Kinda hard not to. I mean, Acheron Records, Mr. *Hades*-ly—the Greek references are a little on the nose, don't you think?"

I blushed again, but this time it was out of embarrassment. "I didn't—I didn't choose the name."

"No worries. I'm not judging you. At least, not right now. It might be a different story when you're up on the stage." Carla laughed, and a bag fell out of her hands. I quickly grabbed it and returned it to her.

"Do you need help taking this to the lobby?" I asked.

"Oh no, it's not for the lobby. I made the mistake of bumping into *Riley* earlier, and the ass asked me to bring this over. Doesn't help that Mr. Hadesly asked me to *personally* take care of him." Her voice dropped a little low like she was afraid someone was listening in, and there was a passing sneer when she said Riley's name. It suddenly felt like I was talking to a different person.

Riley's not a big enough name for everyone to know—just big enough for his rivals to know. His band, Despair, Excavate, was an indie success even before the contest came along.

But rumors said he was too big of a diva, and that was why the band had gone so long without a manager.

Still, the fact that Carla already had to play errand girl?

"Sounds like Mr. Hadesly wants to sign Riley."

Carla rolled her eyes. "Can't see why. I've never met a man with a bigger sense of entitlement—*especially* toward women, if you know what I mean. Between you and me, I wouldn't mind if the guy dropped dead. But anyway, I'll see you downstairs in a few minutes."

She moved on, maneuvering through the hallway and getting out of anyone's way quickly, bumping just once into Essie, who was scanning the hallway for me. Carla apologized and moved along, but I couldn't look away even as I rejoined Nora and Essie in our room.

"Was that Hadesly's assistant? Did she say anything?" Essie asked.

I almost considered telling her how Riley already had a leg up on us, but I knew it would crush her. Instead, I shook my head.

Essie flopped backward on the bed and sighed. "Hey, don't stress it. I mean, would we even be here if we're not good?" Nora took the seat next to her.

I looked away from them. Between the two of us, Nora was

better with words. She was the one who came up with the name of the band, after all.

Besides, my thoughts were swarming with the last thing Carla said.

I wouldn't mind if the guy dropped dead.

Was she talking about her boss or Riley?

"Thank you all for making it here for the Acheron Heights Records contest!" Carla's smile was now cool and professional. How was it possible that someone could have so many different kinds of smiles? "I'm sure you've all gotten the email about how this is going to go, but allow me to go over it again right now. Over the next two days, each band is going to make their way over to the studio just down the street where we will simulate a concert experience. This means you'll *literally* be on a stage and . . ."

As important as it was for me to pay attention to what Carla was saying, I glanced around the room and marveled at the number of black strings there were. The first time I saw a black string, I was in the fifth grade. My math teacher was a little paler than usual, and even though I was too shy to ask about the string over his head, I remembered regretting that I never could—because he was gone the next day. Since then, I had only ever seen two, maybe three strings grouped together at most. It was never easy seeing those, but I was lucky enough to have never encountered a tragedy that struck large groups of people at the same time.

Until now. All around me were black strings. Hovering over every. Single. Band member. What were the chances of that?

The lobby was mostly quiet, with a few other hotel guests coming in and out during our meeting. Unsurprisingly, the loudest person aside from Carla was Riley, who sat right in front of us as he ate chips. I lingered on his string, remembering what Carla said earlier—*I wouldn't mind if the guy dropped dead.*

A girl with pink hair was chewing ice next to Riley, but at least she was quieter about it.

Nora, Essie, and I sat in the back corner on a couch. Other bands either found seats or leaned against the wall as they listened. With all of us here, it was hard to pretend the strings weren't there and even harder not to throw up from overwhelming fear.

Even though the truck hit our car right where I sat, I could see in the rearview mirror that my own string never materialized—

I blinked the image away. This was not the car crash all over again. Get. A. Grip.

The shitty thing about seeing death everywhere was that at some point, it felt like death followed you. And it lingered. The school counselor was really sympathetic when she found out I was there when my parents died—she didn't know I was only there because I thought I could save them. I saw their strings and begged to go with them to their appointment. I thought if I went with my parents on that car ride, they'd still be alive. I thought life was infectious.

It wasn't.

"Mal?" Essie whispered. She placed a hand on my shoulder, and I realized there were tears on my cheeks.

"Bathroom." I excused myself and ran to the nearest restroom. My hands found the cold porcelain sink faster than I realized I was being followed.

"Hey—"

Another hand on my shoulder made me jump.

"Jesus!" Nora held her hands up defensively. "You've been really jumpy lately. What's going on?"

So much death. So much death everywhere.

But I couldn't tell Nora. She'd tell Essie, and Essie would think I was having a nervous breakdown and back out of the competition, and then I couldn't make it up to her for not stopping our parents' death—

I splashed cold water on my face before my thoughts spiraled any further.

"Ah." Nora clicked her tongue and crossed her arms. "I think I know what's going on. You're nervous about this whole competition. You think you're going to drag us all down."

Yeah, to our graves.

"Mal, seriously. You don't have to worry about it. You're a great bass player. Like, on the level of a child genius."

It shouldn't have made me feel lighter to hear those words from her, especially when I knew she'd never share my feelings—but it did. I unclenched my fingers.

I'm good. It's not my fault I can see death.

"You think so?"

"Of course." She patted my back and turned to the stalls. "Now hurry back to your sister before she starts worrying any more. I told her I'd check on you, but I actually really have to go."

"*Pfft*. All right." I checked my reflection again. The black string was still there—but as long as it didn't start unraveling, I had time.

I stepped out of the bathroom and made my way back to

my sister. It must have been a short meeting because it looked like the crowd of bands had dispersed—all except Essie and the Despair, Excavate band members. Essie visibly sighed when she saw me, but I couldn't take my eyes off Riley.

His string was gone.

Essie got in the way. "There you are."

"I was just in the bathroom," I said, craning around her.

I wasn't seeing things—Riley's string was completely gone. Just vanished. That had never happened before unless a person died. Yet he was still sitting there, legs spread out on the couch, licking Dorito dust off his fingers. He looked me up and down and smirked.

Essie stepped back in front of me. "Come on, Mal, let's get back to our room."

"So your name's Mal." Riley was suddenly behind us.

"Stop following us," Essie said. He didn't stop.

"I'm just going to the elevator. You guys are the Fates, Three, right? Where's your third?"

"Bathroom," I answered. We all stopped in front of the elevator. I needed to find out what had changed in the last ten minutes. I didn't know which floor Riley was getting off, and I doubted Essie would let me follow him, so I had to act fast. "Did I miss anything from the meeting?"

More like, how did you cheat death?

Essie pressed the elevator button rapidly. I kept my attention on Riley.

"Carla just wants all of us to be . . . *nice* to each other. No sabotage and all that. You seem pretty young to be in this contest, though."

"I turn eighteen next month."

"Well, if you ever want to practice your technique, I'd be happy to help." Riley winked. "I'm in room 1204." And with that, he walked into the open elevator ahead of us.

Essie gripped my shoulder protectively and gave Riley a tight smile. "You go ahead. We're waiting for our third."

He returned the same expression before the doors shut.

Essie turned to me. "Mal, you need to be more careful about guys. Especially guys like *that*. Do you even know what he really meant by 'practice your technique'? Actually, scratch that—did Mom ever give you 'the talk'?"

The question stunned me so much I forgot Essie didn't know I liked girls. But today was *not* about me coming out, so I answered differently.

"I'm autistic—not naive. And besides—"

My words were cut off by a sudden echo of metal clanging behind the elevator doors. We both turned to it. In the reflection, both our strings began to unravel above us.

Everything in that moment slowed to a crawl. Every heartbeat I felt became hollow. My feet became lead. My blood ran cold. Someone shouted, and before the elevator doors crunched open, exploding with fragments of metal and electricity, Essie slammed into me, pushing us both to the side.

When my body felt like a body again, the first sensation to come through was the sound of screaming. My hands flew up to shield my ears—but Essie's were already there. She covered my ears and held me on her lap like she used to when we were kids. It took me a moment to realize the screaming was coming from her.

Screaming means she's alive, I thought. On impulse, I wiggled my toes, my feet—up until I recognized my body was, in fact, in one piece.

Which meant the blood we were sitting in wasn't mine.

"Essie—Essie, I'm fine." I tapped her repeatedly, hoping to get her to release me long enough so I could take a look at her string.

The screaming stopped momentarily. I finally looked at her—her eyes were streaming with tears, but her string was still in one piece.

I'd never been so relieved to see a black string.

Two bands dropped out. It was unsurprising to say the least. The freak accident that cost Riley his life rattled all of us, but it still wasn't enough to get the contest outright canceled—just delayed for one day. Some bands demanded a room on the first floor. Essie, Nora, and I got transferred to a room on the third floor. It was the best the hotel could do on short notice.

Riley was dead. A malfunction in the elevator as it took him up to the twelfth floor caused the whole thing to come crashing down. There was no saving him. All I could do was try to save us.

I was so freaked out by the whole thing that I didn't even think to check the heads of the bands that dropped out before they left. I had no idea whether their strings went away or not, and that presented me with a new problem: Should I have convinced Essie that the contest was a bad idea and begged her to let us drop out, too?

If the hotel was, in fact, a death trap, we'd live, and the other bands would never see their deaths coming. It was a terrible thing, but that's how it normally was. Nobody *should* see death coming.

And if I was wrong about the hotel? If I was wrong, not only would our lives still be in danger, but I'd cost Essie her dream.

After we both showered and changed out of our bloodied clothes, she gave me a solemn look and asked me what I wanted. "Do you still want to stay, Mal?" She didn't even ask Nora. I knew whatever I said would go.

Flipping the coin in my head, I decided we should stay.

For the rest of the night, we were quiet in our rooms, only speaking aloud once to decide what we were going to do for dinner.

Nora looked over a Wendy's menu. "We can order delivery, but one of us would have to be in the lobby to wait for them."

"I'll go," I volunteered. My feet were getting itchy. I needed to move around.

For once, Essie didn't react in the usual nervous way she did. She just handed me the money and told me to call her from the lobby if anything was wrong. I guessed that with Riley gone, she didn't feel the need to be so protective.

And she probably felt terrible about that.

I was taking the stairs down to the lobby when I heard a familiar voice.

"Are you sure there's no other footage?"

"Lady, this is all there is," a gruff voice replied. "I shouldn't even be showing you this."

I stopped by a door that was slightly ajar. Someone was typing on a keyboard and then stopped.

Suddenly, the door swung open. Carla's wide eyes were red.

"Oh. It's just you." She sighed and rejoined a man at a desk. He wore a security jacket and gave me a once-over.

"Who's this?"

"Get your eyes checked, Zeke. This is the girl in the original footage. A different band member."

The man whistled. "You really dodged death today, huh?"

I ignored his question and asked my own. "What's going on here?" The man sat at a desk with two monitors. Both monitors were displaying several different hallways and some rooms in a slow rotation.

"Carla's blackmailing me to let her review the footage of the accident."

Carla punched him on the arm, and he winced. "Zeke's an old friend who owes me one. And I just want to make sure that the *accident* was an accident."

"What makes you think it wasn't?" I asked. From the little that I knew about Riley, Carla wouldn't have been the only one actively wishing for his death. She'd just be the one with the most opportunity. Was she trying to get rid of any evidence leading back to her?

"I don't know! This has literally never happened before, so it feels . . . off."

Her confusion seemed genuine enough. *Or maybe I really* am *naïve.*

"Look at the poor girl; you're freaking her out!" Zeke swatted

Carla's arm. "Sorry about her. You don't have to worry about anything. I promise, everything will be fine from now on."

Zeke's words did nothing to untangle the knots in my stomach.

"What about you, Mal? Something wrong?" Carla asked.

"I was just coming down to pick up the . . ." My words trailed off as I noticed something weird on one of the monitors. "What's that?"

Carla and Zeke turned to the computer, and I pointed to the bottom corner of the second monitor. A young woman was pounding her chest with both hands in a staircase. An ice bucket lay on its side with cubes of ice scattered around her. I remembered who she was—the pink-haired girl who liked to chew ice.

And like Riley, she had no black string.

"I think she's choking!" Carla went white. "What floor is she on?"

Zeke clicked on the camera and zoomed in. "Shit, that's the eighth floor."

Carla and I ran for it.

"Quinn!" Carla shrieked, jumping up the stairs by two or three.

The silence that followed pushed me faster. My limbs swung out recklessly until my foot caught on a step and I crashed down. A white splintering pain shot through my shin. Carla was zipping faster and faster up the stairs, and I tried to keep pace with her despite the pain. Even though Quinn was choking, we could resuscitate her—the brain could survive for up to twelve minutes without oxygen. Right?

Between the bars, Quinn's face came into view. She was red,

one hand on the railing and the other on her throat. She stumbled and fell halfway onto the railing. Her body teetered on that edge—then both her hands loosened.

And she went into freefall.

I didn't leave the stairwell or come back downstairs until the ambulance took the body away. I didn't want to see what Quinn looked like when she hit the ground—it was enough to know she was dead. No one could have survived that.

I texted Essie to let her know what happened, and Nora ran out to get takeout instead.

Another band down. There were only seven left. Who would be next?

By morning, we were hit with another piece of news—to not delay the contest any longer, we would all enter the studio and perform one right after another. We would be given very little time to reset the stage. It was going to be an in-and-out gig. Maybe Mr. Hadesly thought if we got the contest over with, there would be no suspicions of the "accidental" deaths actually being murders. Fortunately for him, Quinn's death was hardly something that could be caused intentionally. Choking on ice and falling down eight flights of stairs was . . . unusual, but not impossible.

"What was she even doing in the staircase?" I heard Essie whisper to Nora while I was in the bathroom.

"The ice machine on her floor was broken, apparently," Nora answered. "So she went one floor up to get more."

I splashed water on my face and looked at my reflection. The black string was still there, still taunting me. What I didn't understand was—why had Quinn's black string disappeared *before* she died? They always appeared when death was close, unraveling when death was imminent, and then snapping in half before disappearing forever. But just like Riley's, hers was there and then just . . . gone.

I joined Essie and Nora in the hallway outside our room. It was weird being comforted by the black strings hanging over their heads. Like we were just on the edge of a cliff, but at least that meant the cliffside wasn't crumbling.

"Ready to go?" Essie smiled. Her hands were gripping her guitar case so hard that her knuckles were tight. I nodded and followed them. Instead of the stairs, we took the elevator down. It didn't seem like there was a way out of the hotel that wouldn't remind us of these strange and terrible deaths.

When we got to the lobby, the rest of the bands were waiting there. They looked at us solemnly before walking with us out the door.

Were they waiting for us?

It seemed like it. Both Quinn and Riley died alone—maybe the others thought there would be safety in numbers.

I checked everyone's heads twice. Everyone still had a black string. That was good, right? And yet, paranoia kicked in. It didn't feel like we were on a solid cliff anymore. It felt like we were a tight cluster of death flags raised high. Death was coming. I still had no way to stop it.

So instead, I analyzed everything around us.

The street we were on was relatively busy. Cars outside the

hotel came and went, and most people didn't bat an eye at us. Pigeons flew out of the way. I counted the seconds as we walked, staring over everyone's head to make sure not a single thread suddenly disappeared. We crossed the street with every string in one piece. It was confusing, wanting them to stay above our heads like I didn't spend my entire life trying to outrun them. It was like the logic behind the way they work was suddenly being changed. But by what? What could be manipulating them?

Acheron Heights Records was right in front of us—a sleek building made of obsidian with polished windows.

Carla, who looked worse for wear this morning, greeted us at the door. Her hair was pulled back in a careless ponytail, but she plastered a professional smile on her face. "Thank you all for agreeing to do this on such short notice," she began, walking us through the entrance. "Right down this hall, you'll find the stage area. There's a table with a list that will tell you who will go first. I'm going to let Mr. Hadesly know you're all here, and then we'll begin."

We pressed onward. I didn't bother looking at the list. My main concern was trying to get out of this alive. I checked everyone's heads again. Strings everywhere, and yet I was still hesitant to walk into the concert hall. This wasn't the same thing as playing at a venue, where everyone came to have a good time. This was a place to be judged—and if I wasn't careful, it was possibly a place to die.

Without thinking, I blurted, "Hey, wait . . ."

Everyone froze. I stared at the person nearest the door for an uncomfortably long time. A guy with a cobalt blue beanie.

Shoot. What was I supposed to say? What was the plan here?

"Your shoelaces are untied," I said, pointing down. "Don't want to trip."

Snorting, he leaned down to tie them before going inside. Everyone else followed.

"You okay, Mal?" Essie squeezed my shoulder.

"I need to use the bathroom." I quickly left.

In the bathroom, I checked my own black string. Still above my head, still in one piece. My chest squeezed tight. What was I supposed to do? If I did nothing, people would die. I would die. But what other option did I have?

Watch the hands. Dad's advice suddenly came to me.

"Hands." I looked at my hands and slowly reached up to my own thread. I'd never tried touching a thread before—I didn't even know if it was possible. I held my breath as I pinched the thin thread. Shock hit once I realized I *could* touch it. Letting it go, it remained floating over my head.

What if . . .

I didn't finish that thought. Immediately, I grabbed the thread and pulled it down.

"You were this easy to remove?" I scoffed, staring at the thread. It was so small and thin. Fragile. A moment of panic came to me as I wondered whether removing it meant I would not die—but the string was still intact. Not snapping or disappearing. Maybe physical removal didn't cause death to come any closer.

Something else immediately became obvious to me. The threads above people's heads weren't disappearing. They were being removed.

Which meant someone else could see them, too.

I nearly collided with Nora on my way out of the bathroom.

"Jesus! Slow down, Mal!"

But I ran anyway. I came back to the concert hall just in time to see the first band on the stage. I scanned the small crowd, but I saw a number of them were already missing strings.

Including Essie.

"Mal, get over here!" Essie yelled from the front.

On the stage, the guy with the blue beanie plugged his guitar into the amp—and the lights went out. Shots of electricity arced around Blue Beanie, and his hair caught on fire. The smell of burnt flesh filled the air just as much as the sound of screaming did.

Someone pushed past me, and I fell hard in the dark. But I could still hear Essie yelling for me.

"Mal, where are you?" She didn't sound far, but the chaos around us confused me.

"I'm here!" I shrieked, just as the amp exploded.

More feet ran by as the fire spread quickly. Someone tripped over me, and the moment I got up, I saw how the glow of the fire illuminated total chaos.

"Essie?" I shouted. "Nora?"

No answer.

Panic pushed me forward to a twitchy body ahead. I held my breath as I came closer, the sound of pained gargling rising above distant screaming. Blood spurted from the person's neck no matter how hard they pressed both hands against it. Within seconds, they stopped moving. I knew from the clothing that it wasn't Essie, and still I couldn't look away.

Suddenly, I was pulled backward.

"Don't look." Essie dragged me away. Behind us, I realized Nora was nowhere to be found. We got to the hallway just as firefighters rushed in, assessing the damage and tending to the other bands. I looked up to see Essie holding back tears. Her face was crumpled like she'd been hollowed out.

"Hey." I gripped her hand. "We're okay. Right?"

Essie sucked in a deep breath. "Let's just . . . let's get out of here."

Something in Essie died that day. Even after half the competition dropped out due to five more deaths, she didn't have it in her to compete.

She got a job as a waitress while I started community college. Nora hardly came around. I used to think it was because she was too heartbroken over not getting to compete. The dream was just as much hers as it was Essie's.

It took me a few months until I was finally able to piece it all together, and then another few weeks to work up the courage to call Nora.

We sat across from each other at a nearby diner. My stomach was too twisted into knots to eat, but when she ordered a plate of French toast and a side of scrambled eggs, I asked for the same.

"How're you doing, Mal?"

I cut to the chase. Small talk had never been my thing, after all. "Why'd you do it?"

"Why'd I do what?" And she looked at me.

For a few seconds, we stared at each other, and as much as I wanted to look away, I forced myself to hold on.

Her smile soon faltered. "So you figured it out, huh?"

"Riley was sitting in front of us. You could've easily grabbed his string when you got up. And at the concert hall, you went to the bathroom, so you were the only one who was missing when everything fell apart. It was dark, and we were the last group in. You could have easily grabbed the other bands' strings, too."

I didn't know when she had grabbed Quinn's string, but it probably happened when I wasn't around. Essie's was also missing—which made me think Nora hadn't intended to snap hers, but to keep it safe in the midst of all that chaos.

Always watch the hands.

Nora leaned back and stared at the ceiling. "What's the point of being able to choose who lives and who dies if I never *choose*?"

I opened and closed my mouth. I didn't know how to react to that.

"You know, I knew you could see the strings almost as soon as I met you. It's one thing to not like eye contact, but you were always checking over people's heads, like you were looking for an expiration date. I thought about saying something but knew you would just have questions I didn't have answers to. Questions I spent my whole life dodging."

"And Riley? Everyone else?"

"Mal, Essie was *struggling*. You didn't know it but every week, she'd go down to the Roosevelt Clinic and sell her blood plasma just to have enough gas to pick you up from school. I hated to see her like that, so when this competition happened, I jumped at the chance to make her dreams come true."

"So you killed people?"

Nora shrugged. "I would've settled for a light maiming, but the strings are sort of an all-or-nothing deal."

I felt myself deflate a little. This was not how I expected this conversation to go. "But all those deaths . . . don't you feel bad at all?"

Nora looked at me. "Do you?"

Death was a lot of things to me. An end, a great emptiness, a hole that nothing ever climbs out of. . . . Sometimes, it even felt like it was my fault, regardless of how hard I tried to stop it. After Essie and I were taken to the hospital for a checkup, I noticed that my own string had disappeared. Not snapped, like it did when death was on its way. Just . . . faded into nothing. Like it was never there.

"I just wish I could've saved them," I whispered. Riley, Quinn, all the other band members—my parents. What's the point of being able to choose who can live and die if I can't choose for them to *live*?

Nora smiled sadly. "I know. And I'm sorry I don't have any easy answers for you. We can sit and argue about whether or not it's better to do nothing, but we both know that whatever we choose still sucks. I just hope you also choose not to blame yourself too much either way."

I didn't have anything to say to that. For the first time in a long time, I let myself breathe.

When our food came, I ate every bite gratefully.

LOCAL COLOR

EDEN ROYCE

Veronne sat on the floor in the corner of her bedroom, her headlamp the only light cutting through the gloom as she delicately turned the pages of the ancient journal. The book had arrived in the mail only that morning. She'd gotten in trouble with her grandfather for buying it, spending all of the money he'd put in her account to secure the find of a lifetime from the online bookseller.

But she got in trouble with Gramps all the time. Not over typical teenager stuff like wanting to go to parties or dating boys or arguing over her clothing choices. No. She got in trouble for staying up late, reading news articles on people who had been lost in avalanches on Huascarán or to floods in Ghana and Sudan, desperate to find some information about her parents, who had gone missing on an expedition five years ago. Getting in trouble so much used to bother her, but now that she was sixteen, solving the mystery of why her parents had disappeared mattered more.

She tugged one of her twists free of the band holding her

headlamp in place, easing its pressure on her scalp, then turned another fragile parchment-colored page. When she found the ancient-looking journal that claimed to have a detailed list of primitive folklore and mythologies from the American South for sale, she had to buy it. It was so rare to find these stories written down, and her mom and pop would travel just to speak with old people who remembered the tales and passed them on only by word of mouth. Veronne didn't particularly care about those ancient stories herself—they were created by people who didn't have scientific facts to explain the world around them, so they made up gods and monsters to make sense of the unexplainable. But her parents had, and the journal might offer a clue to what had happened to them.

Mom and Pop had been on a worldwide tour, lecturing and repatriating artifacts and treasures stolen during the height of European colonialism to their rightful countries. It was work Veronne admired. Work she intended to do herself one day, if Gramps would get off her back about everything. She wasn't a problem, not like some other kids at her school, stealing or smoking or smashing everyone who moved. It was one more book. And it had just been that single time she drove his car without permission. He'd refused to take her for her driving test after that incident, saying she'd have to earn back his trust. She'd only gone around the block! Veronne sucked her teeth at his overprotectiveness. In another year, she'd graduate and be in charge of her own life. *Finally*.

She returned her attention to the chicken-scratch writing in the margins of the tattered, age-softened journal. An entry caught her attention:

Plat-eye (n.): shape-altering creature of Gullah origin, used to guard treasure of aforementioned people. Said to be able to mold itself into objects from its prey's mind.

She shook her head, sending light careening over the walls. No way. She'd grown up with stories about her people, but she'd never heard about this. Mostly, the stories she knew were about the contributions her ancestors made to society and how the economy of the South was built on the backs of their labor. Stuff that could be proven through historical records. Folk stories were for what Mom and Pop had called "local color," whimsical tales they told to increase investor interest in their future missions.

The cursive handwriting was almost impossible to decipher. Did they use a freaking quill or something? Probably. It was supposed to be, like, two hundred years old. Holding this piece of history in her hands was amazing, and she wanted to share it with someone who would get it, like her parents would have. Gramps didn't. The kids at school definitely didn't. So Veronne ignored them, keeping her journals and her maps and her history obsession to herself.

Except for Lucky Rodriguez.

He was popular, and surprisingly nice. Once he'd seen her in the library, hunched over a dusty old atlas, almost falling asleep. He'd tapped on her table to wake her. When she'd jolted upright, he'd apologized for scaring her, saying with a smile that the place was closing soon, and he didn't want her to get locked in.

She'd liked him ever since.

The book in her hand suddenly felt heavier, like it was trying to get her attention. Veronne shifted her weight, reading the remainder of the entry.

Danger: high
Weaknesses: unknown
Recommendation: avoid

Surely, this wasn't real. It felt like a fairy tale, a grotesque story to frighten little kids. And she wasn't a little kid anymore. She ran her fingers over the endpapers at the back of the journal, feeling a ragged unevenness that suggested the pages had repeatedly gotten wet and then dried.

"Ow!" she cried out, yanking her hand back. The stiff paper had cut the pad of her finger, and she watched the slit well with blood. She sucked her finger, cursing. More careful now, she used her fingernail to pry up the offending endpaper. This time when she cried out, it was with the joy of discovery.

The map's colors were still vibrant despite the age-softened parchment. She scanned it greedily. Charleston was a city that held on to its history, both good and bad, so it wasn't hard to recognize the general area the map referenced, marked with an X and an ellipse with a dot at the center. Was this a treasure map? Didn't X always mark the spot where people buried treasures? If she had the area right, a park now stood there.

She entered "Corrine Jones Playground" on her phone and found a result on the city's website. An afterthought of a park that held only grass, edged by a line of mature oak and hickory trees. What did the ellipse mean? Was it some indication of some kind of treasure? If so, she didn't know what. She shook her head.

It didn't matter, really. Whatever it was, Veronne was going to get it. And she would sell it if it wasn't a clue that would help her find her parents. Any money would help finance her trip to Lake Chad, where her parents had last been seen. No made-up monster was gonna scare her off from finding out what had happened to them.

Veronne flicked her hair over her shoulder and checked her phone. It was almost midnight, so she'd have to leave soon if she wanted to follow the map tonight. The walk to the park was only ten minutes, but there was no way to tell how long it would take to dig up the treasure. No matter what, she needed to get back before Gramps woke up.

Veronne checked on him before she left, and he was sleeping soundly. Back in her room, she tossed the map, journal, and the two-piece shovel she'd bought online in her backpack. Her phone went in her back pocket before she snuck out into a night fragrant with yellow jessamine and honeysuckle. The vines twisted around the porch, and she plucked a honeysuckle blossom, pinched the end of the flower firmly and pulled the stem out, releasing a bead of nectar. She touched it to her tongue, then strode off, the blossom still between her lips. The night was calm, quiet. One good thing about living in a neighborhood of old people: everyone went to bed at a decent time. Wind in the pecan trees and the call of owls out for their nightly meal were her only soundtrack.

Soon, she reached the edge of the park. Lampposts lined the main path, giving off a watery amber light that creeped her out. No wonder no one came here anymore. The brick path curved through the long grass and mature trees, narrowing as it grew distant. Even in the stillness, Veronne didn't feel alone. She felt watched, the sensation prickling the fine hair on her arms. She shuddered, and not from the midnight air.

Steeling herself, she pulled out the map. As she turned the worn paper, she could make out faint, smeared letters underneath the map's images:

STAY ON THE PATH

How was she supposed to do that if she wanted to get to the marked areas? Whatever the warning had been supposed to protect her from couldn't *still* be here. With the help of the compass app on her phone, Veronne followed the instructions to the first dotted icon. She walked forward fifty paces, the brick path sturdy under her sneakers, then turned twelve degrees north. Above her, the almost-full moon filtered its light through the dense branches overhead to create inky, vine-like patterns on the red brick.

She glanced at the map again. Toe-to-heel another hundred steps, it said, and she started counting. At eighty steps, she stopped. The warning rattled in her mind, and a fingertip of worry slid down her spine. Veronne glanced to her right, trying to see as far as she could. Light directly above her was reassuring, but the path dimmed as it wound away from her. Park benches crouched along the path at every other lamppost, perspective making them smaller and smaller until they were little more than doll-size. She then looked left, and there was a shorter distance back to the entrance where she'd come in. Reassured, she took a deep breath. She'd be fine.

But when she looked right again, she let out a small, startled cry. Someone was sitting on a doll-size bench, silhouetted in the dimness. They hadn't been there a moment ago. She would have seen them. She swallowed hard. What could she do? It was a public park, and anyone had a right to be here. Maybe they were an old person who couldn't sleep and had decided to take a walk. It was okay. They were far enough away that they wouldn't see what she was doing. Hopefully they hadn't noticed her at all. She didn't know what she'd do if someone questioned her.

Veronne held her breath as she stepped off the path. When nothing happened, she berated herself for being so gullible. They were stories. Ways her ancestors explained what was inexplicable back then but science had now solved. Final instructions on the map were: *Beside an old elm, hewn down, dig.*

There was no cut-down tree at all, elm or otherwise, and she wondered if she was in the right place. All she saw was a line of dense green bushes full of hot pink azaleas filling the night with a woozy perfume. Still, she fished her shovel out of her bag. Might as well get started.

As she began to dig, Veronne wondered if Gramps was right to be irritated with her. If anyone else at school had said they did the things she did—driving the car, spending a month's worth of allowance on a book, sneaking out of the house in the middle of the night—what would she think of them? Probably that they were doing the most to get in some mess they didn't belong in, but her . . . her purposes were legit. Like, noble, even. Everything she did was either to find out what had happened to her parents or to prepare herself to search for them once she was eighteen.

The only reason she didn't just take the money she'd saved and leave now was that she knew Gramps would get in trouble.

She couldn't do that to him. A part of her still hoped to convince him to come along with her on the search. There was no way she could just give up on him. On them.

Rustling in the darkness made her freeze. Breath held, she nestled next to the azaleas and waited. Nothing else. No footsteps. Her skin prickled, stung like a paper cut. A high-pitched whine cut through the night. Veronne dropped to her knees, heart hammering, and peered through the dense foliage. When she saw the culprit, she slowly released the breath she'd been holding.

"What are you doing out here all alone?" She reached out for the puppy with her free hand, but it darted away, farther into the azalea bushes. The flowers shivered, releasing their perfume. She didn't want to leave her spot, but it was just a little thing, probably hungry.

"Come here, baby," she called, crawling out of her hiding spot. Finally, she found it cowering in the leaves. The puppy came toward her, slowly, unsure, but wagging its tail. Veronne scooped it up, cuddling it close. A lump formed on the puppy's back, pushing through the thin, fragile skin. Her breath stopped as she watched the lump lengthen and contort as it moved along the furry back. It warmed, grew fever hot, then protruded from the skin like another appendage.

"What in the—!"

To her horror, all of the puppy's fur stood on end, then retracted into its body with a snap. She shrieked and dropped what was clearly not a puppy. When the thing hit the grass, its entire body melted into a slick red puddle and soaked into the surrounding ground.

Veronne sprang to her feet. Forget her bag, she'd come back for it later. The warning from the map blared in her head like a siren.

STAY ON THE PATH

Why hadn't she listened? She ran wildly toward the path, half expecting some invisible force field to materialize, preventing her from reaching safety. But she made it without incident. Heart hammering, she spun on the heel of her sneaker and ran toward the park entrance. She got three strides before she ran smack into something that knocked her on her ass.

There it was.

Force field or whatever it was, it was keeping her from leaving the park. Even under the assault of her shovel, it didn't give. She tried to run around it, but her movements were heavy, weighted like she was trying to walk through a hip-deep marsh. The effort was exhausting, so she stopped trying to move around the obstacle in front of her and instead turned back. Maybe she could get out from the other side.

Her breath stuck in her throat.

At every bench lining the winding path, a silhouette stood. No matter how close the figure was, she could see nothing of its features. Each shape remained a hollow absence of light that drew any illumination to itself and extinguished it. As she watched, the figures moved as one, heading toward her.

You shouldn't have left the path.

It was a voice without sound, brewing in her mind, but she somehow heard it as clearly as she would have heard Gramps talking to her. As the creatures neared her, the blossoms dropped and turned the yellowish brown of new rot. She tried to scream, but nothing came out, and the taste of rotting azaleas invaded her mouth, growing on her tongue.

What do you want, girl?

You followed the map.

You are here.

Why? What reason do you have to come here?

"It's a park," she stuttered. "The treasure."

Oh, that. Greedy, are you?

"No, I—"

Aren't you? You were going to take what you found here. I can see it in your empty little head.

"What are you?"

Don't you mean who?

One of the silhouettes morphed, its form twisting into that of her gramps.

No, it wasn't possible. This wasn't real.

But he looked real, down to his slightly stooped frame and his salt-and-pepper beard. Lamppost light reflected off his bald brown head. This time, the thing spoke with Gramps's voice in her mind.

Didn't I tell you not to go fooling around out here in the middle of the night? Why can't you just do as I ask sometime, Veronne?

Hearing her own name was too much. She swung her shovel, connecting enough to disrupt the image of her grandfather. Its body froze like it was buffering, then began a rattling shake that made her eyes cross. The figure liquified, melting into the brick path. Behind her, she could see the sheen of the force field flicker. Without another thought, she turned tail and ran.

Straight into Lucky Rodriguez.

"Ayo! Easy . . ." His hands went around her upper arms to steady her.

She jerked away, breathing hard and rubbing her palms on her jeans to get the feel of that . . . thing off them.

He held his hands up as if at gunpoint. "Hey . . . sorry. Just tryna see if you okay."

"What are you doing here?"

Lucky raised one eyebrow. "I was at a party. What *you* doing here?"

She shrank from him, breath racing through her lungs as she looked back over her shoulder. Nothing was there, not the creature that looked like Gramps or the line of silhouetted figures that had been heading toward her. It was all gone, like she'd woken up from a nightmare. Veronne swung her attention back to Lucky. He was skyscraper tall, and the scent of him was incredible—some kind of beard oil or cologne wafted around him.

"But I guess you cool, so . . ." He shrugged and backed up two steps before heading toward the path that led out of the park.

"No, wait! I was . . . spooked. Something happened and I . . ." She rubbed her temple. That journal had gotten inside her head. She'd seen it, though, right? The dog thing? Gramps? And they had both just melted. *Impossible*.

Lucky leaned against a lamppost, looking at her like he couldn't figure out if she was real or not. Whatever. She felt that way about herself a lot of the time. And she definitely felt that way about tonight. Suddenly, she wished she had never bought the journal and kept her ass home. The last thing she needed was to get a reputation for being weird. But who was she kidding? She already had that reputation.

"It's late," she finished. "I'm tired, I guess."

He continued to regard her for a moment. "Want me to walk you home?"

"No, you don't have to—"

What are you, stupid? Her own voice echoed inside her mind. *You have liked this boy since sixth grade.* Her heart thudded harder than it had when she was frightened. Why now, when she was filthy from kneeling in black soil and sweaty from fear? Her fingers ached from gripping the shovel. Veronne brushed the back of her hand over her face, shooing away a white moth that fluttered all in her face for attention.

Lucky nodded. His tank top was crisp and white under his open hoodie. In the watery lamplight, his skin looked luminous, otherworldly. His profile was amazing: the sharp, strong jaw, high cheekbones, his thin mustache dark against his plush lips. He opened his mouth to speak, then closed it and rubbed his lips together. Veronne scratched at her arm, the memory of what was surely her imagination making her itch. Maybe that map had been laced with some kind of drug. Some kind of ancient hallucinogen that made monsters seem real.

Hands shoved in the pockets of his hoodie, he finally spoke. "I'll walk you home."

If Gramps saw her out this late and with some boy from

school, she wouldn't get to leave the house again until she was forty. "No, maybe . . . maybe just to the park entrance?"

"Don't wanna be seen with me?" His grin was warm, like he understood the concern.

Veronne let out a short, sharp laugh. "I do, but my gramps . . ." She trailed off, not sure how to explain her situation without sounding like she was a baby.

"Gotchu." He tilted his head in the direction of the entrance. "Ready?"

She gathered her bag, shoved her things into it. Lucky slowed his long strides to keep pace with her. The heady fragrance of the azaleas followed, draping them in a magical aura. At the sidewalk that bordered the park's exit, he turned to her. His smile was lopsided, and it was the cutest thing she had ever seen. Her heart raced, and she felt like every thought in her head had evaporated, leaving empty space between her ears. All she could manage was to stand where she was and stare up at him. She blinked a few times, voiceless.

He pulled a hand out from his pocket and pressed his fingertips to her chin, tilting it up. "I can kiss you, right? You want that?"

God, yes, she did. She definitely wanted that. Veronne had never been kissed, certainly not by anyone her own age, and definitely not by someone as fine as Lucky. She licked her lips, her throat dry and pulsing. How did she hold her head? Was she supposed to tilt it, turn it? Her nose . . . it was kinda big, round. Would it get in the way? What did she do with her arms?

Every worry stopped as Lucky's lips pressed against hers.

They were firm and somehow soft at the same time. She didn't need to worry about her nose, or how to move her head, or her long arms. They fit together like pieces of a puzzle. And it was perfect. She leaned into him, and his hands slid gently around her. His mouth opened, and he touched his tongue to the seam of her lips, asking for entry. She obliged. Hot and slick, he slid inside, flicked his tongue teasingly against the roof of her mouth, and she shuddered.

She slid her arms up his chest, her fingers brushing the gold chain lying against his collarbone. The metal links were warm from his skin—so warm. Just as she moved to clutch him closer, he pulled away. This was a moment she'd never forget. She rubbed her tongue along her palate, savoring the flavor of him. She knew he smoked, and she wondered if that was what she was tasting. Or maybe he'd had a few beers at the party.

"You taste . . . kinda smoky, almost bitter."

His half grin sent her stomach flipping over. The clouds overhead shifted, allowing wan moonlight to shadow his face.

"Thanks for the escort."

He nodded, then strolled off down the shadowy, flower-lined sidewalk bordering the park. She wasn't fooling herself enough to think this meant anything. It was a possibility he wouldn't want to be seen with her at school on Monday, but she was prepared for that. This moment was enough. She couldn't go home yet, anyway.

The journal she'd bought was ancient, at least a century old, and it had come from halfway across the country. How could the map hidden inside be of a place so close to home? It couldn't be coincidence. Curiosity wormed its way into her mind, twisting deep. Suppose there was something in the park . . . a clue to where her parents had disappeared to, and she'd just left it? How could she live with herself? She couldn't.

Veronne adjusted her bag on her shoulder as she re-entered the park. There was no way she wasn't going to find what the map marked—whatever it was. Returning along winding pathways toward the first map marker, she again dropped her bag and pulled out the shovel. But before she could celebrate, a shadow fell over her.

Fear clogged her throat, but Veronne turned.

Lucky sat on the bench closest to her, his arm dangling along the back of it, supporting his head. The glow from the lamppost darkened his eyes, highlighted the tightness around his mouth and in what she could see of his body. It was a readiness full of delight, like someone who has found the key to a previously locked room. Or a predator who has cornered easy prey.

"You should have stayed on the path." He delivered those words tenderly, as if he was reminiscing about a bittersweet moment. When he turned around on the bench to fully focus his gaze on her, she couldn't understand how he was so flexible.

It took her a few blinks to connect that it wasn't the flickering of the lamppost's illumination that blackened his eyes. And a few more to understand that no one should be able to move that way, like something else was underneath. The chain around his neck wasn't gold anymore. It looked like leather, frayed but strong, and several small jars hung from it, winking with faint light as they clinked together. The noise they left on the air sounded wrong in this moment, like a celebratory toast after a crushing loss.

"You're not Lucky," she blurted.

"No."

"What have you done with him?" Angry at the tremble in her voice, she clenched her grip around the shovel. Held it out like a shield.

Part of the thing that was not Lucky moved. Its right eye trembled and widened, the skin of the lower lid going slack to allow the eyeball to grow. "He was never here. Your mind is an unprotected orchard, so easy to pluck what we need from it."

"We?"

"The map leads to where each of us was formed."

"But . . ." Veronne's mind spun. The ellipses, each with a dot in the center. Why hadn't she caught that it was the symbol for an eye? There were at least ten or more icons on the map; she'd just gone with the closest. Those X marks weren't the spots for treasure, but an indication of where one of those creatures had been born.

No wonder no one came to this park. Certainly not after dark.

Not-Lucky shuddered, and a silhouette began to peel away from his body. Another. Another. Until a cluster of the creatures surrounded him, their voices all speaking at once. "And we protect what we were created to protect. At any cost."

Veronne swung her shovel.

One of the creatures erupted from the impact, collapsing into a gelatinous mass. Not-Lucky moved out of the weapon's path easily. Its eye grew still larger, pushing the other features of Lucky's face out of the way to make room for itself.

Another silhouette fell under the onslaught of her shovel,

withering to the ground. The rest of the creatures surrounded her, confining her in a wide circle. They wove away from Veronne's repeated swings, chuckling. One by one, they took familiar forms: Gramps, herself, and, finally, Mom and Pop.

"No!" She squeezed her eyes shut. However, they sprang open again at Not-Lucky's next words.

Don't you want to know about your parents? Where they are? What happened to them?

God, she did. She wanted to solve the greatest mystery of her life. The lulling sound of the creature's voice was irresistible. (Oh god, his voice; his taste was inside her.) The sheen of the widening eye, luring her like a candle in the dark. That eye was a pathway, a portal to a place she wanted to go. Dense jungles and bird cries. Rushing waterfalls. Swirling desert sands. The smell of adventure surrounded her, and it would only be a few steps to her own freedom and her own choices and her own life. Without Gramps's rules. Sixteen and free. It was possible. She could see—

The creature's face moved like gelatin, the eye in the center quivering as it held her in its gaze. She shook, too, fear and adrenaline combining to send her heart plummeting into her stomach. Veronne remembered the taste of his mouth on hers, sweet and smoky. No, Lucky wasn't her first kiss at all. It was this monster in front of her.

Her mouth went sour, the earlier sweetness turning to rot.

She gripped the shovel and jabbed it deep into that growing eye. It shrieked, and she swung hard at the rest of the monsters circling her. She hesitated a fraction of a second at the ones that had taken the shape of her parents.

Not them. *It's not them*, she told herself, and struck out again and again. Her bag dropped to the ground, but she didn't stop until she had cleared a path. She ran then, twisting to avoid their hands as they reached for her, trying to pull her back into them. Her breath burned in her lungs as she pushed hard toward home, running at a speed she never thought possible.

Home.

She would collapse when she got home. Her bag, she hoped, would be there in the morning. No way was she going back for it now.

Soon, she saw the house. A light was on, and she knew she'd be in trouble with Gramps. She didn't care. For a different reason this time. She would be so glad to get home that she would happily put up with any punishment he chose.

Veronne knocked on the door, and when he opened it, she fell into the house. He caught her before she hit the ground and helped her to the sofa. She panted, accepting the glass he handed her, and answered his frantic questions between alternating gulps of air and water. The journal, the creature . . . she explained all of it to his increasingly shocked face.

"Well, you home now," he said, draping a blanket over her.

She nodded, closed her eyes. She heard him take her glass to the kitchen and refill it. When he set it back down, she opened her eyes and sat up.

"Someone dropped this off right before you came in," he said, placing her bag on her lap. The bag she'd left in the park when she'd run for her life.

"But I . . . how . . ." she stuttered, her mind not grasping what was happening.

Gramps sighed as his entire head shook, blurring his features.

When he stopped moving, his right eye stretched in all directions as if tugged into place by some unseen person with dreadful intent. His eye became an impossible, shimmering thing. She could see herself reflected in that monstrous ellipse: her own eyes wide with a confusion and horror that no matter what happened next, she was unable to stop it.

"Don't look so surprised. We are created to protect treasures. You, my girl, are the greatest treasure your parents ever had. Of course, they would want you protected."

Veronne whispered, "You're not my gramps, I guess."

"No, he died before you were born." Not-Gramps shook his head, his huge eye glistening under the overhead light. "But your parents wanted me to take on his appearance. They found it comforting."

All Veronne could do was nod. She was so tired, so drained after her sprint. Now she was processing the knowledge that this creature wasn't a tale to provide local color. She herself was a treasure, and always had been.

"Perhaps I was too overzealous in my duties as your protector. But the events of tonight have shown you're ready to search for your parents. Ready for an adventure." Not-Gramps's eye shifted and shrank. Soon, it was once again the same face she knew and loved. Trusted. "Are you? We can go together."

Veronne looked around the house she'd grown up in, at the familiar things surrounding her. The warmth and safety of home and the protector who had always been in her life, ever since she was born. The one who had raised her when her parents hadn't come home. She smiled and settled back into the cozy sofa.

"Absolutely ready."

FOXHUNT

CHARLOTTE NICOLE DAVIS

The crowd would not stop baying like dogs. Every tackle, every touchdown, every extra point: *RUH-RUH-ROOO!* It wasn't just Flex's classmates, the seniors of Arbor Hill High—the boys with their faces painted crimson and gold, the girls with their jerseys tied off above their midriffs. It was the *senior* seniors, too, the alumni, the oldheads, risen from the dead by the trumpets of the homecoming halftime show. They exchanged furtive grins like dirty secrets as they passed each other up and down the bleachers. The air hummed with anticipation. Flex could feel it in the roots of her teeth. She had spent plenty of Sunday mornings after sleepovers being shepherded to someone else's church; she recognized worship when she saw it. But she'd never seen such devotion to a town, to a *school*. What all did they have to be whooping and hollering about? Their team was down by twenty-one points.

It was Flex's team, too, of course, and had been since the start of the school year—but as she watched the marching band arrange itself into one wobbly formation after another, instruments glinting under the stadium lights, she felt only impatience. Her transfer to Arbor Hill had come far too late to be the fresh start she'd been prescribed. She had barely been here twelve weeks. Her classmates had had twelve *years* together. How could she ever hope to be one of them?

And yet, even given twelve years, Flex knew she would never belong to Arbor Hill, nor it to her. Not that anyone had ever told her as much—the people here were nothing if not polite—but there were some things so true they did not need to be said. Flex knew what people thought of her: the "troubled" transfer from out of state. The Big Black Bull Dyke. Always in the gym, always lifting. *Why?* Her classmates let their imaginations run wild whenever they tried to write her origin story. Inner city, they whispered. Guns, drugs. She'd been expelled for breaking some kid's eye socket just for looking at her wrong.

That last part was almost true—true enough, at least, that the knuckles on her right hand still ached in the rain. But there had been no malice to it, or even thought. Just some hair-trigger instinct, that of an animal born in the corner. She'd spooked. She was spooky. Flex had always been that way.

The rest of the rumors, though: pure fantasy. Flex had come from a red-state, white-picket, blue-ribbon suburb just like this one. The guns had been an aisle over from the baseball gloves. The drugs had been prescribed.

It had been bigger, though, her hometown. There'd been more places to hide.

"Ahoy, matey! Eyes starboard!"

Flex startled. But it was only Kirsten, her admin-appointed student ambassador. Tiny, almost translucently pale, with wispy white-blond hair that frizzed as if from her own frenetic energy. She was never without her favorite jean jacket, and today was no exception. It hung loosely over her gameday shirt, its denim covered with cutesy custom patches. A cactus with a mustache. An ichthus. *"Though she be but little, she is fierce!"*

Kirsten had been tasked with making Flex feel welcome at Arbor Hill High, and in this she was relentless. Everyone else ignored Flex, politely, as they might have politely ignored someone they found vaguely embarrassing. Not so Kirsten. Kirsten never left Flex's side, even when Flex might have preferred to be alone. But Flex's therapist had made it clear that Flex was "at a crossroads" and needed to put in "real work" toward integrating with her peers—and so here she was at the homecoming game, listening to a fight song she didn't know the words to, shivering in a sweatshirt that was the wrong color, standing next to a girl who logged their time together as volunteer hours.

"Sorry, didn't mean to scare you," Kirsten chirped. "Didn't think I *could*. You're so . . ." Kirsten hesitated, seeming to think better of whatever she'd been about to say, but she gestured in Flex's direction as if it was obvious. "Maybe we should start calling you 'Flinch' instead. Ha! Anyway, I got us snacks."

"That was fast."

"I keep telling you, Flex, I'm not short, I'm *aerodynamic*. Corn dog?" She held out a breaded hot dog on a stick, shooing away an inquisitive horsefly. Flex couldn't help curling her lip.

"I'm good. I don't eat pork."

Kirsten's face fell. "Oh, sorry, is that like a religious thing? I should have asked."

"It's fine, it's not a religious thing. I'm just trying to eat clean, you know, while I'm training."

Training for what? Flex could see the question written in the wrinkle of Kirsten's nose. But Flex didn't have an answer for her, or even herself. She didn't *know* what she was training for. That was why it was so important to be ready for it.

But Kirsten looked so discouraged that Flex felt a twinge of regret.

"I mean . . . maybe just this once."

"Yay!" Kirsten handed her the corn dog, bouncing back immediately. "Okay, so, who do you want to win homecoming queen?"

Flex didn't even know who was on the court, but she would try to play along.

"Um . . . it's so hard to pick a favorite."

"Didn't you vote?"

"No." The ballots had been passed out during homeroom, to the same secretive smirks and sly glances that Flex saw now in the stands. Was she missing something here? Some inside joke? Suddenly she felt like a guest in someone else's home, among family who understood each other so completely that they could communicate with a twitch of their fingers or arch of a brow. Flex had stuffed her ballot in her bag to deal with later and then forgotten about it entirely.

Kirsten seemed taken aback. "You should've voted. It's important. Everyone has to have a say."

Flex shrugged. "Not me."

"*Especially* you."

Flex's cheeks flushed with warmth. Was it not enough that she was at this game at all?

"Who did *you* vote for?" she deflected.

Kirsten's answer was immediate. "Chloe Beck, obviously—and Caleb Long, I guess, but that's whatever. King doesn't matter. The queen is the only one who matters. Chloe deserves it, she's been preparing for this."

The marching band had finished their set and was filing off the field, clearing the way for the main event. The homecoming hopefuls were already lined up along the straight of the track. Seven girls, seven boys. Flex knew most of their faces, but none of their names, except for Darren, the only other Black kid she had a class with, and . . . yes, there was Chloe, class president, glossy and blond and beaming with benevolence. She shimmered in her crimson gown. Of course Flex knew who she was—everyone did.

After a brief preamble from the principal—*"Legacy!" "Loyalty!"*—each member of the court was called forward and given a moment to speak into the microphone. Flex found she couldn't concentrate on their words for long. She got the sensation sometimes—and she was getting it now—that she was not really *here*, or anywhere. As if she were already dead, her soul departed, and her body just hadn't realized it yet. It was a sign she was overstimulated, her therapist had told her. She was supposed to ground herself in the little things. But the night felt so heightened, so unreal, that every detail she turned to only deepened the feeling. There was something sickening about the fluorescent green of the turf, something sinister in the insistence of the wind. The crowd became wax figures beneath the dull shine of their face paint. The stadium lights became an interrogation. They cast faint, interlocking halos against the black of the sky; Flex closed her eyes and saw them seared into the dark.

She was finally brought back to herself by the announcement of the winners—Caleb Long and Chloe Beck, just as Kirsten had predicted. The crowd did not erupt into applause at this, but more *barking*.

"*RUFF-RUFF-ROO, RUFF-RUFF!*"

"*RARF RARF!*"

"*ROOOOO—*"

Her flesh crawled. "What is that?"

Kirsten herself was jumping up and down, yapping like a Pekingese. She stopped and looked at Flex with wild eyes. "What's what?"

"The . . . *barking*. Aren't we the Wildcats?"

"Oh! Ha, sorry! I should have explained. It's just one of the town's old traditions. From before the high school was built, even. We do it every game."

Flex was not satisfied with this answer. What game had they been playing before the high school was built? What did the barking have to do with it? If it were howling, even, like a wolf, she might have felt better, but these people were baying like hounds.

Chloe was then given not a crown, but a mask—a crude, misshapen dog's head made out of papier-mâché. Pointed ears, pointed snout, pointed teeth. It'd been painted Arbor Hill High red, the color of dried blood.

Flex wet her cracked lips. "Kirsten, why—?"

But then Chloe lowered the mask over her head, and the crowd let loose once more.

PSYCHIATRIC EVALUATION

Dr. William DeVries

Background

Amadea "Flex" Washington is a 17-year-old high school student. Her chief complaint is, "I do not feel safe."

Amadea currently lives with her 34-year-old sister and guardian, Amarantha, who is seeking treatment for Amadea following an unprecedented violent outburst against a classmate that resulted in her suspension. Amarantha describes her sister as a "good kid" despite her difficulty making friends.

Exam

Amadea presents with a near-constant but unspecified dread that appears to interfere with almost every aspect of her life. Her intense feelings of mistrust and fear (unwarranted) have left her with a severely underdeveloped (potentially dangerous?) inability to form healthy, meaningful relationships with her peers.

Amadea denies thoughts of harming herself or others, but there is hostility in her tone. She is incredibly resistant to evaluation and assumes malicious intent, as she reportedly does for all authority figures other than her sister.

Symptoms are consistent with post-traumatic stress, but neither Amadea nor her sister reports any significant traumatic events in Amadea's history. As such, there is no clear precipitant for her behavior.

Diagnoses

Paranoid Personality Disorder

Outpatient treatment in the form of supportive therapy is recommended, but "Flex" will need to be monitored closely for any further warning signs of aggression or deviance.

Flex lay down on the weightlifting bench, pressing the bar up along its guided track. Her eyes closed, her ears trained to the rasp of metal on metal. The rough stubble of the knurling bit into her palms, but it was a good pain, clean, like the ache in her shoulders or the sweat on her back. The weight room rang with the chatter and laughter of athletes and the thunder of weights dropping to the rubber floor, but Flex focused solely on the meditation of her own body at work.

Homecoming had been weeks ago, but Flex had not felt right since. That creeping certainty that she was *missing* something would not leave her. She noticed things now that she hadn't before. Money changing hands in the cafeteria, teachers speaking to one another in hushed tones. Flex was certain people dropped their conversation whenever she entered a room. Even Kirsten had started avoiding her the past couple of days, quickly growing flustered when she saw Flex in the hallway. She would force small talk for only a moment, then scurry off to class. Flex had wanted nothing more than to be left alone, and now that she was, it felt like an ill omen. If a gazelle found itself alone at a watering hole it was probably because there was a lion lurking nearby, stepping lightly so as to be mistaken for the wind in the grass.

But then . . . maybe it really *was* just the wind.

This was how it went, Flex's therapist had warned her—with compulsions, with delusions. You changed your behavior to protect yourself from a threat that had never actually existed, and when the threat never materialized, you only became more convinced: *it's working.*

A chill ran through Flex, head to toe, as it often did toward the end of a hard workout. She slowly lowered the bar for the last time and rested it on the safety catch, opening her eyes.

Chloe Beck was standing over her.

Flex sat up sharply, nearly banging her head on the bar. She blinked away the burn of sweat.

"Thought I'd find you here!" Chloe said brightly. "Amadea, right? Sorry—*Flex.* Because you're always working out? That's cute. I'm Chloe Beck."

"I know who you are."

Flex had never been this close to her before, though. Chloe was dressed in her street clothes—blue jeans and a white lace blouse, chaste makeup, and a gold cross necklace. She smelled faintly of orange blossom. She was clearly not here to work out, and yet Flex herself suddenly felt like the one who had been caught somewhere she did not belong.

Chloe's brute of a boyfriend had tagged along as well, looming behind her in a sweatshirt and shorts. His muscular white calves were covered with coarse dark hair. Flex had often seen him here after school, strength training with the lacrosse team. She could never remember his name—Bryan or Brendan or Bryce or Brett or something like that.

He had always hated her. She didn't know why. It didn't matter. She just knew she would feel it on the back of her neck, like a sunburn, and turn to catch him staring.

"Okay, you're right, that was silly, of *course* we know each other's names," Chloe admitted. "It's not like you can really be anonymous in a school this small, can you? But you sure try!"

"I just . . . don't really see the point of us getting to know each other," Flex said. She didn't even mean anything by it—it was only the truth. "We're all about to graduate anyway."

Brendan puffed up. "Don't be an asshole."

"No, do!" Chloe insisted, letting out a sparkling laugh. "I love it! Kirsten warned me that you could be a little rough around the edges."

Flex's neck prickled. Kirsten wasn't talking *to* her, but she was talking *about* her? To Chloe?

"Kirsten also said she told you a little bit about Arbor Hill's traditions, but it sounds like she didn't tell the whole truth," Chloe went on. "Probably because townies aren't really supposed to talk about this stuff in mixed company. But I disagree, Flex—that you're 'mixed company,' I mean. You live here now, you're one of us. And I disagree, too, that there's no point in us getting to know each other." Chloe sat down at the end of the bench, leaning in and dropping her voice to create a promise of confidence between the two of them. "Admit it, I won't tell anyone—aren't you at least a *little* curious?"

Flex's skin was growing cold and clammy as her sweat

chilled. Some of the other students had stopped what they were doing, huddling together, watching her. The coaches pointedly looked away. Chloe was right: Flex *was* curious. Or, no, perhaps that wasn't the right word. Flex was *exhausted.* Everyone around her seemed to know the answers instinctively. Flex did not even know the questions. Her whole life, fumbling through every interaction like it was a math problem, wishing for the cheat sheet.

So why was she dreading Chloe's answer now?

"There's a game the senior class plays every year," Chloe continued softly. "We call it 'Foxhunt.' It's kind of like hide-and-seek, but with a twist. One of us hides, and the rest of us seek. One of us is the Fox, and the rest of us are the Hounds. On the first night of November, the Fox is released into the woods. They get a one-hour head start. And if they make it across the creek before sunrise without getting caught, they win."

Chloe stopped here, her eyes shining with an excitement that was almost carnal.

Flex couldn't help but ask, "Win what?"

"Win *money,*" Bryan cut in. He seemed to be getting impatient with the whole thing. "Everyone who wants to play has to pay a buy-in. If the Fox gets away, they win the pot. Otherwise, the Hounds who catch them do. Can we move this along, Chlo?"

She shared a glance with Flex, rolling her eyes. *Boys!* "Anyway," she said, returning to a normal speaking voice, "it's part of the tradition that the homecoming queen nominates the Fox. The people pick their homecoming queen, and the homecoming queen picks their Fox. It's fair that way."

"Oh." Flex took a moment to turn this over in her head, looking at it from every angle. She had to admit that this explained the "suspicious" behavior she'd noticed the past few weeks. Cash passed under the table, a Hound mask for the homecoming queen. And Kirsten, probably only avoiding her because she didn't want to spill the secret.

Just the wind after all.

"So . . . who's your Fox?" Flex asked.

Chloe said nothing, but she smiled strangely, and Bryce let out a soft snort. Flex almost recoiled as it hit her.

"*Me?*"

"Who else!" Chloe cheered.

Flex's body rejected the proposal before her brain could even consider it. She drew a shallow breath, her chest tight, and felt the sharp pain of her ribs digging into her lungs.

"I'm good," Flex mumbled. She reached for her water bottle. Her hands were tremoring. From lifting, she told herself.

"'You're good,' what's that supposed to mean? 'Yes'?" Brett pushed.

"No," Flex said shortly. "It means 'no.'"

He crossed his arms over the *AHH* emblazoned on his chest. "Yeah, you can't just say *no*."

The hell she couldn't? Flex was getting flustered now. Her mind was threatening to untether as it had during the homecoming game. The other students were still watching them, pretending not to.

"Ladies, please!" Chloe broke in, holding a hand up to placate them both. "Of *course*, Flex can say no. But Flex, why would you want to? It's a huge honor, being the Fox."

"Then you should give it to someone who's been looking forward to this since they were five."

"*Or*," Chloe countered, "I should give it to the new girl, to prove to her and everyone else that she's as much a part of this class as the rest of us."

Flex hesitated. Did she have any reason to say no other than the hum of premonition building at the base of her skull? Did she have any reason, really, to "assume malicious intent"? How Flex hated being this person! It had been hard enough before, when she'd only mistrusted others. Now she didn't trust herself, either.

"Did Kirsten put you up to this?" she asked finally.

Chloe let out another sparkling laugh. "No! Flex, is it really so hard to believe that *I* might want you there? That we *all* might?"

Flex flicked her gaze back over to Brendan. He was still scowling, but he gave a grudging nod.

"You're in shape. It'll actually be a challenge keeping up with you. That's what makes the game fun."

Flex refused to be flattered. They had cornered her, here in her most sacred of places, and it would never feel safe again. She wanted only to go home.

"I'll think about it."

She stood up to leave. Some shadow passed across Chloe's face for an instant, so quickly Flex might have imagined it—but then Chloe was all smiles again.

"Okay, but don't take too long, Flex! Foxhunt is only a week away."

One hot shower and two turkey burgers later, and Flex was starting to feel better. Silly, even, for how she'd reacted. Letting Cornball

Chloe ruin her workout like that. Flex was determined to put it out of her mind—now she was nestled in a pile of laundry on the swaybacked old sofa in her bedroom, working through her assigned reading for English. Her room was small and cluttered, cramped with her grandmother's hand-me-down furniture, the chipped walls covered with peeling posters of professional women's basketball players. Her sister, Amarantha, took her to a game every year for her birthday.

Flex had told Amarantha about Foxhunt over dinner. They kept no secrets between each other. She'd expected her sister to reject the whole thing immediately, as Flex had. Instead, Amarantha had been excited that Flex had been invited to something. She'd even started strategizing about what to wear to stay warm for a night in the woods. Who was this person? The real Amarantha would not even go in the backyard because she'd seen a possum once. Flex had shut down, cleared her plate, and hurried to her room. She'd felt bad about that, but she would put it out of her mind, too.

There was a soft knock at the door.

Flex's stomach twisted. She closed her book.

"Come in!"

Amarantha cracked the door open, poking her head in, her hair wrapped in a patterned headscarf. The two sisters were opposites in many ways: Flex, short and stocky; Amarantha, long and lean. Flex, reclusive and reserved; Amarantha, bubbly and boisterous. But, in other ways, Flex felt like they were two halves of a whole: the same person, and the only one she trusted.

"Hey, Dea," Amarantha said gently. "Can I come in?"

Flex nodded, sitting up. Her sister opened the door and came to sit on the corner of the bed, offering up a plate of cut fruit. Flex picked out an apple slice and took a nibble.

Amarantha let out a long breath. "Listen, I'm sorry about dinner—"

"No, I'm sorry."

"Aht! Let me finish. I wasn't trying to pressure you into anything you're uncomfortable with. I was just . . . trying to understand. You're always talking about how hard it is out here, not knowing anybody. Then here comes this girl, trying to get to know you, and you want nothing to do with her."

Flex's face warmed. "We don't have anything in common."

"So what? You don't think you'd have a good time anyway? We had a game like this, actually, back when I was in school. 'Last Man Standing.' All the seniors would buy these cans of washable spray paint. We'd hunt one another down and tag one another with them. I think the admin shut it down a few years ago—it doesn't work, you know, in today's climate. But it was fun, is my point. I want you to have some fun, too, before this is all over."

Flex took another bite of apple rather than speak. She did not know how to explain, even to Amarantha, that she did not find it "fun" to be among other people.

But her sister knew her too well. "Dea, if it makes you uncomfortable, that's all the more reason to do it," Amarantha said quietly. "I see you out here, every day, working on yourself, getting strong. You have to treat your mind the same."

Flex's throat tightened. "Have you been talking to the therapist?" Because the therapist was always saying things like this. Fear had its place, apparently, but when it was constant, like Flex's, it became paranoia. It had to be challenged.

But that white woman did not understand her. Amarantha did.

Amarantha's voice was pained. "You know I would never cross that line. But I see things, too. I just don't want you going through life afraid—"

"I'm not afraid." Flex could not believe it: that trapped, panicky feeling, here, at home. She fucking hated this—the injustice of being seen as a coward, the shame that came with it. She was not *afraid* of anything. She was simply *ready* for it.

"Dea, come on, I didn't mean it like that. I just . . ." Amarantha continued to struggle for words—such a rare thing for her. Flex felt the clenched fist of her heart loosen. It upset her, seeing her sister upset, and feeling like she had caused it. Whenever Flex suffered, Amarantha blamed herself.

Just go, Flex thought then, resigned.

Maybe Amarantha was right, even.

Maybe it would be *fun*.

The night of November 1 fell cold and clear, with a bright blue moon. The pale light filtered down through the branches to the frostbitten floor. Flex savored the crunch of leaves as she hiked north toward the creek, flashlight in hand. She was not yet worried about giving her position away. It had only been half an hour, and it would be half an hour more before the Hounds started after her.

Flex had had to make a mask for herself out of papier-mâché—a cunning Fox to Chloe's Hound. All the other seniors had done the same, outfitting their Hounds with flashes of personality. Viking horns and Spartan plumes, jersey numbers and cupid hearts. This was Arbor Hill's Halloween.

Flex would have been content to scrawl *FOX* across a paper bag and call it a day, but Kirsten had actually gone and made a mask for her. Flex had found it hanging on a hook in the locker they shared. Unsurprisingly, Kirsten turned out to be incredibly crafty, and she'd put together a Fox mask that popped with fiery streaks of orange and red paint. Flex was sweating beneath it now, the damp heat of her breath chilling instantly in the cold. Her insides felt loose, but she wasn't anxious, no. She was *alert*. There was something energizing about the autumn air, even as it cut her lungs with each breath. It was liberating, the way the woods demanded the attention of all her senses, leaving no room for idle thoughts. Her therapist was always talking about *being present*—Flex finally understood the appeal.

A branch snapped somewhere to Flex's left. Flex froze, listening intently. Chloe had reassured her there were no dangerous animals in these woods and hadn't been in over a century. The townies culled any wildlife bigger than a house cat.

A patch of shadow, slightly darker than the night, was moving toward her—*definitely* bigger than a house cat. The flashlight might only aggravate it. Flex half crouched, readying herself to fight or run.

"Flex!" the shadow stage-whispered.

Flex hesitated, squinting. ". . . *Kirsten?*"

She swung the flashlight around. Kirsten's face was hidden behind her Hound mask—the left half painted comedy, the right tragedy—but Flex knew it was her. She was wearing that damned jean jacket.

Kirsten held a hand up in front of her eyes. "Turn that light off! Someone will see us."

Flex would do no such thing. "What are *you* doing here? Chloe told me I had an hour. It's barely been thirty minutes."

"Right! About that. Chloe doesn't know I'm here," Kirsten said. Her voice was high and thin, with an edge of hysteria to it. She seemed . . . *charged*, somehow, more than usual, all fidgets and twitches. "See, I'm not trying to hunt you, Flex, I'm trying to help you."

Flex could not believe it. How was it that she couldn't even shake this girl *here*, in the middle of nowhere? And helping wasn't allowed; Chloe had made that clear. It wasn't like Kirsten to break the rules.

"Kirsten, I don't need any help."

"You do, though!" Kirsten said, still with that same strained cheeriness. "Now follow me, we're wasting 'daylight.' Ha!"

She set off, and after a moment, Flex flicked her flashlight off and ran after her, bewildered.

"So . . . you're talking to me now?" Flex mumbled into the lengthening silence. She hadn't meant to sound so childish, but there had been—and she was only just now realizing it—a child-like hurt at the thought that even Kirsten had given up on her. That Flex's efforts to push her away had actually worked.

"Oh, yeah, sorry I've been weird! Not very ambassadorial, huh?" Kirsten said. She did not stop or even slow, stepping deftly through the darkened undergrowth. "I heard people saying Chloe was going to pick you, and I didn't know what to do.

I couldn't talk to *you* about it, obviously. And I couldn't talk *her* out of it, either. And then I felt bad for even trying."

Why would she have wanted to talk Chloe out of it, Flex wondered? But just as suddenly, the answer came to her: *Kirsten* had wanted to be the Fox. Was there anyone else half as committed to the bit as her? Probably Kirsten thought she deserved this. Probably she did.

If that was the case, Flex thought, it was only fair to let her tag along.

They toiled in silence for what felt like a mile, maybe more. Kirsten set an aggressive pace. Flex was strong, yes, but she hadn't built her body for hiking, and she hadn't dressed for it either, wearing the same high-top basketball shoes she always wore. Her toes were growing numb with the cold, making her clumsy over the rough terrain. Exposed tree roots, sliding rocks, little pits and ditches just the right size for turning an ankle—it would have been hard going even in the daytime, but Kirsten remained adamant that the light stay off, and the moonlight only grew fainter the deeper into the woods they went. Still: Flex had always been an athlete, always been competitive, and some part of her relished the challenge.

"*RUH-RUH-ROOOOOO!*"

The sound of baying, still far-off.

"Does that mean they're coming?" Flex asked. She could hardly catch her breath, but a thrill of excitement ran through her.

Amarantha had been right. This *was* fun.

"Yes." Kirsten's eyes were owlishly wide behind her mask, and there was a new note of fear in her voice. "We're not even halfway to the creek."

"Why is the creek the finish line, anyway?"

"It's symbolic," she said impatiently. *Of what,* Flex was about to ask, but Kirsten was single-minded. "Come on, we have to pick it up. They're fast, Flex. The others. They've been practicing for years; they can navigate these woods in the dark as easily as if it were their own home. So can I, obviously, but I have to deal with *you*."

"Not too much, now," Flex said, feigning offense. But Kirsten didn't respond with one of her typical witticisms. She was all business, throwing tight glances over her shoulder—not at Flex, but beyond, into the ripening dark.

Flex began to feel the first gnawing worm of doubt work its way through her.

"*RARF-RAAARRR!*"

"*Hurry,*" Kirsten pleaded.

From then on, not more than a moment passed without some punctuation of barking and yipping from the Hounds. The different vocalizations meant different things, apparently, because Kirsten adjusted their movements every time. Flex asked if she still knew where she was going—if she was *certain* they wouldn't get lost.

"Of course. You can't get lost. The creek runs the length of the whole woods, you just have to keep heading north. I have a compass. Save your breath, Flex, we've still got a long—"

"*Ewww-uh,* Ryan, get that thing *away* from me! *Stoppp*-uh!" A girl's high-pitched laughter cut through the silence, so nearby it made Flex startle. It was followed by squeals of delight. A boy shouted something unintelligible; another shouted back. Someone broke a bottle.

And then, from the opposite direction, farther away but growing closer:

"Arbor Hill, Arbor Hill, let's-see-your-strength, let's-see-your-skill! Arbor Hill, Arbor Hill, for the win, for the kill! *ROOOOOO!*"

"*Shit!*" Kirsten hissed. She stopped, spinning from one direction to another, pulling at her hair. "That has to be the main group. They're on our trail. But we can't double back because—*shit*!"

Flex had never heard Kirsten swear before. Somehow, this shook Flex more than anything else that had come before.

"Kirsten, stop, look at me," Flex said softly, touching her shoulder. Kirsten flinched away from her. Her breaths were short and shallow, rapid bursts of fogged air, and she had that look in her eyes—too wide, too white, fixed on some horror that had shown itself to her alone.

Is this what I *look like?* Flex realized suddenly.

Is this what everyone sees?

"Flex, you have to keep going." Kirsten was clutching at her chest now. "I'm sorry, I don't know what's wrong with me, but—"

"You're having a panic attack. You're going to be okay," Flex said, keeping her voice level. Perhaps the therapist *had* known a thing or two. Flex fumbled with half-frozen fingers for the water bottle she'd stuffed in her jacket pocket. But Kirsten only slapped it away.

"*No!* Flex, you have to keep going! Just leave me, I'll be fine—"

"Jesus, Kirsten, it's just a game. I'm not leaving you, you could freeze to death."

"Arbor Hill! Arbor Hill! ROOOOOOOOOOO!"

Good, Flex thought. Let them find her. Let it end. She was beginning to tremble, and not with the cold.

"Flex, please—"

It was the first group that found them. Three Hounds emerged from the shadows, their silhouettes sharp and black against a flickering yellow-orange light—not a flashlight, Flex realized, but a vintage oil lantern. The girl Hound held it high, leading the way, her mask garnished with a flower crown. The two boys followed her, an unsteady sway in their gait. One's mask had been painted a mottled military green, the other's sporting longhorns and a gold ring through the nose.

Both boys carried hunting rifles on their backs.

Flex went still.

"*Shhhhh*," the girl hissed. She sounded like she was struggling to keep a straight face, a trickle of giggles leaking out from behind her mask. She lifted a hand, signaling the boys to stop, and raised the lantern higher. "Is that . . . ?"

"*Fuck, it is! That's her!*"

"*Hurry up, I think she sees us!*"

"*Take the shot!*"

The boys fumbled their rifles from their backs.

Kirsten was crying softly now. "Flex, I'm so sorry."

To Flex's surprise, her immediate reaction was one of overwhelming relief. It was as if a great weight had sloughed off her shoulders. Because she'd been expecting this, hadn't she? Not *this*, but *something*. Eventually, inevitably. The dread had only been in the waiting.

But Flex was not afraid anymore.

She stood, lifting Kirsten up with her.

"Stop! *Stop!*" the girl in the flower crown cried suddenly, swatting the guns down. "She has a hostage, can't you see? Who is that? Let her go, you monster!"

"Toss me your guns first," Flex ordered.

The Hounds hesitated, seemingly shocked by the steel in her voice. They leaned together to conference among themselves. But the main hunting party was already closing in. Their baying cascaded through the dark.

"ROOOOOOOOO!"

"RUH-ROOOOOOO, RUH-ROOOOO!"

"Ha! Clever, Flex," Kirsten whispered through her tears. She did not fight back against Flex's grip. "Maybe I'll be able to save you after all."

No! Kirsten did not get to do this. She did not get to make herself a martyr, not now.

"If you wanted to save me, you should've *said* something," Flex whispered back harshly. Her mind was beginning to dissipate in every direction, but her voice shook with a hurt and rage that her body could not deny. "God, Kirsten, I really thought—I thought you were *real*."

"I am!" Kirsten was sobbing now. "I wanted so badly to tell you. I wish I had. I wish I'd been brave. But I realized if I could just at least get you over the water—"

"And then what?"

"And then nothing! Flex, I *swear*. I know how it looks, but I swear, *no one* will come after you. Tomorrow they'll pretend none of this even happened. Not just the hunt—all of it. The sex, the booze. And more, and worse. Because tonight doesn't count, see? It's the in-between. Autumn and winter, life and death. Childhood and adulthood. My oma called it God's blind spot, but I don't think He misses anything. I think sometimes He just . . . looks away. And that's what we do, Flex, we look away—"

"*Hey!* Fox! You win, okay? We're tossing you the guns, okay?" the flower-crowned Hound shouted. She spoke so slowly and clearly, it was plain she wanted to be overheard by the other groups. "I repeat! We are tossing you! The guns!"

They were not going to toss the guns. Flex could see it in the set of their hips as the Hounds squared up not to throw their rifles, but to fire them—hostage be damned. Everything around Flex seemed to slow then: the Hounds moving with the clumsy sluggishness of alcohol, Flex herself moving with the sudden surety of adrenaline. She ducked just as they pulled the triggers, pulling Kirsten down with her. The sound of the gunshots tore through the tissue-thin remnants of her sanity, a bullet tugging at the air as it went just wide of her temple. Flex dropped Kirsten to the ground and sprinted forward. The Hounds were already fumbling to reload their weapons. She slammed into the nearest one, the Hound with the horns, and wrapped her bicep around his throat, the crook of her elbow pressed tight against his Adam's apple. He let out a strangled cry and dropped the gun, scrabbling desperately to pull her arm away. He smelled of cheap beer, of expensive cologne, of sweat, of fear.

She inhaled sharply. Flexed.

The boy went limp in her arm. She held him fast until the flutter in his throat faded, then let him fall to the ground with a *thud*. She picked up his rifle. It was heavier than she'd have guessed, cooler to the touch. Flex swung the barrel around, fixed it on the remaining two Hounds. The Hound in hunting camo took a half step back before doubling over to heave up his dinner. The Hound with the flower crown collapsed, her skirt a puddle around her feet. She'd dropped the lantern in the dirt, and the flicker of its firelight did something hellish to her face, shadows licking up from below, twisting her features.

"You *monster*, we'll *kill* you for this—"

"You were going to kill me anyway," Flex said calmly. She had no idea how to use a gun, but her shoulders, her back: she knew them intimately. She flipped the rifle around deftly and swung it with all her strength, the butt of it cracking across the girl's jaw with a starburst of blood. The girl's words devolved into shrieks of agony. Flex slammed the butt of the gun down—once, twice—until she felt it give.

She turned to face the last of the three.

"Hey, man, listen—" he said shakily.

WHAM.

He fell to the ground.

Flex knelt to pick up his Hound mask and gently wiped away the blood from its temple. She removed her own mask, taking a moment to savor the cold of the wind on her flushed skin, then fixed the Hound's face over her own. Was that really all it took to become one of them?

All around her, half-human howls rose and fell like sirens at the end of the world. Flex had a minute now, at most.

She turned to face Kirsten, who remained rooted to the spot where Flex had left her. She was still sobbing quietly, the words of prayer now riding the flood of tears.

"Greater love has no one than this: to lay down one's life for

one's friends. You are my friends if you do what I command. I no longer call you servants, for—"

"How did this whole thing start?" Flex said softly.

"Flex, please—"

"How did it *start*, Kirsten?"

She let out a shuddering breath. "It doesn't matter. It was a long time ago. Things are different now." Flex waited, implacable. As if she had lifetimes, not seconds, before her classmates closed in for the kill. Kirsten's red-rimmed eyes flicked down to the rifle. "It . . . it was a kindness, really," she said finally. "Back then, most people . . . you know . . . they kept slaves. And in Arbor Hill, once a year, one of those slaves would get a chance to escape. Just because we made a game of it doesn't mean . . . Flex, they *begged* for the privilege of being the Fox. It was considered an honor. It still is, even now—"

Flex turned away, suddenly feeling sick. Not because she was surprised, but because she wasn't.

"I guess you're going to kill me now, too," Kirsten choked out through her tears.

Flex did not have it in her to comfort Kirsten, resented her for even asking. She could only shake her head. "God looks away, right?" Tears rose in her own throat, sharp as stones. "Don't follow me."

Flex set off, her feet heavy as her heart. She was beginning to fall back into herself—to crash, really—her adrenaline replaced not by fear, but by grief, terrifying in its infinity. Some part of her understood now that she was profoundly broken, and it was a fault line that spread not just forward, to her future, but back, to her beginning. She'd felt tonight's aftershocks when she'd taken her first step. She'd never known steady ground. Sometimes disaster only raised children capable of surviving it. Sometimes madness precipitated itself.

No: Flex would not come back from tonight whole.

But she *would* come back. She was sure of that.

Fresh howls filled the night. And Flex, free at last of the burden of pretending, let loose a triumphant animal cry of her own, racing toward the river on feet that were suddenly lighter than air.

ABOUT THE AUTHORS

Named one of *The Root*'s and BET's 100 most influential African Americans, **L.L. McKinney** is an advocate for equality and inclusion in publishing and the creator of the hashtags #PublishingPaidMe and #WhatWoCWritersHear. A gamer, geek, and adamant *Sailor Moon* stan, her works include the Nightmare-Verse books, *Nubia: Real One* through DC, *Power Rangers Unlimited: Heir to Darkness*, Marvel's *Black Widow: Bad Blood*, and more.

Kortney Nash is a Black American writer with a love for anything and everything supernatural. She graduated from UC Berkeley with a Bachelor of Arts in 2021 and has been working in children's publishing ever since. When she's not reading, she can be found sewing or practicing new spreads with her tarot cards. Kort is currently based in Jersey but grew up in sunny South Los Angeles. You can keep up with her on Twitter @quarrtknee.

Erin E. Adams is a first-generation Haitian American writer and theater artist. She received her BA with honors in literary arts from Brown University, her MFA in acting from the Old Globe and University of San Diego Shiley Graduate Theatre Program, and her MFA in dramatic writing from NYU Tisch School of the Arts. An award-winning playwright and actor, Adams has called New York City home for the last decade. *Jackal* is her first novel.

Desiree S. Evans (ed.) is a writer from South Louisiana. Her writing has been nominated for the Pushcart Prize and *The Best of the Net* and has appeared in literary journals such as *Gulf Coast, The Offing, Nimrod,* and others. She is a contributor to the young adult fiction anthologies *Cool. Awkward. Black.* and *Foreshadow: Stories to Celebrate the Magic of Reading and Writing* Y.A. Desiree loves writing for children, teens, and adults and is a 2020 winner of the Walter Dean Myers Grant for children's fiction awarded by the nonprofit organization We Need Diverse Books. Visit Desiree on the web at www.desiree-evans.com, and on Instagram and Twitter @ literarydesiree.

Zakiya Dalila Harris is the *New York Times* bestselling author of *The Other Black Girl,* which was adapted into a Hulu original series and was named a Best Book of 2021 by *Time* and *The Washington Post.* She received her MFA in nonfiction writing from the New School and her BA in English literature from the University of North Carolina at Chapel Hill. You can find her writing in *Cosmopolitan, Esquire,* and *The New York Times.* She lives in Brooklyn with her husband and their growing collection of plants.

Justina Ireland is the *New York Times* bestselling author of numerous books, including *Dread Nation, Deathless Divide, Rust in the Root,* and the award-winning middle-grade novel *Ophie's Ghosts*. She is the author of numerous Star Wars books and one of the story architects of Star Wars: The High Republic. You can find her work wherever great books are sold, and you can find her at her website, www.authorjustinaireland.com.

Daka Hermon is a writer from Chattanooga, Tennessee. She has a degree in English literature and creative writing. She spent her childhood huddled under blankets reading and writing. Her love of children's media started with an internship at Nickelodeon, and she is currently a staff writer on a preschool animated superhero series. She loves sweet tea, chocolate, cupcakes, and collecting superhero toys and paraphernalia. You can find her online at dakahermon.com.

Brittney Morris is the bestselling author of *SLAY, The Cost of Knowing,* Marvel's *Spider-Man: Miles Morales—Wings of Fury,* and *The Jump*. She also writes video games and has contributed to projects such as *The Lost Legends of Redwall, Subnautica: Below Zero, Spider-Man 2* for PS5, and *Wolverine* for PS5. Brittney is an NAACP Image Award nominee, an ALA Black Caucus Youth Literary Award winner, and an Ignyte Award finalist. She has an economics degree from Boston University. You can find her on Twitter and Instagram @BrittneyMMorris, and online at www.authorbrittneymorris.com.

Camara Aaron is a Dominican American writer and filmmaker, passionate about telling coming-of-age stories for and about Black women and girls. In 2021, she graduated from Yale University with a BA in film and media studies. She is currently based in New York and working in documentary film production. Camara hopes to one day see her very own soukouyan. For now, she is content to hear stories of her family's sightings. You can find her on Instagram @camaraife.

Maika Moulite is a Miami native and the daughter of Haitian immigrants. She loves writing: books, think pieces, journal entries, never-ending lists, you name it. When she's not scribbling every random thought into her Notes app, she's sharpening her skills as a Howard University PhD student. (That means more writing.) Her research focuses on representation in media and its impact on marginalized groups. She's the eldest of four sisters and loves audiobooks, fierce female leads, and laughing.

Maritza Moulite graduated from the University of Florida with a bachelor's in women's studies and the University of Southern California with a master's in journalism. She's worked in various capacities for NBC News, CNN, and *USA Today*, but her favorite roles were Head Start literacy tutor and pre-K teacher assistant. She loved working with young people so much that she is now a PhD student at the University of Pennsylvania exploring ways to improve literacy through children's media. She clearly couldn't get enough of school. Her favorite song is "September" by Earth, Wind & Fire.

Saraciea J. Fennell (ed.) is a Brooklyn-born Black Honduran American writer and social entrepreneur from the Bronx. She is the founder and CEO of The Bronx is Reading, a social impact venture that empowers the next generation of readers and writers, and the creator of Honduran Garifuna Writers. She is the board chair of Latinx in Publishing Inc. and the editor of *Wild Tongues Can't Be Tamed. Good Morning America* included her on its 2021 Hispanic Heritage Month Inspiration List, and *Bitch* included her in its 2018 Bitch 50 list alongside changemakers like AOC and Roxane Gay. Fennell is an advocate for marginalized voices, especially within the Black diaspora, Honduran, and Central American communities. Please visit www.saracieafennell.com for more information and follow her on social media @sj_fennell.

Monica Brashears is an Affrilachian writer from Tennessee and author of her debut novel, *House of Cotton*. She is a graduate of Syracuse University's MFA program. Her work has appeared in *Nashville Review, Split Lip Magazine, Appalachian Review, The Masters Review*, and more. She lives in Brooklyn, New York, where she is at work on her second novel.

Vincent Tirado is a nonbinary Afro-Latine Bronx native. They ventured out to Pennsylvania and Ohio to get their bachelor's degree in biology and master's degree in bioethics. Their first novel, *Burn Down, Rise Up* (2022), was recognized with a

Pura Belpré Award and nominated for both the Bram Stoker and Lambda Literary Awards. *We Don't Swim Here* is their latest novel. When they're not writing, you can catch them playing video games or making digital art. Find them on Twitter @v_e_tirado or visit them on their website, www.v-e-tirado.com, for more information.

Eden Royce is a writer from Charleston, South Carolina. She is a Shirley Jackson Award finalist for her short story work and has written articles for *Writer's Digest* and We Need Diverse Books. Her debut novel, *Root Magic*, is a Walter Dean Myers Award honoree, an Andre Norton Nebula Award finalist, a Mythopoeic Award winner, and an Ignyte Award winner for outstanding children's literature. Find her online at www.edenroyce.com.

Charlotte Nicole Davis (any/all) is the critically acclaimed author of the Good Luck Girls duology and contributor to young adult sci-fi/fantasy anthologies *Tasting Light* and *A Phoenix First Must Burn*. A graduate of the New School's Writing for Children and Young Adults MFA program, they've been living and writing in New York ever since. Find them online at www.lnk.bio/cndwrites.

ACKNOWLEDGMENTS

We're two Black women who love horror. As teenage girls, we collected teen pulp horror paperbacks like Alvin Schwartz's *Scary Stories to Tell in the Dark*; R. L. Stine's Fear Street and Goosebumps series; and Scholastic's Point Horror series. On our bookshelves, teen horror novels by Christopher Pike, Lois Duncan, and L. J. Smith sat alongside adult horror classics by Stephen King, Anne Rice, Clive Barker, and Charlaine Harris. Movies such as *Night of the Living Dead*, by Cuban American director George A. Romero, changed how we saw the genre. It was the first time we saw a Black man—Duane Jones—in a leading role in a horror movie.

Eager for more horror tales, we rushed home from school to finish our homework so we could watch shows like *Tales from the Crypt*, *The X-Files*, *Buffy the Vampire Slayer*, *The Twilight Zone*, and so many others. But Black characters were never the "main protagonist" in those shows, always side characters. The few places where we found horror that featured Black characters as leads, in movies such as *Queen of the Damned*, *Blade*, *Vampire in Brooklyn, Candyman, Tales from the Hood*, and *The People Under the Stairs*, made us eager to find those protagonists in books as well.

So many of us come to horror in order to be shocked, thrilled, and, more than anything, scared. As one of the oldest literary genres, with its roots in our cultural folklore and campfire tales, horror is a safe space for us to confront our imagined, and sometimes all too real, monsters. Yet, in the hundreds of horror books we both read as teens, we can't recall one that featured young Black girls like us as the protagonist, as the heroine at the center of her own story. We were always in search of a Black Final Girl.

As horror expands, as it becomes more imaginative and inclusive, now is the time to ask: Who gets to tell scary stories? Who gets to be the hero, the monster, the villain, and the savior in these stories? Where are the Black Final Girls? This anthology is our attempt to answer that question by bringing together an amazing array of Black women and Black nonbinary writers to craft new and exciting horror stories for young adults. The kind of stories we always wanted as teen horror fans.

Today, we are seeing a new generation of Black writers claiming space, using speculative tools to tell the stories of Black girls as heroines, warriors, magicians, and princesses. It's so important that these new voices also get a chance to use the horror genre to tell their new stories. We hope that this anthology finds a home in this growing movement for Black voices in horror.

The Black Girl Survives in This One was a dream project for us both, and it gave us a chance to bring together a wonderful group of writers to respond to our call for more Black Final Girls. We are so grateful to the team who came together to make this

dream project of ours a reality. We want to thank our amazing team at New Leaf Literary & Media, including Patrice Caldwell, who championed this idea from the start and helped to sharpen our vision for the anthology. We also want to thank New Leaf's Jordan Hill, Trinica Sampson-Vera, and Donna Yee for their support. Thank you to our friends and family for supporting us, feeding us, and cheering us on throughout this publishing process.

We are so grateful to our incredible editors at Flatiron Books, Caroline Bleeke and Sarah Barley, who believed in this anthology and guided us in making it the best collection we could make. Thank you to the rest of the Flatiron team who helped bring this book to life: Sydney Jeon, Amelia Possanza, Bria Strothers, Maris Tasaka, Eva Diaz, Morgan Mitchell, Emily Walters, Kelly Gatesman, Erin Gordon, Keith Hayes, Louis Grilli, Malati Chavali, Megan Lynch, and all the other countless book workers from folks in sales to the warehouse team. We appreciate your efforts to get this book into readers' hands. A special thank-you to visual artist Monet Alyssa, who created our incredibly beautiful and eerie book cover!

We are so thankful to the wonderful group of writers who agreed to be part of this collection: Erin E. Adams, Monica Brashears, Charlotte Nicole Davis, Zakiya Dalila Harris, Daka Hermon, Justina Ireland, L.L. McKinney, Brittney Morris, Maika and Maritza Moulite, Eden Royce, and Vincent Tirado. Thank you for trusting us with your Black Final Girls! We want to give a special shout-out to our two New Voices winners who answered our open call: Camara Aaron and Kortney Nash. Thank you to all those who submitted stories to us during the submission window. Keep writing, your stories are necessary! Last but not least, we want to thank the amazing Tananarive Due for sharing her wisdom and history of the genre with us and crafting a wonderful introduction to this anthology.

The writers featured in this collection are all working hard to craft rich and complex stories that are making space for Black women, girls, and nonbinary protagonists in speculative fiction across the board. Thank you all for coming on this wonderful journey with us. And to you, dear reader, thank you for picking up this book and devouring these stories. We hope you find a new Black Final Girl to champion.

—Desiree S. Evans & Saraciea J. Fennell